WOMEN'S JUSTICE

CHRISSY WISSLER

BLUE CEDAR PUBLISHING

Created with Vellum

To my parents—
For all those trips to museums, ghost towns, and mine tours.

PROLOGUE

Every sound imaginable filled the air: discordant keys striking hard on a piano, the shrill shriek of a violin. Yells and cheers as money was lost and won from one gambling house or dance hall or saloon; it truly didn't matter. They were all one and the same and they lit the chill, wintery night as Norma stumbled about in their shadows.

At least they would have lit the night, if not for the blackness. The smoke hanging so tight and close she could barely see one foot in front of her.

The noise throbbed against her head until it became nothing more than a dull ache no amount of alcohol could take away. Which was well enough. The noise, if not her eyes, at least told her this was the way home.

Norma accepted this small bit of comfort, for that's all it was.

That's all she had left.

That, and that light stirring bit of wind. Not enough to help her breathe or see. To push away that heavy, thick smoke hanging over Butte like a black halo, from all those smelters pourin' out their blackness, not caring a whit about the folks who lived there.

Day and night, they went on and on. Day and night, they kept on with their burning of the ore. Great heaps of it.

And the smoke, it stayed right where it was cause the wind, the little tickling thing that it was, wasn't strong enough to do much else than make her shiver. Make her wish for the coat that she'd... lost somewhere.

Which, for the moment, was no matter because the sharp sting of cold helped. It cleared her mind, just enough, anyway. The kinda cold that went straight through you. Right into your bones without so much as a by-your-leave. And it stayed there, too. Stayed in you as yet even more of it came rolling down off those far-off, snow-peaked mountains. Ones she'd never been to but had always dreamed of. She'd had many dreams as she'd gazed out the rickety door of her little one-room crib, gazing off into that distance, so close and yet so far.

A dream she'd almost had, too.

But almost didn't get you nothin' in this place, just kept on pushing you down into the muck and mud until that's all that you had left. Until it was just you stumblin' about in the blackness, stomach ready to revolt right up your throat, hopin' like hell you could actually make it home before that happened.

Not that wind cared 'bout her dreams. Or whether or not she made it home.

It didn't. It rolled straight on down the hill, laughing all the way. Taunting her with it presence.

Or perhaps the laughter was all in her head.

Laughing or not, the wind at least brought another small comfort. A small one, yes, but a comfort nonetheless: It stole away the bits of sweat lining her forehead.

Though why the sweat was there, she didn't know. And couldn't much think straight, either.

Had it been from the heat of the Lucky Horseshoe, all those hours she'd spent there, earning her coin just like the rest of them? Bodies stacked up against each other from one wall to the next, so tight, desperate, almost as if there weren't another four dozen just like it?

Her head spun. Black dots dancin' right about in that darkness.

Norma pressed one hand against a building's brick wall, which turned her fingers blacker than even this black, hell-bit of a night. Not that she could see much, eyes stinging red, burning from that sulfur-laden air. Smoke that was both bane and blessing. They and their mines, giving miners their steady stream of money, a steady need to laugh and relax, to seek comfort from any willing-enough woman they could find after trudging hours beyond imaging in that dark underground of Butte's great and rich Hill.

Norma welcomed them, as did many others.

And this time, she'd managed to claim some of that coin for herself. A decent bit, for once.

Maybe even enough to get home.

Home.

That very word... it sent a longing straight through her, seared through her. So powerful, so strong, she felt it right to her soul. The only way to keep it from burning her whole was to keep walking.

But... the word just wouldn't go away... wouldn't leave her with this small peace that she had, this little amount of coin and the chillness of the night, whether or not she could see. *Home.* As if such a place were still open to someone like her, her and her brother, but well, a woman could dream. Could... long for.

So, she did.

She longed, and she walked. It was the only way to survive in this town. The only way to keep head above water was to keeping pushin' forward, never pausing long enough cause if you did you'd sink right on down to that bottom and never get it. She was so close to that, too. So close to just laying down and giving in.

Because she'd been a fool.

She'd wanted it all, and what she'd really wanted, that whole time, was home.

Something she could never have again.

Norma followed along that brick building, feet thudding on the rotting, shifting, plank way. Her stomach, its ends, turning and twisting something so fierce she actually lost her grip along that brick wall a few times and nearly crashed right down.

Something... wrong. Not... not right at all.

Horses and carriages she couldn't see from beyond the blackness creaked by in the street. Except for the noise from the carriages, from the saloon whose steady beat she could nearly feel right through that blackened brick, it felt like she was completely alone.

Walking alone in that blackness.

Her other hand clung tight to her shawl, now dipping so low it'd give any passerby, if they was close enough to see in the smoky-dark, a glance at her bare shoulder. At some point while she worked the saloon, offering drinks to customers and offering a bit more to anyone with a hint of willingness, before the owner had declared her too drunk for good business and thrown her out, some-time then... her dress had caught on some piece of nail, or ripped, or...

She could no longer remember.

Something had happened.

Her mind got even more tangled. Sluggish. But she focused on that rip in her dress like it were the lifeline she needed to see her home.

It wouldn't be an easy easy thing to mend, let alone replace. And her missing coat, too.

Except... she couldn't quite understand why such worries mattered much.

Only that it hurt, this truth. As if her body alone were all the proof and reprimand she needed, that she'd never go home.

That she didn't deserve it, neither.

Once creamy smooth, her shoulder, where the fingers of the most wealthy had once caressed her, held her, devoted themselves to her, it was a changed thing, now. Smudged as it was with dirt and grease and black powder. She could even see the imprints of her last customer, the swirls of his fingertips as they'd ground down hard into her.

At least... if she could see straight, anyway.

Which she couldn't.

Norma moaned. Her stomach twistin' like it was about to knot itself good and tight and never untangle. Her head pounding, it was getting hard to think let alone breathe. She pressed a soot-smudged hand to her forehead and it felt like a fiery, hot poker was being stabbed into her, again and again. So hard and fast the rest of her was starting to go numb.

Fingers shaking.

Legs weak.

Could she have drunk more than she'd thought?

Not the opium. She knew the feeling well enough, and she hadn't had enough money to push herself into a more lengthy state of pure bliss and calm.

This, though, this was different.

Her stomach churned and burned, and she sagged against the wall. Felt like it was the only thing on this hill keeping her upright.

Something slipped into her own drink?

Possible.

She... she hadn't been in her right mind tonight. Not with the pain still so fresh, and then, her final... rejection. Too good to be true. She'd taken a risk, such a foolish one thinking it'd bring her happiness, and it'd failed her. And tonight, it had felt like every man in the place knew it, too, and wanted to enjoy their good fortune while she wallowed in her own misfortune.

It hadn't taken her long to lose her last shred of decency, the desire to be the lady she'd once been known for, certainly in the face of alcohol and its promises of dulling this too-painful world. She'd easily lost count of how much she drank, of how much and what exactly, as the others, no longer her gentleman callers for sure but men all the same, men willing and men spending, as they poured whatever they had right into her cup.

And she hadn't cared.

A swirling image of another man slipped through the pain tearing into her skull. A man who'd both fit and didn't. His clothing, looking like all the others, but treating her with kindness and caring like she was still one of Grace's ladies. And oh, he'd been her heaven in that moment, that little joy, the reminder of the woman she'd been before. And then he'd given her this brilliant, promising smile, and she'd soared. The sting from earlier, gone. Rejection after rejection, and knowing too the wrath that was about to fall down on her.

But for that moment, it had been enough.

He'd been her last customer for the night and he had paid her a hefty price. He'd caressed her forearm like she was indeed the treasure and not the coins he was parting with.

It was a touch she still felt, still caused a shiver of pride. Felt even through her splitting head. Even her breasts, too, as they pushed out her too-tight, breath-stealing corset.

She stumbled at that moment, her worn shoe catching some uneven plank on the walkway. It caused the ribbing of her corset to gouge into her soft skin.

She gasped.

Got only a mouthful of smoke that burned.

Her pride burning, too. Silly, foolish woman she was, she'd believed him, believed this man when he said she'd been worth every coin and more.

Once, she'd been that girl.

A girl with a smile, who lived with joy and enjoyed sharing it with others. No longer.

Red—a sudden pain seared through her head. So fast, so complete, her vision turned to blackness. It came so suddenly. Violently. Nothing like before. Nothing that she could see through, see around. It was her everything. Shrinking her whole world down to that one sight, that one feeling.

She cried out. Doubled over.

From somewhere far off—or close, she couldn't tell, not around the pain, not around the red—she thought she heard the clomping of horses. Hooves smackin' into the beat-hard dirt. They came nearer. Towards her?

Impossible.

She was no one. A nothing.

Now, anyway. She'd long ago lost the glittering jewels and silk and dresses fashioned straight from Paris, which she'd worn like the dazzling primrose she'd been while at Gardens. A world so far gone it felt like decades rather than months.

Her own fault. Her own weakness.

The pain came again. This time it felt like it split her in two. Right from her head all the way to her groin.

She crouched on the ground. Panting, moaning, crying.

Was... was she crying? Did she truly have any tears left?

Surely not.

There was a shout. Feet rushed towards her. Then... hands pressed against her head as if that would make it all go away. Soft and gentle hands, of the kind she hadn't felt in many long months. Caring hands, and they were cool, too, not like the wind cold, but cool. Comforting. Though they did nothing against the fire that was on her skin.

Those hands felt her head, lifted open her eyelids. She thought maybe something cool pressed against her chest, listening to her poor, straining chest. Her lungs that desperately fought for a clean breath of air, or any breath really, through her corset, through that smoke-thick air, and each time failing a bit more than the last.

"Norma? My dear girl, how could this possibly be you? What happened?"

What happened was she'd been a fool, thinking she was in love, and turned out she was wrong.

Yet again.

Somehow, she opened her eyes, and at first, saw nothing but the pain and fire and darkness.

"I, I can't see."

But that wasn't fully true.

The image of the man slowly came together. Blurry and full of shadows, but enough to make out his wrinkled, bone-white skin. The long, back cloak that looked close enough to the darkness she found herself in. A man she recognized.

A tear slipped past.

The man, this doctor who'd reluctantly tended to her before she'd given up her life of glitter in hopes of a better one, a decent one with the promise of a full life that, even now, burned like a secret flower in her chest.

"You're burning up," he said. "We need to get you to a hospital. Immediately. Driver!"

Who he called to, she couldn't see. Could, in fact, barely see him and his so sad face. Even now her vision was darkening as if it was reaching right up from her soul to finally take the rest of her.

The doctor had always looked at her, at all the girls really, with such overwhelming sadness.

His hands though, they'd always been kind.

"Who did this to you?" he asked.

Her hand, black from all the soot, black as her soul, lifted. Touched his cheek.

"Doctor. Thank you."

It was all she managed.

That, and one last smile. She had no idea she still had one in her, but it was there.

And for a moment, she felt that joy again. Just like she felt his kindness, one last time.

The pain became too great then. Too great, even, for the great and kind Doctor to heal.

She would die and no one, beyond the doctor, would care. Not for her, not for any of the fallen sisters like her.

No one.

CHAPTER ONE

C at stepped off the Butte train and walked right into hell.

A heavy, black smoke hung about the hill. So thick, so dark, forget seeing any of those narrow, wooden frames she knew were out in the distance. Gallows, really, marking the entrances to hundreds of the copper mines the city was so famous for (and damned rich, too, if the stories held true).

And the railroad station? Those folks in charge were smart to string up lanterns all about the place, otherwise their paying customers would be lost right quick.

Hell, it looked like it were about midnight and she knew darn well it was just past noon.

Ashes drifted down, so fine and thin that at first she thought she'd imagined it. Then she saw those ladies disembarking from the train, all lace and yards of fabric bustled about their persons, wrapped up tight in their fancy coats and furs even though it weren't that cold, certainly for the mountains. They pressed their dainty, flimsy, pure-white handkerchiefs to their delicate little lips to keep themselves from breathing in the noxious, disgusting air.

As if that would do a damn thing.

Certainly not when those pearly-white handkerchiefs were already takin' on the ashy, gray color themselves.

The burning sulfur and what-not already stung Cat's eyes. Probably lookin' red-rimmed and bloodshot like she'd downed herself in the bottle the whole jostling ride over from Miles City.

There was a bit of wind, the late winter kind, so chill it reminded your bones that snow still lay hidden in those mountain peaks and had no intention of giving way to spring, just yet anyway. Or anytime soon. But as pleasing as that bit of wind was, it wasn't nearly enough to cleanse this poor air of the smoke that fouled it.

Butte looked like hell, no doubt about it, and she, the whole of the city herself, didn't seem to mind one wit about showing her true colors to the world. There was certainly some grace in that.

Honesty, too.

Just as Cat had been promised.

She tucked her scarf into the protective covering of her overcoat. The faint, flowery pink somehow still holding onto those dyed threads even after all these years. The rest of her could handle the ash and soot just fine. Her blouse, the best one she had even with all them stains and wrinkles, not to mention her blue jeans, getting a bit worn round the bottom, but still hugging her hips in all the right places.

Fact was, she drew about as many glances from the newcomers to Butte as well as the ones who lived there.

The men trudged around in tough-looking boots meant to carry a man miles underground, protecting his toes from heavy rocks and slabs ready to crush him silly. Nothing like the kind of boots that slapped-on spurs and carried about a pound of muck soon as you slipped 'em on. Then there were those smart, slim-cut jackets and more manner of shined shoes than she'd seen in a whole year workin' in Miles City.

Not to mention those squashed caps the newsboys wore, just as soot-stained as the rest of 'em. One in particular studied about everything and everyone shuffling off that train, those sharp eyes of his missing nothing, including Cat. All them newsboys cried out their headlines to the overflowing passengers, waving their ink-stained fingers like the whole stack was about to blow away if one didn't hurry on over and get the latest.

And not a cowboy in sight.

Butte was a city all right, but not like the usual ones out here in Montana.

All that put together, plus Cat herself not looking like the respectable part of a lady (or of any kind, for that matter), well, it made perfect sense why her fellow passengers tried to bustle past her. Those fancy, lacy skirts and dresses, and not an inch of fabric ever touching Cat's person.

Which, considering the flood of bodies flowing off the train then stopping right in their tracks as Cat had done, was fairly impressive.

Course, there were also those in their matchin' suits and vests best known as the upper gentry. They at least gave her the most curious of glances. More than a few were filled with revulsion, which was all right, but none of them could deny it:

They all looked.

They didn't dare come near, though. At least, not now, anyway.

Certainly not with the empty holster for her revolver hanging loose at her hip. The gun was stored away in her bag, as most cities likened these days, but the holster was reminder enough for most folks. They gave Cat her space, and she watched as they fled to the hordes of waiting hacks, drivers and horses seeming to appear and disappear right before her eyes, materializing in this unnatural light.

Or un-light, as the case were.

Through this all, this constant movement, the ringing of bells and whistles and clomping hooves, for the first time in years, Cat felt a weight slide off her shoulders.

Not a whole lot, cause it weren't ever gonna go away, couldn't, but now she felt lighter.

Comfortable. Content.

Part of her hoping, praying even, that her dear sister had found some measure of this same peace during her final days, all the while

Cat knew that she hadn't. Couldn't. That just weren't the way of the world, when ill luck fell hard on a woman, even a righteous and good one. *Especially* a righteous and good one. Especially, too, when they stuck to that path even knowing the end result, something neither God, nor man—certainly no woman—could change.

Alice had agreed to her fate, accepted it even, hardness and all.

Cat hadn't.

Or she had, but just in a different way. A path she wouldn't be on now if not for her sister. Of the last memory she had of Alice—her eyes, saddened, alive still but lifeless, and how she'd told Cat to leave and never come back. Standing there in that thin dress, the fabric barely hanging off her bones, and her straight, pale hair. It hadn't mattered that she was finally free of her wretched, hateful husband, who'd been inches away from finally stealing her dear Alice's life— and it hadn't mattered.

Not to Alice, the good and righteous woman that she was.

The memory would never, ever let Cat go. It would haunt her to the end of her days, but maybe, just maybe, Butte could help lessen that burden. Because perhaps, right here, there was a place for someone like her. Someone who'd do what she could for those the world didn't care none about. It might only be a small act, but it'd be something.

It'd be justice.

Cat had no doubt, none at all, that this was the place she was meant to be.

Needed to be.

CHAPTER TWO

Truth was, there was only one place to find the happenings in any town, big or small, likened enough to hell or not.

In this, Butte was like any other.

The newsboys stood where train station met street, their squashed hats and ink-stained fingers waving about their papers and yelling about somebody who died out in the wilds of Chicago or New York. They didn't stop, not a once, even with the constant roll and crunch of hooves and wheels as hack drivers loaded everybody they could into their carriages. The whistling of those trains and whatnot. Even further off whistling in that blackness, which Cat only assumed came from the mines.

Dear lord, she'd never been to a place that made such a noise.

And those newsboys, why they were made of stern stuff because they kept on going without even a pause or need for breath, it seemed.

Except for the boy with sharp eyes.

He'd been studying Cat the moment her boots had smacked onto the hard platform, and unlike his fellows, he hadn't gone back to selling his papers. Instead, he kept on watching her. Waiting. Green-gray eyes of his, as if there was more than a mix of curiosity there, almost like a daring.

Now, however, his eyes narrowed, focused, right on her.

Somehow even in this blasted black smoke that green of his eyes cut through like a sharp knife. They never once left Cat's face.

She recognized him for what he was.

A shadow soul.

Someone living on the edge, on the fringes of society. Someone who hadn't yet failed, or if he had, he'd gotten back up before life trampled him under the muck and ash. Someone who made his livin' at surviving and didn't bother hiding it none.

A shiver slipped through her.

Carried right down passed her overcoat as if that chilly, still winter air was its own doing and not the actual truth.

Instinct.

Cat knew this truth, through and through. It tingled all up and down her body, and she'd learned long ago to trust in her feelings. Let them guide her.

Cat slapped her wide-brimmed cowboy hat on her head. Thing was, she couldn't stop herself even she wanted to, the urge was just that powerful. And never say curiosity itself wasn't powerful in its own right.

Cause it was.

So, Cat let it be what it was, and headed right towards him.

She kept the boy in sight as she moved around the passengers, trying not to trample on the enormously long and ridiculously impractical dresses some ladies thought travel necessitated. Not that the boy was trying to disappear or nothing, but she had this itch between her shoulders.

Instinct, again.

It dangled in her gut like a fish teasing her, ready to slip on free of its hook before heading back towards the murky-dark waters of home.

Something important, she simply knew, and she couldn't let it get away.

Maybe it was the way he looked at her, with that daring of his, or maybe it was leftover from her own resolution to come to Butte.

Whatever the reason, it was there, and this feeling, well, it stirred within her, pushing her forward and she followed. Besides, if there was anyone who knew about the inner workings of Butte, both above ground and what took place below, it'd be a kid like this.

Her boots clomped on the wooden platform and her bag slung across her shoulder, heavy and feeling just the way it needed to. Behind her, the train whistled something fierce, starting up a whole litany from others she couldn't see through the thick, heavy smoke.

"Offer you a paper, Miss?" the boy asked when she got close enough.

Not Mizz or ma'am.

She noticed, too, that he had a few different stacks with a few different names leaking across the fading pulp. *The Miner, Anaconda Standard, Butte Bystander.* All being sold by one boy? She hadn't a clue what was the norm in a city like Butte, but compared to the boys nearest him, they each had their one stack and that was all. Even the nearest kid, of the tall, beefy variety with narrowed, squinty eyes that about lost themselves in his freckled face. He looked the kind that wouldn't stand for some green-eyed, skinny kid outselling him.

Yet, there beefy stood and Green Eyes here, well, here *he* stood. Right on that corner, in the coveted spot and not a one of the others challenging him or his three papers.

Definitely a shadow soul, no doubt about it.

And exactly the person she needed to talk to.

"I'm looking for some news," Cat said. "Of the local sort."

Cat tossed him a coin. It twisted once and then twice in the air, just a glimmer of its copper-gold gleaming in the poor lantern light. The boy snatched it right quick from the air before it got even a second turn in. And whether he stashed it in his coat pocket or some hidden fold in his sleeve, Cat didn't know. His movement had been so fast and fluid.

Shadow soul, indeed.

Green Eyes tipped his cap up with an ink-smudged finger. "Local news, eh?"

"That's right."

"I'd recommend *The Bystander*, then. Some interesting bits in there."

She noticed he didn't bother to recite the headlines like the others, just told her, straight-a-way, which newspaper suited her needs.

"Course," he said, "depends on just how local a story you're lookin' for."

Cat felt the tingling again, crawling all up and around her spine. Testing her, perhaps?

"The kind not a whole lot of folk care about," she said.

He glanced at her hip, specifically her empty holster. "You plan on staying long, Miss Justice?"

There it was. The tingling.

She didn't fight it. Instead, she embraced it.

"Depends," she said, "on how the wind blows and what turns up."

"It's quite foul, I'll warn you right. When the wind turns wrong, you'll have never experienced anything of the like before, I promise you. You'll know it when you smell it. At least, that's when the wind blows wrong. When it blows right?"

This time, it was his turn to shrug.

"Well, fresh mountain air, for one. A thing of beauty, really, even here in this eyesore of a city. For the rest, though? I guess it'll just depend."

"Depend on what?"

"You, I suppose."

And there it was.

That look again. That kind that cut right on through her, taking her so far back like this kid could see back to the days of her being at home, when ma and pa were alive, when it was just her and Alice and when it felt like they had the whole world to themselves.

So naive and foolish they'd been. Little bitty dreamers that they were.

Dear God, did she miss those days... did she miss Alice.

Green Eyes slapped out the paper to her without a wasted movement or word. "Still interested in local?"

"I am."

She took it from him. Felt the weight on her shoulders shift yet again, settling almost. And... there was a feather-cold touch along her fingers, too, as if her sister were right beside her, reaching out for that paper and accepting more than they both realized.

Alice, of course, wasn't there, but this kid was, and Cat got a dusting of ash and ink on her hand.

She nodded to him. "I'd appreciate a recommendation of where to start. Rather big town you've got here."

"Page four, then. 'Bout midway down. Might just find a good place to rest your feet for a spell."

"Thanks."

Cat opened the paper, which crinkled in her hand. It rustled, too, as that chill winter wind suddenly swept up and between them, like it was planning on snatching the paper good and quick before she could stop it.

It didn't, though.

Cat held on, and for a moment felt like it was her breath that had been stolen. At least, what the smoke hadn't already burned right out and through her lungs. Especially as the words themselves, in that tiny, blocked print, like it was the most insignificant piece of news in the world, jumped out of the page and landed squarely against her chest.

The place where her heart still ached and beat because Alice was finally gone and Cat had failed her, time and time again. That same place that had driven her to Butte, and now to this boy.

But the words themselves were somehow clear, even in this shifting lantern light:

Woman Found Dead on Galena Street

CHAPTER THREE

All around Cat the bustling and muscling continued, passengers leaving the railroad and its noisy station behind. Hacks and horses clomping, pushing their way past one another on a street so dark you couldn't tell one horse's rear end from the next. Or if it were even a horse to begin with and not a small, fat gentry's butt.

But all of that, it faded to some hazy, dull, faded thing as her own focus narrowed to the story in her hands. A story that gripped her and wouldn't let her go.

Not that she wanted it to. Not when, right here, was her reason for coming.

She embraced it—words, story, and all.

Woman Found Dead on Galena Street

A woman, real name unknown, died on Galena Street late Saturday night. A passing doctor saw the woman in distress, and due to the nature of his calling, attempted to rescue the fallen woman. He was unsuccessful in his valiant efforts. Police believe this was an occurrence of too much drink or other such desires. The doctor, reportedly, believes otherwise. The woman in question was well known in her profession, though having fallen even further in recent months. No witnesses or suspects have been identified.

CAT'S EYES burned from the effort, not that she couldn't read, but that foul smoke and even fouler lighting had made it all but impossible. Fact was, it amazing she could even see the tiny print at all. But she could, and those words about demanded her attention and focus, same way that her daddy had taught her.

His teaching which came back in one whoosh of a memory.

How her breath had slowly slipped back out her lungs as her cheek rested on the cool barrel of her rifle. The constant symphony of the forest around her, the grasshoppers and their humming neighbors, the scream of some hawk circling high above her head. It was all there, all around her, and yet... distant. Instead, she focused her whole self as the buck bent its head, pushing past the last lingering snow to reveal grass hiding and awakening underneath. Tall and graceful, antlers stating his age just as they were, plain and simple, while he lifted his mighty head. Wide, all-seeing dark eyes that stared right back at her.

All the while, she breathed.

So, too, did Cat breathe in that sulfur-tinged air. Air that burned her lungs and made her want to wretch.

But still, her focus held.

And right at this moment, with this newspaper in her hands that felt both weightless and impossibly heavy, she felt her daddy's reassuring hand on her shoulder.

And she read what *wasn't* there.

Read in between the lines, the words that were left unsaid, invisible unless one really looked, or even cared to look. A woman, known openly in her profession, yet one that wasn't named. Neither the name she was given, or the one she gave herself. Her given name, it was no surprise there. The ladies, like Cat, who walked and lived in these shadows, kept their names hidden like jewels, little secrets of themselves that the greater world and the homes they'd left behind must never, ever find out.

So, no great surprise to have not written the woman's name, but her professional name? Usually newspapers and the righteous who ran them were always so eager to spell out those women who dared fall from their place in the world. Loved to tell each one of their readers every detail they could about her... while leaving any other parties, certainly those of the male variety, safely, carefully anonymous.

But that was not the last clue this article gave. In fact, the whole piece, as short as it was, was written in such a way that, if read by another, one of the more gentler class, as women were ought to be and not such pitiful, fallen things as the lady who died, that it would not disturb such important sensibilities.

The readership in and of itself was a clue. As to how the city viewed its creatures who lived in the shadows. Lived and profited from, she had no doubt at all.

And Galena Street itself?

Cat squinted at the printing, made sure she was reading it right with that dim, awful light.

Yes, it was Galena Street. To be so openly named and in such an unsurprising way meant only one thing: This was where the lowest of the ladies would work.

And where they would walk, alone.

Then there was the doctor... a hero the writer had tried to make him to be, stopping for such a poor, fallen woman when he did not need to *because* she was fallen.

And yet, he'd stopped anyway. That alone was a curiosity, to both the writer and to Cat herself.

Why had the doctor been there in the first place, driving this route? Or was it a common route for the drivers? A question only a local would know.

Cat filed that away, continued to focus, narrow down even further. Just as her father had taught.

Her breathing, slowing. Not daring to miss one small detail.

The doctor *had* stopped and not only that... he'd suspected some other reason for the lady's death. One which the police, not to Cat's surprise in the least, didn't agree with.

They were more willing to blame the death fully on the woman in question.

The victim.

But this doctor had spoken out. To the police. To the writer of the paper.

Would he speak with her as well? Would he dare to, or care enough about such an insignificant life as the woman who'd died?

Cat gripped the paper, almost crushing it.

She forced herself to relax, to breathe again. This was not the time nor place for anger. Later when she was alone, had her own quiet and her own mind, perhaps then she could explore it.

But not now.

All this while, the boy still watched her. She didn't miss this, nor it seemed, did he miss this either. Both were studying the other. Both letting the other one be, yet both watchful.

If anything, his gaze felt heavier than it had felt a moment ago.

Another test, then.

Cat ignored him and again focused on the questions that her mind was already piecing together from what little this article was willing to say.

So few details because people like this, people like Cat, simply didn't matter. They did not deserve anything, though others might grudgingly admit they had their place in the grand scheme of life. Someone to take the edge off all that darkness those living down in the mines faced day in, day out, but they certainly did not deserve justice.

And yet, the writer still gave her clues, much as he wouldn't have wanted to. In fact, would have been disgusted with himself if he ever learned otherwise.

Like, "falling farther."

This meant that, even if the woman's name was not provided, she *was* known. Perhaps as an upscale prostitute, one of the fine ladies in a parlor house. Were there many here? Again, Cat didn't know, but it would be easy enough to learn. Or perhaps this was just a woman many men thought of as kindly, much as they had with Cat when she worked the line.

Possibly.

Cat closed her eyes. Reached out further with her awareness, no longer just focusing on the paper and the boy with green eyes who, interestingly, hadn't begun selling any others. Hadn't moved on to other clients, all those passengers practically running off the station into what they perceived as safety in those hacks.

Clearly... this moment with her... it was important to him.

Another piece falling into place.

This boy, he'd known her. He'd known this woman who died. Somehow.

And yet, he hadn't said anything to this fact, nor would he.

Cat knew this like she knew how to ride.

She let the matter slide away.

Instead, focusing beyond the two of them to the *other* newsboys. Specifically, the headlines they were crying out... somehow heard even over that chorus of head-piercing whistles and snaps of whips in that ashy air.

Not a one said a word about this woman. No mention at all of her death.

Truly, Cat hadn't expected less.

But Green Eyes *had* told her. At least in a 'round about fashion.

"Boy..."
She opened her eyes, planning to ask him more...
Except he was gone.
He and all his stacks of papers, simply gone.

CHAPTER FOUR

Green Eyes might have disappeared, but he'd given Cat more than enough to get started. And not just with the poor woman, but also where Cat might go next.

A place to board.

Cat flipped the paper back open, squinting her aching eyes to see (and read) yet again. They burned something fierce and kept watering, no matter how much she wiped them with her mostly clean scarf. She really needed to get out of this air for a bit, give her lungs and her head a chance to clear and settle.

Sure enough, right where Green Eyes had said was a tiny ad calling for boarders:

Mrs. Allen's Boarding. Single men, families, ladies welcome. Provided at $5 per week.

More than affordable for Cat without her having to work any extra business, which she had no interest in getting started out here in Butte. She had enough saved to keep her well off for a time until she could find the right kind of place for herself and for this real work she wanted to do.

Like the deceased lady in question.

Her fingers brushed across the article one last time. Felt this little surge, like the new electricity starting up or instinct, call it what you like, but it was there. Just like Mrs. Allen's ad was there as well, and that Green Eyes had recommended them both.

Cat tucked the paper in her bag and hefted it on her shoulders.

There was only one way to find out both the deceased woman's name and history, as well if this Mrs. Allen would be interested in takin' on a boarder of Cat's like. Especially since if she stood out here much longer, these noxious fumes of Butte would about turn her blonde hair into an ashy-gray.

She did not have much vanities, but she liked her hair just fine, even if the darn thing knotted up at the slightest wind tugging on it. However, blonde going gray at her age was simply not something she was interested in.

Cat hailed a hack and by golly, one materialized straight up and out of that smoky-black like Hades himself had sent it to her. Those double-black horses also helped that image some, 'cept for that splattering of mud about their coats and legs, but maybe that just made them actually seem real. It certainly helped that they did, as the driver himself, look quite the skeleton. Long and narrow, top hat pressed smartly on his head, and a dark goatee trimmed to a small point. He looked like he was half-in the grave, and the buffalo-skin overcoat looked like it was gonna swallow him whole.

But the grin he gave her just about sparkled, even with the cigar clutched there between his yellowing teeth.

Apparently the smoke of Butte wasn't enough for the man, and he needed to pour a bit more of the stuff straight into his lungs.

Still, she grinned right back.

As a matter of point, she didn't like people instantly. You couldn't truly know a person, or even half of 'em, until you'd spent a lifetime with them. And upon meeting someone for the first time? That was a fool's game, a lesson which Alice and her devil-born, deceased husband had pounded hard into Cat.

She'd learned quickly on that one.

But this driver here, though, he was a person of Butte through and through. The open and honest sort who saw all sides of life, dark as well as the light, and still grinned as much as he darn well pleased.

She couldn't help but like that about the man.

The hack rattled to a stop in front of her, horses stamping their hooves on the crushed gravel, dark tails swatting at their behinds.

"Well, now."

He didn't bother to pull out his cigar, just kept on talking with that thing sticking out of his mouth.

"I thought I about knew everyone of interest that came to Butte. Lookin' here like I mighta been wrong about that."

"Just got in." Cat nodded towards the train. "Can't blame a man for not seeing the future."

"Indeed, indeed. Wish we all had the luck of that around here. You needing a ride, Miss Cowboy? I'd be mighty obliged to take you there."

Her brows arched up at that.

He just grinned bigger, that cigar somehow staying in place. Though she might have caught a glint of gold in those teeth of his.

"It's my job, after all," he said. "And an interesting sort such as yourself, well, now. I wouldn't mind the tale that comes with it."

The man really was all Butte. A place she was getting the sense of the longer her feet stayed on this dark, bruised ground.

"Well, all righty, then," Cat said. "You know of a Mrs. Allen's boarding house?"

He stroked his goatee from where he perched on his cab box, watching her, that darn sparkle reaching all the way to his eyes. He held the reins loosely in his fingers, as if that were all the touch he needed to get his team under command, skeleton that he was.

"Well, now," he said. "Not many askin' to go her way these days, what with the big and fancy hotels openin' up shop uptown."

"She was recommended to me."

"Oh?"

Again came that tingling feeling in her gut.

The bait and the fish, dangling right there in those murky waters. And again, she didn't fight it.

"Saw it right here."

Cat held out the *Butte Bystander* to him. Her fingers, though, didn't rest on the ad itself. Instead, she'd placed them just beside the article about the poor deceased lady.

The driver's dark eyes widened some, almost disappearing right on up to his hat. "Well, now indeed. That is something. Something, indeed."

"Is it?"

His eyes met hers. Held there for a breath or two, and she didn't waiver her gaze, not one bit.

"Wasn't aware she'd put out an ad," he said. "Mrs. Allen, I mean. But... I reckon she'd accept the look of you. All of you."

At this last, he nodded at her gun, or at least the empty holster.

"Don't see many ladies wearin' openly like such. You come from a rough patch?"

"Where in Montana isn't?"

He cackled at her, his laughter just as rough and thin as the rest of him, but there was plenty of pure joy in it and it made her like him all the more. No wonder he sought out interesting characters like herself. She'd probably given him a month's worth of barbershop tales from these few minutes alone.

"True enough, my fine lady, true enough. Fat Jack's the name, and I'll get you and your precious cargo to where you likin' to be."

The name surprised her, seeing how it was the exact opposite of the man, and she imagined there was quite a story there. Though, at least for the time being, he clearly had no interest in telling it.

Instead, Fat Jack hopped down from his cab and opened the door for her. It creaked and groaned, not much different from the man himself as he moved. He grumbled off a group of boys who'd come swarming around, looking to hoist her bags for an extra coin or two, as was their way, but apparently Fat Jack's way was a might different because they danced away right quick at his glare.

Cat settled herself in, and then held on.

CHAPTER FIVE

H olding on.

That was about the only way to describe the experience of riding with Fat Jack.

The damn smoke stung her eyes something fierce as they took off, heading west. At least she thought it was a west-like direction. Certainly once they got going and rode straight into the thick of it, Cat could barely tell up from down. And that smoke, it felt like she was getting punched with the stuff as they practically flew down those sloping streets. The carriage wheels practically rose right off the ground as Fat Jack took one turn and then another so hard and fast it was amazing they didn't flip right on over.

Amazing, too, they didn't crash headlong into some building or street lamp considering how he and his poor horses couldn't see two licks in front of them.

They didn't crash, though.

Small blessings, indeed.

She mighta picked herself one crazy-ass driver, but he was at least one who knew the way. Or at least, his horses sure did.

Except... probably for the first time in months, ever since she'd gotten the letter about Alice, Cat was smiling.

Oh, she was holding on right tight, but there was still the joy in simply *moving*. And moving fast. Especially when that fast came from these two competent horses, and she daresay, a darn good, if not wild, driver.

It felt something an awful lot like happiness, or close enough to it.

They might be making a headlong dash through the darkness, but it was plain as day that the man and his horses knew what they were doing. And that the horses, even puffin' as hard as they were, were well-cared for... and lovin' every minute of excitement.

As if noting her interest, Fat Jack managed to speak a few words about them, though truth to tell, Cat only heard about one word in three. Still, it seemed she'd drawn his interest, at least on the horses, and he told her how he worked 'em hard, and then they had themselves a few days' rest.

"Streets of Butte. They'd lame a horse right fast if not cared for properly. Every driver worth his salt knows this, some better than others, course, and the ones that don't, well, reckon they pay the price with what they get."

Of course, that's what it sounded like he'd said.

As they moved through the streets, even if she couldn't see a whole lot, she got more a sense of Butte. It was one of her gifts, the quick knowing of a place. Directions and weather and the like. The people and all their ilk and class.

See, a place—from the very ground itself right up to the air—they all had their own feelings and temperament. Moods. And sure those moods changed with the seasons, more often than the fine ladies in those fancy houses changed dresses, but they were there and they could be relied on.

The moods. Not the ladies.

Miles City had been like breathing the wild. You could tell instantly simply from the way the wind tore right through you, picking apart your clothing and your hair. It was quite up for grabs, thanks very much (along with any lady foolish enough to don ribbons and other such niceties). The moment your boots touched down in Miles, you quickly learned there were some places on this earth that just weren't interested in being tamed.

That was Miles City, no question 'bout it. And Butte? Well, she was another type of place altogether.

Dark and dazzling. Somehow one and the same, neither side hiding behind the other or behind any fancy skirts. Butte was upfront 'bout who she was, which Cat got to see, even if she was traveling at Fat Jack's pace of fast and barely slowin' down two-bits.

She kept a hand on her hat to keep from the losin' the thing altogether, and still, she smiled.

Specially, too, when she saw the dark swarm of miners trudging on up the hill, tin pails in hand. She couldn't tell if they were heading into work or just getting off shift, or taking their lunch. She didn't know enough about the working of Butte, especially the mines, but she could still see the weariness in about every inch of 'em.

And there was a lot of 'em, too.

They each seemed to have lines wearing hard round the eyes, boots so darn heavy and thick like, by themselves, they must have weighed five pounds each. Or maybe that was just the weight they all felt and it didn't change none from day to day, except maybe coming home when they were either exhausted beyond measure or they were thrilled they'd survived another day down where no sun could ever, would ever, shine.

But somehow they kept on walking, one heavy boot in front of the other, wearing that crunched gravel and stone street down to an even finer dust.

They were real people here, real people who did their darn best and worked hard, tempting fate every day they entered those God-forsaken mines and all that endless darkness.

There was something quite honorable in that, and no mistaking it.

And Fat Jack, driving as fast as he darn was, noticed her smiling. Truly, he was a kindred soul.

"You got some plans while you be here, Miss Cowboy?" Fat Jack hollered back to her.

It truly was amazing she could hear him at all.

"Just calling on Mrs. Allen," she said. "Then maybe following up on an interesting bit I saw in the paper."

"Huh."

Fat Jack spit out something black, which thankfully did not hit Cat as it flew by.

"The woman who died," he said, matter-of-fact.

Cat's eyebrows lifted. She leaned closer, feeling the swirls in her stomach begin all over again, and wished she'd declined the ride in the cab to instead sit right on top with him. Damn it.

"You know her?" she asked.

Course, right at that point one wheel found a nasty bit of hole, one that was about determined to unseat her, Jack, and the horses, and all in one swoop. Jack held on, and the horses—heaven almighty, they were quite the team—did not lose their footing. Possibly a shoe, though she'd have to trust Jack to take a good look at the poor animals.

She, at least, didn't lose her seating either.

Who'd have guessed years of riding and herding cattle would keep her from losing her life just a few minutes after rolling into Butte.

Jack glanced back, and again she saw a glimmer in his harried, tired eyes. Not quite respect—after all, she was who she was—and it wasn't simply acceptance either. Perhaps, though, some place in between.

Almost like Butte herself.

And Cat had a really, really good hunch that he'd done that fancy bit of driving on purpose.

"You knew her," Cat said.

It was not a question, not in the least, and they both knew it.

Jack slowed his hack down a tad, enough that there was an actual chance for Cat to hear without no mistaking his meaning or words. That was also most likely by design.

"Aye, I did," he said. "Fact is, I know about everyone in town, and I've driven 'round everyone from ladies like yourself to the great Copper Kings of Daly and Clark and the like, though don't you go telling 'em. They'd be quite belligerent over their bums sharing the same seat as such."

Jack laughed at this, though this time he didn't have the same joy. No, not at all.

Instead, there was a heaviness about him, one that Cat knew herself, and all too well. About seeing the wrongs in a place, or in a people, and being completely helpless to stop it. Or seeing it and knowing, even if you could do such a thing, nothing would change.

Life would become harder for you, and that was all.

Cat reached up and fingered the scarf still tucked safely in her jacket. Yes, she knew that feeling all too well.

"What was her name?" she asked.

"Norma. At least, such is the name she gave me and every other person who met her in Butte. Her real name, well, I'd doubt that greatly, as you, yourself, know."

Cat nodded at this, as it seemed he was expecting this.

Norma. She had a name now.

"I reckon," he went on, "that it was a sad thing that happened to her. Sad, indeed. She was a lady who liked to smile and smile kindly. Always appreciated around here, a smile. One that wasn't charged for neither. She'd smile to smile, simply cause it was part of her character. You'll see for yourself, soon enough. A smile is in short supply these days."

"There a reason for that?"

"Butte's not an easy place to live. Those gents on top, Clark and Daly and the like, they worked hard for it. Had quite a bit of brains to start with, and an even larger douse of luck, but mostly brains, I reckon. Brains and money already backin' enough behind 'em. The rest of us, though?"

Fat Jack shook his head. "We work for what we got, every bit of it, every inch of it. And those who got even less? Well... let's just say it's a life too easily fallen into and one not even a smile, kind or not, can get you out of."

"Like Norma."

"Norma had herself the world, then lost it, bit by bit. Even the smile."

Norma.... who the newspaper writer had said had fallen even farther. And Cat knew from walking the line herself that even on this darker side of life, the side that those good mothers raising their good Christian children would never want their young ones, certainly their girls to know... that even on this shadow side of life, there was an order to it.

And an order of exactly how you fell, and how far.

Cat had never hit that bottom herself. She was a bit of an... irregularity herself, being able to ride like the men and choosin' to when she could. Riding herd. Ranching. And earning the other kind of coin. The kind that was only reserved for those fallen ladies like herself, but she'd done it. Earned herself a different place in life, a different kind of respect, and she'd never fallen as low as could.

Even now.

There was always still room to fall. And it sounded like this Norma mighta fallen pretty far indeed.

Which, in and of itself, was yet another clue. Another piece to the puzzle. And there was the doctor's testimony to consider as well...

Cat leaned forward on her seat, as far as she dared without actually letting go and grabbing onto Fat Jack himself.

"What happened? Do you know—"

Jack pulled on the reins and, as if materializing right out of the smoky black, was a house. It was a darn good thing Cat *hadn't* moved all the way on up, otherwise she'd have flown right over his head and the horses' heads to boot.

Well, she didn't.

There were also plenty of houses around like this one, strung together side by side like some weather-worn tree ornaments. Hardy ones, though. Even with the white picket fence running round its side, that little porch with a rocker and swing, the two stories of pleasantly washed windows and laced curtains. All the windows, of course, were snapped closed to keep out the smoke.

The home looked just as worn and bruised as she felt on the inside. Nothing like the sprinkling of mansions she could see just peeking out of the smoke not too far down the street, giant monstrosities that hadn't an inch of ash coating their brick, like they had someone to specially keep the red nice and shiny bright. Couldn't believe, honestly, that those things were parked right up beside these other ones, the ones that had people who actually lived in them, cooked their meals, and shat in them.

Personally, Cat would accept the worn-in look, something honest and true, rather than the new and fancy any day.

"As promised," Jack waved his hand towards the house. "Mrs. Allen's place."

She was no fool. The timing, right there, had been a little too perfect.

Like the boy with green eyes, Fat Jack knew a hell a lot more than he planned on telling her.

Jack hopped off the seat, lanky body and all, and did not break or snap a bone when he landed. He opened the door for her, which actually surprised her.

She walked openly to the world, declaring who she was, but declaring it in a different way than her sisters in their fancy make-ups and even fancier dresses shipped in straight from Paris. And because she stood her ground, because she was who she was, makin' no bones about it, the world generally tended to shut its door in her face.

Kindness. Gentry. All such simple things the rest of the world took for granted were continually denied her.

It was her calling, and her punishment. She did not harbor ill will, but kindness? Chivalry?

Not in the least expected.

Jack just grinned, yellow narrow teeth and all, like he could read her mind.

She had a feeling he could, to a degree. Probably made him the best hack driver in town, knowing his clients with just a glance.

She definitely needed to keep him in mind, hear his tales, and learn just who this skeleton driver named Fat Jack was.

Certainly, more than he first appeared.

"Is there anything else you can tell me?" she asked. "I'd be most grateful."

Or what he was willing to tell her.

Jack shrugged, the kind that was neither confirming nor denying. Apparently the test she'd passed earlier, of even seeing and caring about the news clip, of holding onto her hat and breeches as he sped through Butte, only went so far.

For now, anyway.

No use pushing him harder. She had no doubt they'd cross paths again.

"I thank you, then," she said, tipping her hat to him, which only made the man grin harder. "You've given me a place to start. It's much appreciated."

A place to start looking, and possibly to start living again.

Cat glanced at the welcoming home and felt a slight twist in her gut. Nerves, possibly? It'd been awhile since she stayed in any place resembling an actual home. A home that had been lived in by a family.

Not just a parlor house or brothel. Not a boarding house either.

A real, honest to God home.

That's exactly what Mrs. Allen's felt like. What the very earth here she was standing on was telling her. Sure the ground and the mud might be frozen hard, but there was no mistaking the feeling.

The only mistake was in her taking these few last steps and knocking on her door.

She didn't want to disrupt the feeling of this place, intrude upon it. She'd done that enough in her life.

Jack lifted down her bag. "You tell Mrs. Allen I sent you. She'll give you a few more breaths, seeing as she runs a respectable boarding house and all, for families and the like, as well as the miners, at least before throwing your hide out."

Which, Cat had expected.

"In that case," she said, "I thank you again."

She accepted the bag, easily slinging it over her shoulder. She turned, boots thumping on the small wooden stairs, that darn knot in her stomach tightening even more. It was time to face the kind a woman who won the respect of a driver like Fat Jack and the perspective newsboy. Time, indeed, to find another place to start. Another chance, a place to make it right.

Any little bit of it she could.

Her hand was reaching for the knocker when Jack called out.

"One last thing, Miss Cowboy. Who told you 'bout Mrs. Allen, anyway?"

Cat shifted and turned.

Again, she felt her senses come alive. Her focus sharpening.

"A newsboy," she said. "Sharp lad. Perspective."

"Sharp, huh? He got a look to him?"

She turned even more.

Again, felt the tingle slip through her stomach, carrying all the way to her hands.

"He did," she said. "Green eyes. So green I could see straight through that black smoke."

"Well, now." Jack tapped the brim of his hat. "I reckon you might just make it to the living room if Dusty gave you the all-clear."

"Dusty?"

"That's right. That's his name. A good enough, lad, if I do say so."

Jack didn't explain more. He waved her goodbye, then went to patting his horses, whispering to them in some language she didn't understand, or perhaps just grumbling. He ran his hands down one leg, then another, checking for injuries and lost shoes, she imagined.

Certainly after the ride he'd given her, which clearly had been his intent.

Then, Fat Jack vaulted back up, black overcoat flappin' like he was a great important thing himself. Then he and his hack took off, kicking out bits of gravel and stone which pelted her legs and arms.

She watched him leave, disappearing into that smoky black when anywhere else in Montana she'd be watching a searing, beautiful sun blazing down at her as it slowed made its way overhead, slowly reaching towards the west where it'd sink right straight behind those black, crag-like mountains.

Not here, though.

Not in a place like Butte.

Just like now more than before, she felt the rightness. To be here. This place. This porch.

Her instincts had carried her this far, it was time now to see where they'd lead her.

She touched her scarf again, and for a moment she felt Alice beside her. The old Alice with her smile, so warm and encouraging. And this time, Cat felt her own smile light up. Just a little bit, anyway, but enough.

Somehow, it would be enough.

She reached up and smacked that cold, brass knocker hard.

CHAPTER SIX

While Cat waited on the little family-style porch of Mrs. Allen's, she couldn't help but marvel at the whole street itself. She'd never before seen this... this way classes and society here seemed to brush up against each other. It was, in all of Butte it seemed, like they was made to rub elbows, as opposed to the other way around. How they were all these homes, for families and the like, then boarding places like Mrs. Allen's, yet sprinkled in between all that were these giant, monstrous mansions with more rooms than the inmates probably knew what to do with. That, and their legion of servants needed to keep those places spick and clean.

Cat gave another swift knock, and this time the door opened.

It was a Chinaman who answered.

A short man, his head barely reaching her shoulders, with a wiry beard of gray that matched what little hair he had on top. He wore simple black pants and shirt, loose fitting in just about everywhere. He looked nothing like the done-up pictures she had in her head, the few pictures she'd seen on her travels, of Chinese dressed up in their silks and robes that about reached their knees, lookin' a might similar to that of a dress.

He looked liked any other man, though one clear as day from the Asian homeland.

He sure sounded like one, too, certainly when he opened that door wider upon seeing her. That's when he started talking. She couldn't understand a single word he said. Not that she was supposed to, as it wasn't English he spoke and she certainly didn't speak Chinese.

His smile, though, was all kindness and welcoming. And then he began bobbing his head like a duck, up and down, and gesturing her to come in, come in!

Bowing?

To her?

Yet he kept on going. Didn't seem to mind how she was dressed one bit. Up and down he went with that little head of his, as if a guest at the door was a guest at the door, regardless of how she looked.

Which it should.

Matter, anyway.

She was no lady, that was for darn sure.

Cat tried to wave his gesture and welcome away, but apparently that was simply a signal for her to come inside, and he practically bustled her right in, somehow without even laying a hand on her, which was quite impressive.

"My name is Cat. I'm here about the boarding—"

That's was all she got out before he about whisked off her bag, so fast even she hadn't quite realized his intent until her bag was resting on that smooth, polished floor. Then he was hustling her towards some fancy-like chair, the cushion and fabric worn from so many sitting before her. Then the Chinaman was gone. Slipping away on soft shoes and then through some heavy door down the hall, which thudded shut behind him.

Cat could only blink.

This was not a reception she'd ever counted on. Not that she'd had a whole lot of dealings with the Chinese; they mostly kept to themselves unless a business transaction, such a laundering or some damn fine noodles, were needed.

And if she were being honest, which she tried to be, her perception was a bit off. Especially since she hadn't expected one to be employed here. In general, it was not their place to work in a home such as this. She knew some of the parlor houses, the upper class of the line where her sisters worked, were not uncommon. But a boarding home?

From her experience, those were usually run by family members or others of the same nationality. Hirin' out help, especially women and mothers who couldn't get much else in the way of jobs. But a Chinaman? And in a home that looked exactly like her own mother's home?

Because without a doubt, this *was* her mother's home. Or the exact mirror image of what it once was, what it had once looked like. At least before the weight of the world slammed on top of Cat and Alice and all those happy childhood memories turned to ash.

Just the sight of this place brought tears to her eyes, tears she'd long thought gone and dried up. She should simply leave. Grab her bag and find another place to reside in. One that fit her better, that wouldn't intrude on the families and the like who clearly lived on this street, or who might even still live in this home.

This place wasn't meant for her.

And yet, she couldn't help herself.

It was like some tether held her tight and pulled her forward.

Instead of opening that door and headin' the way she came, she left the entryway and walked into the home, feeling a shiver run right up and down her back, never once letting her go.

A simple staircase led up to a second story, and a tidy rug, red and worn from the press of heavy boots and shoes but still cared for, slipped on down each step. But what drew her attention and make no mistake, was the sitting room just off the entryway. She couldn't help it. Couldn't help her feet being drawn in further still, like a call of a nightingale that she simply couldn't ignore. A call she felt thrumming right down and through her body.

The windows overlooking the street—not that she could see much the street through that smoky black—well, they were washed and cleaned. Handsome, heavy curtains were pulled back as if to capture whatever sunshine managed to poke on through the thick ash.

Cat moved about the room, her fingers trailing along the tops of chairs. Her ma would be appalled at her manners, at her not keeping her hands to herself.

Truth was, she couldn't help herself.

She needed to feel, to touch that fabric with its mix of soft and coarse threads. To see that this place wasn't made up of her own imagination but was real.

Real as her own two feet walking about the place were.

Her boots, the soft thuds they made, along with the small smattering of dirt and ash that trailed behind her like a warning.

Her stomach tightened.

She *should* go.

But then, her feet really did seem to have a mind of their own at the moment. Or maybe it was just every inch of her not caring one wit about what was logical as she walked in this place, this place that whispered of home, of the good times. Of the love and all that joy, and oh, she could feel it in this place.

Feel like it was in the very bones themselves of the building.

The couches with their wooden armrests and feet practically gleamed like they'd just gotten a new dosing of polish recently, and it made those worn cushions even more inviting to sit on. Not cause they'd been polished and cleaned, but 'cause they were used. Well used, and lovingly so. They looked solid and sturdy like they could bear the weight of any who sat in them. The weight of a body, and the weight of all they carried inside them.

The whole place itself looked and felt like it was meant to be a home, one meant to be lived in.

Her stomach twisted again, like it was trying to wrap itself into one knot until it got so painful she just turned tail and ran.

She didn't, though.

Not even when the smells swept in from the kitchen.

A mix of cinnamon, spice, and... nutmeg. Apples and baking bread. She could almost feel the fluffy bits in her mouth as they flaked off. Like she could reach out into the air and touch them herself and then they'd be right there, in her hand. The lingering warmth, the smells, all of it, felt like it had seeped into the very place itself and every time you breathed you just dreamed of pie and apples, like no amount was ever enough.

Cat's knees shook. She braced herself on the back of that couch and just focused on breathing.

On keeping herself upright.

On keeping the tears back just a bit longer.

She hadn't known, truly, that she had any left in her. But then again, she'd never walked into a place that felt like her mother, that felt like the life she and Alice had once had.

What a long journey, long road, really, just to find herself back here.

Home.

Or where the home of her past had once been.

She felt her heart simply ache from the loss... of losing her mother, as if it had happened just yesterday and not years before.

A tear fell down her cheek.

She wiped it away. Probably left a smear from all the dirt and ash she was covered in. But that was just the one and no one else had seen her moment of sorrow seeping through. Not a weakness. No, she'd never believed that, but sadness and tears were only for those who could afford to let the whole world see. Or for herself, to feel.

She was not that person anymore. Couldn't be. Not if she wanted to keep on living. Keeping on putting one boot in front of the other.

She'd also thought she was completely alone.

She wasn't, though.

And again, she'd lost count of how many times in just this one day, this short time since she'd stepped off the train and onto that crowded, bustling platform of Butte, that Cat was again surprised.

Another *was* in the sitting room with her and clearly, like the day outside was night, had seen the evidence... of Cat's tear like a lightning bolt, now stainin' her cheeks.

"I reckon," the woman said, "you've got a good reason for coming into my home."

CHAPTER SEVEN

It took all Cat's control not to whirl. To not reach and draw for her gun, the one that was still packed safely away in her bag, as the law here liked. But that instinct, to react, to defend, it had bled into her from the day she'd started on this hard life.

And while her gun wasn't there, her hand still rested on the empty holster.

Which was not at all polite. Certainly since she was the one intruding on another woman's home. One which they both knew Cat didn't belong in.

Cat let go and turned to face the woman. Which, at least for a moment, made all those feelings brought up by this house—the apple pies and the dough her ma had baked every fall when the apples ripened in their small corner of the world—fade away.

Instead Cat focused on where she was and on the woman in front of her.

A woman with her hands cocked on her hips, her full dark skirt sprawling about her ankles. She stood there confident as all get out. Loose blouse posed like she was ready to go into battle, even with the white flour dusting all about her person, from her apron all the way up to her face.

It was also clear that this was no woman behind in the times. No, she was sportin' the latest style, sleeves good and tight except for the appropriate puff at the shoulders. And yet Cat still glimpsed a fair few amounts of stitchin' and sewin', certainly along the skirt's hem.

This, clearly, was not a starving woman desperate for boarders, which probably made Cat's chances of boarding here pretty darn slim, no matter what the kid Dusty and Fat Jack mighta thought. Especially the way this woman, clearly this Mrs. Allen, stood there on that polished wood floor like her hands were restin' on her own guns, ready to draw and shoot and clearly defend if necessary.

The woman's narrowed gray eyes were like twin daggers, and they glared down at Cat like she was an intrusion on her small domain.

Which she was.

The flour—cause clearly it was her doing the apple pie bakin' and rollin' out the dough—found its home in her hair, too, though that was mighty hard to tell since she also had a healthy streak of gray sportin' in her coal-black hair.

Even with all this, the perfect image of domesticity, Mrs. Allen was far from defenseless, make no mistake.

Specially when that hard gaze landed square on Cat and her empty holster.

Cat tried her best at a smile, though a smile was the furthest thing she felt like, seeing as she was staring at the ghost of her ma, at least the ghost when her ma had gotten worked up in quite a fury over something her pa had done. She'd been a range banshee through and through when that happened, and Cat had learned early to steer clear and take cover.

She didn't now, though.

Instead, she stood her own ground and kept on mustering some semblance of a smile.

Behind the formidable woman, the Chinaman peeked out his

head. Tiny eyes wide. He said something that Cat hadn't a clue about 'cept that she thought it was English, though with his accent so heavy it still sounded like a bunch of mumbling to her. She did hope he was at least informing Mrs. Allen it was *him* and not *Cat* who'd pushed her inside when she'd been inclined to turn back the way she came.

Which she was now makin' a right mess things, her poor manners and all. Ma would certainly skin her hide if she'd been standing there.

"Forgive me," Cat said.

She swept off her hat. Felt the sweat and stickiness of being too long in a train car and not enough time in fresh air. Not that there was any here either, fresh nor air. Also, her hair was quite the mess, even tied back in a braid as it was, already unraveling and sticking about her forehead. She probably looked the part—the dangerous, uncivilized wild woman Mrs. Allen thought her to be.

"My name is Cat. I do pardon the interruption, Mrs. Allen, calling on your home unannounced. I was told you were a boarding establishment. Though those who recommended me hadn't been clear on the... the type of boarding you ran."

One that was too much like a home. One that wasn't right for a girl like her, even if she'd donned her dresses and frills and the like.

Those gray eyes narrowed further if that were possible, and they were far, far from being kind.

"I am Mrs. Allen, and yes, I do take in boarders. I'd suggest checking with the other female boarding residencies. There are plenty in this city."

"I imagine so, but I'm not looking to work as such—"

"Good. For your kind of employment does not happen under my roof. This is a respected place. A place for men needing a hot meal and a warm bed, families and their mothers, too."

Cat nodded. "I do understand. I'm sorry for putting you out as such."

She really should have considered wearing the dress, even as wrinkled as it was, maybe even the awful, breath-stealing corset that partnered with it. But no. She'd wanted to appear as the woman she was, straight and true. It looked like she was paying the price for that... and if she were honest with herself, she'd expected it right from stepping off that train.

Or even more truthfully, when she'd stepped onto it in the first place.

What was done was done, though.

Cat placed her hat back on and gave a small nod. "I didn't mean to cause you discomfort. I'll be on my way."

She grabbed her bag and as she did, the *Bystander* flopped out. She would have reached for it, but Mrs. Allen, for whatever reason, retrieved it instead. Maybe it was her own sense of manners that were kicking in, regardless of Cat's ill look about her.

Mrs. Allen glanced at the paper, which Cat had left folded open to the advertisement, and quite strangely indeed, Mrs. Allen frowned. Her whole forehead looked a mass of wrinkles, specially when she turned that hard gaze back on Cat.

Mrs. Allen, however, did not hand back the paper.

She must have seen the article. Of that, Cat had no doubt.

And since there wasn't anything left to lose, and remembering Fat Jack's warning about her getting kicked out on her hind, she pressed on. If there was ever a chance to state her intent, this was it.

"I told you true," Cat said. "I'm not here looking for employment, not in your home and not in any house of ill fame. I came to Butte for my own reasons."

"And those are?"

Cat shifted. She hadn't been prepared to answer the question so soon, to give voice to it, as if doing so would make it real. And when something was real, stated like such, well, then you could actually fail. Try and fail and then where would she be?

She certainly hadn't planned on saying as much to the stern, aging woman before her. But then, if she were honest and she was sure trying darn hard to be, she would never be ready to answer this question. Too much at stake and all. Too much risk by speaking the words and making it real.

And then, possibly—probably—failing.

Just as she'd done with Alice.

"I can't quite say for sure," Cat said. "Cause I'm not really sure myself what I'm searching for would look like. Another kind of employment, I reckon. The kind of job where people who don't have much else, or no one else, can turn to. The kinds of people most folks don't care about none."

Cat nodded at the paper.

"I doubt it'd pay much. Or at all. A problem I'll come to soon enough. But my reasons are to try. Try and help those the rest of the world don't care none about it."

It felt like her ma was staring down at her. Cold and hard, as if she'd sensed a lie when she heard it.

Cat hadn't a doubt Mrs. Allen had this ability as well.

"Justice, you mean." Mrs. Allen straightened, but she did not look away from Cat.

Now it was Cat's turn to straighten, to feel herself under the rolling loop of a noose as if it were closin' in. Tightening. Something else, too. Something deeper in herself she couldn't begin to guess at.

Justice.

That'd been the second time today she'd heard the word. The second time she'd felt the rightness of the word... and how darn hard and scary it was.

"I reckon maybe so."

It was all Cat could say. All she managed with the way her throat closed itself up.

"Of all the boarding," Mrs. Allen whispered, "all the houses and options you got in this town, and you came here."

"I did."

Mrs. Allen took in a deep breath. Flour dusted off her like white snow, which was better than the black ash falling down outside.

"Who recommended you, then?"

"Two folks," Cat said. "Well, no, one actually. A boy, selling news-papers at the station. He's the one who told me first. Then the hack driver seemed to approve some."

"A boy?"

More flour sprinkled off Mrs. Allen. She started just a bit, just that little upward lilt of her voice. Eyes widening just every so slightly. Shoulders rising.

Mrs. Allen was both surprised and... something else. Almost like she cared about the opinions of a boy. A child.

Or maybe not just any child.

One in particular.

Cat's senses did their tingling again and she felt her awareness expand further. She pulled in yet more pieces of this puzzle she found herself in. Or more accurately, the puzzle surrounding this boy who'd practically challenged her as Mrs. Allen had just done, for Cat to name her business here.

And then daring her to actually do something about it.

About this woman who died. Norma.

Cat shook her head, pulling herself back to the sitting room with the clean windows lookin' out at the ashy, black world outside. Those welcoming couches, the apples and cinnamon that about coated Mrs. Allen's person. Every bit of the place, a contrast. A every bit both fitting and yet not.

Different.

Mrs. Allen who'd be willing to consider the thoughts of a boy and not throw Cat right out on her ass.

More than a story resided here, and Cat felt a little tingling of hope. Hope that she might stay... and surprise in herself that she wanted to.

She clamped down on *that* thought right fast.

"The driver, himself, was quite the character," Cat said. "Got me here right quick and managed to even scare me some back there."

Mrs. Allen closed her eyes for a moment, as if she needed to steady herself. "Fat Jack, correct?"

"Yes, ma'am. I told him, too, about the boy cause he was surprised I asked for your place as well."

Cat stepped forward. Her boot makin' the slightest thud noise on that smooth, polished floor.

"He told me the boy's name. Dusty."

Mrs. Allen went pale so fast Cat thought she might have to call for the Chinaman and ring for a doctor. She didn't faint, though, but got herself recovered so quick that if Cat was anyone else, she'd have thought she'd imagined it.

She didn't, though, imagine it.

Mrs. Allen knew more than she was letting on—about Dusty, about the article in the paper she held. A paper which was now crumpling up good in her strong grip.

"I never thought..."

Mrs. Allen shook her head. She smoothed the paper and handed it back to Cat.

"Well, I guess that's that. No matter. I suppose it's a settled matter, then. For a better or worse, well, that'll be for time to tell."

"What is, ma'am? Better or worse?"

"You, I suppose. You indeed. Well then, come in, Miss Cat. Let's see if we can't come to an arrangement."

CHAPTER EIGHT

It turned out that when Mrs. Allen was referring to an arrangement, she also meant one where her guests was cleaned and scrubbed up. All her dust and dirt stained travel clothes sent off, promptly to a nearby Chinese laundry, which the Chinaman, who Mrs. Allen called Chin Lee Fung, delivered himself. Then and only then, cleaned and appropriate like, at least enough, anyway, Cat found herself sitting down to a nice afternoon tea. There was a slice of heavenly pie set out on a table with all the trimmings, including dainty napkins and a white lace sewings covering up the table.

Course, the view outside that sitting room window was anything but nice. It was still black as all hell out there, reminding her that no, she was indeed not home in Miles City and that yes, this was likening a bit much to hell.

Except for that glorious smelling apple pie drifting in from the kitchen.

And yes, her mouth was watering something fierce, reminding Cat quite clearly just how long that train ride had been, jostling and uncomfortable and all the like. And precisely how long it'd been since she'd put something of substance into her belly.

It was amazing just how accurate her body was at telling time.

Still, hungry or not, this was the very last place Cat ever expected herself to be. Certainly when, by all appearance, they *were* about to have a right little ol' tea party, just the two of them.

An image that was instantly destroyed by Cat's dress, or lack thereof.

And Mrs. Allen hadn't blinked an eye when Cat came down the stairs in a clean pair of blue jeans and boots. Her boots were cleaned o' course (her mother had raised her right; made sure she didn't trail in any mud and such into people's homes, and that was a fact). While Cat sat on the chair with the worn but so comfortable cushions waiting for Mrs. Allen, she nearly lost herself in the feeling of this little room, this quiet, welcoming little house.

Heck, the cushion itself was as close enough to a feather straight from heaven after the long, jostling right in the train with an even harder place to park her rear.

There was no extra setting at the table, so clearly it would just be the two of them coming to their "arrangement" as Mrs. Allen had called it.

Were there no other boarders here?

She'd listened for them while she'd been changing and scrubbing off her travel grime. She hadn't heard any commotions in the two rooms next to hers. No coming and going up the stairs except for the Chinaman, though she'd quickly learned to identify his nearly silent, swishing feet on the carpet.

Clearly, she was the only boarder.

At least, the only one *living* here.

On a small table near her was a large pile of letters. They sat there mostly in a neat stack, with the gloomy haze of the outside world shining through those windows. She didn't look too close, that wouldn't be polite, but they were there and Cat had learned early to study her surroundings. So, she did, and her focus was on that odd piling of letters.

Letters written in scrawling handwriting which graced each

envelope that she could see. Not that this was unusual, nor that most were hard as all get out to even read. But what *was* unusual was they were written by different hands. And each one addressed to a different lady. In fact, she couldn't see one to Mrs. Allen herself.

Not that Cat was about to rifle through them, that would not only be impolite, it'd break the trust Mrs. Allen had already placed in her.

So Cat just sat and waited, taking in every curtain, lace, and fabric, everything she could see, her mind puzzling through each detail, each clue, slowly adding them up.

Finally Mrs. Allen appeared, bringing a heavy tray with said apple pie slices, and she immediately swooshed Cat away when she was about to get up and help.

She might wear boots and blue jeans, but her ma had taught her right.

"Nonsense," Mrs. Allen said. "I can see a heavy soul clear as day, specially one that's past time for a hearty meal."

While apple pie did not qualify as hearty, Cat's stomach growled quite fiercely in agreement.

The Chinaman was nowhere to be seen, so Mrs. Allen served them both the pie and the tea without any comment or pause at all. Cat's eyebrows raised at this, but she said nothing.

In fact, she waited until Mrs. Allen was ready to begin with the speaking, especially the questions.

It didn't take long.

Not when Cat's fork finally scraped off the last bits of flakey brown crust, the bits of apple juice that had spilled onto the small, porcelain plate. When Cat put her fork down, it clinked bright and true on that plate, and Mrs. Allen set her own down. She entwined her fingers together and sat back.

Ever the image of the patiently waiting matron. Very well, patient or not, it was clear Mrs. Allen was ready to get right to business. The small respite of cleaning and eating was done.

Cat nodded. "I imagine you have questions for me."

"I imagine you have a few yourself."

"I do. First and foremost, though, was why you were willing to let me on. Though, the longer I'm here, the clearer that becomes."

"Oh?"

Mrs. Allen's gray eyes widened, though not much, like the lady was quite the hand at cards and knew to hide her tells. The fact that Mrs. Allen was even aware of them and was clearly workin' hard at keeping them calm and under control was quite unusual as well.

Just another mystery piling on top of all the others.

But while Cat had a few guesses to Mrs. Allen's person, she also didn't know the lady. The last thing she wanted was to offend.

However, Cat had found, at least from experience, that she simply got better results when she was clear and to the point. Often blunt to a fault, as Alice would constantly warn her of.

A trait that, unfortunately, had both helped and haunted Cat in her line of work... both being a lady of the evening and this, this other one that was still as yet takin' shape.

But she'd come here promising to be who she was. No point on stoppin' that now.

"If you don't mind my speaking openly, Mrs. Allen, but you are a former lady of the business."

"Am I?"

"That's why you were willing enough to allow my board. Though, truthfully, it was mostly my explaining that I had no interest in startin' up the trade again."

"Most girls don't," Mrs. Allen answered. "But then, life often has other plans. Jobs of any kind really, but certainly ones that pay more than a mouthful, are not easy to come by. Even in Butte."

"Usually, too, how they got into it in the first place, ma'am. Life and some pretty poor choices."

If any choices at all.

For a woman, especially one who mighta lost her husband, who might have a clutch of mouths to feed. Or hell, just a child barely outta her bows and pigtails with no parents alive to care for her, or her for younger siblings. In this life, this particular... well, calling wasn't the right word, and yet one that every other person seemed to slap on them just fine... but in truth, there were rarely any choices.

Any at all.

Mrs. Allen's finger drummed once on the table. "And how did you go about surmising that I was a former... lady?"

Cat nodded to the table. "Your letters."

"So?"

"They aren't addressed to you, and no, I didn't go through them. I like to believe I'm a woman of honor. But those I saw just sitting there so, they were written all to girls, different girls in different hands, and not a one to you."

Mrs. Allen shrugged. Her blouse rose up and fell, the puff about her shoulders giving a little sway.

"I have many friends. I do run a boarding establishment."

"With no boarders yet, that I can tell. Other than me."

Mrs. Allen's mouth tightened just a bit around the corners. "A recent development, one I do not expect to last. My pie, after all, is quite renowned."

"I don't doubt it, but still doesn't change the fact that those letters aren't for you or your boarders."

Cat crossed her arms and leaned forward. Her hair, now nicely braided and not the unraveling weave it had been before, slid down her own shoulder.

"Truth is," Cat said, "my family is dead and gone, so I never had a need to hide. Hide who I was, the job I was in. But others? Others who still send money off to their own mothers, who are in a desperate need of their own, barely making enough to feed all those younger brothers and sisters? For them, for those ladies, the need is quite high. Hide the truth, as such. So, they find themselves a respectable place to have letters mailed and received, to keep family from knowing the truth."

The horrible truth that would blacken a woman faster than stepping out into Butte's daylight air would.

Mrs. Allen let not a whip show. Not a sign of concern or surprise.

Made Cat want to shift her bum on that worn-in, lovely cushion. She didn't, though, cause that would be showing Mrs. Allen a tell of her own, and she had no intention of doing so.

"Is there more?" Mrs. Allen asked.

Well, yes. Indeed there was, as Cat explained.

Mrs. Allen's sense of fashion, for one. She might not be sportin' the latest in silks and lace, but it *was* the latest fashion. Also the fact that there were *no* other boarders (which Mrs. Allen still did not comment on). And then there was her association with the green eyed boy, a boy named Dusty.

Cat said all this, and through it all, Mrs. Allen gave not a sign away. Simply tapped a finger on that table, the slight clink of fork and plate playing a gentle game of tag, if you will.

Or a dance.

An interesting dance, indeed.

"But," Cat continued, "not only did you get out of the business, you carry a respectable quality about you. By others. Fat Jack, for one, and I have a feeling if I wandered around town long enough, the list would get quite long. You are respected and that's something not lightly done."

Mrs. Allen shrugged. "This is Butte. She is a strange town."

One where the underworld stood out stark and bright, right where the eye could see, clear as day. Yes, Cat had seen that for herself.

Cat crossed her legs. Her blue jeans pulled 'round her knees, but she leaned back in that chair feeling settled, confident. The sense coming again that yes... yes, this was right.

The right place.

Even Mrs. Allen, her and her home that carried along this constant reminder of a family. One that still got to her, hell even now sitting here after she'd given herself a few minutes of grief alone, upstairs. The feeling wouldn't leave her.

Instead it stayed right there, right at her throat. An emotion ready to burst on out if she let it.

Finally, Mrs. Allen set her own plate down.

"The truth of the matter is, curiosity itself is a mighty powerful thing. And you, Miss Cat, are a walking curiosity. I have no doubt that's why you found yourself in Fat Jack's care. I have no doubt that's why it was Dusty who gave you that paper."

A paper that Mrs. Allen slipped out from underneath the tray. Hardly jostling the forks and plates, caused the apple pie—the half thing sitting there not yet devoured cause there was politeness to consider—with its thick bits of the juice and apple chunks to jiggle a bit as Mrs. Allen removed the paper from its hiding place.

Which Cat hadn't noticed was even there.

Hadn't noticed the slight—very slight—uneven balance to the tray. Or the way her tea had tilted just a bit too much to the right instead of being nice and even like.

Oh, there was no doubt Mrs. Allen knew of the evening, but more than that, she knew of the shadow world. Her awareness, how she paid attention to all those details, a cool patience, and more than just a bit of daring—she'd accepted Cat as a boarder, after all. But there was that a healthy dose of cunning. A required trait if one wanted to keep one's boots on.

Mrs. Allen gently laid out the paper onto the table, though careful to keep it far from the pie itself and the stickiness of their unclean plates.

"You are right, Miss Cat, on many accounts. I was lady of the evening and yes, yes, I knew the woman."

Mrs. Allen sat back a moment, still sitting so straight and tall, but there was no mistakin' the sudden pain that clouded her eyes before she shuttered them.

As if she didn't dare let Cat or anyone else see.

Except, Mrs. Allen did open her eyes and she did not hide the swell of water there. The tears that she didn't dare shed because, well, how could she mourn for a fallen woman? How could any of them?

It was simply not allowed.

And yet, the tears were there. And she was showing them,

showing them to Cat even though she was now a respectable lady of society. Someone who'd gone and shed her shadowy past and this place here, this city of Butte, had decided to tip its hat in some kind of acknowledgment. Or arrangement.

Yet still, this didn't change the truth.

A woman had died, and regardless of who she was, someone or many someones mourned the loss.

Respectable or not.

"Who was she?" Cat asked.

"Her name is—was, Norma. And she was my friend."

CHAPTER NINE

Cat sucked in a deep breath. Breathed in the baked apples and cinnamon and nutmeg spices, then let it out again. Breathing was one of those tricks she'd developed to help clear her mind, to rustle up that focus her pa had taught her.

So, she did it now with what she knew of Mrs. Allen as they sat there together, this little slice of domestic life while the blackness of Butte's midday glared at them from the windows. The white lace, the table cloth, the heat of tea still blowin' out the top from her small, dainty-like cup.

Yet, there was Butte, dark as night, black as all hell, watching over them and what they were discussing there.

Somehow, this seemed fitting.

A dead street walker, suspicious circumstance, and both ladies, in their own way, mourning her passing.

Norma.

There was, however, another matter to discuss before Cat asked some hard truths about Norma and Mrs. Allen's relationship with her. The truth was, everything they discussed now, shared at this little table with the little cups and plates, all that hinged on this other matter. It was the true reason Cat was sitting here right now, belly full of pie and tea and not riding on some bouncing, jostling hack through the black to some other establishment that would accept the look and truth of her.

Cat gave a nod to the newspaper. "I came to Butte, for this. For those like Norma."

Like Alice.

Cat gently pushed aside the thought.

"But first," Cat said, "you wanted to discuss my arrangement here. Seems to me this is 'bout the right time to do it."

Mrs. Allen let a small smile peek out. It caused her face to wrinkle even more, making those laugh lines and other, harder lines, more pronounced. But the smile was a more nod to Cat than a one of joy or happiness, or anything else of the like.

Maybe even a nod to herself, as well.

"Very well," Mrs. Allen said. "I see your reasoning. Then let's put the cards on the table, if you will. Justice. That's what you aim to do here in Butte, even if you don't see it as such yourself. At least not yet, anyway. But... that's what you're aiming to do. And frankly, that's what we're needing."

"I am no law officer. I'm not riding around in any Black Maria clanging the bell, as such. You know, on that end I can't do much for justice."

"Neither can they. Neither *will* they."

Cat tipped her head in acknowledgment.

It was a truth they all knew well. A justice that was overseen by judges and their like, who already had made their stance quite clear towards those who walked on the shadow side. Oh, they gave a nod with their overly large chins, a 'thank ye well' for all the money them fines and whatnot brought into a city, but justice? Or hell, even a fair hearing?

Mrs. Allen rose from her chair, and Cat followed suit.

It was a mix of manners and politeness, and perhaps, too, cause there she was, wearing men's clothing and now... now discussing a path for her, a vocation, that wasn't at all suited to a woman and yet one that would only be dared filled by a woman.

At least, a different kind of woman. The kind that simply had nothing else left to lose. No children. No family ties to keep secret, keep hidden. Just the ghost haunting her, Alice and all the others she'd known along the way, who'd been treated by the worst of society and then simply discarded. Uncaring. Unloved. And here she was, a woman, and one who both wanted and needed... to seek justice.

Could she?

Dare she?

Yet, regardless, this idea took hold and held her something fierce. Again, the feeling... of rightness.

And fear, too. A right healthy dose of it. Cause there was Alice to consider, and Cat's failure there. A failure she could very well repeat now with Norma, with Mrs. Allen's request.

"As I told you, Miss Cat, we're needing justice. Corruption rules in any city, anywhere in the country, and, I imagine the world, too. But here, though, Butte is... different. Our way of life is different. Those at the top, as I'm sure you've heard, our self-appointed 'Copper Kings' who openly flaunt the wealth reaped off the backs of our miners, our folk living down in the muck and shadows who see a bare dime of it. Then there are our girls, living in that same muck, who get by with barely enough food while others take whatever profit she earns and doom her to that life for an eternity."

"I noticed Butte doesn't worry much about hiding her colors."

"No, she does not. In fact, I think she takes pride in it."

Mrs. Allen gestured to the window, the smoky blackness outside, all that falling ash. "This is a sight you'll see all through winter, and why? Because those businesses running their mines can do so whenever they damn well please. Burning their ore in the open pits while the rest of us are barely breathing, lungs and chest filling with all that foulness. And those unfortunate who get sick? They'll be dying off, right quick. And no one, anywhere, does anything."

Mrs. Allen turned to Cat. "Not our mayor nor our *esteemed* judges. Not the chief of police. They can't do anything."

"If that's the case, what is it you're expecting, or wanting me to do? Like as not, I can't go cleaning the air for you."

Cat moved away from the tight little corner she'd sat in. Careful to not knock over the table or any of the delicate plates and bowls resting there, which even now waited to be swept off and cleaned. This image here, one of the domestic, of a quiet, civilized life, would have sure made Alice smile. And yet, that was not at all the conversation they were having.

The two sides of Butte, standing hand-in-hand.

"I want you to find the truth," Mrs. Allen said. "Wherever that truth takes you. About Norma. About what happened to her."

The truth.

The words vibrated through Cat, humming, growing more powerful the more she thought on them. And Mrs. Allen, she didn't give Cat a moment to consider, or reconsider, too hard.

"I've already asked the law for help and been denied," Mrs. Allen continued. "The officers will not look further into Norma's death. They wouldn't even give the name of the doctor who tended her in her last moments."

"That was a bit brave of you, askin' after a woman they know to be... fallen."

After all, Mrs. Allen had her own reputation to consider and it was no light thing to put such at risk.

"I'm getting old enough," Mrs. Allen said, "to not really care about such things. At least, in some ways. I am well off enough, in money, in the reputation of my boarding house, where I don't need to rely... strictly on the officers' goodwill. Not that I'd ever dare their full wrath on me, but we all know my business is legitimate."

She meant harassing her.

It was something Cat knew from her time at the brothels. Hell, all the ladies knew it. The 'payments' madams made to certain officers to allow the doors to remain open, the tip offs when a raid was due to come in. And a lady, especially a former one of the night, yes, Cat could see how officers, certainly some, wouldn't care so much if that lady changed her stripes and started dawning the respectable cloth again.

Just give 'em an excuse and they'd be there. Ready and waitin.'

Mrs. Allen glanced at Cat in quite a significant manner. "And I do expect my business will continue to remain above reproach."

"As well as one can," Cat agreed.

Because the very fact that Cat was simply staying here would bring this into question, at least to anyone who wanted to come and stir up trouble, law officers or not. Still, that was Mrs. Allen's choice and risk to bear, though Cat would not bring in any doubt the morality of the business here. She would not be taking in any "side" jobs, as it were.

Mrs. Allen nodded, accepting Cat's unspoken promise. They'd both share this risk together, then.

"And the officers," Cat said, "are there any that you'd willingly trust? Or are they all taking pay in some manner?"

"There are a few, though not many. Jere Murphy is one. He's an honest man with an honest upbringing. A family man, too. You'll hear of him right quickly enough. He's a friend of Marcus Daly but never been in the pay of him, from everything I've heard. Though Daly, himself? Never trust that man, nor his declared rival, Clark."

"And you would have heard? About Murphy being on the cut?"

Another small smile. "I would have. Along with those officers that Jere Murphy has taken under him, bringing them up along, if you will. Though there are so few of them, as well."

"Their names?"

"Paul Sanders. Richard Fowl. Christopher Blake. Though, I warn you, Christopher's not a sympathetic ear. He does not like our kind. But he's not under the pay of city officials or the Copper Kings, which is something all its own."

"Any of 'em willing to answer some questions?"

Mrs. Allen shook her head. "I tried asking and they won't answer. Not a one of them."

"Afraid?"

"I don't know. Don't know if they're under orders not to by their boss or some other person. The not knowing, *that's* what concerns me most."

Mrs. Allen tugged at the sleeves of her blouse, the first display of uneasiness Cat had seen in her.

Other than the unshed tears, of course.

"I have this sense," Mrs. Allen said, "there's something bigger in play otherwise... why not tell me? Not even the doctor's name, surely that would bring no harm, yet they wouldn't. Norma was nothing to them, to anyone. At least, not anymore."

Cat remembered the article. Its hint that she had fallen very far indeed. Fallen to the role of street walker. And while Mrs. Allen seemed the kind to know all sorts of folk, the ones she actually associated with? Those she dared name friend? That person, Cat had no doubt, would not be some lowly street walker. Not some woman working out of her crib, barely big enough for a bed and maybe a little nightstand.

Mrs. Allen turned to the windows, wrinkled fingers clasped together. "My proposal to you is a simple one. I want you to shed light on the truth, wherever that truth brings you to, whoever it brings you to. In return, you may stay."

"Stay?"

"Room and board, and Chin will handle your laundry as well."

"And the cost?"

"Two dollars a week."

Cat's eyebrows lifted at that. "That's some generosity, Mrs. Allen. Specially as you have no other boarders."

Mrs. Allen waved her wrinkled hand. "That will change. It always changes. Truth be told, I'm sure word will get out of your staying here and we'll have a few visitors."

"I thought you said no—"

"For the tales, Lady Cat. Stories of meeting the Lady Detective. Or simply tales of meeting Cowboy Cat. Yes, that certainly does have a nice flare about it."

Mrs. Allen smiled.

Cat shook her head. The woman might no longer walk the line, but she certainly remembered a few of the tricks, one of the first and most important being the name.

Memorable, to say the least.

"Yes, yes," Mrs. Allen continued on. "They'll come here to meet you, and make no mistake. As well as a few slices of my pie. I'll inform Chin. Also, Mrs. Beats, who helps with the cookin' when we have a fair few extra mouths interested in eating. Yes, I'll send word, for sure. To Dusty as well. He knows all the right places, all the right people to get the word out. Someone will bound to come by that knows."

"Knows?"

"What happened, of course. We'll be sure to let that bit out, too, that you're interested in Norma, in finding out what happened to her. Sympathy, if you will, for a fellow night lady."

Mrs. Allen's eyes got a calculating look to them. Cat had no doubt that she was counting numbers and bags of flour and whatnot, seeing it all in just those few seconds, before nodding her head in that crisp, firm way.

"Yes, yes. I think that will do nicely. Draw out the right sorts and the wrong, if we're lucky."

"And earn some money, too?"

Mrs. Allen smiled. "Isn't that what life's all about?"

Cat wasn't quite sure how news of her staying here, even as strangely dressed as she was for a lady, would mean learning some news of Norma. But then, this was Mrs. Allen's town. If she thought someone might come by interested in meeting the woman looking into Norma's death—yes, that may be the case.

Especially if Green Eyes, or Dusty as Mrs. Allen called him, spread the news to the right folks, indeed.

There was only one way to know for sure.

Mrs. Allen shook her fingers at Cat, completely unconcerned that Cat was focused on her own thoughts.

"Regardless," she said, "don't concern yourself with my affairs. I know them quite well. So, if you're willing, I'd like to hire your services. Find the truth about Norma, however long it takes you. Is this arrangement fair to you?"

"More than I expected, honestly."

Mrs. Allen was nodding, already turning away to sweep up that tray of plates and the still warm, wonderfully smelling apple pie, but Cat wasn't done. She reached out and gently touched the older lady's arm.

Mrs. Allen glanced up.

"The arrangement is fine, but I do need you to answer one question."

"Yes?"

See, Cat needed to understand. Everything. Not just what it all looked like on the surface, all nice and tidy and wrapped up in little ribbons and bows. She didn't make no deal, ever, without understanding the real stakes in the matter. The personal ones, to be clear.

"Why?" Cat asked. "Why is this so important?"

"Calling her a friend isn't enough?"

"No. Not when you'll be risking everything you've built here."

And it would.

Respectable now or not, if word got out that Mrs. Allen was looking into the death of a prostitute, a street walker at that—and let's be truthful, it *would* get out—a lot of unfriendly eyes would be drawn their way. And what would those eyes want? What would they be looking for? What risks would Mrs. Allen, and by association and her own digging, would Cat be taking on?

She didn't know. Couldn't.

She simply didn't know the city well enough—the players, the movers and shakers. She didn't know the secrets buried here nor the lengths that some would go to keep them this way.

"You are indeed more than your appearance portrays," Mrs. Allen said.

"I thought my appearance was quite clear."

Again, the smile and the deliberate glance at Cat's still empty holster.

"Indeed. Indeed," Mrs. Allen said. "Maybe it's because we haven't been graced with a woman of your stature in some time. Or at all. Well, Miss Cat, it's important because I'm not blameless in this matter. Or many others. My past is my past. I've moved on from it, have a family, too, though mine are grown enough and away on their own. I've walked both worlds, my dear, and I'm done tired of watching them get trampled on. Those... those people who've just lost all the luck in the world, while others, somehow, managed to hold onto it."

Mrs. Allen looked up. Met Cat's eyes. Her gray ones filled again with shadows and unshed tears.

"People like me, Miss Cat. People who never quite ran out of luck and managed to walk away. The rest? They didn't. They died, and I played my part in it, too."

"So, guilt then."

"Guilt? Yes, but that's much too simple a word. There are many things I've done, that I've been party to, or simply stood by and done nothing. For most, I'm too late. I cannot atone for my sins or change the outcome, but now, even if in this small way, I'd like to start, to try, anyway. With Norma. She was a good person, a kind soul who simply got lost along the way. Or maybe the way lost her."

Mrs. Allen took a deep breath, eyes still shining and bright, but not a tear falling. Perhaps, like Cat, she just never dared cry for it would never be enough.

Nor would it change anything.

"So," Mrs. Allen said, "do we have a deal?"

Cat looked away.

Her gaze settled on the black world outside, past the once-clean window frames, the glass even now carrying a black shimmer from the ash makin' it its new home. She thought maybe she could make some movement out there. A glimpse of a hand, perhaps legs hurrying as fast as they dared along the boardwalk. Maybe even the black rump of Fat Jack's horses.

Cat closed her eyes.

Took her time.

Simply breathed.

Felt the focus, as her pa had taught, settle in about her.

She'd known, not consciously but deep down, she'd known. Known this task she'd set out for herself, coming here to Butte, searching for a life of justice, truth, too... would not be an easy one. Would be dangerous, more than she'd ever imagined. Certainly more so than living in Miles City had, partly as a prostitute, partly as a rancher ready to leap on a horse and forget the world and all its troubles.

Again came the image of Alice.

The feeling of her hand as it touched her shoulder. A chill she felt to her toes and straight into her heart.

She'd come here for a life... a life just like this one. Like the one that Mrs. Allen was standing there offering to her. All she had to do was say yes.

Risk and all, failures and all.

Possibilities endless. And the lord only knew, if he cared anyway, just where she'd might end up. Or who, exactly, might come her way next... asking for help.

The ones that already had been forgotten.

But not, it seemed, by Mrs. Allen.

Or by Cat.

"Mrs. Allen, I'd say you have yourself a deal."

They shook on it, and to seal the deal they finished off what was left of Mrs. Allen's pie. All the while as they enjoyed the last bits of flakey brown crust and apple drippings with that perfect dusting of cinnamon, Cat kept on thinking about the woman named Norma and wondering when she'd last tasted something so divine. Or, truly, when she'd last had a decent meal of her own.

And never would again.

Her and about a thousand others like her. Women. Children, both boys and girls. All of them real people with no hope left in the world except to fall further and pray they and their loved ones kept on livin'. And yet, those same people were faceless to those living on the civilized side of society with their Sunday dresses and coats. Their family meals.

And right there with all these thoughts came that tingling feeling. It raced on up her arms and legs and settled there, right in her chest, right above her heart.

Cowboy Cat.

It did have a flare to it.

CHAPTER TEN

True to her word, Mrs. Allen did get the word out about Cat staying at her boarding house. About the lady cowboy wearing her blue jeans and cowboy hat. About the lady who made no bones about her feelin' toward guns and knowin' how to use one.

A police officer came round too, but Cat didn't catch more than a passin' glimpse of him. Streak of blond hair standing out like a blazing Montana sun even in that deep, smoky haze while she ran an errand for Mrs. Allen, one she'd insisted would help Cat get the lay of the town and the hill. So, Cat donned her hat, her coat to ward off at least some of winter's chill bite, and gave a nod to Mrs. Allen. She went out walking through hell again, freezing as it was, but keeping herself warm as she could as she made her way to T. J. Bennett's. It was a Cornish grocery store where Mrs. Allen frequented, getting all the fixins' for her famous apple pie and other such stuff for supposedly kindly prices.

Course, Mrs. Allen could have just sent Chin, which meant she had a couple of purposes for Cat takin' this particular stroll. Sure, she got more in regards to understanding the city, learning the lay of the land, if you will. And it was a good reason. But was there another?

No doubt 'bout it.

Certainly when every two steps she took, boots slappin' down hard on board walk or crunched up cobblestones, depending on the street of course, about five heads turned her way. Watched her with eyes about falling out their faces. Kids running after her and all around, but not getting too close, never that.

Word was getting out about Cat, and make no mistake about it.

But—and here Cat had quite the hunch—Mrs. Allen was the kind of woman who never did any one thing when, in practice, she could get another three out of it. Every decision, every calculation, thought through and probably to the greatest detail. If, of course, yours was the kind of mind that thought in such a manner.

Mrs. Allen seemed the type.

And it was entirely possible, by Mrs. Allen's design or maybe a carefully placed remark from the mysterious Dusty, who Cat had not laid eyes on since she arrived in Butte two days earlier, that was the reason for the officer now following her.

And Cat knew it was one, too. No mistake about it.

Hard, sure steps on the boardwalk. Determined. Focused. The kind of steps that didn't give a damn about the muck and dried black bits from the street and its horses, who'd probably flung it about the place during their overnight runs and scrambles and deliveries. Steps that ventured right onto the crumbled, gravel-stone street when she'd veered into T. J. Bennett's street, not carin' one whit about what he might be stepping on except for keeping an eye on her.

Which Cat had been doing the same to him.

Or trying to.

Damn the man was good at keepin' himself hidden from view, even with that blazing blond streak of his. He went on hiding right behind all those other folk who'd gotten their eyeful of Cat and were now continuin' on with their lives. Those folk who'd mustered up the courage to venture out into the blackness or merely ventured out cause life simply couldn't stop even if the day itself resembled hell.

Dishes and laundry didn't wash themselves, even if they never got quite clean. Kids still needed to get themselves to school, though she'd never seen the sight as like. Whole flocks of them stumbling 'bout through that blackness, some even holdin' hands, makin' sure everyone, oldest to the youngest, got to where they were needin' to go. And laughing the whole way, too, though Cat seriously doubted their mas would think it funny.

And then, of course, were the mines, and well, those never stopped.

Nor the miners who trekked up that hill with their backs already bowing under the weight of the day—a day that was just getting started.

And while Cat got more of a feel for this place, for Butte herself and the people who lived here, she didn't catch more than that one glimpse of the officer. Sure, she got a sense of him, his purpose and that steel-like determination, all of which was another of her gifts, but that was all.

He'd kept himself hidden and right good at that.

No point being frustrated. Sooner or later, whenever he was ready, he'd show himself. Make his purpose, for good or ill, known. And she'd watch for it.

She always did.

Always would.

Cat let the door of T. J's slam shut behind her, the delicate glass shaking like the whole thing was gonna pluck right on out. It didn't.

She picked up Mrs. Allen's order, a couple of boxes and other such goods straight from the Mr. Bennett of T. J. Bennett's himself. The man gave her a kindly old smile, one that about burst out from underneath his very large, very curvy mustache. Oh, he sure took a gander at her, dressed as she was, but he was certainly a friendly soul and peppered her with so many questions Cat could barely keep up.

Or keep track of time.

Before she knew it, it was pushing the noon meal and she hadn't yet started on digging in and finding some answers. Not that she expected Mr. Bennett to have detailed knowledge of Norma, but little hints. Clues, if you will.

And Mr. Bennett did have a few, even if he didn't quite know it.

She also got the sense he'd been in Butte for a time and seen his fair share of oddities. Nothin' quite like her, though, which he proclaimed with that same kindly smile. A twinkle in his eyes too, specially the one that was startin' to cloud up.

No doubt word be spreadin' like fire after this.

Which, no doubt, had also been part of Mrs. Allen's design.

Cat was beginning to see how the woman was so respected, especially considering the past she'd had. A shrewd, calculating mind, and make no mistake. Former lady of the night or not, she was a straight up good business woman, and Cat had a hunch the business people runnin' Butte knew it too, and let the woman alone.

Like Mr. Bennett here.

Who, Cat was guessin', had known Mrs. Allen during her days of walking the shadow life. Perhaps not intimately, but in a respected sort of way. Which again started fillin' in those holes of the story between Norma and Mrs. Allen. Little ones to start, anyway. Little ones cause she didn't have the whole story as of yet.

Which was getting to be a might bit frustrating.

Still, Cat did what she could. Asked Mr. Bennett news about the town, if he'd heard of Norma, and if he did know about her death and considered it relevant news, he didn't share it. Not that Cat would have expected much more, a businessman, well off to boot. He wasn't the type to have associations likenin' to Norma or probably on the infamous Galena Street, right smack in the middle of the Red Light.

Cat let thoughts of Norma fade and instead focused on Mr. Bennett, who'd been playing fair during their entire exchange. He treated her as a lady n' such, even though she was dressed like a herd wrangler straight in from ridin' the range (though without the dirt and dust cakin' her in about every crease possible). It wasn't long before he insisted on carrying the boxes out himself, but then, so did Cat.

They compromised.

She called a hack to take both her and her goods safely home, while he hollered for some boys to do all the heavy lifting. One boy even kept an eye out for other ruffians lookin' to snatch a free meal or can o' beans.

Truth was, Cat didn't mind the help or the coin it cost her. Not when she had the chance to pause there, breath coming out in white puffs right on that street, to look for her shadow. Her officer with his determined, hard-stomping boots.

Nothing. Nowhere in sight.

Not a single streak of sun she could see.

Cat didn't quite know what to make of it, and neither did her senses, or instinct, if you will. Curious indeed, though.

And also, maybe a bit of disappointment.

It meant this meeting, confrontation or not, was put on hold.

For now, anyway.

There'd certainly been intent in his following of her, which meant they *would* meet. But whether his purpose was for good or ill, she still didn't yet know. Couldn't, at least, until she shook the man's hand, looked in those eyes before she got a real sense of him.

For now, she'd mention it to Mrs. Allen and keep an eye out. It was the only play she had left to her right now. For the time being, anyway.

And yet... she felt disappointment.

Maybe it was cause she still didn't fully understand this place. Or maybe its cause she *did,* and it was Norma and the mystery surrounding her death, something that really caused her senses to prickle, that didn't sit right. Something about it that just made Cat feel unsteady. Like she hadn't quite got her grounding between the place she was beginning to know—Butte—and what'd been reported in the papers—and all that *hadn't* been said.

Like the name of the doctor.

The doctor who'd been telling the police, right from the beginning, that someone, or something, was playing foul.

And Cat hadn't learned anything new from Mrs. Allen, which,

truth be told, was quite the source of frustration. Fact was, the woman had waved off Cat's questions 'bout Norma, saying they'd get to them when the time was right. That she had all these preparations to make, what with Cat staying there and all. Two days, and she still didn't know the two ladies, their relationship, how their lives interconnected. Didn't know Norma's past, at least here in Butte.

How the hell could she go on solvin' what happened, finding out the truth as it were, without knowing those details?

Fact was, she couldn't.

And for whatever reason, Mrs. Allen seemed disinclined to tell her now that she and Cat had come to their arrangement.

Something, definitely, just not feeling right.

Cat was a patient person. Mostly. But this officer, her shadow followin' her and like and with such care, it set her shoulders itching.

Something already in motion.

Something that neither she nor Mrs. Allen would see coming.

Maybe it was the black smoke giving her this sense, this uneasiness. The sulfur and ash clinging about her person. Hell, it felt like it. The smoke which kept on spewing out the top of those chimney stacks, the ones that lined the hill right along with their counterparts, those great gallows frames which looked like they were waiting for a good ol' time lynching.

Not that she could see the darn things, but dear lord could she feel them.

Her eyes stinging and burning, feeling even redder today than yesterday, like all the mines were, for whatever reason, doing double-duty.

Cat tucked her scarf further into her coat, wishin' she'd had the guts to leave it back in her room where it'd be safe, but unable to part from it.

Something was indeed coming.

The moment she got back to Mrs. Allen's, she'd insist that it was time. Maybe not the time Mrs. Allen was wanting for, and maybe that time would never come despite her need to learn the truth of

Norma's fate. And hell, maybe Mrs. Allen wasn't too keen on reliving that part of her life, the part that Norma had played in it, and while Cat could understand that, the time for waiting was ending.

Cause clearly, the rest of Butte, or at least the shadow with the blazing blond hair, was taking that decision out of her hands.

Out of both their hands.

Cat climbed into the hack, thankin' the boys and the Mr. Bennett of T. J. Bennett's with a tip of her hat. She crossed her legs and her blue jeans pulled tight on her knees and hips. She shifted, feeling that itch again, right there between her shoulders.

Not alone.

Someone, somewhere, was watching her.

She kept searching for him, as if her gaze could pierce right through that black, smoky haze.

Nothing. Nothing at all out of place or unusual.

Any other person would shrug their shoulders. Laugh off the unease as silly paranoia. Not Cat. She wasn't the type to shrug off the feeling, the warning that something wasn't right. It was how she'd survived so long. Why she was here and breathing, and Alice, her dearest Alice, wasn't. And why, when she finally did leave this world, she'd been a mere shade of her former light.

Two sisters. Completely different. One alive, and one who'd died long before her breath had actually stopped leavin' her body.

So, sure, could be that this officer was comin' round just to make sure Cat knew the laws and such about guns. To which point, she still only wore her holster empty.

But... Cat didn't think so.

That explanation, while a simple one, and while there was nothing wrong with simple, this time simply didn't feel right. Not with the determination and steel that thudded in the man's footsteps. Why he'd worked so darn hard to hide himself. The simple explanation simply didn't add up.

Her hand drifted to her empty holster. She fingered the worn leather. Leather that had seen both the hard, parched sun and the thundering rains that about knocked your hat right off.

Even now, as her driver got his horses movin' (and a right normal speed, too, nothing at all like Fat Jack's ride through hell), she knew without a doubt that she was being watched.

Unseen eyes still followin' her.

Studying her, even now, as she fingered that empty holster.

CHAPTER ELEVEN

Cat didn't drop her hand away, gun or no gun, until they arrived at Mrs. Allen's. Her street with all its personality, the big mansions with their cleaned windows and green, growing plants. Not that they were actually growing. Nothing grew here in Butte, as declared by Mrs. Allen, though the big folk in their big folk mansions did their best to prove otherwise. A battle they were losin', which Cat could see clear as day. The ash and smoke that dusted every single leaf and blade of grass until they shriveled up and died like the rest of 'em before another poor gardener was sent out to replace the whole lot again.

Foolish.

And downright stupid.

Mixed in right with all that money and upscale living was the simple look and feel of Mrs. Allen's and others just like hers. The inviting white fences, rocking chair and swings, all of which stood there, unmoving, in that cold, still air.

Remnants of home, like little breadcrumbs.

Bits and pieces of a simple life long gone, when she and Alice had chased the chickens and geese round their yard, laughing and giggling and getting their stockings into such a state their ma would tongue lash them for days. Then there were those few moments when their ma actually sat down there on that rocker, stopped with all those thousand chores and errands that simply needed tending to, and instead enjoyed the peace and stillness of their world—stillness except for her two ruffian daughters, that is.

Those were the memories, the simple and quiet ones, that Cat held onto. That brought her both a smile and a sorrow to her heart something fierce. How could it not? How could she not see Alice sitting beside her right then, a matching smile on her face as if she could see Cat's memories, too? A smile that faded into nothing. Eyes that slowly leached all the joy and light and life to become these dead, hard, and cold things.

Eyes that Cat felt turn on her.

A cold she suddenly felt race down her spine that had nothing to do with the Montana chill weather.

Cat shook her head.

Some bits of her straight, blonde hair once again escaped from the braid. They tickled the side of her face, her cheek.

Hard to believe that this house, just looking at Mrs. Allen's place, could stir up so much. So many images and feelings she'd long ago thought were gone and buried. But then, maybe, the truth had a way of coming out. Of never staying hidin', regardless of how much you wanted it to.

Her driver pulled her right up to Mrs. Allen's, right at the little gate with its little opening, the kind that kept toddlers in but which tall folk could simply bolt on over if they wanted. And it wasn't until that moment, when the horses came to a clopping stop on the crushed gravel street, that Cat finally dropped her hand away from her empty holster.

Part of her wanted to go right on inside and retrieve her gun.

The other part of her, the part that her pa had taught about breathing and stillness, learning how to get a feel of a place and its people, that part of her knew darn well why she wanted it.

Fear.

Which meant that now was not the time to strap it on. Not when she wasn't the one in control. Especially when even now her heart was still racing.

A feeling that she'd been followed. Watched. One that didn't leave her the whole drive home.

Not a first time for her. Wouldn't be the last, either. Of course folks watched her; they couldn't help themselves. This, though... this had been different.

Deliberate. Careful.

But the real problem was she hadn't seen him. *Cat* hadn't seen him. And she saw everything. Everyone.

Cat got down off the hack, boots crunching the gravel, and thanked the driver again. She started hauling in her load along with some help from boys that she swore appeared right out of the cold, smoky black the minute they sensed a coin or two was to be earned.

She accepted their help and before long had a nice pile waiting to be taken into the house. She'd call for Chin, see where all this stuff usually went, but truly her mind wasn't so much on the task.

Instead, she moved quicker than she had earlier. Back then, what felt like days ago but really was only a few hours, she'd been frustrated at Mrs. Allen. How she kept on waving off Cat's questions about Norma and their past.

Now it was different.

Now, thanks to her shadow, the need to learn, to understand, pressed in on her hard.

No more sidestepping or waving her away.

The first thing Cat was gonna do was venture right into Mrs. Allen's kitchen, or wherever the hell her landlady was, and get some answers from the woman.

And as to be expected when walking into Mrs. Allen's were the glorious smells coming out from that kitchen. Little tendrils of delight that made your mouth water and your stomach growl. Two days and Cat was accustomed to this. Also, too, this could be one of the reasons why she *was* moving faster. She was, after all, hungry and her stomach had no qualms about reminding her n' such.

Loudly, too, apparently.

But what Cat *hadn't* been expectin' was a smell so darn glorious it about smacked you silly. Smacked you so hard on the head it made you stumble back a step or two, to the point you just might stumble right on off the front porch with its two creaking steps.

Heaven.

Pure and simple, heaven. No mistake about it.

And that's what nearly happened.

Cat nearly did stumble right on out the door, box and all. She didn't, though. Thought her pa might be proud of her at that, keepin' her wits, at least somewhat, when there was nothing but pure heaven blowing out that there kitchen.

Any lingering bits of sulfur and ash clogging her nose, gone.

Her frustrations of trudging through Butte, not seeing more than that one glimpse of her shadow, the uncertainty in her own abilities, the little worm of fear that was working hard, burrowing itself even deeper into her, faded away.

Just two steps into Mrs. Allen's and just like that, everything else simply fell away. Didn't matter so much anymore.

Cause heaven, truly, was all in the cooking.

Cat closed her eyes and simply breathed. Imagined Mrs. Allen doing her thing in that there kitchen, probably with some extra hands or two helping out, while Chin did all the carrying. Bringing in those great heavy bowls onto the dining room table. Chicken, oh yes, definitely chicken. And with all that fat drizzling and baking round it, melting butter straight into a giant pot of creamy-like mashed potatoes.

Pies, too, she sincerely hoped.

Oh dear lord, could she picture it all.

So could her stomach, which groaned and grumbled even louder. Why the heck was she still standin' there, it demanded? Get a move on, girl!

Cause there was also coffee to consider, recently brewed from the smell of it. And dear lord, it practically grabbed her by her braid and yanked her on forward.

She couldn't say no to coffee. Not ever.

And all that right there set off all the warning whistles and bells inside her head. Cause, while Mrs. Allen was a heaven-sent angel in that kitchen, the noon meals were usually a simpler fair, not some grand gathering with all the fixings, inviting in all the neighbors and their friends of friends, or heck, just strangers off the street. All except one day, one day that, no matter what side of a state or country you stood on, remained a steadfast exception to the rule—

Cat swore aloud.

She'd been so wrapped up in learnin' about Butte, in teasing what she could about Norma out of Mrs. Allen (and frustratingly failing at that), she'd completely forgotten what day it was.

Sunday.

The big day that was sort of a celebration for all the folk, big ones to the small ones, rich to the poor. A time for the church-goers to get together and meet, for families to join and catch up on the week's comings and goings. At least, that's what it had been like for Cat back during those kinder days before she'd lost everyone. And that norm had continued while she resided in Miles City. It stood to reason it'd be the same here in Butte.

Cat *should* have been expecting this.

The very first Sunday after Cat's arrival... of course it'd make sense that Mrs. Allen would mark today as the big day, the big opening to meet the lady cowboy as Mrs. Allen kept on saying, kept on telling anyone willing enough to listen.

Yet again, something so obvious she missed it.

What the hell was it about this city that made her stumble? Making small mistakes like this? Or maybe it wasn't so much the city but her purpose here.

Norma.

And her promise. To Alice.

To hell with it. Like she could give a reason for why she was making mistakes, missing the small details, something she never did before. Letting some house dredge up memories of her ma that made her want to turn into the same sniveling ladies she'd openly disdained as a child.

A Sunday gathering... and she'd straight-up missed it. But even putting that bit aside, why the heck had T.J.'s been *open*? Was that normal for businesses here? Or was it all part of some grand scheme by Mrs. Allen?

"God damn it."

Cat was about ready to dump the box right then and stomp into that kitchen and give Mrs. Allen a right good talking to about her practice of "arranging" Cat into the position *she* found most suitable, when she heard voices.

Lots of them, in fact.

Male, mostly.

All ages. The old, grizzly types with voices as rough as that gravel road outside, and they mixed right alongside with young ones, their voices still sweet and high, not yet roughened out from both age and darker times. And the accents... dear lord, she'd never heard so many different ones in all her life. Hard to tell, though, as it was mostly muffled, there being a door separating her and them, but there was no mistaking the differences in tones and vocals carrying on there in the dining room.

They were already here.

All these thoughts flashed right on through her mind. Then they settled. The chill, cold feel of realization sliding into place.

Cat kept her breathing even, though she felt her heartbeat quicken, her face getting red with a touch of anger.

Definitely a touch.

She was no pawn to be moved 'round as Mrs. Allen damn well pleased. No matter the reason. No matter the intent.

She was done being that pawn, the know-nothing that no one anywhere cared about. Or cared if they hurt.

Well, this damn well hurt.

Why the hell it did, so soon, after only two days staying here, Cat hadn't a clue and she wasn't about to take the time to figure it out. First, she needed to surmise just what was going on, what she was about to walk into...

Cat concentrated on breathing.

Did her best to keep the mouth-watering sensations from distracting her. There was a reason she'd done so well for herself, survived when others didn't or couldn't.

The facts started filing in.

All the sounds, the hustling and the bustling, the heavy stomp of boots on the polished wood floor. Definitely a full dining room, she knew. Seating for at least twenty, maybe more if one didn't care so much about things like elbow room and place settings.

A lot of folk, then, and probably from all walks of life.

This, this right here, had been Mrs. Allen's plan right from the beginning.

Get word out about Cowboy Cat. Open the doors to anyone who'd stay and board, and for those not interested in a place to lay their head, offer up the best food on the west side. Fact was, they'd all been gearing up for it. Cat, too. She'd played her part in helpin' Mrs. Allen and Beats and Chin all get ready.

Mrs. Allen just hadn't told Cat *when* that day would be taking place.

Even this right here had been part of her plan. Cat standing there in the damn entryway, arms aching from holding up one of several boxes she was responsible for seeing home safely. Sending Cat out for most of the morning, right to a fellow who didn't mind Cat wearing blue jeans like the men, only too happy for an attentive audience as he regaled tales of the old days.

The real question that remained was: *Why?*

Why set Cat up like this? A surprise on the doorstep? What had Mrs. Allen been hoping to gain?

Cat didn't know. Couldn't. Didn't know the woman well enough, didn't know Butte well enough.

She figured, and sure as hell hoped, Mrs. Allen had orchestrated all this with some good intentions in mind—and they better be pretty damn good intentions, too.

None of these thoughts, though, settled her. Not in the least.

Didn't ease the sudden tension right there behind her eyes. The tightening along her shoulder muscles. Tensing, as if... as if her trust had been broken.

'Cause it had.

Again.

Cat dropped the box right there on the floor. Not too hard to damage the bottles clinking inside. Manners and all died hard. But she was frustrated and make no mistake. Being put off for two days, not getting any discussion whatsoever about Norma, the *real* person Cat had been intent on helping. And truthfully, she was just darn tired of being surprised, of being off balance in this place.

Something about Butte—well, she was done being caught surprised.

Done, too, waiting around for answers.

And so was Alice.

Cat felt her sister, the ghost that was sitting right there on Cat's shoulder, the constant reminder of her failed promise to keep her safe, how even now Alice's memory sent a chill so fierce it practically turned her lips blue.

She took two steps forward, fully intent on busting into that kitchen and hauling Mrs. Allen to a side room for a little chat. Landlady or not, respectable or not, no one pulled Cat's strings.

Not since Alice's bastard husband.

Never again.

Cat reached for the door handle, the one that'd take her straight to the kitchen. Started to turn the knob when she heard the unmistakable opening of the front door. A sudden breeze of ash and sulfur assaulted the heavenly smell from the kitchen, and for a moment even won.

And the unmistakable creak and thud that this particular door needed to actually get itself closed. She'd a feeling that Mrs. Allen knew the door needed some tender loving care and purposefully left it just the way it was.

Cause no one anywhere in this house wouldn't hear *that* front door getting closed.

She heard a light shuffle of boots on the floor. Soft and quiet, almost like a cat as the person eased themselves in. There was no stumble or heck, even a quiet bump against that clinking box of glass and bottles and whatnot, the one that Cat had literally dropped down right smack in the middle of the front door.

A larger person would have to bend down, pick the whole thing up, and move it if they had any hope of actually walking into Mrs. Allen's boarding house. Certainly with dignity still intact. Jumping over boxes, after all, was the sort of business reserved for child's play.

Cat slowly dropped her hand away from the knob and straightened.

Now instinct, it was a powerful thing. If bred true, if you honed it to be the fine instrument that it actually was, surpassed even the everyday motions and memory of the body, of muscles working together, remembering repeated actions like they were as natural as breathing.

See, instinct was that and more. Much more.

The more came from an actual knowing outside yourself, sensing the moods of others, premonition, gut sense, all that, and then reacting. And it was reacting without thought, without your conscience getting in the way and screwing the whole thing up. It was also 'bout reacting in the *right* way. Recognizing what all your senses told you, whether those feelings were telling you defense or joy, didn't matter; they all came from the same place.

For whatever reason, Butte had been playing hell on her, muddling up what details she saw, what she pieced together, and more than a few she'd been missing, like this Sunday gathering for one, but the one thing that *hadn't* changed was her gut sense.

Her instinct.

If anything, that piece of her had only sharpened since she'd come here, since she'd stepped into Mrs. Allen's home, bringing out all those ghosts Cat had long thought buried.

Alice, her ma, all of it.

As she stood there, hands resting alongside her jeans, breathing in all the glorious goodness slipping by underneath the door, the roasting chicken and mashed potatoes and butter, her instinct was working hard.

She could almost see with just her senses alone. No eyes needed.

Instinct was simply that powerful.

She didn't have the same unease as earlier with her shadow. The police officer with his blazing blond hair. His hard, focused intent as he'd followed her, studied her. Hell, every moment he'd had his eyes on her it felt like the whole back of her neck had been prickling.

Itching almost, but not quite, to reach for her gun.

The gun that was still, of course, resting safely up by her bed. Tucked away, nice and safe. Which was certainly something she might need to reconsider, at least until she determined the officer's actual intent with her. Better to be safe and slapped with breaking some ordinance of the city since firing off weapons of any sort was not looked on kindly.

Or she could be dead.

Now, however, there was no tingling. No warning, at least, driving her to reach for the gun that wasn't there.

And make no mistake, she *was* being studied. Watched.

This time, though, it was more a curiosity. And something else. Like a daring, perhaps. A *need.*

Cat felt it all without actually seeing. The way the person moved 'round the room. Again, those light steps like a cat bounding from one spot to the next, barely seeming to touch or slip on that polished floor. One step then another. The kind of movement someone wouldn't even hear or notice unless they were paying attention. Like her.

All grace. All silence.

And Cat knew then why the presence felt familiar. Why it pinged all her senses but not in a way that warned of danger. Yet, anyway

Shadow soul, indeed.

Cat tipped back her hat and turned and came face-to-face with the boy, those piercing green eyes of his. The boy who she'd met immediately stepping off that train and into Butte, with its fallin' ash and smoke that turned those other ladies in their white lace a gray, muddy-like color. The day she'd walked into a life that wasn't yet hers, but one she'd wanted.

The same life this boy right here had seen in her before she'd known it herself.

Cat shook her head in sort of a wonder... and amazement.

Truth was, she couldn't even quite begin to grasp how this boy fit into all this. Sure, she saw the ends of some threads, or felt them more like, but the actual knowing? The actual understanding? Not yet.

He'd pointed out the newspaper article on Norma's death and then directed Cat to seek boarding with Mrs. Allen. They very same Mrs. Allen who'd hired Cat and then mysteriously decided talking about her former lady of the evening wasn't quite as urgent as the day before.

Cat's blonde hair, the bits that had fallen away from her braid, brushed her cheek, her nose.

Again, she got that tingling feeling.

Not dangerous, not a warning, but the sense that something else was right there.

Why come find her after two days of silence? Of her keepin' a sharp eye out for a newsboy carrying more stacks than the rest of his fellows?

She'd not seen one sight of him.

No glimpse. No nothing.

And yet here he was now, at the apparent big reveal of Mrs. Allen's new boarder, the curiosity she'd named as Cowboy Cat. That same little bit of news that this boy here had helped get out there to run like fire through the city. This was certainly if the loudness of the voices coming from the dining room was anything to go by.

But why was *he* here? And now?

Only one thing for it.

Askin' directly.

And Cat... well, she always favored the direct approach. When it was warranted, anyway.

"Green Eyes," Cat said. "Wasn't sure we'd meet again."

"I knew we would, Miss Justice. No doubt in my mind."

At his nickname of her, he smiled.

But... his smile, there... it didn't have the same spark as earlier. That sharp edge which... well, while it hadn't been joy, at least not the same kind of joy found in kids who wanted for nothing, who'd never starved or faced life on the street, he'd still *had* joy. Of a kind, anyway. Like he'd clearly managed to find some manner of happiness even living in these hard, shadow edges that he did.

But that joy, however, was now gone. Vanished. Like it'd been snuffed out quick as if blowin' on a candle flame. There one moment, burning bright and strong, and then nothing but a trailing bit of smoke that tingled the nose. Not even the leftover orange embers from that blackened wick.

Nothing.

Cat felt her instinct again, almost like a too-chill breeze brushing the back of her neck, makin' the hairs there stand up on edge.

Something had happened.

Something, even if only in some small, subtle way, had changed everything.

CHAPTER TWELVE

Cat itched to ask. To pepper Dusty with questions, to find out what'd caused this change in him. The hairs on her arms rising, standing up straight like they was cold even with her warm coat still on. Her instinct, her whole sense, it was practically buzzing, begging to ask. To say *something*.

She knew better, though.

She'd seen that look too many times.

On herself.

And sure, he was now standing across from Cat, with his squashed cap on his head, dust and ash smeared across his forehead, his cheeks, all the while standing right center in the middle of Mrs. Allen's entryway. All those trimmings and trappings of the nice, civilized life, something they'd both left behind a ways ago. The lace and the curtains, the little rug running down the length of the room. And there on that delicate little table were even more delicate little cups without a chip on them. A teapot gone cold, not a single whisper of steam pouring out its spout. Little spoons, too, on those delicate little plates. For stirring, of course.

Really, it was the most complete picture of domestic you could ask for. The "acceptable" life. And yet, here they two stood, right smack in the center. Heck, the only dirt and ash in existence was what Cat and Dusty had tracked in. And yet none of that, the lacing or the little teacups, changed the person she saw in front of her. Or where they'd both come from.

Dusty's eyes were still piercing and undeniable, and well, they cut right through all the lace like it was nothing. Sliced through the pretendings the rest of the folk got to live in, with their church and school and meetings, gettin' to close their eyes shut good and tight. They, who got to look the other way when the dark side reared its ugly head, this shadow side, and pretend like it didn't exist none. And when it did, when it came front and center in their little lives, well, it was *only* for those folks who were fallen. Unredeemable. Unsavable.

Never mind the fact that this dark side, well, it was just as essential as those mines and all the copper they were hauling up to the surface.

Dusty, though. Dusty was the kind of kid who knew all that. Like it lived in his bones, his essence and whatnot, and there was no hiding from it. Except now... something had certainly shifted.

He wasn't quite haunted, but if she were honest, pretty darn close.

The kid had a way about him, make no mistake, but there was more going on now. This... this shadow. It was new. Not there the last time. It clung to the boy, literally hanging right off his shoulders like it was his own cloak of midnight and for whatever reason, he was trying to keep that darkness from reaching right out towards her.

Curious, indeed, the difference in two days.

Made Cat's itching grow even stronger. Cause it all circled back to what she'd realized moments before: Something *had* happened. Something had caused this shift. This change.

What the hell was it?

Sure, he was still the same boy with those ink-stained fingers. Same eyes, too, intense and all knowing, but there was a definite heaviness to them. A sadness, too, that told her it'd never be lifted, either.

And that, surely, was what being haunted looked like.

Again, something she saw in herself whenever she dared look in a mirror.

The inkling, the knowing, danced right along the back of her neck and Cat knew she was right. Make no mistake.

A small cloud of ash had followed the boy inside and floated there about the air like little dust bits, except some pieces were a bit large. All of them to a one were black. Black and cold as that daylight outside. Black as the ash coating Dusty in about every place and every way possible. Cheeks. Nose. Tips of his hair.

Not an inch of him was spared, and she'd a hunch could be where the name came from.

Because Dusty *didn't* dust himself off or anythin', now that he was standing inside. He just simply stood there. But no longer the easy, confident stance of the kid she'd met at the station. The kid who'd been sure of his place and who he was. Whatever had happened had shattered that confidence. Took it and slammed right hard against some brick wall leaving only the pieces there, standing before her.

Cat managed to keep from swearing. Barely.

Cause this, clearly, was not the kind of kid who scared easily. If ever.

"Green Eyes?" he asked, recalling the nickname she'd given him.

He was doing this on purpose. Keepin' the conversation light, unimportant almost. As if it could be. With that shadow hanging on him, the intense look he was given her, bordering on... well, on something, their meeting here was anything but unimportant.

For both of them.

Something Cat had learned to do while living on the line was taking what was in front of her naturally and going with the flow. To simply... shrug and follow with where her client's mind and thoughts were already going. It made the person you were talking with easier to understand and manipulate at times, though this was not always necessary. Or needed.

See, truth had a way of comin' out... whether you'd be laying across the bed from a fellow, or hell, riding across the whole damn plains with 'em. Truth didn't matter who you were or where you were, and it certainly didn't like to stay buried. Truth was a funny thing like that.

So, Cat shrugged and followed Dusty's lead.

"Needed to call you something at the time. Even if it was only in my head. I heard from a driver, though, that you go by Dusty."

He gave her a little half-grin at that. Which again didn't carry that same spark, and she filed the detail away.

Still, his smile told 'em both he knew darn well *who* that driver had been. See, Cat had purposefully left out Fat Jack's name. A test of her own, one that Dusty passed clear as day. At least, would be clear in any city other than Butte.

Again, Cat could only shake her head in a bit of wonder. It wasn't much of a surprise he'd survived so well, so long on his own.

Until recently, anyway.

Did he want her help? Was that why he was here now? Was this still about Norma? Or something else entirely?

She wasn't quite ready to ask.

And she'd a feeling he wasn't ready to answer yet either.

Again, she followed her instinct and focused on what she did know. Dusty was a person of interest to her... in her, well, "case" wasn't the right word, but it was all she had. Her search for the truth, anyway, about Norma. Cause, after all, it had been *this* kid, this one right here, who'd pegged Cat for what she was and what she was hoping—no, needing—to do.

Again, there was that tingling...

There was some laughter of the extra-loud variety that came pounding through the wall separating them and the dining room. No kidding, shook the windows and the black view of the outside.

Dusty flinched.

And the shadow hanging off him wrapped tighter and tighter until she could barely see him and those green eyes anymore.

His half-smile dimmed.

Instantly.

"You gonna tell me what's goin' on?" she asked.

Dusty tilted up his head and she glimpsed a bit of his former self. Confident. Sure. Defiant as all hell.

Which made Cat grind her teeth.

Sure, she could be understanding. Sure, she saw way too much of herself in this kid, and more besides, if she was being truthful. But seriously, she was gettin' darn tired of the fronts these people were puttin' up around her. She'd come to Butte to help, find some answers about the people no one else cared 'bout, what happened to them, give their ghosts some amount of peace. Closure, too, if it were possible.

Instead she had Mrs. Allen stonewallin' her out of nowhere.

She'd tried asking her about Norma. Tried askin' about the people who mighta known her. Instead of learning the truth, Cat got a rosy smile and a pat on the head for "helpin' out 'round the house."

And when Cat had wanted to follow in Norma's footsteps? When she'd wanted to walk Norma's path in life, and then finally the place where her steps had stopped? She'd been sent on errands for jars and cans of dried fruit and whatever else that got cooked up in that kitchen.

Oh, and got a surprise Sunday-gossip gathering for all her efforts.

"You're mad," Dusty said.

That caused Cat to start a bit.

She'd forgotten, if just for a moment, where she was. And who she was standing in front of. Shadow or not, haunted or not, that kid missed nothing.

Like how she was getting herself worked up and hopping mad.

Again.

Cat blew out a breath. Pushed aside the annoying hair that was falling right across her nose and itching it.

"Yeah, I'm mad. In fact, I'm frustrated as all hell."

"Because of Mrs. Allen. 'Cause she didn't tell you about today."

"That's right. And more."

Damn perceptive kid.

But... she took another deep breath.

She wasn't gonna take her frustration out on him, though. No point for that. He wasn't the one who'd gone and made the decision to keep her on the outs, to keep some pretty important information from her, and for what? What the hell reason did Mrs. Allen have for keeping Cat in the dark about today? About *not* answering questions about Norma, the same woman she'd only been to eager to find out what had happened the day before?

Still...

The frustration, the anger, it was still there and mighty strong at that.

Which wouldn't do.

Couldn't think straight and clear if all you saw was red.

So, Cat took yet another deep breath, this time getting a noseful of delicious mashed potatoes, also maybe some kind of spice that made her nose twitch a bit, but in a delightful sort of way.

Food... later.

Focus first.

It *hadn't* been Dusty who'd given Cat cause to mistrust. No, that mantel fell clearly on Mrs. Allen and it was Mrs. Allen that Cat needed to relay that anger to.

Even if that meant walking away from some delectable cooking dishes, damn it.

Cat nodded to the door, the one with all those smells slipping through the wood, under the doors, finding any crack or split it could like it was nothing. Which, of course, *still* had her stomach rumbling, traitorous thing it was, not giving one whit that she *was* mad and eating the woman's cooking was not the order of the moment.

"Actually," Cat said, "I'm about to march right on in and demand an answering from her."

"Don't."

"Why the hell not?"

"It would embarrass her."

"I imagine it would take a whole lot more than me dragging her out to cause embarrassment. Unless I twisted my fists 'round her hair and hauled good and hard. I'd expect that'd get some attention."

He didn't smile.

Which, was fine. He'd probably seen the sight one too many times in his short life.

"Look," Cat said, "I'm not gonna do that. I was raised to be civil and the like. Besides, I know her past. I know she walked both sides of the line, and my talking to her and when I do it, even if I'm in a bit of a huff—which for the record, I *will* be—it wouldn't be enough to embarrass a woman like her."

A woman made of steel, really.

Hell, shadow steel.

Something they'd all been forged in it, after all. Mrs. Allen. Cat. Probably Norma, too, and well, look where that got her. Sometimes even the strongest steel wasn't enough. Sometimes your luck just came up short.

Or someone else cut it off for you.

Again, there came the tingling... that something she wasn't seeing, or at least, not quite clearly.

Dusty reached up, slipped off his cap. He twisted it, just once, in his fingers.

"You don't know all of it."

"Not my problem," Cat said. "Mrs. Allen's the one who set the board pieces. She's the one who's been putting me off for two days, not answering my questions, keeping me in the dark."

Not to mention the secret of today itself, the gathering here of folks that she'd purposefully wanted to get Cat in front of. Definitely for the money, which she'd made no bones about at the time. Had she been hunting for information, too, from these folks here?

Probably.

Most likely, in fact.

Cat's gaze narrowed at Dusty. He didn't look away, just stood there and took it.

Accepted it.

Like it was his fault.

Another piece fell into place. And so, too, did her tingling grow. Just a bit.

"Which," Cat said, slowly, "you already knew, didn't you? All of it."

He paused just a moment, as if weighing his options. Finally, he nodded.

The itch came again. The whisper of... *something more.*

But Dusty just stood there, his worn, black shoes rooted to that floor... and his mouth zipped up tighter than a clam. Not willingly gonna say anything. Not willingly gonna break his oath, his silence.

Fine, then. He could keep on playing it his way, if that's what he wanted. In return, he'd see exactly what it meant to play with a person like Cat.

"You're not gonna tell me?"

"Not sure what you're talkin' about, Miss Justice."

"Alright then, fine. I'm not done askin' you questions, since you clearly knew Norma. If you didn't, you'd never have sent me here in the first place. But, what I am gonna do is settle this matter with Mrs. Allen first."

His green eyes got wide.

Just a bit. Not enough that someone who wasn't a studier of persons would have noticed. But they did, though, get just a bit wider, and Cat saw it.

Saw everything.

Him fighting, him trying to be that same boy outside the train station with his newspapers, the confidence that had about lived in every inch of his body. Confidence, assurance, feet like a cat knowing just where and how to step to keep on livin'.

And he was fighting to hold onto that. Fighting to get himself back to that person.

Something *had* happened, make no mistake. And it was a big something.

One he wasn't gonna say squat about without the right amount of backside nudging.

So be it.

"Now," Cat said, "if you'll excuse me, Green Eyes—"

She marched the last two steps to the door. Boots smacking hard on the polished, delicate wood. Leavin' in her wake who knows what manner of black and mud bits, and not caring in the least.

There was a strangled-like surprise sound coming from behind her, proving that he was, in fact, losin' that fight within himself. But she didn't pause, though, not for one second. Not even one breath. She reached for that knob, ready to make good on her promise—

"Wait."

"Why?"

Dusty didn't say nothing.

"I'm not playing here, kid. And I'm sure as hell not letting anyone, not you, not Mrs. Allen, play me."

Again, no response.

"Fine."

Cat turned the knob just a bit more—

"Stop, al'right? I'll tell you."

She did, but kept her hand right where it was, leaving that knob half-turned. All it'd take was just a bit more and the whole thing would click on open. All those smells would pour right on in, the same ones running 'round that kitchen, chasing themselves silly, just waiting for a little opening to take over the rest of the house.

Her stomach, though, it had finally stopped growling and was now focused on the job at hand.

Again, she felt her breath slow. She exhaled once, then let the world still around her, just like her pa had taught.

And the truth, the very thing that had a way of working its way to the surface, refusing to stay buried... well, this time you couldn't miss it. Couldn't miss the truth the kid was trying so desperately to hide. Because shadow soul or not, he *was* still a kid...

And he was afraid.

For himself, but also for Mrs. Allen.

"Why are you protecting her?" Cat demanded. "What would be so damning if I were I stomp in there, into her kitchen, and haul her ass out for a nice chat?"

"Because... she's not there. And no one can know."

CHAPTER THIRTEEN

Cat rocked back on her boots. Her body thumped quietly against the closed door.

Not that anyone could hear. Not with all the loud, roarous laughter and whatnot taking place just on the other side of her. From the kitchen, sure, but also from that dining room, which she guessed by all those voices was filled to the brim with folk waiting for their helpings of roast chicken and beef, mashed potatoes with so much melted butter their plates would be swimming in the yellow stuff.

No one heard her quiet thud.

No one heard that slight moment, admission, of Cat's surprise.

Cause out of all she'd scenarios she'd imagined, she certainly hadn't seen *that* one coming.

Once again, here she was standing in Butte, and she was surprised.

"What do you mean," Cat said slowly, "that she's not here?"

Dusty shook his head. His cheeks, dusted as they were with ash and soot, actually managed to turn a slight pink color.

The stirring came in her again.

She breathed in, then out.

Instinct... it pinged her insides like she was a jackrabbit bounding on away from the heavy stomping feet of hunters who were totting their rifles after her. So close they could almost grab that fluffy white tail.

She didn't let none of that show, though.

Instead, she glanced back at Dusty, still keeping her hand on that doorknob, both as threat and promise.

"I came here a trusting person," Cat said. "And I feel like that was broken. I'm not one to let the matter lie."

"Trust's important to you."

"So is honesty."

"Then you can be mad at me."

"Why? You're the one standing here, talking to me. Not Mrs. Allen. She had two days for that. Now you're telling me she, the woman who orchestrated this whole event, isn't even here?"

"That's right."

"Why the hell not?"

"Because..."

Again, she heard that fear. Just a little bit. Just enough... to make Cat pause.

She kept on breathing.

Slow, deep breaths to keep herself clear and focused.

All that lingering smoke and ash, clinging to both of them still, right alongside the roasted chicken. And, dare she say, the soft undertone of baked apples and... cinnamon. Where ever the hell Mrs. Allen had gone, she'd managed to roll out a few pies first.

And yet there they both were, the light side and the dark. Both daring her, daunting her. And maybe even... challenging her. Just like Butte herself, and it seemed no matter which way Cat turned or looked, there was certainly more going on here than she'd first imagined. Two sides, same coin.

One shiny and bright.

The other dark.

And someone, somewhere, was afraid of the dark getting out. Or knowledge of it bubbling up to the surface...

Which was when another piece fell into place.

Son of a bitch.

Cat would have slapped herself on the back of her head if she could reach, just like her daddy would do when she'd done something really silly, something that clearly said she had cotton for brains.

It made sense now.

Of course, the first thing Mrs. Allen would have done would be to reach out to the very person who'd set Cat on her doorstep. Dusty. She'd have talked with him, if nothing else just to make sure that Dusty agreed with her own assessment of Cat. And whether or not she'd be a trusting person, someone who could be told the details of Norma's life and hopefully, some clues about her death.

So Mrs. Allen and Dusty would have talked, probably sometime late that very night... and the next day, Mrs. Allen's walkin' a different tune. She's suddenly all gunshy on any conversation having to do with the dead Norma.

Because of Dusty.

And because of whatever he'd said.

"You're the one." Cat said. "It was you who'd asked Mrs. Allen to be quiet. She'd been all ready to tell me about it, but then the very next day I couldn't get one word out of her."

Dusty, he just nodded.

But he wouldn't look at her though, and Cat wasn't having none of that. Oh, no. Certainly not that. She was still darn mad, after all. And now? Now she was definitely feeling a bit on the pinkish mad side and definitely considering just picking up her bags and finding some other person in need of some truth learning.

Cat let the kitchen doorknob click back into place, crossed that short distance separating her and Dusty. Her boots stomped on that polished floor, leaving bits of smoke and hard, dried mud in her wake. And she, for once, not caring a single bit about it, either.

"Tell me, right here, right now, what's going on or I'm leaving."

Dusty looked up at her and paled. "You, you can't leave. She needs you."

She stayed right where she was, eyes narrowed down at him. Cause she needed to know. Needed to understand.

They had looked at each other that day there on the train station, and it'd felt like her soul had been mirrored right back at her. All the worst parts of her, the worst parts of what she'd done, what'd she'd probably do again. But that wasn't the real worst part, or really the scary part. It was everything she was trying to do different... trying to *be* different. He'd dared her to be different, and now she was pushing him to do the same. Taking a chance. Trusting in her.

Now, now she was daring him to do the same.

To trust. In her.

"I will leave," Cat said. "If you don't give me a reason to stay."

"We need you."

"Don't look that way to me, seein' as how you're still not tellin' me nothing."

"*Please.*"

Just that one word.

She'd never have believed it, not when they'd first met, so sure and confident he was. Hell, she could barely believe it now, but there it was. Truth. This kid here could shatter. Would. Make no mistake. The very idea of Cat leaving, grabbing her stuff and walkin' on out that door, and he'd shatter.

A kid who Cat had only talked to for a handful of minutes. That was all. Just minutes. But then, it wasn't so much about her, really, but this other thing. Something she knew well but hadn't felt in many, many years.

Hope.

And with the hope, well, there came the fear right along behind it. A real large dose of it, too. You couldn't have one without the other.

But fear also wasn't something that lived daily in a kid like Dusty. Couldn't. Not unless it was something big. Huge. When you lived the shadow life, fear got dulled after a bit. You just got numb to the whole experience, starving and beatings and all that, stuff that became normalized and the real thing you feared was actual, honest-to-God hope.

And Cat, if she walked out right now, would take all that with her.

Truth was, she was still surprised. She'd *seen* the kid's resolve that day on the station. Hell, he'd challenged *her* that day. He's the one who'd dared her to get on this path in the first place and now he stood there, practically shaking at the knees at the very idea of hope.

So... what had changed?

Only one thing for it: to ask.

Cat touched his shoulder and waited until he looked up at her.

It didn't take long, neither.

They both had the sense, after all. The instinct to survive. The sense that the rest of the citizens wearing their Sunday bests right now, all their bows and ribbons and fancy hats, didn't even know existed. Couldn't, cause they hadn't gone and lost everything yet.

Probably never would either.

And as frustrated as she was 'bout being lied to and manipulated, pulled and strung along, she also felt those same feelings blowing away like they'd do back when she was riding the range 'round Miles City, that warm breeze pullin' at her braided hair, trying its damnedest to snatch that hat right off her head. God, were those glorious, wonderful days. And that breeze, it would just pluck off all those feelings and they'd be done. Because that's how you learned to survive.

As shadow souls.

"Why?" Cat asked. "Why did you ask Mrs. Allen to do this?"

Again, there went that tightening of his lips.

He twisted his cap even tighter in his grip. So tight the knuckles were pure white even with all the ash layered on him.

"You gotta tell me," she said. "I can't help otherwise. I can't *do* what you want me to. I can't help Norma, can't find the truth, without knowing."

She paused. "That's what you *do* want, right? The truth?"

"Yeah. It is."

"All right, then. Choice is yours, Green Eyes. You tell me, and I can help. You don't... well, there's not a whole lot of reason for me to stay, now is there?"

"I don't share. I don't tell people things."

"I get that. What I'm askin' ain't easy, but I'm still asking."

Cat knew the score on his life, on surviving. Well, it was time to add herself to the table, but not as a pawn.

Never again as a pawn.

"You want me to be a knight in your game," Cat pointed out, "you better start treating me as one. Otherwise, I got no reason to stay."

Dusty let out a breath. Both dust and ash shook off him, falling to the ground in little floating bits.

"Mrs. Allen," he finally said. "She did all those things, keeping you in the dark, sending you on errands, because I asked her."

Cat nodded. "All right. I figured as much. What else? You said she's not here. You ask her to do that, too?"

"No."

The word came out a bit pained, like it hurt him.

And Cat, as she likened to do, started putting in all those details from the moment she'd walked in Mrs. Allen's homey door with the rug running down the center. The box, right where she'd left it, glasses and whatnot still intact, still right in the way of anyone else wanting to walk on in. Seemed a lifetime ago, but just moments, really. And those moments? She remembered every one. The sounds and voices. Lots of 'em, too, all different tones and nationalities, and not a single female among 'em, though.

She turned all those bits and pieces, round and round, until they fit. Until she started to see a shape, a picture, taking place.

"Well," Cat said, "this is her big event, with a lot of good money waiting to be served on that table. I imagine a lot of big types in there, too. The kind who feel mighty sure of themselves."

And their positions.

Secure. Important.

No doubt about it, there were a couple cultured voices in there, for sure. The upper gentry. How high and mighty, though, she couldn't tell until she walked in and got a feel of the place. Still, no doubt, those upper types were chatting right alongside others whose accents were so thick she could barely pick out one word in three.

Quite a collection in there, and knowing a woman like Mrs. Allen, each one of them in there for a purpose.

"I imagine," Cat went on, slow-like, thinking all the bits through, "that they're the kind of people who'd be pretty darn mad if they learned their hostess had gone and deserted them at such a fine, Sunday hour."

"That's right."

It'd be the kind of blow a reputation like Mrs. Allen's *couldn't* ride out, couldn't survive. Not after she'd been the one doing the inviting, bringing in all those colors and flavors under her roof and all.

A roof that was housing a new, interesting face in town. Of the like even Butte hadn't seen before.

Too much risk.

"So, why did she leave?"

Dusty stayed silent.

Cat managed, barely, not to sigh. It was getting a bit hard to not let loose her own frustrations.

She didn't, though. Instead, she swept her hat right off her head, not caring about all those stray wisps that bounced about every which way. She wore her own dusting of ash and smoke that stuck about her person, turning those blond wisps into a gray-like mess, which wasn't a surprise. Heck, just by stepping outside you got covered in the stuff; there was just no escape from the dark side of Butte.

She didn't care that she looked a sight. That she looked nothing at all like some romanced version of the lady cowboy, decked out in her blue jeans and heavy coat. Maybe even sportin' a rifle at her side, ribbons darned in her hair. A regular ol' Annie Oakley. But that image was not Cat, not in the least. And she didn't care. Not even if one of Mrs. Allen's special invitees walked through the door and took a gander at her, unimpressive as she was right now. She wouldn't have cared.

All her focus, all her attention, was on Dusty.

He needed her help, and she needed him to trust her.

It wasn't just for Norma, either, she realized. He needed help... for himself. And maybe, too, it was something he hadn't yet realized.

Everything 'round her, even the telltale sounds of laughter and joyous company drifting through the thin walls, the promised Sunday meal clearly ready to be served, and those voices getting a bit on the annoyed side, which was understandable considering all that glorious food waiting to be served, and it clearly hadn't been. Not with the hostess herself missing.

But none of that mattered. Not at that moment.

Cat knelt in front of Dusty, scrunching her hat against her chest. She needed to reach him. Needed, for both their sakes, for him to open up.

To trust.

Which was nearly asking for the moon when you lived in the shadows, when you were, through and through, a shadow soul.

"That's not enough, Green Eyes," she said. "Not if you want me to keep my boots right where they are and not go hauling off back onto that train and straight outta town."

"*You* can't leave."

"I will."

He took another deep breath.

She had the sense that he didn't notice the lingering aroma from the kitchen either, the glorious roasts and potatoes, the traces of freshly brewed coffee. Probably didn't notice the bustle and hustle just on the other side of that wall, either.

But no... the people on the other side, what they were doing, what they were saying, he probably *did* notice. Hell, he probably even knew exactly who was in there, smokin' their cigars, getting ready for their large slice of pie. Probably knew their names, their professions, their rank in this city called Butte.

That's how he'd survived, after all.

Which she confirmed when she caught him sneaking a right quick glance at the walls separating them. Again, just the barest flicker, but it was there, clear as day to Cat:

Fear.

Was Dusty expecting someone to come barging out? Demanding where the missing Mrs. Allen was? Or was he nervous about himself being seen here?

"You wanted my help," Cat said, "but now, all a sudden, something's changed. You're not telling me about Norma, and on top of that, Mrs. Allen is gone."

His lips got all tight again and white.

Again came the feeling. Getting close, and closer still.

"Where is she? What happened?"

And as soon as the words got out, Cat felt it.

Felt this, this certainty. It settled over her like a warm, fraying quilt, but it was still warm, still sturdy. Still good at its job despite the rough bits 'round the edges.

Whatever situation she'd walked into two days ago, Dusty, who'd cautiously though gladly pointed her here, right to Mrs. Allen's front door, but that particular situation, whatever it'd been, wasn't the same no more.

Oh, no. Something *had* happened.

Something *had* changed.

And Mrs. Allen, for whatever reason, was right in the middle of it.

CHAPTER FOURTEEN

Cat looked right at Dusty who was still holding his black cap, but now it was twisted so tight it looked more like a coiled rope. He was hiding none that he was concentrating on the other side of that wall, the dining room there where all Mrs. Allen's gets were waiting.

And if sounds were to be judged, gettin' a might bit rowdy that the food wasn't yet being served. A few voices, one booming one in particular, gettin' so loud it felt like the windows were shakin'.

Cat felt time slipping by, knowing it was now or never for her to make a decision. It was her turn now, whether or not to trust again, and without knowing all she'd needed to know.

She swore softly.

Felt that exact same moment when she'd met Alice's betrothed, and that feeling in her gut, stirring in the wrong way, knowing there was something they were all missing here. But hey, couldn't be choosers, not when there were two young ladies without an adult watching over them, caring for the needs, lodgings and all the like.

Both she and Alice had trusted in the fortune that had come knocking on their doorstop, and they—and yes, that included Cat—

had greeted him with... well, open enough arms. Trusted him to come into their family and ultimately destroy it.

Now, here she was again. The choice to trust, or not.

Voices, getting louder. That booming one in particular feeling a bit more intense, heated. Pushing, almost, for the meal, perhaps for Mrs. Allen. Cat didn't know. She didn't have a cat's hearing.

Or Dusty's, for that matter.

Still... while she felt that press of time, she gave herself this breath, this moment. Felt the world around her still as she focused... on herself, on all those feelings whirling up hard and fast in her gut. So many emotions that she didn't want to think on now. Just the very thought of Alice, of her husband—no, now was not the time.

Tears and the like, whatever it was she'd needed, that'd come later.

When she was by herself.

When she had time.

For now, all she had was herself, her instincts, and this little but important thing called trust.

So be it.

"Okay, then." Cat slapped her hat back on her head and straightened. "Okay."

"Okay?"

Dusty, she noticed, had changed in those few moments she'd been checking in with herself. Actually, it was those green eyes of his that had changed. Shifted. The anxious, afraid kid was gone. Now he stood there with those eyes boring right into her. His cap even now resting loosely in his hands.

The shift, it had happened so fast, and if Cat hadn't seen it all herself, hadn't been part of the conversation, as one-sided as it was, well, she might have not believed it.

Or maybe Dusty had just needed to get his truth out there. Or part of it, anyway. He'd been the one pulling her strings, knocking her around that game board like a pawn.

And, for whatever reason, Mrs. Allen was now paying that price.

A price that'd cost her dearly, no doubt about it. Perhaps everything she had built for herself, certainly if she were found missing at her own little gathering. But where exactly she was, that was a question Cat hadn't teased out yet.

Not enough information.

Not enough time, either.

Boots, and there were quite a few, at least three pairs, thumped closer. Not happy ones, not if the way they were banging on that floor was any indication. Hell, sounded like a whole herd of them were ready to pile out into the sitting room, leaving all the glorious smells and meal behind—

And there, right beside that very entry way, was where she and Dusty stood, plain as day.

And dirty and dark as the day outside itself.

Nothing for it. Nothing she could do. That alone would probably take a bit of a dip in Mrs. Allen's original plan, when all those folks saw she was no Annie Oakley. Could have been helped if she'd known the gathering was today in the first place—yet another piece she didn't quite understand. But that was for another moment.

Right now, the cards, they'd fall as the lady herself wanted. Cause how Cat appeared to those barging into the sitting room and how they perceived her, well that was out of Cat's hands now.

The rest, though, like knowing what kind of snake's nest she was about to stir up, maybe she could do something about that.

"Where is she?" Cat asked.

"You gonna help?"

"Not unless you start trusting me."

Dusty's mouth thinned, like the kid had just swallowed a lemon whole.

"Your turn to trust, Green Eyes. If I don't know what I'm walking into with these folk—"

"Police station."

Not what Cat had been expecting. Not in the least.

Dusty kept on, glancing at the dining room door, then back at Cat. His words quick. Fast.

"She's at the station being questioned. Jere Murphy himself picked her up."

"What the hell for?"

"Don't know. All I know is they'd waited until now to call her up. You know what that means."

She did. Someone, a definitely important someone, a powerful someone, the kind of someone with the clout to send out officers, and at just the right time to hurt Mrs. Allen the most. And it would, no doubt about it. The cost for her, missing this event, would be high. Cat didn't know the players yet, but between Mrs. Allen and Dusty, the folks they would reach in both the world of light and shadow, they'd be important. No doubt at all.

Also, that someone had sent the one honest cop to pick her up. That didn't bode well. Not at all.

No wonder Dusty had been scared. No wonder he hadn't wanted to trust her. Cat being here, not even two days, and their world was getting turned upside down.

Perfect timing.

Just not for them.

Footsteps getting closer. Voices getting louder. 'Specially, too, from that booming one. No doubt about it, that one was mad. She could hear him quite clear. Clear, as if he were yelling right two feet from her.

"I've been quite patient with Mrs. Allen. I *am* a busy man, after all."

An Irish man, definitely. His accent clipping right at the end of his words, making some hard to understand, others rolling right off the tongue. But the anger? Well, that was still pretty darn clear all on its own.

Businessman? Politician?

Someone important, clearly. Or, at least thinkin' he was.

Another voice chimed in, this one high pitched and completely unintelligible.

To Cat, anyway.

That alone made Chin a pretty distinctive person, and it was clear he was doing his best to stop the guests from all leaving—which, knowing the feeling towards the Chinese, it was probably pissing off Mr. Irish even more.

"If our hostess," the man said, "cannot grace us with her presence, then I have no intention to stay. Nor do my fellows."

Every *r* sound the man made was rolling, hard and strong. And loud.

But he didn't sound wrong, either. Not when there were a whole bunch of additional murmurings and "ayes" being spoken. So Mr. Irish just kept going on, rolling right over Chin's determined protests and pleas with his *r*'s, and that was that.

He was coming and Cat, she was outta time.

No time to plan or speculate or even guess who *that* particular person was, and what his beef was with Mrs. Allen. All Cat had was the sudden tingle she got at his words, the force behind his anger. Her instincts telling her something else was at play, something else was off about him.

Other than that, she was on her own.

Or maybe not.

'Cause there was Dusty standing right next to her, knowing a hell of a lot more than he was saying. He'd been the one to get the word out, after all, sending out those rumors about Cat so the right people would hear. That Cat herself would be digging into the death of a fellow night lady.

Cat grabbed Dusty's arm, squeezed.

"The folks here, they all know Norma? Either as clients? Associates? Friends?"

Dusty gave her that half-grin, which honestly was so darn good to see on him that Cat released a breath she hadn't realized she'd been holding. Damn. She'd missed that grin. Confidence, too.

She needed them both for what was coming, make no mistake.

"They, to a man," Dusty said, "knew Norma. Each and every one of them."

That was all he had time to tell her.

Not when the door itself opened, the one Mrs. Allen had opened to the sitting room that first day Cat was here. Her arms heavy with a loaded tray of tea and apple pie, who'd refused Cat's assistance and served them both herself as they'd discussed Cat's arrangement for staying. God, it seemed a lifetime ago, not two days.

Well, this time that door banged open so quick and fast the poor thing bounced off the wall. That doorknob bit right into the wall there, spewing a piece or two into the air, joining the still-floating bits of dust and ash and smoke.

And that was all she had time to notice.

Not when the angry Irish man himself, complete with his hard and rolling *r*'s, also being a good size bigger than her both in height and girth, strode out. Boots stomping down so hard they about shook the wood panels underneath hers. His once pale, pasty face, the kind that about never saw the sun, was now a bright red except for a few strangling hairs of white up top his head and his curling mustache.

Angry as all hell, and clearly looking for a fight.

Especially when those sharp blue eyes narrowed right at Cat, who was standing there... right beside Dusty. A pair of eyes that narrowed even further, like they were dual slivers spoutin' smoke straight from hell itself.

Definitely looking for a fight.

One that Cat doubted she was ready for but was gonna walk into anyway.

CHAPTER FIFTEEN

See, Cat knew her way 'round a fight.

She'd had her fair share of them growing up, even without brothers in the family, least the ones that lived long enough to get to the brothering, fighting age. And Alice, of course, was Alice. But there'd always been boys about, and Cat found herself following after them, joining their battles and gangs and wars. She'd done her share of leading them, too, throughout the years.

As a general rule of her person, she'd chosen the outside world, as dirty and daring as it was, as often as she could instead of darning clothes on dolls or helping in the sewing or the mending with her ma and Alice. Cat liked learning from her daddy, riding and shooting and the like. And thinking and using her brain. Seeing what everyone else missed, as busy as they were, as focused on themselves as they were.

Those were the skills Cat had sought. Craved.

Though, to be fair, she'd also eventually learned to mend her own damn socks, as Ma had insisted both her girls know their fair share of needlework. Which, in all fairness, had come in just as handy as knowing how and when and why to pull a trigger.

Fighting, though, that just came hand in hand with child's play. And as much as Alice had denied it, Cat knew for a fact she'd been involved in fair share of 'em with the girls. And in complete honesty, Cat had had her fair of fights as an adult, too, either walkin' the line or riding on the range.

Fists. Guns. Heavy-ass iron pots.

You used what you needed to survive. To keep on breathing and to make sure the person across from you was the one with more broken bones and bruises and bleedings than you. That they be the ones who wised up and left you the hell alone.

Cat's gun, of course, was still upstairs.

And tempting as it was to have on hand, it being a right good comfort and all, this was one particular battle that needed neither fists or guns.

Words would be the weapon of choice.

Even if the anger behind them—and the emotions—was enough to *want* to draw a weapon. Meaning, it was the best time of all to not have one.

But it would be words in this particular battle, and every instinct she laid claim to screamed it. Because, after all, that was how the gentleman settled their disputes.

Words, and money.

Which was fine as well. Cat had the training there was well, living the life as both Mrs. Allen and then Norma had done, and the many thousands more like 'em.

Confidence and perception.

Those were the night lady's weapons of choice.

Oh, sure you could probably throw in desire and the like, but the truth of the matter was in order to be desired you needed to narrow down on the fellow, see right inside his heart, his mind, find out exactly what he wanted, and make sure that you, and you alone, gave it to him. Not the other four girls standing next to you.

Perception was everything.

Confidence, even more so.

Now, this particular Irishman was *not* one you'd call 'prim and proper.' Oh, he looked the part, well enough. The smooth, expensive fabric of his black pants, jacket, vest. All matching, all tailored, nothing at all like the ones found in a catalog or ready-made. Nope. No, sir.

Course, not all of him looked the perfect part.

Certainly not the way his vest buttons strained as they did, drawing far too much attention to the girth he'd recently acquired. Which did not fall into the Gentleman of Standing category. Not the girth part necessarily, but the *hiding it* part. Gentleman usually went to great, great lengths to hide the... discrepancies life tended to throw their way.

But the rest of him, though?

Oh, definitely high and mighty.

And no question 'bout it, wealthy, too.

His nicely pressed, crisp jacket. The white shirt underneath not showing one speck of dust or black ash, while the same damn stuff covered about every inch of her and Dusty. He was also wearing the quite fashionable black bowtie, and from what she could see, it was in perfect arrangement as it circled around his large neck like a noose.

It was certainly, too, in the way he stood there, commanding everyone's attention. Or demanding it, more like, especially with all those others.

Others just like him.

Wearing those same black suits and jackets and ties, wearing, too, the same scowling and unhappy faces. Those other men filed into the sitting room right on Mr. Irish's heels. His own little herd doing his bidding and his will, whatever their own individual reasons were for doing so. And because he'd stopped just outside that doorway standing there and glaring at Cat, they stood as well.

Each and every one of 'em, taking a good hard and long look at Cat. Surprise showing in each of their faces.

Except, of course, for Mr. Irish.

His face got even redder, even puffier. Sweat lining 'bout his brow, never mind that it was still right chilly outside and here Cat was still wearing her winter coat, and *she* looked nowhere near as hot and huffy as he did.

Maybe he'd just keel over right there of heart troubles and it'd save her from sparring with the man. Although... that probably would not help Mrs. Allen's situation. Quite possibly, it would make it worse.

So be it.

She'd play her role in this, and make no mistake, she was aiming to win. For Mrs. Allen. For Norma. For herself really, cause damn did she hate those like him in the world, walkin' about like they owned the very ground and earth bits just 'cause they got into some money at some point in their lives. Or their parents or parents before them.

Especially, too, when they were up to no good, and this man here, this Mr. Irish, certainly was.

Instead of being intimated by him, his presence, Cat simply straightened and grinned from ear-to-ear.

Again, perception.

She tipped her hat at them like she would to any lady she passed in the street. Her gaze, her grin, the one that said confidence and nothing but it. She met each of their eyes, holding them, too, and makin' a few dance in discomfort. Of those that she could see, anyway. A few bustled in the back, pressing close as they could, sensing that something interesting was about to happen, especially at Mr. Irish's sudden stop. She'd bet money those in the back were the 'unimportant folk' in Mr. Irish's eyes. Probably just the laborer types around town. Miners, probably, blacksmiths and the like. Maybe a shopkeeper or bookkeeper. Bartender? Dear lord, did she hope so.

Certainly hoped that Mrs. Allen had something stronger on hand than just the coffee.

Still, each of them to a man were all hear to see her, the woman who dressed herself like a cowboy and went walking around town as such, and comfortable as the day she was born. They'd heard some interesting enough tales and had come to see the real life being for themselves. And, of course, to carry on with the most interesting bits, to spread through the town like fire.

Which it would, no doubt about it.

And no doubt either, a few had other reasons for being here. Like, as Cat was suspecting with Mr. Irish, his purpose not merely based on curiosity. At least, about her.

About what she was doing, however, and about Norma was another story entirely.

So, Cat stood there grinning and met each and every face that she could. Met them eye for eye and waited until a good few of them looked away first while a whole bunch more got a bit pale and open mouthed. She inwardly shook her head at those. They weren't even trying to do the decent thing and hide their surprise at seeing a woman before them wearing jeans, a wide-brimmed hat, and the like —not a single item of clothing that their lady acquaintances and family members would ever be caught dead in.

And yet there she was.

Taking her time, acknowledging the power that *she* had at making the whole room go silent. Finally, her gaze landed square and true on Mr. Irish. And stayed there for quite a bit longer than the others.

"My name," she said, "is Cowboy Cat, and I believe you gents came here to see me."

CHAPTER SIXTEEN

C at's words seemed to break through whatever shock had taken hold of Mr. Irish. Or maybe not shock so much but pure out-and-out frustration at her getting in his way.

Which she'd done.

After all, she was literally blocking his perfectly timed, disgruntled tantrum at Mrs. Allen for making him and his important fellows wait on this supposedly Sunday noon meal that hadn't yet been served. Now, why any of them were here and *not* home with their families was yet another question to throw on top of all the others, though, if she'd hazard a guess, assumed 'business' was at the forefront of their reasons.

Still, there was no mistaking that by standing there, right smack dab in the middle of the sitting room with the lace and the curtains, meant that she'd single-handedly ruined his chance of tarnishing Mrs. Allen's reputation with a few well-placed, unkind words. Before stomping right out the front door, of course.

To which Cat's smile only got bigger.

And Mr. Irish, well, he just got redder. To the point that, perhaps, they might consider calling for a doctor. Just in case. And who knows, maybe they'd even get lucky on the doctor that got sent over...

"What is the meaning of this?" Mr. Irish asked. Demanded, more like. "Who are you? What are you doing here?"

"Well, I thought I made that quite clear."

Cat gave a glance at Dusty, makin' a show of needing some confirmation, which he did, playing his part as young boy nicely, nodding gravely and the like.

"You were, Miss Cat, quite clear with the gentleman."

"Well, then," she said, "perhaps there was some *other* confusion? Though I was under the impression that Mrs. Allen decided to throw this little gathering as a... well, a welcoming as it were, to Butte. And here you all are!"

Cat gave them a most charming smile, clasping her hands together like she about won some great prize. "Now, Mrs. Allen, she wanted me to meet with you fine folk—"

"Speaking of Mrs. Allen," Mr. Irish busted in. "We have been kept waiting long enough. Good manners, indeed—and here I *thought* this was supposedly a house reliant on manners. We've been kept an hour or more, and not one sighting or greeting from our hostess. This is unacceptable, *lady* Cat."

Well, there was no mistakin' the disdain curling off that man's tongue as he said the word 'lady,' and just exactly what he'd thought about her.

Chin tried pushing his way round Mr. Irish, but he got bounced back and out of sight. No help from him, and she'd have to watch just how much she turned to Dusty, seeing as how she was the one at a disadvantage not knowing the players, the power that she knew, beyond a doubt, was bouncing off this room like the ringing echoes of a mining bell.

Careful, indeed.

No tellin' what she was 'bout to step into.

"I demand," he said, "to see her at once. We all demand it."

He swept large, sweaty hands to the fellows behind him. There were quite a few murmurs and nods, though also quite a few who missed their cue. They were a bit busy still caught up and staring at her because, as Mrs. Allen had predicted, Cat certainly *was* the sight, the kind that certainly drew all kinds of attention.

Mr. Irish, though, he didn't seem to notice. He was too busy gloating, giving her a half-smile, the kind that pulled at one corner of his mouth, smug and defiant, as if to say, 'I won.'

But again, instinct and circumstance pointed the way for her, and she followed.

"Oh, well, dear me," Cat said, keeping her voice gentle, soft. "I'm not so sure that'd be wise, Mr. ah...?"

The man straightened even further, clamping his mouth so tight and still managing a smile. He had his little power move, that was for sure, her not knowing his name, and he not planning on giving it any time soon. Regardless of how rude and improper it was.

Not at all a gentleman. Just a man with a money and a trifling amount of power.

Curious, indeed.

But Dusty, the smart lad, was right there with an answer. He touched her elbow gently.

"This here is Mr. Seamus O'Neil, Miss Cat. A high banker at Daly Bank and Trust."

O'Neil's attention narrowed on Dusty like he wanted to squash this dusty little cockroach with the heel of his shoe. His nose was twistin' too, as if he'd caught a real whiff of something foul.

After a determined pause, O'Neil nodded. "The lad is correct, though I'm curious to how he knows of my person. For the record, I am also a good, personal friend to Marcus Daly himself."

Well, that was that, then. Cards on the table, at least the ones not up the man's sleeve, and she was bettin' there was a good half dozen missing.

"Now," O'Neil said, "about Mrs. Allen—"

"Well, sir," Cat said, cutting him off with her sweetest tone she could muster. "I *am* sorry to inform you, especially since you and all these other fine gentleman have been waiting for so long, tummies about growling if I'm hearing things right. But Mrs. Allen, well, she's not here."

There were some shocked exclamations and surprises from the group. And those icy blue eyes of O'Neil's? Oh, they twinkled something fierce, like he had a snowstorm taking place right then and there.

Victory, he thought.

Hell, she *felt* his triumph coming off him like a reeking black swirl of smoke. Even Dusty was stunned at her, announcing the truth just plain as day, as it were. His fingers, digging into her elbow.

"What are you doing?"

His voice was so soft, so quiet, that if Cat hadn't been expecting the response she'd never have heard it. Dusty was simply that quiet.

That good.

She patted his hand, soft and reassuring. "I'm asking you to let me do what I came here for."

"But—"

"And right now, that means trusting me."

Then she slipped free of him.

After all, she was playing the part that had been given to her. Following the lead as best she could, and most importantly, according to *who* she was.

Deception was part of the game, had to be if you wanted to survive. Whether you lived on the light side or the dark, or the shadows smack-dab in between both worlds, deception was everything. So, too, was confidence and the knowing... knowing when to follow where the wind took you, and when you dug your boots into that parched ground and held on for everything you were worth.

Like now.

Cat smiled at O'Neil and all his important associates, smiled like she was, in fact, a lady herself, even dressed as she was in jeans. As if the calling of her sex was so strong it didn't matter what she wore— she was ready to serve these men some pretty fine biscuits and mashed potatoes and apple pie. To sit down right beside them and laugh away a few hours.

It was both truth and deception, and all the while her eyes were gleaming right on one goal, and one goal, only:

The truth.

O'Neil hadn't a clue what he was walking into, the danger that stood before him. A woman for sure, and one who knew her own mind and wasn't afraid to use it. Or everything at her disposal, either.

He was clueless. She was simply so far beneath his understanding, his world view, that his mind couldn't wrap itself around the possibility of what she was and what she could do. That her, the shadow soul that she was, made her dangerous. A threat. Dusty, too.

And the man before them, with his straining vest buttons and sweat-lined forehead, hadn't a clue. He just kept on nodding at his fellows, a full-on grin splitting his red face, completely unaware, thinking he'd had the whole affair wrapped up neat in a little bow.

How wrong he was.

Chin, the resourceful man he was, had snuck in through the side door and was watching her, ready and waiting to respond.

Good.

"You see?" O'Neil said. "It's just as I told you! It's a travesty that a woman of Mrs. Allen's background be allowed to sit here amongst us. That she do business beside others, legitimate ones with the proper, moral upbringings—"

"Ah, thank you, Chin." Cat swept off her hat. Her jacket. "Please dust these off as best you can. It's a might-bit ashy out there."

Chin had responded with barely a nod from her to come and assist, and as he did, he bowed all the while.

Smoke and ash covered the rest of her, making her pink scarf from Alice take on an even more faded tone. A reminder. She touched it, just a bare press of finger to cloth. It was enough. Enough to give her strength to keep going, to not let either Mrs. Allen or Norma down.

She wouldn't.

The same ash dusted Cat's face, clung to her hair, and she knew she looked the sight, and make no mistake. She also made no apology for her appearance to these gentleman. And none at all for who she was.

Hat, jeans, and the empty holster at her hips.

A holster that O'Neil noticed immediately.

Eyes going wide. Back straightening. The barest flickering hint that perhaps he was not so sure of the outcome. How could he be when he didn't understand the very person standing in his way, preventing him from leaving.

Not to mention the box Cat had dumped right in the middle of the floor, and she doubted O'Neil could move it without pulling some muscle or breaking his foolhardy back.

And still, she gave no apology.

Not for the ash coating her with its own unique coloring. Not that her form was entirely female, and everything she wore, from the jeans to her blouse, made it easy enough to take in all the curves the Lord herself had blessed Cat with.

O'Neil sputtered at the sight, as if her being there was simply too much for his 'sensibilities.'

"There will be no need for that," O'Neil said. "As I said, we are leaving—"

"Which is quite the shame, I must say."

He'd had his chance to take control of the moment. He'd lost. He just didn't realize it yet.

Cat maneuvered her way closer to the others, almost as if she were leading the crowd back into the dining room with all those wonderful smells, and sure enough, steam slipping out from under the closed kitchen door where Mrs. Beats was working her magic, keeping everything piping hot and simply waiting for the signal to get started.

And all the fellows, including O'Neil and his important companions, they all followed her, inch by inch, without ever realizing it.

She turned her attention away from them, focusing instead on the others. Those who'd been deemed lesser simply by their placement in the group, who were now doing their best to crowd around and get a good look at the wonder that she was.

They were exactly the folk she'd been expecting. Miners. Blacksmiths. Shopkeepers. The kind of folk who'd wash their hands a hundred times and still never remove that black stain about their nails, fingers, as if the color were simply part of the creases along the knuckles. The weariness, too, that pulled at their eyes, their shoulders, as if they spent their days hunched over with the weight of the city on top of them.

Which many of them did.

Cat hid nothing of herself, certainly not to them, and certainly not the true joy she felt being around these working folk.

Also, she was sure to work the charm on each of them, the charm and camaraderie she'd been known for when she'd worked at Mrs. Brown's house in Miles City.

"As I said, gentleman, I *am* sorry that you've been kept waiting for so long. Really, a sad affair that Mrs. Allen had to attend to."

Another man slid around O'Neil. His suit, with those carefully ironed creases, looked almost the spitting image of O'Neil, as if they frequented the same tailor. But that's where the similarities ended. This man was a handful of years younger, had a full head of dark, black hair. Not to mention his own vest wasn't one that strained about the buttons. A curling mustache that about touched his nose, and quite different from O'Neil, he also had a quiet intensity that told Cat this was a man who didn't miss much.

Including her.

"And what, exactly, is this affair, lady?" he asked. "You must understand that this is quite upsetting for us, to be kept waiting all this time, waiting in quite the anticipation, I might add, only to learn that the lady who organized our gathering isn't even here."

Cat nodded. "I understand completely, sir, which is why Mrs. Allen sent for me. Called me up to make sure that each of you were personally taken care of—"

O'Neil about bounced the thin man, throwing the full weight of his fury at Cat. "How dare you! We are honest men, coming from good homes with good families—"

Cat pressed a hand to her blouse, wounded. "Well, my heavens. There's no need to be crude, Mr. O'Neil. What *I* was referring to was your enjoyment of this fantastic meal that Mrs. Allen has prepared. You do know she went to great pains to see that it was perfect for you gentleman on this fine Sunday."

There were some quiet murmurs, especially from the men with the black staining underneath their nails.

"After all," she said, looking right at O'Neil, "isn't *that* why you came?"

O'Neil straightened.

He said nothing.

"Or perhaps," Cat went on, "there's another purpose for your visit?"

Like making sure Mrs. Allen got a giant black mark on her reputation, disappointing all these gentleman. Could *O'Neil* be the one pulling the strings? Did he have that kind of power? Enough to demand that Mrs. Allen be picked up by the police at this most inopportune time?

Or was it another person entirely?

Cat didn't know. And Dusty hadn't either.

Something to keep in mind, to keep watch over.

Especially when the second man came forward yet again and patted O'Neil on the shoulder as if they were, in fact, equals and not one following on the heels of another. A pat, she noticed, that was both calming and... lasted a bit too long.

Like the fingers gripped the shoulder just a bit, tightening. As if in warning.

Of something.

The movement was so quick, and just like that, it was gone.

The thinner man dropped his hand and gave her his own understanding nod. A grave one. "Why, of course this is our reason for coming. We all know from personal experiences, Mrs. Allen's fine cooking. It's simply not an opportunity to miss. Not to mention you, my lady. You are much more to behold than even the rumors convened, which is quite the feat."

He gave her a slight bow, and of course, his kind, charming smile again. Disarming, too, to any other woman.

But not Cat.

She smiled back.

O'Neil did not. And again, the degree of red in his face, starting to border on purple, which truly did have her thinking of calling for a doctor...

"I would like to ask for my coat and hat, please," O'Neil said. "Where is that Chinaman of yours? I see no reason to stay, to break bread in the house of a woman who has been called upon by the *police.*"

Dusty stirred behind Cat but this time couldn't reach her, couldn't warn her of his displeasure for speaking the truth as she'd had. There were too many others standing in the way, and Dusty had no subtle way of warning her to keep her trap shut.

Which was fine cause she knew he was upset with her. Felt it the same way she felt these men stirring around her. They, too, were concerned of this news, especially since O'Neil's carefully placed remark had done its job. Just as the man had intended.

Cat ignored Dusty, keeping her smile, keeping her understanding tone directed at O'Neil but making sure his gaze traveled about the room, including everyone in that simple, fluid action.

"Well, by all means," she said. "If this is how you feel, then I see no point trying to convince you otherwise."

She motioned for Chin, who responded with a bow and then disappeared into some closet.

"Besides," she said, "I see that you've your mind made up and the truth, well, perhaps the truth only matters to a few of us."

For a brief moment, O'Neil's face lost a bit of that reddened intensity. No longer the dangerous purple shade, though he certainly hadn't paled, either. Oh no, the man was clearly too angry for *that* kind of reaction.

But certainly, her words had caused a reaction and not one to be discounted.

Along with the reaction of this other man with his waving black hair, who now had this look in his dark brown eyes... a sharp, burning look, and one that was quite bright indeed. And he wasn't the only one, either. Many of the other fellows around her had a similar look. After all, this here, *this* was the kind of gossip a city like Butte simply thrived on.

And they each, to a man, waited on pins and needles, practically bouncing to hear what she had to say.

And Cat, well, she just kept on smiling.

After all, she was the perfect hostess, the perfect replacement for the missing Mrs. Allen, and this sad, sad business with her being summoned by the police.

"Forgive me," the thin mad said. "My manners are just as deplorable as my friend here. My name is Jim, Jim MacDonald, lady. And I must say, you have me quite interested in this tale of... of Mrs. Allen's. Is it, is it she who's in trouble?"

"No, no," Cat said. "It's not her who's in trouble. But a friend, I'm sorry to say."

O'Neil snorted. "Yes, well, we can all assume, and assume rightly, where Mrs. Allen met this 'friend.' Also, too, what business the police have with her, unless, of course, you have those details for yourself?"

Cat ignored the jab at her profession. Former or not, once you were known to walk the shadow side, that was how you'd always be seen, always be known. Unless you were Mrs. Allen. Regardless, it didn't matter to Cat. She was the one alive. Alice was not.

She shrugged at O'Neil. "I haven't yet learned the details of their friendship. I've been quite busy helping out since I arrived. But yes, the friend was a former night lady and one, I'm sorry to say, who came to a bad end."

There was a slight stir among the men. As if many, too many, shifted on their feet. Looked away.

Cat locked her eyes right on O'Neil's blue ones. Neither looked away, not even when several heartbeats passed.

"Perhaps," she said, "you've heard of her."

Mr. MacDonald stepped in, breaking their stares, a jovial, easy smile on his face. "Well, I'm not so sure any of us can claim such knowledge. Mrs. Allen has many she calls friends, including, well... all of us here. At least, I do hope she counts me as one—"

"Her name was Norma."

CHAPTER SEVENTEEN

T o say the whole room froze would have been an understatement.

Norma.

Her name seemed to echo about the large dining room. As if the walls had purposefully kept the sound in, the very cadence of the word right there. Right there, out in the open. Unable to be denied, to pretend the matter of her existence and death didn't matter or happen. It was like the whole of the room had trapped each letter of her name, a ringing sound that stayed in the ears. Like it swirled around the piping hot steam from the kitchen as if it were a living thing, mixing right on in with the cinnamon and apples, the roasts of chicken and ham ready to be carved into.

And yet, the name stayed. Haunted that very room, and everyone knew it. Everyone felt it.

Norma.

Hell, even if Dusty had gone and suddenly let open the front door and all the windows, the side doors to boot, allowing all that winter-chill air to come rushing in along with the ash and smoke and whatever else was floating on those currents like all those bits owned the whole town, it still wouldn't have come close to the reaction of Cat saying Norma's name.

The room, so still, so quiet, even though there were over a good two dozen men cloistered around her.

From outside she heard the faint clomp, clomp of horseshoes smacking onto the hard, gravel road. The crack of a whip. The needing cry of some babe a few doors down.

Cat heard it all, along with the name of a woman she still knew too little about, and yet a name that managed to hold this entire room of men completely and totally still. There wasn't even the shift of feet on creaking floorboards. Instead, just stillness, just silence.

She watched everything and everyone and missed nothing.

Not even these two powerful men, O'Neil and MacDonald, both whose breath had caught right and true in their chests. She knew what they were thinking. Knew, because that's what all the guilty thought about, or, at least those who had something to hide:

If they breathed, she'd know their secret, right then and there.

Which, in fact, the opposite was actually true. By *holding* their breaths, well, that was all the confirmation she needed. Secrets... something both of these men were hiding, and ones which, somehow, were directly tied to Norma.

No wonder why O'Neil had been in such a rush to leave, to call out Mrs. Allen on missing this gathering of her guests; he'd have wanted to halt Cat's little investigation right from the start. What better way to throw dirt over a budding fire than blackening the reputation of the local matron organizing things?

And yet, it still wasn't enough.

Cat needed details, facts, if she wanted to learn what really happened to Norma. And if any of these men here were responsible for her death.

Still, it was a start.

To which Cat kept on her beaming smile. All charm, all polite and kindness, the kind of woman that'd have made her ma smile if she'd only glimpsed Cat in this moment.

Well, except for the jeans and the ash clinging to her person.

"See?" Cat said. "I *thought* you knew her."

Cat's words echoed off those wood-paneled walls the same way the name of Norma had done. Ringing, filled with truth, and not a single man here willing to deny it.

Not when the fellow standing next to them knew otherwise.

No one looked at her, certainly not in the eyes. Embarrassed, perhaps. Or maybe just afraid... afraid of what she just might find out.

"Now come on in, gentleman. I believe a meal was promised, and if my nose hasn't yet deceived me, it smells like we've got quite the serving for you."

Which it was.

Mrs. Beats poked out her head out of the kitchen, face flushed from all that heat from the stoves and whatnot, sweat dottin' about her forehead, sliding down her cheeks. She gave Cat a thankful nod before darting back inside, only to come bustling right back out with a giant tray and a steaming silver pot on its center.

The food, clearly ready to be served.

But that wasn't all. Far from it.

Cat felt her focus narrow, like she was back on the range with her daddy, wind tugging at whatever strand of hair it could snatch away and play with. Her daddy's calm, steady hands on her shoulder as she stared down the rifle's sight. She felt it all now, clear as day. Felt her finger, relaxed but ready around that trigger. Her own breathing, even and calm.

There was the truth to consider, and right here in this room was someone who knew more about Norma's demise than they were willing to admit.

A truth she was finally on the hunt for.

———

TRUTH WAS, Norma's name became a mantle hanging heavy about

the room, wrapping each and every person in it. Didn't matter that trays of food were brought in and laid out on this grand table with a white-clean tablecloth and shining dishes just begging to be filled up and used.

The gathering had changed.

No longer a jovial affair, one of old friendships and new, a shaking down between classes and all the layers in between them. It was the kind of mingling that Butte was known for, at least, as well enough was possible when you had people who labeled themselves 'copper kings' and all. Still, there were the fancy houses living right alongside Mrs. Allen's and *that* was certainly not the way you'd find in just about any other city.

And yet, whatever camaraderie she'd first heard was gone. When Cat had stood outside those doors, trying to decide if she should bust on in and drag Mrs. Allen out for a talk or just pack her bags and try again. But that original tone, though, of these men gathered here for this fine Sunday meal, was gone.

Because of Norma.

The single name of a dead woman. A night lady who, in any other circumstance, in any other situation—or hell, any other woman, including Cat herself—would never have gotten this kind of reaction.

Never.

Not this tense atmosphere that pulled at each of these men, making it harder to breath, to move. As if the very act of moving towards the serving table and shoveling all the glorious food onto those shining plates was almost impossible, as if their bodies were made of lead or wood and could suddenly not move right.

This... this fear—and no mistaking, it *was* fear—and it was almost a living thing, competing nose to nose with all of Mrs. Allen's finest offerings.

And winning, too.

All the while, Cat kept close watch on each of those faces around her. From the miners to those rich banker friends of O'Neil with their clean nails and washed hands, their dark suits completely free of any lingering bits of smoke or ash.

Cat didn't know their names, though Dusty would, and she'd bet some good money that he'd already memorized each and every person here, as well as the drivers who'd most likely dropped 'em off in the first place. And while she didn't have names, she *did* know the look of them, and those images, those impressions, they stayed with her. All she had to do was close her eyes and a whole image of a person would snap back up, right along with all the bits and pieces of their puzzle.

Just as she knew, without a doubt, which of these gentleman were generally sorry to hear Norma's name spoken aloud, and which ones were not.

Cat knew by feeling alone, by seeing their small reactions, movements, which of these men had been graced by Norma's smile and enjoyed it for enjoyment's sake. The same smile Fat Jack had kindly spoken of, and now hearing Norma's name spoken aloud, sorrowed them that she and her smile were gone.

Cat learned enough to know that it wasn't death itself that had delivered the final blow to Norma's smile. For whatever reason, she'd lost it months earlier, long before her fateful evening stroll on Galena Street. Cat hadn't quite teased out what exactly had happened, but this story alone was important.

Why the sudden change in Norma's character? From a woman who smiled to the whole world and then, almost as if overnight, became a woman who saw that world like she had nothing left. As if she'd fallen so far that she'd lost the joy she'd managed to scrounge up in life.

Cat knew from personal experience and from living beside others that this was an important piece.

Something had happened, a big something, to fully and completely change Norma's character. It wouldn't be the little things adding up over time, the years that wore a woman down until she was nothing but threads and rags of the person, the soul she used to be.

That process took time. That process happened so slowly you'd blink and you'd miss the change.

Something like this, though, with Norma, it *would* have been big. And without a doubt, it was a story that'd help Cat make sense of what had happened to her that night and why.

And quite possibly a reason for her murder.

Not that Cat even had *this* much evidence yet, that it was a murder and not an accident. She only had her gut instinct here and those of Dusty and Mrs. Allen. She needed to speak with the doctor, and the very least, find an eyewitness to the event, someone who'd seen enough to know that it wasn't what the police had originally suggested.

But for now, what she had wasn't evidence or facts but feelings. Feelings over Norma's death... sadness, sorrow, indifference, fear, and... something more.

It was no far leap to say that the feelings in *this* room were running the gamut and had little to do with the full bowls and plates of mashed potatoes and the thick brown gravy soaking through.

Just like... those gentleman who were, in general, *not* sorry or sad of Norma's passing.

And there were quite the handful of those gentleman here.

Cat knew exactly who they were. Watched as they about rushed to fill their plates with the steaming roast chicken, browned in all the right places, juices sliding down from all sides. These men? They didn't even stop to notice those glorious smells. They were rushing. Putting as much stuff as they could onto their plates, needing a distraction, needing their hands busy, their focus on something else than the *other* men in the room, all who'd been called out, a big light of attention, on the fact they each knew in some manner a night lady.

Norma.

And what these gentleman in particular wanted, more than anything else, was to *not* have the attention on themselves.

Again, it came down to fear.

Fear that, oh yes, these respectable, fine folk did *indeed* have knowledge of this night lady—intimate knowledge, in fact. And here they were, locked and tied in with a group that undeniably had known her as well. See, it was one thing to have these little... affairs on the side. To go out in the night, leaving their wives and brood at home, so long as that's where they stayed. Outside. In the dark. Not a single shine of light illuminating those... unpure actions.

These types of men, Cat understood all too well. Had to.

In fact, all the night ladies did. It was part of the job, after all. Part of the role they played, entertaining these high-born, well-off men. At least, for some women. For most it was a dream to be in such a position, to entertain a man of such high means. And entertaining was certainly the name for it.

From the bits Cat had learned, she suspected Norma had at one time been one of these ladies. One of those first-class women living in one of those big parlor houses, an establishment whose name Cat hadn't yet been given but that someone here, certainly a few some-ones, would have knowledge of.

It wasn't a hard thing to imagine for a woman like Norma, with her legendary warm and kind smile, to live that kind of life. Glorious and dazzling with all the jewels and dresses straight from Paris, step-ping in to fulfill whatever role the gentleman requested of her.

And chances were if the hints from the newspaper were any indi-cation, Norma had filled the role perfectly as she went out for a night on the town, arm in arm with a respected individual. Or perhaps simply staying inside for a warm, cozy night away from winter's chill and the constant falling of smoke and ash.

Nearly every night lady Cat had met during her time on the line had hoped to win herself a husband. Any husband would do, even if not the richest, because they were a way out for these girls. The dream to start over. To charm a client so well, so completely, that he swept them both far away. Bought themselves a ticket on some train, riding off into the sunset to someplace where no one knew of the lady's past...

It *was* a dream. Cat had only seen or heard of a handful of ladies who'd achieved it, and for many who did, keeping the dream was another thing altogether. As Mrs. Allen had and yet, even for her, there was still this constant, lingering threat that it could, and would, be taken away.

Certainly if the O'Neils of the world got their way.

And yet... as Dusty had told her moments before Cat found herself the center of the gathering, the newly declared hostess, that this had indeed been Norma's dream.

Had she achieved that dream?

Cat fingered her poor, faded scarf. Could almost sense her sister beside her. Her chill touch as Alice reached up and tugged Cat's hands away from the scarf. The pale, long hair of hers, and her sad eyes as she slowly shook her head as if declaring for both of them the truth.

No.

Norma hadn't achieved the dream. If she had, she'd be alive and on that train and still smiling, smiling with more warmth than she'd probably felt in a long, long time.

Still, the simple act of touching the scarf, that faded, worn fabric, sent a bolt singing through Cat. Not electricity, not that strong, but something pure and powerful. Something... true.

Again, it was just that feeling.

Norma had wanted a new life and didn't get it.

But... had she *thought* she'd found it, only to later—a few months later, in fact—learned differently?

Yes.

The feeling, the word, so strong that it about sung through Cat's whole body. It stole away the last chills from that cold winter outside.

There was an answer here, no question 'bout it.

And she didn't plan on leaving or letting any of these gentleman leave until she found out what it was.

CHAPTER EIGHTEEN

Cat wasn't one to waste time, not when she was holding that rifle steady in her arms, breathing in and out. Knowing that the time she had was ticking slowly down.

She watched as the men began moving in slow groups towards the serving tables or sitting down with their plates full of carved ham and chicken bits and pieces. Chairs that were pulled and scraped on the floor, heavy boots dragging and scuffing. The quiet hum of voices finally taking over the silence. Not loudly. There was still too much heaviness, too much tension for that.

But enough noise to provide just the sort of mask they all needed. A mask to pretend the word Cat had spoken hadn't actually happened.

Norma.

Of course, there was still the matter of O'Neil and MacDonald and where exactly those two high-profile, obviously rich men fell into Norma's life. Cat had a feeling they were in a category all their own, and one she was just beginning to tease out.

No doubt, O'Neil had a deeper role to play in this.

She could have used Mrs. Allen right then, with her insight and understanding of the powers that worked underneath the surface of Butte, powers that clearly coursed pretty true and strong in this very room itself. Of just how these men were tuned into the shadow world, what roles they played in it. Were they all just clients (or in the case of a few, merely passersby—at least in the establishment Norma originally worked out of) or was it possibly that some of these folks actually ran parts of that shadow world? And if not directly, were still tied into it?

Too many questions, and Dusty, well, he wasn't much help at all right now. Sure he was watching and studying everyone without seeming to do so. And sure, he'd fill her in when he could, when it was safe enough to do so. But right now, right at this moment, she was on her own.

Except for the feeding part, which she was mighty grateful for.

In fact, Chin and Mrs. Beats handled all the actual feeding and such. Chin who was even now carrying a out second tray of food and bowls that were nearly the size of him. Steam slipped out from underneath the shine of metal pots and brought along all those smells from the kitchen that had finally been allowed to escape, to roam freely in the dining room as if they were living beings all themselves.

And just as Cat had guessed, no one was leaving.

Now, Mrs. Allen and Mrs. Beats's fine cooking did most of the work true enough, but it also helped that these men followed another code, the 'civilized' rules set down by society. They simply couldn't risk the appearance of anything less. So they would stay to a man, until the designated, unspoken time in which leaving early was then deemed appropriate.

And that meant Cat had time. Not a lot, but enough.

Time to ask, to listen, to learn.

To find out how these men had known Norma, and just what, if anything, they knew of her death.

As hungry as Cat was, she did not serve herself much. Just grabbed a biscuit, slathered it in as much butter as her stomach could tolerate, and set to work. She needed her attention focused but in a soft, unassuming way, and biscuits meant she had one hand free. She'd learned early, thanks to those childhood adventures, to always have one hand free. But it'd also been a good rule to carry in her shadow life. Best to not get tripped up even if a battle was taking place over biscuits and cream instead of fists and teeth. Didn't need those pesky forks and porcelain cups getting in the way.

Of course, Dusty poured her a good helping of coffee, pressing it into her hand, along with a hard, cold look in his green eyes. He didn't need to speak for his warning to be clear:

Don't mess up.

Well, she had no intention of losing this opportunity. It might not have been Mrs. Allen's original plan, but so far it was working, and working just fine.

Cat was getting a feel for the room and the men there. There was also the curiosity of Mrs. Allen herself and the police that was starting to make the rounds again. One man touched Cat's arm lightly, eyes wide and curious as he asked:

"What *did* she do?"

And Cat's answering smile. "Wouldn't we all like to know."

Followed by a wink.

The man, of course, blushed from his face straight down to his neck, and his fellows laughed good naturedly.

Except for O'Neil, who'd heard the exchange just fine. His face, however, had turned back to its purple sheen. Although to be fair, that was mostly cause she gave him her own dazzling smile.

Sure her face and hair still sported quite a few signs of the ashy soot outside, but that part of her appearance didn't matter as much. It was those other bits—her interaction with these men, playing the part of a lady though still looking very much as she did, cowboy and all— that would keep them there, bums glued to those seats. Keep them curious even when the acceptable, polite time to stay had come and gone.

They would still be there.

Curiosity would hold them.

Were *all* these men of significant in Norma's life? An interesting thought, but then that couldn't be true. Fat Jack wasn't here. Also too in their profession, a woman met many kinds of men, certainly if she was on the lower rung of that ladder. Which, Cat knew, had been Norma's situation over these past few months.

Still, she had enough to work with, enough to ask the right questions and see who was willing to answer. And surprisingly, it was Mr. MacDonald who was the first to offer comment.

Cat was walking about the big dining table, most of the chairs filled with warm bodies who were happily focused on the glorious chicken roast and the red-like jelly spread they were dunkin' those legs in, while the others were serving themselves at the even larger table, putting as much as possible on their plates. Many offered her a chair and she smiled politely, getting a gauge and a feel for the man, letting instincts guide her if this was someone to pursue further. At times the answer was yes, at least yes for filling in those bits and pieces of missing information.

There was a bit of blushing to be had whenever Cat asked of Norma, and quite a few wouldn't meet her eyes as she did so, which was fine. She was, after all, at times asking straight out, while for others her questions were more subtle and soft. A tact that many appreciated and opened up freely, too, as she was respecting their unspoken wishes regarding the light on them and all that attention.

And yet, even with all the dance and play of words slipping round between the servings of food, the slice of apple pie that she simply could not pass up, or yes, alright, *two* slices of pie, she finally learned Norma's story.

At least, parts of it.

The real story, the whole story, had probably only existed with Norma herself. Still, Cat leaned that Norma had worked for a year at one of the big parlor houses on Mercury Street—Grace's Gardens, it was called.

"Not that I'd ever a chance to go there myself," one miner told her, Mr. Rippi, a thin Finnish man. His whole mouth grinned at her, dark teeth and one shining gold one. "But a man can right up and dream till the day he dies, yes?"

A place to dream of? Certainly. From everything Cat had heard of the Gardens, it was only for the elite of society. The men who'd easily pay a year or more in salaries equal to that of a working man like Mr. Rippi here, and instead of fainting when the madam handed him the bill, he'd instead wave it away and schedule another appointment with his favorite girl. There'd be no hesitation to come again, certainly if the girl had been worth the experience.

Those girls, in particular, excelled at providing an experience.

Cat asked him where the Gardens were located and he told her.

"Can't miss it. Just few doors down from the Dumas. Can't miss that one, either. Good rivalry going on between them two houses. Both big ol' brick buildings. Lovely windows out front, even lovelier ladies waving out 'em."

Rivalry? That's a curious thought. Enough for a girl of one house to harm another? Though, truth be told, there was enough infighting among girls of a single house that Norma probably had her hands full of clawed enemies.

Cat certainly had herself, and she carried a gun. Didn't stop a bunch of harpies from trying to do her in, from time to time.

No point asking Rippi here about any of that. Cat would need a visit to the Gardens itself to determine that vein. Instead, she focused on what Rippi *would* know: Which parlor had the lovelier ladies?

"That's a question a man gets himself in trouble over, lady Cat, and make no mistake."

Vow of silence on that last question or not, Mr. Rippi had indeed been helpful. Honestly, more so than Cat had ever been expecting, certainly from a miner.

But then, she had Norma herself to thank for that.

Rippi, as many of his fellow miners here, would often stop by the Gardens when the windows were open, when the breeze was blowing just right and a fellow could actually breathe. The lady Norma herself was there, playing court to those fellows just heading off shift, trudging on home after living in the dark for twelve hours, to find themselves a piping hot meal from their boarding establishment or from home. Hard, long days they'd had, and then there was Norma, smiling and offering a kind word or two.

Sometimes even a small kiss on their cheeks, especially for those who had close calls down there in the mines.

"She'd never needed to do that," Rippi said, "and we all knew it. Most of them ladies there didn't, nor cared, as we walked by. Beneath them, we were, but not Norma. She noticed us. She cared."

And that had been Norma, from the moment she'd arrived at the Gardens. This act alone would have further spread the tale of the newest flower, this Norma.

Cat was no fool, though, and saw Norma for exactly who she was. Or, had been.

The woman might have been kind and warm to these men, these hard-working miners just pulling off twelve hours in full-black darkness, a darkness only broken by what candles and lanterns they had on 'em, but no doubt there'd been a calculating mind there as well. A mind that knew and understood the game of the big parlor houses.

Gentleman, the silly, puffed-feather beings that they were, assumed only ladies existed in the big houses, with all the glamor and silk they feasted their eyes on. When, in truth, it was the big houses that were more cutthroat than the streets.

Much, much more was at stake there.

Something Norma had clearly known.

Only the most beautiful and dazzling ladies caught the finest men and could hold that attention. Beauty... well, it was a fleeting thing in this profession. It never lasted, not when time and life itself were workin' against you.

Hell, just look at Cat's hair. What used to be fine, glimmering gold no matter what time of day or cast of light, now the shine was gone no matter how much brushing she did. And here? In Butte, in this cold winter with the air that hung right over head like a bowl, trapping all that smoke and ash, not a breeze stirring to give them and their poor lungs some manner of relief?

She was looking more gray these days than blonde, and she'd only been here two days.

What would it be like to live here, year after year? Living life on the line? How quickly *would* that toll take on a body?

And on a mind?

Norma must have known the stakes. Known she'd needed something more than beauty to stand out, to take center stage, as it were. And she'd found exactly that. A smile, a kindness that had carried right off the lips of miners, right off their cheeks in some cases, and word of her spread.

Spread like wildfire through town, the same way that Cat herself was now doing.

Grace's Gardens had been Norma's home for a year, and it was quite a home to have. Yes, it had its rival houses like the Dumas and the Victoria Hotel, where each fought for the wealthiest men to reside for the evening or to simply dance and enjoy the food and over-charged champagne. In fact, Cat was surprised to learn that both the Dumas and the Victoria only had four girls in residence. Four. That meant one evening with them was quite the cost. Could probably even weigh that cost in gold. No wonder there was a rivalry going on. Did Butte have enough of the upper gentry to even support three upscale houses? Apparently so, because from everything she'd heard, both the Dumas and the Victoria were neck-in-neck when it came to shining, even though the Gardens had a few more girls.

And thanks to Norma's smile, she was one of them.

Where Norma came from before that, however, neither Mr. Rippi or none of the others here knew. But make no mistake, each of them swore they knew the moment that Norma *had* entered the scene in all her shine and dazzle, with that smile that couldn't help but draw the eye, to cheer a downed soul right on up.

Again, from everything Cat had learned, it was the warmth that had radiated from her, the smile, the kindness, that had been Norma's secret.

Men were drawn to her light like moths to a candle flame, and it didn't take a hard guess—certainly not as Cat made her rounds about the room—that more than a few got burned.

These, of course, were not the miners like Rippi, but actual clients, and not necessarily ones that had been intimate with the lady. These were all the well-off men in the room, with their gold vest watches and canes. Those fine matching suits with their shirts and jackets neatly pressed, and not by a wife or child, but by a servant or another in their employ.

And yet even among these particular men, Cat didn't get the sense they'd been burned by Norma's light in a bad way, either. Instead, it was as if they genuinely believed they weren't good enough for her. She'd been kind and polite from all accounts, and surprisingly one of the absolute few working ladies who'd ever declined a patronage. This fact alone still surprised quite a few of them. And yet, for some strange reason, they still held no animosity or ill will towards her.

This was certainly not the normal interaction Cat was used to seeing, and while she hadn't seen everything, her experiences and those of other girls she'd known weren't nothing.

It was like the burn of Norma, of her light, instead of causing animosity and anger had the opposite effect. It made her all the more desirable.

At least to those who'd admit as much to Cat.

She'd a feeling some of these men actually felt otherwise. But then, she didn't need them to tell her. They did it just fine all on their own, without them being the wiser. It was in the little things—grabbing onto a napkin, pressing that cloth too hard and too long to their mouth, the way they white-knuckled the thing the moment it'd been lowered to the table.

And yet, there was a piece missing...

How could a woman who'd been so desirable, been in such a

place of prominence with clearly a mind that understood the stakes and how to maneuver herself around the big parlor houses, how had she fallen so far? And overnight, it seemed?

One moment Norma had been the single most desired, loveliest flower of Grace's Gardens, with enough power and prestige to turn *down* those men who weren't to her liking or her plan. Only to end up working the street as it were, the saloons and gambling houses and the like. A woman who'd gotten herself kicked out of one of the biggest parlor houses in Butte to the streets of Galena where, after a few months, she'd died. A mysterious death, in fact, that a doctor hadn't believed had been of her own causing.

There was a story there. A link between the parlor house and the street, that moment when everything had been going so well, and then suddenly, it all fell out.

Something clearly had happened.

A call out with the madam, perhaps? A lover she'd planned on running away with, to live that dream that Dusty had known about, and he'd left her? Died?

Cat shook her head. Strands of her hair, the unruly ones that refused to stay tucked and braided away, tickled at her cheek and nose.

She didn't have time to ponder these thoughts, not when it was MacDonald himself who waved Cat over. And it was here she learned another piece of Norma's story. The story of a man who'd indeed been burned and still carried it with him, despite his charm, despite the warm smile he gave her.

Almost as if he'd learned the smile from Norma herself.

CHAPTER NINETEEN

Cat slid into the chair MacDonald had pulled out for her, the empty one beside him, and conveniently as well across from O'Neil. The first thing she did was put down that empty mug of coffee, a free hand and all, cause with O'Neil across from her there would no doubt be a battle.

He might even draw a fork on her if she weren't prepared.

Not that her cup stayed empty long.

Not when Dusty himself came to refill it, steaming and hot, somehow managing not to get her hand or that white tablecloth. Which was indeed a feat considering he was looking right at her the whole time, with that same warning look in his green eyes, his dark hair bouncing off in about every direction.

She nodded, accepting his concerns.

But instead of relaxing, Dusty got more uptight, more tense. His movements jerky, especially when he clearly glanced at MacDonald and then at O'Neil.

He was nothing at all like the smooth boy she'd met at that train platform, who'd scooped her coin up in the air and disappeared it within a blink. He clearly knew more about these two men than he was letting on or was able to. Also, he kept glancing in the direction of the sitting room and the front door, as if he expected Mrs. Allen or someone else to come barging in at any moment.

But the doors all stayed closed, and whoever he was worried about—worried they'd take away this chance to learn of Norma and the story that had found her alone that fateful night—it didn't happen.

Not this moment, anyway.

And with the time ticking away, clicking closer to the acceptable, 'it's time to be gettin' home' hour, Cat needed all her focus on these two men. She'd learned enough of Norma, of her story, to follow her instincts with them, to see exactly where they took her and how they would try and play her.

And there was no doubt they would. None at all.

Even now, they were waiting and watching, two powerful men of Butte who were expecting her to play the part they demanded of her.

O'Neil, as expected, was the one to make the first move. He huffed and snorted, shifting his large frame on a chair that was only barely managing to hold him. A fork held like a death grip in his hand, red jam dripping off the prongs and staining the table like blood.

"I see no reason," O'Neil said to MacDonald, "why you insisted on us staying. A black mark for us all when word gets out—and it will. There's only one reason a woman of Mrs. Allen's standing should be questioned by the police and not this... this tale that *she'd* have us believe."

Cat's eyebrows rose. He was *still* focusing on the police?

She'd listened in on their conversation a few times as she'd worked the room, but it'd always been of a financial bent, banker talk and the like. So she'd assumed, anyway. Was O'Neil bringing the police back up just because she was now with them?

Most definitely.

"Tale?" Cat asked. "I was under the impression that it was considered fact when a person was found dead. After all, I read it first in the papers... your, your *Bystander*, I believe it was."

"That may be," O'Neil said, "but it's a solved case. This woman, sad affair that it was, was the cause of her own destruction. Nothing more... more nefarious than a fallen woman unable to escape the trap of her own making."

He had not said Norma's name, as if he didn't dare.

Several other fellows nearby leaned in closer. The word 'police' tended to have that effect on people.

So, too, did Cat.

Leaned over far enough that her braid slid off her shoulder and thumped on the table. "If it's a solved case, as you say, than why are the police still investigating?"

O'Neil's mouth opened wide. His face started casting that dreadful deep purple sheen again, when Mr. MacDonald waved his hands in an attempt to calm them.

"Now, now..."

MacDonald's voice was just as smooth and calm as before, and completely directed at O'Neil. Except there was a warning tilt, too, his cadence like a sharp sting at the end as if reminding the larger, volatile man to keep control of himself.

Cat did not miss this exchange. Not even that flickering glance O'Neil sent to MacDonald before his face started taking on a more healthier red tone, if that were possible when the man still looked the color of a tomato and pretty much had since she'd first laid eyes on him.

"Now, Seamus," MacDonald was saying, "I thought we'd promised to play the role of polite gentleman to the lady Cat?"

"*Lady*," O'Neil huffed.

MacDonald, however, was clearly not to be deterred, for he gave Cat a polite, apologetic smile before pestering O'Neil again.

"After all," MacDonald said, "it's not *her* fault this business happened, and now at this most inopportune time."

"Yes. Exactly. And the police surely would not have if—"

"And we all know Jere Murphy is a fine man, an even finer cop, along with those he's taken under his care."

Cat blinked.

How had he known about Murphy—?

"Especially," O'Neil said, cutting her thought right off, "since she now has in her employment another with a... past such as *hers*."

His voice rolled thicker and harder with each *r*, making no mistake or argument to the table, or the whole room since it seemed everyone had quieted down and they were all now listening in. There was no mistaking, none at all, regarding what O'Neil thought about the 'lady' sitting across from him.

Cat's eyebrows rose. A bit of... shock, really. Polite society had indeed provided an armor for her, for her profession. It was something that was seen but not spoken of—ever—at least so openly, because doing so sullied the person doing the speaking and this was never allowed.

Despite her utmost intentions, she felt her own anger rising. Felt her own cheeks flush red. It was all the men like him that had finally gotten her tired and fed up with this life. How they could walk whatever line they damn well wanted and never, ever have to pay the price. The high price in human life, in happiness.

Because they were men.

Because they were the gentleman with the money and not a thing could touch them. Ever.

And when someone or something came close? Well, then they just went around blaming the girls for the sad state they and their beloved cities and societies had fallen into. It was their fault, this temptation that they provided, and never once considering exactly *who* was to blame.

Cat's scarf felt like a noose round her neck. Tightening, reminding her exactly *why* she was sitting here. Not here for her own righteous calling, not even to reach across that table and smack O'Neil and all men like him until they got some clue in that puffed-out brain of theirs just *who* was at fault here—and it was not the fault of the dead woman.

Norma.

The very word caused a shiver to race through Cat.

It was enough. Enough of a reminder that she felt her own mask, her own role, slide right into place.

She gave a small shake of her head, disappointment and hurt living in each action, each movement, as she looked right at O'Neil, knowing the whole room was their audience.

"I must say, Mr. O'Neil, your words stun me. I've only been in town two days and you've already taken my character under attack."

"Lady, the proof stands before me."

"Seamus!" MacDonald interjected. "I'm sorry, Miss Cat, so sorry for my friend's manners. This is quite at all not like him."

Cat waved him off. "It's, it's quite all right, Mr. MacDonald. I know quite well the reaction I cause in many folk."

She looked right at O'Neil, never once dropping her gaze. Predator to predator. She was not afraid of him, and he knew it.

"Perhaps," she said, "my very appearance is all the proof you need, that I am not worthy of civilized, polite conversations."

O'Neil snorted, a chortle that sounded like it got caught in his throat. "There's hardly a question of that."

O'Neil, of course, ignored MacDonald's second attempt at chastising him for his impolite manners, but again, Cat simply calmed the man. This time, she placed a hand on MacDonald's arm, firm and solid, nothing at all intimate, and yet, as always, her touch had the desired power on him.

He stopped instantly.

Because that's what she was asking him to do, without using a single word or phrase or even glance. It was by touch alone, her intent and will, to fight this battle on her own.

She always fought her own battles. She'd earned that right.

Cat turned her attention directly to O'Neil. "If that's the way you feel, Mr. O'Neil, than allow *me* the same courtesy."

"And that is what... *lady?*"

"Honesty."

"I am nothing but honest, and I certainly will not stand for some harlot saying otherwise."

Now, the room truly quieted. Not even the chewing of food. Not even the clink of silver against plate nor the loud slurping of coffee or drink.

Simply silence.

A heavy one, too.

Even from across the room, without turning or looking, Cat felt Dusty's hard gaze on her, as if he wanted to burn her right into the ground where she sat for stirring up such rattlesnake den. Because, of course, the other reason such things were not openly discussed because of the utter and complete ruin of the person in question, the person who did, indeed, live on that shadow side. There'd be no victory for that person and yet here she was, pushing O'Neil right down that road.

Cat merely gave O'Neil a small half smile.

"Mr. O'Neil, I'm glad to hear you're an honest man. So, as an honest man I would expect an honest answer. And because your manner with me is so upfront, I hope you'll allow me to act the same."

He shrugged in response. Probably too dignified to even speak.

It was more than enough admission for Cat.

She leaned forward farther still, leaning across that table, braid barely missing her steaming mug of coffee, untouched and forgotten.

"What are *you* doing here?"

In a room filled with these fellows who'd known in passing, in a smile, or by actual carnal knowledge, of the woman once known as Norma.

Norma.

O'Neil's triumphant smile finally dipped. Waivered. As if finally sensing the trap wrapping round his foot, ready to spring, ready to fling him into the air and smack hard on the ground with a sickening thud, just like any good trap you set when hunting.

But Cat wasn't done. Not by a long shot. Not when she held that rifle steady in her arms. Her breathing slow, even, and paced.

"What business," she said again, "did *you* have with the woman named Norma?"

A single bead of sweat slipped from the side of his nose and dropped. "I—how dare you. You accuse me of such, such—it was Mrs. Allen who'd invited me here, I'll have you know. Trap. Trap. Trying to catch me when I've done nothing."

O'Neil's face had finally lost any sign of purple or even red. He'd gone so pale that he about matched the whiteness of his shirt, untouched as it was by smoke and ash.

Unlike Cat who was dropping bits of ash as she leaned across that table like little black snowflakes.

"Allen's the one," O'Neil said, "she's the one been called by police and you're trying to trap *me*—"

O'Neil stood. Moved so fast he nearly tipped the whole table over the way his large knees caught the underside like that.

Plates and forks and cups jostled and toppled. Swears suddenly went up, probably a hot spill that hadn't been expected or seen, not when O'Neil and Cat were taken center stage as they were.

Cat rose as well, fluid and graceful even as she wore her jeans, her empty holster.

A holster that again O'Neil's blue eyes fell right to and held there. Held there.

Fear, perhaps? Or something more?

But then MacDonald had risen as well, waving his hands for calmness, pleading almost with O'Neil to simply sit back down and it'd be quite all right. But O'Neil wasn't having it. Didn't even seem to care that he had a yellowish-gold stain on the front of the shirt from Mrs. Allen's famous apple pie from when he'd stood so quickly.

"I will not stand here and be accused as such!" He waved a meaty, pale finger at Cat. "And *you* will certainly not be hearing the last from me."

Cat hadn't needed to ask for Chin to fetch O'Neil's belongings, his top hat and coat. She might not understand a word Chin said, but the little man seemed to know everything they all said just fine. He was right there, right in the doorway, bowing and bowing and holding out O'Neil's things, who snatched them from him, squashed the hat on his head until it pressed down to his ears, and then he was off.

Gone.

The front door slammed hard, making all the plates and silverware jostle again. And again, there were more swears as hot liquids spilled and splattered.

But Cat, who despite what O'Neil said, *was* still the hostess, and she smiled in polite calm, apologizing for the behavior, and at her urging, they all again began to eat and enjoy the meal. And regardless of O'Neil's abrupt and angry departure, enjoyment was certainly an apt description for the meal, this Sunday gathering orchestrated by Mrs. Allen.

No doubt within two steps of all them leaving out the door, the whole of Butte would know what had happened here, and Cat wouldn't be surprised in the least if she had another more, formal visit from some officer.

No doubt O'Neil would see to that. Insist on it, more 'n likely. Maybe she'd finally meet her shadow with the blazing blond hair.

But wearing pants wasn't a crime, and while her words may have bruised O'Neil's reputation, words alone were also not a crime.

Not yet, anyway.

Hopefully not here. God, it'd been nice if she'd known the players before that meal had started. If she'd known the real movers and shakers of Butte before stepping her boot into this snake pit.

Nothing for it now.

Cat slid back into her chair and sipped her now cold coffee, using it as more a shield to study those around her... their reactions, lookin' for any sign that they knew more than they'd been lettin' on. Like MacDonald. She felt his presence so easily, as is he were touching her, when in fact he wasn't. His emotions were suddenly so open, like he was a swirling tornado of frustration and something else, something deeper and colder, and try as she might to focus her rifle's sights on him... she simply couldn't get a firm read on him.

But, there *was* simply something off and make no mistake. Something... she couldn't quite put her finger on.

Then the feeling was gone as he sat heavily in his chair beside her. Cat quashed her concentrated focus, not wanting him to see.

"I'm terribly sorry, Miss Cat. My friend's behavior." He shook his head. "To even accuse you..."

"As being someone with my past?"

"Yes, yes. But and truth to the matter or not, it is simply not done. A lady is a lady, regardless of dress, and you've been nothing but kind. A perfect, attentive hostess, in fact. You've done nothing at all to deserve his behavior. Please, please allow me to make it up to you. This business..."

His gaze shifted about the whole of the room and all the men there.

He'd of course meant *her* business. And Norma's. And every woman like them who found herself alone and bereft job or prospects, with only one way left to feed themselves and clothe themselves and shelter themselves.

"This business..." MacDonald shook his head. "It's not a thing I'm proud to be a part of, any of us here, I'm sure."

"But you are. You're a part of it."

"I am. I am. I won't sully your honor any more than it's been by denying it. So please, for the sake of our, I do hope, our growing friendship and mine with Mrs. Allen's, let me tell you my story. My story and Norma's."

CHAPTER TWENTY

Cat sat in the same chair she'd been in earlier, that first day when she'd discussed over apple pie with Mrs. Allen her arrangement for staying here. The worn cushions as they folded around her legs, pressing delicately into her back. This time, though, instead of wearing her jeans and the ashy smoke from outside, she was bundled up in a warm, comfortable coat, thick, woolly stockings, and her loose night robe. Hair also hanging loose.

A mug of coffee sat untouched on the small table, still holding a coil of steam tipping on out over the top even with the frigid air still living in the sitting room.

A gas lamp gave off a low glow, enough to push back a bit of darkness, but that was all. Together, she and her coffee sat in silent vigil as she watched out that dark window.

True darkness this time, the kind where in Miles City—or anywhere else in the world for that matter—you'd look up and see a sky full of sparkling white stars. A silver of moon, maybe even peaking its tip around some dark clouds that were threatening rain or snow, it being winter and all.

Here though, there was still no sky or stars or moon. Just blackness and cold.

In fact, it looked so much like day the only real clue that it was actually night, at least if you were to pull back the curtain and have a look, was the people. Gone were all those families and mothers hurrying home or rushing about their business, errands and such. Heads bent, cloth and bits of fabric wrapped tight around their mouths as if that little strip could keep out all that ash from breathing in and wreaking havoc on their bodies. They'd sure hurried, too, as if the whipping horses of hell with their fiery eyes and nostrils were constantly after them.

Now, though, the only people who were about, walking around on those streets lit by lanterns, were the men.

Men trudging home from their shift work at the mines, wearing their overalls and heavy coats, even heavier boots stomping the ground flat as if the act was needed to keep themselves warm, to keep that chilling night air from stealing the breath right out their bodies. A breath which, most likely, was a bit tart and strong from liquid courage more than a few had needed, stopping at one of the hundreds of saloons before heading home. Or maybe not courage so much but a desperate need for that burning fire to remind them they were alive.

Still... alive.

Another day of living, of breathing. Something Cat could very much understand.

Night wasn't silent here in Butte, either. Not with the constant movement of train cars, all that clinking and chucking, hauling their heavy loads over iron tracks as numerous as there were mines. And then there were the whistles, too. They didn't stop, either, because the families and day workers of Butte were fast asleep—or trying to be. Those mine whistles were a high-pitched chorus that sounded off, from one to the next, signaling shift change or some other code she didn't know.

Never ending, too, it seemed.

Residents probably got used to them to the point they might not hear 'em anymore, but Cat sure heard 'em.

She didn't know what time in the evening it was, though long-time residents probably knew just by the whistles alone. She also hadn't a clue there'd been that many mines, either. Sure, she'd heard the stories of all those endless miles underground, but to sit here and listen...

It was all the proof she needed.

Especially when her eyes hadn't actually seen all those endless gallows frames dotting the hill, lowering those same men down into that darkness and hard rock below. And then doing it the next day, then the next. Those same miners who'd sat across from both her and the bankers today, without a blink of being uncomfortable or feeling out of place.

Each of them had belonged here today, sitting there enjoying Mrs. Allen's home-cooked meal just as she had, just as the bankers, reliving tales of life, of the smiles of a woman now gone from this world.

Yet, each of them had belonged, even with the various degrees of class and social distance between them. Cat had never seen anything like it before.

Which made the mystery and question surrounding Norma, her fall from grace, as it were, and finally her death, all the greater.

The whistles finally stopped their chorus, and it seemed like the night had a slight pause, as if it was taking a deep inhale before the next noise took up the chorus and kept all of Butte tossin' and turning on their beds.

Though to be fair, it hadn't been the whistles or jostling train cars that had gotten her up, had kept sleep from claiming her again. She'd no one to blame but herself... and all the unresolved questions floating round in her head. Weighing heavy on her, as if adding another cart full of ore to her soul.

There was so much yet of Butte she didn't understand.

Too much.

Thoughts and ideas, impressions, emotions, they all raced 'round her mind, and she couldn't help but feel with a right strong certainty that she was missing something.

Something important.

But... it was also more than that. It'd been the whole lunch affair today, the whole gathering, and it had stayed with her. Hanging on her, haunting her the same way Alice's ghost now did.

A silent companion with a touch that felt chiller than ice.

The dining room and all those men... it'd been overflowing with tension and anger, certainly when O'Neil had been present, but even that was too simple an explanation for what she'd felt. Like a heaviness had hung about them, a feeling that had come from Norma herself, from her story. A piece of her story which now lived and breathed inside each of those men—and they'd known it, too.

Known they couldn't get rid of it, get rid of *her*.

So many had wanted to forget, to move on, and yet Cat wouldn't let them. She'd brought them there with Mrs. Allen's help to ask them questions. To get a story of a fallen woman, someone they all *knew* should just be forgotten, swept up under the rug and moved on with their lives, looking for the newest and brightest flower to grace Grace's Gardens. The life of a prostitute, no matter how graceful, no matter how much her smile had warmed the soul, simply didn't matter enough.

And yet, she had.

Because try as more than a few had, their thoughts had still remained with Norma... even after she'd gone from the Gardens for a good couple of months. She'd fallen so low as to work the streets. Heck, she'd probably been headin' home that very night to work the one-room crib she lived in, barely big enough for a bed and what probably cost her the most in expenses, that and the necessary fees to police to allow her to keep operating from it.

Norma *should* have been forgotten. Swept under the rug. Her death exactly as it'd been reported in the *Bystander* where she was barely a footnote.

And yet, something about it all, about her, had taken a different turn. Where the paper itself hadn't released Norma's name—which they almost always did. After all, a death of such a fallen lady was a good warning to them all, to the little girls growing up who could easily loose their way in such a dangerous city.

Heck, even propel those socialites to take up their cause even more, shutting down the district for good and chucking all its ladies out on their asses.

Cat let out a heavy sigh. She pressed fingers against her temples and rubbed.

Too many thoughts running around in circles, too many that just weren't adding up, making sense.

Why the heck *was* Norma still in their minds?

Like folks like Mr. Rippi, who'd smiled in good cheer for this same woman. A woman who'd once graced him and his fellows with a smile that had felt like all their own and no one else's.

If Cat were honest, Norma was haunting her now, even if she'd never known the woman in life. It certainly felt like she was getting to know the woman in death.

And that, right there, was the real reason she hadn't been able to sleep.

The haunting that had gotten her up out of bed, stocking feet touching down on the chilling cold wooden floors. There'd been no point sitting in bed letting her thoughts run themselves 'round in circles, chasing their tails as it were. So, she'd gotten up. Gotten her body moving a little, and just the act of coming down here, staring out into that darkness with those handful of lanterns hanging from homes or the floating ones tied up to the hacks calmed her.

Enough that she could sit and think, at least a little, and get a different kind of feel for this city, one that was both hidden and open all at the same time.

The heat had fled Mrs. Allen's home with the sun, so Cat had bundled herself up good and warm with the quilts that had been left along the sofa just for this purpose, as if Mrs. Allen, or maybe it was

Chin, had known this type of night vigil was necessary from time to time.

Then again, Chin *had* heard Cat's soft footsteps on the floor. Either he'd been waiting up for Mrs. Allen or he was just that light a sleeper, but he'd made her some coffee, placed it on the table, and then was gone.

No bow this time, though. His mouth had been remained pinched into a tiny, thin line as he looked at her, his eyes wide with worry.

He had looked just as unsettled as she felt, which was understandable.

Mrs. Allen hadn't come home.

There'd been no news either. Dusty had sent word through the shadow world, but no answers had returned. Cat herself had sent a runner to the police station, and the boy had returned with a shrug of his shoulders saying Mrs. Allen was "indisposed."

So Dusty himself had gone, and he hadn't returned yet either.

Sure, Cat could have followed as well, but she'd a feeling, a sense, that that wasn't the place she needed to be. Not that she *knew* where that was.

Which was still yet another reason why she couldn't sleep.

She was getting tired of those reasons adding up. She liked knowing her path, knowing her way forward. Seeing patterns and the truth that others were blind to.

Now, it was her sitting there in the cold dark, in the middle of the night—though it looked the same as daytime—thinking and wondering about the woman named Norma who'd been stumbling her way home in this same kind 'a blackness.

Finally, Cat took a sip of her coffee.

Black with no cream, just as she liked it, and she felt herself let out a slow, exhausted sigh. That small bit of heat was enough, slipping down her throat and into her belly, warming her just a little bit. It was enough, though.

God, she *was* tired.

The whole gathering had taken more of her than she'd first thought. The minute the last guest had left she'd wanted nothing more than to curl up in her bed, pull that quilt up to her chin, and ward off the bits of cold that always managed to sneak in past the window frame, under those tiny cracks of the door, making her toes freeze at night.

Which she couldn't do, not with Mrs. Allen still missing. And when the time had finally come for sleep, sleep had decided it was taking the night off.

Which again was normal for her.

Too many mysteries and not a one of them adding up, making sense. Too many pieces of Norma's story that Cat had purposefully not been told, had been kept in the dark over.

And she knew it. Knew it right to her soul.

Just like MacDonald and his half-story. His was yet another one that she wore away, like she was chewing a piece of hide. She remembered each and every word he'd spoken, his cadence, his tone. And more importantly, the feelings behind the words... and the ones he'd purposefully left out.

Or changed.

She kept working his story, looking at it from all angles, trying to understand the real bits, the false bits, and the bits he'd just flat out left untold. And still, try as she might, it didn't feel right.

He'd said that it was him, MacDonald, who'd been Norma's lover.

Her *real* lover.

The kind 'a lover most madams wouldn't stand for their girls to keep, not when they were expected to pull in their share of the money. It was one of those funny little inconsistencies of their trade. Girls wanted to get out of the life, but to do that they needed to make a lot of money and save it (meaning not drinking or gambling it away). Or a girl could find herself a man, one who was head-over-heels in love with her, who swept her away from this life, riding out into the distance with her in his arms.

It was a nice dream to have, anyway.

For most girls.

Truth was, a girl couldn't properly do that second part, to find and keep a man like that while she still worked in a house. And that was most definitely true of the high-class parlor houses. A girl couldn't properly shower her attention and graces on one man, or several over the course of an evening, while she was in love with another. At least, thinking she was in love.

But MacDonald had claimed to be that man.

Of course, he hadn't outright said as much, and certainly not in so many words. But he'd dropped in the right ones, in the right places, to suggest that's who he'd been.

And his explanation of what had happened? Of what had ended their romance?

That she'd left him. Dropped him, high and dry, and leaving him heartbroken and crushed. Completely out of nowhere, like he was taken completely by surprise.

To which, Cat called horseshit on.

"Norma," he'd said, "was... special to me."

His voice had barely been above a whisper, as if he was both worried and sure the other men would hear.

"I'm sure you understand," he'd said. "She was... quite the light and I couldn't stay away. I didn't want to, either, which was on me. I am not blameless in this matter."

"And your family?"

He gave her a small smile. "I'm not like Seamus. I don't have a family of my own, not yet, though... I'd been planning on..."

His smile faded.

"I mean," he said, "Norma and I... we'd been planning..."

He'd closed his eyes then, as if in terrible pain, as if he was living an agony so strong it ripped right through his body.

And Cat, playing her part as the concerned, sensitive woman, reached out and squeezed his hand. Not that this gesture would be appropriate for most women, but then, she no longer lived in that echelon of society. She walked her own path.

"Were you gonna run away?" she asked. "Together?"

Again, pain seemed to rack his face for a moment. "It... it wasn't meant to be. She'd wanted more than I could offer. I, alone, wasn't enough for her."

And that's all he'd said.

Well, not all. He'd said she'd left him, and he knew no reason for this sudden change of heart. In fact, he'd never seen her again.

"I went to the Gardens, as was my usual for a Friday night, and she was gone. Not even Grace herself was willing or able to say what had happened."

Or why, apparently.

Not that Cat was inclined to take his word on the matter, or this Madam Grace. The madam would probably be a bit unhappy to learn that her newest, most valuable flower was plotting to take away one of her best clients.

Truly, as far as explanations went, MacDonald had said a whole lot and nothing at all. There were simply too many stories in that simple explanation. Had Norma wanted marriage and he couldn't, or wouldn't, give this to her? Or had he wanted her love and she wasn't *actually* in love with him? Or had there been another lover entirely who'd captured Norma's attention, a man like O'Neil?

Course, the O'Neil explanation was a bit hard for Cat to swallow. Though that didn't mean there *wasn't* another man. Just not O'Neil, at least in the role of doting lover. How exactly O'Neil came into this story was still yet another mystery.

Too many mysteries that were making her head want to split open, right down the middle.

Especially cause she didn't have the chance to get any further with MacDonald. Before Cat could comment, could question MacDonald and his little explanation, he was excusing himself from the luncheon. His movements swift but no longer smooth. Jerky and most definitely uncomfortable. He'd apologized to Cat, not once looking away from her even as he took his abrupt leave.

Again, there came her senses, her tingling, especially as she watched him don his coat and hat and leave, just as O'Neil had done.

Cat took another sip of her coffee. It had just the tiniest tendril of heat left, slipping off over the top like that, then she set it down. The glass made a slight clink on the little plate and the sound cut right through the heavy silence in Mrs. Allen's boarding house.

MacDonald's pain, she could believe.

But the kind of pain he was claiming to have? To be so lost and broken over this woman, a woman who'd been his lover and one he'd planned on running away with? That he would actually walk away from this, his clearly secure position in Butte society, which was certainly true if his relationship with O'Neil had been any indication.

Cat wasn't buying it.

Especially when MacDonald's story still didn't account for the missing few months when Norma *had* worked the streets, when her smile had gone and vanished. He'd claimed to have no knowledge of this, even though he'd asked around at Grace's Gardens. He'd learned nothing. Had, in fact, never seen her again.

Horseshit, and to all of that.

Either he didn't want to know, therefore he was not told the truth by the madam and the ladies at the Garden, or he'd never asked. And Norma dropping a man like him, completely of her own choice? A man with all that wealth and clear power?

Unlikely.

Cat tapped her chin, her fingers chill in the evening air. He was too much a fine catch for Norma. And if Dusty's accounts could be trusted, she'd wanted out of this life.

MacDonald was the dream ticket out, make no mistake.

And yet... MacDonald hadn't felt the need to finish his story about Norma. He hadn't told Cat *exactly* how it'd ended and why. Because there was most certainly a 'why,' and whatever it was, that there was the real truth.

A truth she'd learn one way or another.

Right now it was MacDonald's word against the word of the street itself.

Dusty, of course, had overheard this whole exchange. Not that Cat was surprised. What *had* been surprised her, however, was seeing fury in the kid's blazing green eyes. Like he was about ready to reach right on over and yank that black tie right off MacDonald's neck, wrap it around him tight, and pull.

Cat shook her head at the memory. Her hair, unbraided and actually combed for once, tickled the side of her check.

Too much wasn't adding up. Too much not making sense.

What she needed was Mrs. Allen's guidance, her knowledge of Norma's past and this city, how all these players in power actually moved and danced. Instead, she was left with another mystery—where the hell Mrs. Allen was and what the police were keeping her over—and a boy, also now missing, who'd no intention of breaking his silence and explaining why *he* was mixed up in all this.

Talk about a blazing headache.

It was enough to make Cat want to throw her coffee, cup and all, right out that window into the blackness of Butte's hell.

Which she didn't.

A good thing, too, cause she very well might need to throw the cup at the stranger who suddenly opened Mrs. Allen's front door and showed himself inside.

CHAPTER TWENTY-ONE

For the love of—

Cat shot to her feet. Got behind her chair. A single movement, nothing wasted. Couldn't be. Couldn't get trapped by the table or the lace. She needed space, distance.

The chill floor, so cold it bit right on through her stockings and raced up her legs.

She needed shoes and a weapon. Had neither.

She ignored the cold, ignored the way her heart raced. Thumped so hard it seemed like it was gonna leap right out her chest.

She still had a grip on her coffee cup, wishing like hell it was still piping hot and scalding. It wasn't, but it'd be enough of a weapon if it was needed. She needed her damn gun, but it was still upstairs, tucked away nice and safe, and she was certainly about done with *that*. Butte might want to be this respectable, well-known city, but what she wanted and what the city actually *was* were two different things entirely.

Certainly true as Cat watched the tall, dark shape of a man come inside the dark house.

And the house *was* dark except for Cat's single lantern and that dull glow of a light. He'd probably seen her from outside clear as day as she sat there, perfectly accessible and visible to anyone who was passing by. Or anyone staking the place out. It also pretty much shot her very much needed night vision about now.

Because she hadn't seen him.

Hadn't even sensed his presence outside, staying to those shadows as she'd mulled over all those mysteries, everything that was goin' wrong in her investigation, all the things that weren't adding up. All the while she sat there completely exposed, and her without her gun handy.

Foolish. So foolish.

She knew better. Life in the shadow world had *taught* her better.

No more mistakes. No more getting caught unawares.

If, of course, she survived this encounter.

The man's shadowy movements were smooth and deliberate. No hesitation. Confidence radiated from his whole being. And there was no doubt in her mind that this was a man. The shadow didn't tell her much but enough. The larger, bulkier frame. The heavy shift of a weight on the floorboards. She heard no telltale shift or swish from the numerous layers and yards of fabric, clothing that always rustled and got under foot regardless of how stealthy a woman attempted to be.

She knew from experience.

So no, it wasn't Mrs. Allen finally returning home.

Though this being a boarding house and all, the doors hadn't been locked. Not when the purpose was to allow those who stayed here the ability to come and go as they pleased. Which Mrs. Allen had clearly seen to, even though Cat was currently the only boarder. Which also meant the doors were open to anyone, including strangers, to come and go as they pleased.

In the dark.

In the middle of the night, even.

Cat glanced down, realized she was holding her coat as if it needed to be kept secure. Which it didn't. It was cinched well enough around her waist, and yet she'd still felt this instinctive need to hold onto it. The gesture, so immediate. As if in a single moment she'd felt this deeper need to protect herself... and her inappropriate state underneath. Sleep robes and stockings were not attire fit to receive anyone in, especially if it was the middle of the night. Ladies, after all, did not receive strange, midnight visits.

Damn it.

Even with all her training, all her experience and awareness of walking this life, her ma's teachings were *still* there. Still buried inside her. A harsh reprimand in her mind, complete in her ma's own up-pitched, no-questions-asked voice, that Cat should race upstairs right this moment and put something more appropriate on.

Again, this place—Mrs. Allen's home and all of Butte, it seemed— threatened to unravel her, to take her back to a place she had no interest or need of going back to.

She was who she was, and that was that.

Cat stayed right where she was, keeping one hand on the cup with the lukewarm coffee. The other lightly touching the back of the chair, ready to shove the whole thing or duck, if needed. Her stocking feet set in a wide stance, her long hair completely undone and completely in her way. She wanted to shove the whole mess behind her but didn't dare.

She might need the movement later. A distraction. Anything, anything at all to give her the advantage.

And the shadow?

He was watching her, and make no mistake.

Took one heavy step into that house and stopped. Not freeze or anything so dramatic because why should he? He wasn't at all surprised that she was there. In fact, he'd clearly known of her pres- ence before he'd ever walked in, probably even that she was in such an unpresentable state, and he'd come in anyway. And it was quite clear he hadn't been surprised by her sudden movement as she'd repositioned herself to a... slightly more defensive position.

Well, she could stand there shivering in the dark with her toes going all cold and this little glow of light, or she could find out just how much this man knew about her—and what was needed to keep herself alive and breathing.

"I'd ask if I could help you, sir," Cat said, "but considering the time of night, you've no business being in this home."

He said nothing.

His face, his body, hell, everything about him was completely hidden by darkness, which meant she couldn't get a read on him. Or what he wanted. Although in her case, with that damn lantern, he saw everything *she* did. Every inch of movement, even the way her breathing was hitchin' up and picking up the pace—to which she purposefully forced herself to take in a deep breath and let it out. Then again.

She needed to center herself. Calm. Be prepared for anything. And as she did this, got her breathing and racing heart under control, as if the man had been waiting for just this sign, he finally nodded.

Which told Cat he already knew plenty about *her*. Making this a right more dangerous situation than she'd first thought.

"You're right," he said. "I've no business walking into respectable homes. But then, that doesn't count this one. Or the business you've been stirring up."

His voice was deep but soft. So soft it was almost like a whisper. A hard kind of whisper, though, one that literally spoke the exact same confidence she'd first sensed from him. Both a confidence and hardness, the kind of unyielding hard that said he'd already made up his mind and wasn't gonna bend, no matter what.

He wasn't hiding, not one little bit, of who he was.

Or what he thought of her.

Pure contempt. Disgust, through and through, to be standing there and talking with a woman like her in a boarding home that'd welcome someone like her.

Cat didn't move from her position behind the chair. Her fingers digging into the soft fabric.

She'd been expecting him to make some dramatic gesture. That they'd have the kind of standoff the wild places in Montana was still known for, including Miles City, certainly when too much whiskey and such was flowing. The most dramatic action, of course, being him pulling his own gun and letting those bullets fly. And yes, he was wearing a gun. She could see the slight shape of his sidearm in the darkness. The telltale movement of someone completely comfortable and at ease with having one strapped right to his hips. And those bullets? Well, they'd rip right towards her, sure enough. Completely uncaring of Mrs. Allen's worn and comfortable sofas, all the lace and trimmings that made the sitting room feel like an actual home and not just a place to lay your head, cause bullets never cared. Didn't care about the place or the person they were being fired at. They just did their business, as instructed. And they tore right through everything they came in contact with, leaving nothing but swissed-up cheese behind.

That kind of dramatic gesture, no question 'bout it, would end her investigation into Norma.

And it'd see to it that no one else would pick it back up. No one would dare go any further or even care for that matter. And Mrs. Allen? Dusty? Who knows what'd happen to them, though more than likely, they'd simply disappear. They'd be forgotten, just like all the others who lived and walked in the shadow world, and Cat... well, she'd just be a little two-bit article in some newspaper. Probably unnamed, as Norma had been, because whoever was orchestrating this whole thing didn't want names to get out there.

Names made something real, something tangible, something that could very well be worth investigating. Unless, of course, you'd been running from a past like Cat had, the kind that haunted you until you'd no choice but to do something. Anything.

Be more than the person you'd ever thought you could be.

She was expecting the worst, was prepared for it.

But this man, so comfortable with the gun hanging right from his hip, comfortable hiding out in the darkness he so despised, surprised Cat.

Again.

Instead of going for the dramatic gesture and ending things right then and there while she only had her lukewarm coffee cup, he did the exact opposite.

He turned and gently closed the door behind him.

Cat blinked.

In fact, he was so gentle with that front door she got the distinct impression he didn't want someone... certainly someone with Chin's exceptional hearing, to hear the small creak before the nudge-nudge slam. The usual force it took to get that door closed good and proper.

Almost like... he knew this particular door.

Knew how it liked to stick right before it clicked closed. Knew, too, the sharp-eared and quite concerned Chinaman sleeping not two doors down from them. Someone who would undoubtedly rouse immediately if he heard the door and its particular forcefulness.

Which didn't make sense. He'd been quite clear on his opinions of this house and of Mrs. Allen. To know the place so well and avoid the one sound that'd get Chin up faster than a herd of buffalo tearing down on his heels?

Cat opened her mouth, ready to question this, when he took another step into Mrs. Allen's house. The floorboards groaning and shifting just slightly under his larger, sturdy frame. And she heard, quite clearly, the familiarity in those steps.

Determined. Hard.

And the glow of her lantern gave off just enough light to catch the unmistakable blond of his hair, barely visible underneath a wide-brimmed hat.

He was the police officer. The very one who'd been following her earlier that day.

CHAPTER TWENTY-TWO

I t's you," Cat said.

She kept her voice pitched low, instinctively picking up his need for quiet, though she couldn't quite say why he cared or why she was even following his lead on this.

After all, she should *want* Chin to hear.

Not that the smaller man could do much unless he went right for a gun, though she doubted this was in his nature. But Chin's arrival would be just the distraction she needed to get out of a such a vulnerable position. Her standing there, no weapon except for the dead-on accuracy of throwing rocks, which she'd maintained since she was a child running wild in play.

But lukewarm coffee was in no way a match for bullets.

And yet, she found herself *not* calling out or getting loud, not drawing attention to the fact that she was no longer in this house alone.

Cat's hair tangled around her fingers and hands, getting in the way even as her mind fought for the best maneuver, even as she tried to see all her options and what the best one was. Except she didn't exactly have any *good* options... not when she hadn't a clue who this man really was, other than he'd followed her earlier.

And was darn good at it.

Heck, she didn't even know his name. All she knew was that he was an officer, and clearly he knew the business she and Mrs. Allen were a part of, both as former night ladies, and their interest in Norma's death. Information was the real power here, not weapons. And he wasn't acting like he was planning on drawing his any time soon. So, she'd follow his lead and keep following along until she got a better sense of her own footing and what moves she had open to her.

If any.

Like why he was so interested in a woman like Cat, a woman with the same kind of past as Mrs. Allen, as Norma, all of which clearly disgusted him on principle alone.

"I'd a feeling we'd meet again," Cat said, "though, truth be told, I wasn't expecting the hour."

Or here, for that matter.

"You prefer," he said, "I follow you down some dark alley. Or maybe even some small room where you conduct your... business."

Contempt? Disgust? Oh, he wasn't hiding his opinion of her or her profession, former or not. But what she hated most of all was that he hadn't asked it as a question, either. He was pegging her character simply based on the life she'd chosen. As if he knew everything there was to know 'bout her *because* of that choice. A life which, in all honesty, had never left her with much of a choice at all, certainty not if she'd wanted to keep on living and eating.

Cat, whose only real choice had been to stay behind like Alice had, still breathing but dead all on the inside, or take a stand. This man, this *officer*, he didn't know the first thing about her, her choices, her life.

It was equally infuriating 'cause she didn't know why this man, this one in particular, was working her up like this. It's not like she hadn't met like a hundred like him before. Those who thought they were above all the rest of them because by the grace of God they'd been given the kind of luck that kept them free of the harsh, gray areas of life, kept 'em from falling down into that darkness, and then fallin' even lower than a person ever thought possible—

Cat shook her head.

His opinion didn't matter. She was made of sterner stuff than this.

And yet at the same time, she couldn't help it. That he was standing right there hiding himself in darkness and judging her like *he* knew all about her—

Her senses got to tingling again. Another piece of the puzzle fell into place.

She knew. Knew exactly who this was.

The tension Cat had felt pulsing through her shoulders, making her fingers curl around that cup like they wanted nothing more than to fling the whole thing at him, relaxed. Eased.

It'd been a passing comment of Mrs. Allen's right after Cat had first arrived. In fact, when they'd sat right here for some tea and apple pie. How Mrs. Allen had talked about a younger officer, one of those being trained by the respected Jere Murphy. The very same Murphy who, if rumor was to be believed, had Mrs. Allen picked up before the luncheon gathering. Same cop, too, who was even now holding her for questioning.

But *this* man in particular, this man still mostly shrouded by darkness, visiting her here, doing his utmost best to keep his presence a secret, *he* didn't care for Cat or her kind. Didn't care for those who lived in the shadow world. Had probably been raised as a good, religious boy with loving parents. Probably still had them, too, his parents. In fact, she guessed he was regularly over there for Sunday dinners, being the good and loving son that he was.

At least, when he wasn't following a woman around.

A woman who, until recently, had worked the line.

Cat straightened, came around the chair and placed her cup on the table with a hard clink. Black droplets spilled over the side, staining the white lace of the cloth.

She didn't care.

She was mad, which was perfectly understandable, though perhaps not the intensity. And yet, she couldn't help it. Here she was facing yet another person who thought they could come into her life and start pulling her strings. Control her.

Not today. Not ever again.

Even if he was an officer of the law.

"So you think you know me, Christopher Blake."

He straightened, sudden like.

He was surprised, make no mistake. She felt that in him like he was ringing a noonday bell. Though that was the only sign he let slip loose. Clearly a master of shadows, master of composure. He'd learned it from somewhere, much as he was trying to hide or deny otherwise.

Course, there'd been a time when Cat could have described herself this way as well, someone who let nothing slip by unless she wanted it to. Her cold and calculating way she took in every detail, assessed each and every one and then finally acted. All the while never letting her own emotion through. It'd been a lesson Alice had taught her, that day her sister had said goodbye forever. Emotion, good or bad, was a sure way back to yourself, a way to hurt you so deeply, so truly, and without you ever being the wiser.

Not now, though. It was as if something about Butte just kept her off kilter and didn't let up. She couldn't help but *feel*. Knew she was doing it and yet couldn't muster up what was needed to keep it all in check, check from showing her hand.

Like how she wasn't bothering to hide her smile at Christopher Blake's sudden start at hearing his name.

Nor did she want to, either.

Part of her wanted him to learn. Wanted him to see just what kind of fire he was playing with, and he was sure damn lucky it was her standing across from him and not someone else, someone desperate enough to reach for whatever defense they had and use it without abandon or care. If he was hoping to keep on being an officer of the law, especially if that meant patrolling the shadow world, he'd better get rid of that arrogance. Damn fast, too.

And if that duty fell on her? Well, then. So be it.

She was sure as well going to enjoy it.

"Yes, I know you," Cat said. "I know your name. Can't help but hear the contempt you have for me; it's screaming out 'bout every inch of you. A woman who's fallen so far in society I'm no longer worthy of breathing the same air as you."

The disgusting and foul air as it was.

"Like," she said, "it was a choice I ever had."

"There's always a choice."

"Says a man. And a cop."

She planted her stocking feet wide and set her hands right on her hips, glaring at him. Didn't bother closing her coat as it pulled open slightly by the movement. If he blushed or flushed in anger, she couldn't tell, not half-shrouded in darkness as he was.

But then, she didn't care much either way.

She *was* gonna stand her ground.

"And yet," she said, "here you are. First, following me while I was going on about my business, errands and such, just like any good citizen. And now you're sneaking into the home I'm boarding at, hiding in shadows because clearly, you've got a problem with my being here."

"I told you. You're stirring up trouble; makes a place not safe at night."

"Is that right? Didn't realize looking into a death your fellow officers claimed as 'accidental' caused such of a stir 'round here. Especially because she was a harlot."

Blake jerked back.

Which she'd been expecting.

See, working the line, there was a certain kind of sensibility that was demanded. And in all fairness, it came from both sides of that line. The respectable, civilized side where women had their places and played by the rules dictated to them by their betters. But calling out her trade for what it was? The dirtiness, the darkness of it, something that got summed up by one word and one word alone?

That was simply not done. Both sides, in fact, tried to avoid it.

Usually.

But Cat didn't stop there, either.

Oh, no. Not after the day she'd had. Learning about Mrs. Allen's and Dusty's deceptions, God, which felt a lifetime ago. The half-truths and hidden anger from MacDonald, then there was O'Neil and his not-so-hidden anger. Cat's head was swirling from it all and she just goddamn wished everyone stopped running 'round the truth and got to the point already.

Norma was clearly more than the newspaper had first called her out as. She wasn't just some forgotten, fallen woman whom no one cared about or remembered. Hell, Norma was more than each person Cat had met claimed she was. And the more Cat got to digging into that truth, the more she learned she didn't know squat at all. Because to someone, someone very important and powerful, Norma was *more* than she'd ever dreamed.

Probably, too, than even Norma herself had known.

Which was really, really darn infuriating, especially when her allies into this little investigation were keeping their traps shut tight, preventing Cat from finding out just how high up this spiraling mess went.

All in all, it was a god-damn heap of frustration.

Meant, too, that she was *not* about to stand there and let this man judge her.

Nope. Not gonna have it.

Cat moved around the table, advancing on Blake. Coat swishing around her, pulling open just a bit more revealing her sleep robe. Her fists clenched, like she really was gonna take a swing at him.

And dear lord did she want to.

So sick and tired of all these games when all she wanted, *needed*, was to find the truth of some poor woman who hadn't the same chance at life as she'd had. Same as Alice. Trapped, unable to break free. Both of them, dying before they'd found that freedom. Both of them, not having the determination to keep on going, to keep fighting, even when life fell to its lowest, its worst.

Cat crossed the short distance. Stocking feet stepping light on the floor, not making a single creak on the boards.

She'd already memorized which ones to avoid.

Blake, though, he stood there, wary like a cat waiting to see if he needed to pounce... or scurry on off. He was still hidden in shadows, preventing her from really getting a sense of what he was thinking, feeling, but she saw enough. Like how his eyes about leapt through the darkness, as blue and brilliant as Dusty's had been green, as if the darkness couldn't hide whatever he felt burning inside him.

Nor would he let it.

His hatred for her?

Oh, yeah, burning bright, and no mistake.

Then there was his face, something she'd not even a glimpse of when he'd been following her to T.J. Bennett's, but those curves there, like they'd been chiseled out of some great marble stone, held the same kind of hard lines she'd heard in his voice.

Hard and unyielding, and no question 'bout it, handsome.

There were probably some stories behind that face, behind the hardness. Stories that fueled this unhidden contempt for her and everything she clearly stood for. Maybe, too, a past where he'd shared a tender moment or two with a woman such as herself and had gotten burned. Maybe even heartbroken, though she doubted it.

She'd a feeling this wasn't a man who trusted easily, especially with something so valuable.

Still, there was something definitely there.

But one thing though was quite clear: Christopher Blake was certainly nothing like O'Neil, a man barely keeping his heart pumping from overindulgence and over... well, over everything. And unlike O'Neil, who let his temper control the reins and damn the consequences, Blake was the exact opposite.

A man chiseled out of some fine stone, like he hadn't a soul hiding underneath it all. Well, except the dislike of her character.

And yet... there *was* more. More that he was working hard to hide from her. As if he wanted to throw the viewer off, something that, unless you went looking for it, unless you were the type to notice all them details... the way his cheek muscles cinched, just a bit of tightening 'round the eyes, and that same pull along his lips... as if the man couldn't help those tiny little bits of reaction...

Of emotion.

Of course, his eyes were a different story altogether. One that you had to be strong enough to stand your ground and look right at him, to see it. There was nothing he could do to hide what she saw there, no amount of training or conscious effort. Whatever inner battle was going on, it practically leapt right out of his singing blues, especially as he stared at her—

Glared, more like.

She'd wanted to get this close to Blake earlier, back when he'd been following her. Had needed to, to get a clear sense of the man. Well, she sure did now. And being this close, she knew, without a doubt, she'd been right. He hated her on principle, on simply being who she was. A lesser, fallen being like herself, who truly didn't deserve breathing in the same air as him and the respectable folks living in the city.

And yet, he *was* here.

Despite all his feelings, he was here. In the middle of the night, in Mrs. Allen's home, a woman who'd been hauled off for questioning or some other reason. All because Blake or his boss, Murphy, needed something.

From Cat, in particular.

Otherwise, why have her followed earlier in the day? Why come to her now, and like this, when the gathering had specifically been about Norma and those who'd known her. Unless... Murphy and Blake didn't want anyone to know their own interests.

Regardless, Blake was standing there, swallowing his pride and his dislike, 'cause he needed to.

Well, she wasn't gonna stand for that. No, sir.

Cat crossed her arms. "I deal only in truths, Mr. Blake. And if you can't find the decency to be truthful to me, you can leave."

"You do not wish to know my thoughts, lady."

At least he had the decency to keep the word 'lady' from sounding like a swear word, unlike O'Neil. Blake here, except for those eyes, was obviously a man of control.

Usually, so was she.

Not tonight, though. Tonight, today, hell her entire existence in Butte so far, had been pushing her here, pushing her to this moment. She was just plain fed up with all them half-truths and half-lies. What she wanted, more than anything, was an honest-to-God straight answer.

Might as well wish for the moon.

"I'll tell you once, Mr. Blake, and I won't say it again. Do not ever belittle my intelligence. I know *exactly* your thoughts and what you think of me. You think I can't see? Can't hear it in your voice? The way you stand there?"

He sighed, as if dealing with temperamental females was exactly what he'd been expecting and part of the job he desperately hated.

"Lady, I really don't care—"

"I am certainly not done, Mr. Blake."

Cat moved forward then, pointing at him. Got so close she was just a few feet away, and then, to show that she wasn't afraid, she got even closer. Got to an inch of him, but didn't stop there. She thrust her finger right into his hard chest.

Hard, just like the rest of him.

Certainly like his heart who didn't care for those who'd fallen on such a low existence.

"You," she said, "you who are so righteous, you come slinking in here, in the middle of the night. You stand here, hiding in the shadows, passing your judgments, yet can't even sit down across from me and have the *decency* to tell me what the hell this is all about."

She kept her voice low, not wanting to bring Chin in on this, but the ferocity in her voice? Her manner?

Oh, she didn't hide one ounce of that. She was done acting the part of lady.

"You want to judge me?"

She jabbed her finger again.

"You only want to see the woman you think I am? No, sir. I am *not* gonna let you get off that easy. I came here of my own choice, looking to do some good. Help those folks who no one, certainly not you or your officers, cares about."

Her whole body was shaking with both a rage and a hurt she hadn't ever thought was possible. She'd thought, long ago, she'd stopped caring about the opinions of others.

Apparently not.

Well, that'd be what it was, but she wasn't about it to let it get in the way of what she needed to do here. And that was prove her point. And make a stand.

Blake hadn't moved an inch. Not even with all her finger jabbing. He'd stayed right there, man made of stone that he was.

Not that she cared either way.

She didn't.

Cat didn't jab again, though, but she kept her finger right there, pressing hard into his chest showing him that she wasn't afraid. And that she certainly didn't care about *his* opinion.

"Now," she said, "you clearly need something from me and I need answers. The way I see it, you've got two choices: you can either come sit down at that table and have a civilized conversation with me. Or you can arrest me for whatever charges you think you've got. But one thing I will *not* do is play your games."

Cat stood there, wearing her warm stockings and coat, mostly hiding her night robe underneath, somehow still feeling the bite of the cold room even with all the fire lightin' her blood right now. But she didn't move one inch, even if that inch meant her finger was still pressing into that chest of his, and just the barest space between them for a breath.

She put the whole thing in Blake's hands and she'd wait, for as long as was needed.

He'd wait, too.

She could see it. Could see him thinking and thinking hard, not in the least intimidated by a woman like her standing so close. Maybe she'd been wrong earlier. Maybe it wasn't her that made him uncomfortable. Maybe it was something else entirely.

Still, he was more than likely used to his suspects fidgeting before that hard, blue gaze of his, if they were strong enough to meet them at all. Like having the great eyes of the law lookin' down meant you were gonna come undone right at the seams, as if you didn't have what was needed to hold up to the scrutiny.

Not Cat, though. She was totally and completely comfortable in the silence.

Finally, Blake reached up, took her hands, freezing cold as his were from all that time outside in the chill, frosted air, and gently pushed hers away.

And they *were* gentle, which surprised her.

She'd been expecting the same kind of hardness as the rest of him, certainly towards her. Hell, she hadn't expected his willingness to touch her at all. And yet... there was a softness there—

Blake stepped away then, closer to the door, giving them some more acceptable space. He didn't rush or hurry, either. If anything, he was showing her, quite clearly, that he was completely comfortable with the closeness she'd purposefully imposed on them.

And his blue eyes?

Oh, they were still sparkling, still had a battle going on, but it felt... like the edge on his rage had slipped. Not a whole lot, to be fair, just a bit really. But something clearly had... maybe not changed, but certainly shifted.

Maybe, too, something more. Not that she'd go so far as to say respect; not from this man and not towards a woman like she was, with her past and all. But there'd been a change, no question 'bout it.

Blake tipped his hat to her, ceding the very point she'd been thinking.

"Point made, lady Cat. Or, should I call be calling you Cowboy Cat?"

Now it was her turn to struggle a bit on the inside, not sure about this change. He was being a gentleman, that was all, like MacDonald and the rest of the boys had been. Just Blake's training kicking in, like her own. The kind of childhood instructions and lessons that was branded to you, that stayed with a soul as much as you hated and denied it, yet the darn thing found the most inopportune time to poke its head out.

A change in his character or not, she wasn't fully gonna trust him.

Not yet.

If ever.

They still stood in the shadowy darkness of the doorway, too far from her little lantern and its glow of her light to get a good read on him. He was keeping his emotions in check now, enough that she couldn't quite nail what he was thinking and feeling. And strangely enough, though they were standing even further apart, she was noticing her own very slight discomfort.

She did the smart thing and ignored it.

"The name Cowboy Cat was Mrs. Allen's idea," she said. "But Cat works just fine for me, please."

"You sure? I heard another name you're hoping to live by. A lofty one, too, considering."

Cat shrugged, hoping to look like she didn't care. "I've been given a lot of names over the years. Picked a few out myself."

"Not this one. This one... sounded new. Untested."

She felt a sudden tingle right down the back of her neck. Sharp and stinging, and it roared right down through her, from her belly straight to her toes.

Somehow she managed to find her voice. It was strong. Enough, anyway.

"And what name would that be?" she asked.

His blue eyes met hers, and they sparkled just as fierce as before. He said one word, only one.

But it was enough. Just that one word was more than enough to make her knees shake and her whole body wobble. Somehow, she kept herself upright, if barely.

"Justice," he said.

CHAPTER TWENTY-THREE

C at flinched.

Couldn't help the reaction. Wished that she was holding onto something, the wall, the chair, anything to help disguise her reaction. It came so sudden, so out of the shadows, she hadn't, *couldn't*, have expected it. Thank goodness she'd moved far enough away from her lantern and that dull glow, could only hope it hid at least some of her surprise... and how much the name both hurt and overwhelmed her.

Only Dusty had called her that. A joke, she'd thought, surely. Though, she'd known, too, he hadn't been laughing. He'd been serious and, hopeful.

She managed to breathe.

Justice.

"How—"

Cat cut herself off.

Couldn't give away her confusion, her uncertainty. That was too much power Blake would have over her and she couldn't allow that. But... how had he known? Did Dusty know him, *trust* him? Or, was this just another rumor Dusty had planted to draw out those who'd been involved in Norma's death?

God, when she finally did see the boy again she'd slap him silly. Or just yell. Really, really loud.

Another damn piece of the puzzle one of her allies had and hadn't seen fit to tell her before going off and getting themselves missing.

She wanted to swear. Barely kept herself from doing it, too.

What did he and Mrs. Allen think? That she was made of miracles or something? That she could just close her eyes and find out whatever truth they were hoping to learn, all without telling her *shit?*

"I see you're familiar with the name," Blake said.

"I heard it, once or twice."

Course, all the while Blake stood there in the shadows, keeping whatever he was thinking tucked up close. It seemed, too, that Mrs. Allen's home had grown dimmer since they'd first started talking, as if the lantern's glow also wanted to hide what was taking place here. A conversation that couldn't take place during the light of day, well enough for Butte, anyway, not to mention actual clothes and not sleep attire in a house that had taken the chill winter cold as its own name.

And as mysterious as the visit itself was, there was nothing untoward taking place. And yet... somehow... it felt like there was.

She was, after all, wearing her wool stockings and night robes, even with a good coat keeping out the rest of the cold.

Yet here he was, Christopher Blake, a proclaimed 'good' cop by those in the shadow world, someone who despised what they stood for and yet wasn't taking a bribe or payoff from the big players or self-appointed copper kings. At least, not that anyone knew of, anyway.

An officer of the law, of the peace, coming to Cat in the middle of the night... and for what? Because of a silly name a kid named Dusty had given her, the name 'Justice?'

It was foolish.

And yet Blake was watching her as closely as she'd watched him earlier. He knew damn well that he'd put her footing off, ruined her breathing and calmness. And... that had been exactly his intent. He was testing now her as surly as she'd tested him moments earlier when she'd gotten up close, getting into his space. He was more aware of her and who she was than she'd first given him credit for. Almost like he himself was a studier of humans, same as her.

It wasn't a comforting thought. Especially since the whole city of Butte had been putting her off balance, getting under skin and the like. Not good at all for her chances of staying ahead and getting to the bottom of Norma's death.

Norma, Cat reminded herself. All *this* was about Norma.

So, Cat pulled together everything she could of herself, pushing off those feelings of discomfort. She focused on her breathing and the calmness she so desperately needed right now. And somehow her heart actually started beating a tad bit slower.

Sure, it was still racing, just not quite as fast as when Fat Jack had whipped her about in his hack.

Blake took off his hat, revealing the blazing blond hair she'd glimpsed what felt like a lifetime ago. It fell just past his shoulders, unruly in a few spots, as if there were indeed pieces of him that could not be tamed even by the law.

He nodded to her. "Justice. That's a curious name to go by."

"It wasn't one I chose for myself. Still not sure it suits me."

"Me neither."

Now, the floor had been starting to feel a bit cold again, the way it was seeping up through her socks, almost to the point where it felt like she was standing there barefoot. At least until Blake went and opened that mouth of his. Just like that, she felt her fire come roaring back. Whatever uncomfortable parts he'd been making her feel, well, that was long, long gone. Burned away with just those words leaving his mouth.

Cat crossed her arms. "I really don't see how that matters much to you, just a name some kid gave me."

"See," he said, ignoring her comment, "here in Butte, they care mostly about fairness, 'specially with the mines. Fair wages, fair hours, fair employment opportunities. Don't matter what nation a person hails from, each and every one of them cares about fairness."

"Seems reasonable."

He tapped his hat in hands, slow and methodical like, as if he wanted to draw her attention to his hands and not whatever else he was trying to slip past her.

Trying, being the important word there.

"The thing is," he said, "justice isn't something most people care about. And yet here you are, arrived only two days ago, three if we count the lateness of the hour, and yet you've already been given the name."

She shrugged. "Like I told you, the name was given to me."

"I want to know why."

"You'd have to ask Dusty."

"I did. He told me to come here. Talk to you."

Cat felt the air, cold as it was, leave her chest. Of course he'd talked with Dusty; that's the only way Blake have known it in the first place. But... why? And had the talk been a matter of trust? *That* was the important question, and she'd no way of askin' either, at least not Dusty.

"Well," she said, "you're the one standing here, talking with me, aren't you? Have *you* figured out why the kid gave me the name?"

"I've a hunch or two, but they're not adding up, considering your line of work."

"Former."

"Or former line of work."

The hardness was back again, both in his eyes and his voice.

There he went again, summing up who and what she was because she'd had no other options, because survival meant doing what was needed, regardless if it was what you wanted.

Once a night lady, always a night lady. As if the world itself only dealt in absolutes, in black and whites areas, as if gray simply didn't exist.

Cat's fingers dug into her arms. It was all she could do to keep from going at him again, thrusting her finger into his chest until he actually opened his damn ears and listened.

Somehow, she kept breathing.

Somehow, she got herself centered enough to speak and did it without yelling, which was quite the feat.

"Justice," she said, "it matters *because* of my life. Because I've stood there too many times and seen too many ladies like Norma or others living in the shadows get tossed aside by people like you."

"Like me."

"Yes. All of you who sit there on your shining white chairs. Your city council members, your founding fathers, your sheriff and all their like. People who've never fallen so low that the only option is surviving or death. Not just of you, either, but of your family and your children. Have *you* been faced with that, Mr. Blake? Have you been faced with that choice?"

He said nothing.

"Exactly. We *know* the truth. Know darn well that our lives don't matter, and that means we don't deserve justice, certainly if it means knocking off someone important from that chair of theirs. Especially then. Even when we're the ones deserving of justice, and the very last thing that you or your justice system can give us is that."

Like what had befallen her and Alice, and now, like Norma.

Cat's fingers were about ready to pierce through her coat. Every word she'd spoken like she was renewing her promise, that day she'd taken a chance and left Miles City to come here. She didn't even realize how hard she was squeezing until Blake and that cold, blue gaze of his glanced down.

She dropped her hands immediately.

"I think I'm done answering your questions about my character, Mr. Blake."

She was suddenly feeling so very tired and so very alone. Alone in a city she didn't quite understand, with all its complexities, like how on this street alone there were fancy mansions from the exact people she'd just been talking about, the kind who literally *lived* on top of those white chairs, who'd never even had to dust off the darn things. And there, right across the street from those big houses, was a boarding home being run and maintained by a former madam.

But the real inconsistency was that everyone in Butte knew about Mrs. Allen, too. An open yet accepted secret.

Too many inconsistencies, too many nuances she just didn't understand—didn't have time to understand, not if she wanted to find Norma her justice.

Cat glanced at the door, wishing Blake would just be gone and let what had happened here and all the dust he'd kicked up in her thoughts, her past, all of it just lay where it was. Hopefully forgotten. Both of them.

She doubted she'd get so lucky.

"Mr. Blake, you clearly have news of my associates. You're welcome to come in like a civilized person, sit down with me and have a chat, or you can leave. I'm tired and I'm in no more mood for your games."

She turned away then.

Needed to move. Needed the space. Needed... to breathe.

She hated how this place, hated how just being in this house with this man put her back on her family's ranch, a ranch that had turned from her childhood home, with all those good memories and love and light, into what it had become: a helpless situation where Alice and her pain had been their only savior. At least until Cat and her temper had had enough. When she'd taken the only other way out she had.

It'd destroyed her name and her family's forever. But for her, the freedom had been worth the sacrifice, especially now with Alice gone, though gone from this world. She was still right beside Cat, haunting her, sitting right at Cat's shoulder like she was. Alice's presence was a coldness that the floor there couldn't begin to compete with. A coldness that went right to her soul and stayed there.

What had she been thinking? Thinking she could possibly do some good? Could change something, *anything*? Dreams of the dreamer, as Alice had always called her. What a foolish dreamer she was, as if she could reach a man like Blake, someone who saw her as one thing and that's all there was to it.

Except...

Blake hadn't yet moved from his spot by the door.

Their eyes met and he kept standing there.

So be it. She'd been honest with him, truthful, too. And she *was* tired.

Cat was about ready to grab the lantern and head back upstairs when his voice, both hard and soft, said to her:

"Some people believe they're above justice, Miss Cat, above even the law."

She glanced over her shoulder. "I was sensing as such."

He stirred, stepped forward. An inch closer to her and the lantern's dull flame.

"From your conversations earlier, at the gathering?"

"Some," she admitted.

"They were your fellow night lady's acquaintances?"

Her eyes narrowed at him. There he went again, lumping her and her character all into one.

Blake... hesitated, as if sensing he'd overstepped.

"I imagine," he said, "most were friends, actual acquaintances and not clients. That only a few there could actually afford her services, at least when she worked at the Garden."

Try as Cat might, much as she wanted this man gone, her insides tingled.

Norma.

All this was about Norma, not about Cat and her feelings and sensibilities. It was about finding justice and this man, much as she hated to admit it, knew something.

Hell, he clearly knew a lot, no question 'bout it.

Just like there was no question in her mind, whether a rational one or not, one formed in fact or just by feeling alone, that someone who believed themselves above the law had had a hand in Norma's death. The how... the why... all that, well, it just didn't make sense, didn't add up.

Yet, anyway.

"Norma," Cat said her name, voicing it, giving it the power it had earlier in that day, hell, this very room.

And it did, too, the way it echoed off the walls, hanging in the air like it did. Not loud, and yet still powerful.

Blake nodded. "Norma."

"Why is she so important? She *was* a night lady. She was someone who shouldn't have mattered."

"But she did."

This time, Cat's insides skipped on the tingling bit and went right into rolling. Knew, without a doubt, she was more than onto something... she was on that small trail, the kind placed down by game on hooves or softly furred feet. Just a hint of a trail leading to some nesting spot or watering hole, but no doubt 'bout it, it *was* a trail.

All the while Blake and that blue gaze of his didn't once move or waiver. He looked right at her, promising, in that brief moment, what he could.

The truth.

Norma *had* mattered, and more than likely, more than she'd ever known when she'd been alive and breathing.

Cat nodded to him. "You're an officer of the law."

"I am. And yet... I'm here."

She understood what he hadn't said. That he was here, talking with a former night lady. A woman who wore jeans and a cowboy hat, a woman who was trying to do differently. Trying in her own small way to find justice. And... here Blake was, the very last place he wanted to be because either he or his boss Murphy believed in it.

Believed in her.

No doubt about it. There was something about Butte that was a shock to her system, and there wasn't a damn thing she could do about it.

Well, not entirely.

Cat reached across and rang the bell to alert Chin.

The sound caused Blake to start, those blue eyes of his widening till they about swamped his face. She could almost read his thoughts, wondering if he should bolt for the door or stay right where he was, cause he needed to be here. Needed to know what she'd learned today at the gathering, no doubt.

Something, too, that he couldn't have learned from Dusty, if Dusty was even talking with him.

Cat waved her way towards the sitting room, her coat sleeves dangling above her wrists.

"If we're gonna do this, we're gonna need something stronger than my cold coffee. You'd at least want your own cup, especially considering your feelings towards me."

For a moment he stayed right where he was, safe in those shadows, but then he stepped forward and she was glad for the distance between them. Mrs. Allen could have at least warned her about the size of the man and just how handsome he looked, even covered as he was in Butte's ash and soot.

Well, there was his distaste of her, too, and that was there, clear as day. Something else, too, though nowhere near enough to respect, but a softness nonetheless.

She'd take it, though. It was as much as Blake could give and she did need an ally. Someone, at least, willing to actually open their goddamn mouth and talk with her.

"You got any of Mrs. Allen's pie leftover?" he asked. "Jere Murphy asked me to bring him back a slice. A good-sized one, too."

CHAPTER TWENTY-FOUR

A couple heaping slices of apple pie, heated up, too, and Cat found herself sitting at the same table she'd sat at three days earlier, counting the lateness of the hour after all, with Mrs. Allen as they'd filled their tummies and sipped tea. They'd devoured those slices of gooey apple pie, with that cinnamon just about bursting out with every bite and those perfect-sized apple chunks. Even the sitting room was just as it been that day, with all the lace and curtains and porcelain plates, as if they'd come flying out of the past and her ma's own home to rest right here, haunting her.

Except now there was no Mrs. Allen joining her for said apple pie.

Instead, this time it was the handsome and hard Christopher Blake. Who, after a few hard chews of his pie, as if he was finding it a bit difficult to be sitting across from Cat, finally settled in. Course, Cat figured the deliciousness of the apple pie, and not her presence, had been the reason for the change, slight though it was.

Regardless, it was him who was sitting there, hard blue gaze of his watching her, studying her. And to be fair, she was doing the same of him. Neither really trusting the other, but willing enough to have this middle-of-the-night conversation.

Ash and soot still dusted Blake's cheeks, turning his blazing blond hair a tad bit darker, not much, but enough that it didn't glow like a rising sun over those mountains to Butte's east. Course, there *she* was, wearing a coat and night robe underneath, which she'd cinched up a bit more when she sat down. She'd crossed her legs, too, with her warm enough stockings hiding feet and toes and such.

Quite the sight they made, though it'd only been Chin who saw it with his own eyes.

Chin, who after his initial shock at seeing Blake, his small eyes widening until they about met his eyebrows, had brought them the warmed-up food and got an even warmer fire going. He'd quickly ducked out of sight.

Whether he'd gone back to his own room or was eavesdropping, Cat couldn't tell much. Or that she cared, honestly.

The Chinaman had been an uptight nervous chitter since darkness had fallen and Mrs. Allen still hadn't returned. The first thing Cat had done, after asking for the coffee and pie slices, was give him a good nod—one that, she hoped, indicated she planned on finding out what happened to their missing hostess.

Still, the fire was a nice touch and it sparked sparks in the corner nearest them. The heat took away some, while not all, of the room's chill, enough of winter's bite to make the room a might bit comfortable. Enough as could be, considering the shared company and the conversation.

Norma.

Blake had helped himself to one slice, then another, while Cat was still working on her first. Midnight conversations didn't exactly stir her appetite, but she liked having something to do with her hands, something else to focus on than the mysteries surrounding her and the man, this one in particular, sitting across from her. They weren't seated nearly close enough for their knees or anything untoward to brush under the table, and yet there was a different kind of weight about the room now. It wasn't like that heavy tension from earlier, when she'd been head-to-head with the arrogance of O'Neil and the fellows who followed him.

This one was different.

The kind of weight she wanted to see out that door and out of her life as soon as possible. The why of that, well, she wasn't interested in looking too closely.

She was here to do a job, and that job was Norma.

Cat's fork clinked on the plate as she set it down. She leaned back just a bit, signaling Blake she was ready to talk. Blake's eyebrows lifted at that, and he leaned back, too, though he didn't set his plate down.

Course, he had half a slice waiting to be finished.

Still, it was time enough to get this conversation started. The sooner it started, the sooner they'd get it over and done. Sooner, too, for Blake to be gone and out of the house, taking his opinions and judgments with him.

Blake tilted his own fork in her direction. "I imagine you've a few questions for me."

More than a few, in fact.

"I do," she said. "But first, tell me about Mrs. Allen. Where is she? Why did you bring her in?"

Blake smirked, the kind of smirk that made his face more roguish and handsome than arrogant and frustrating.

Cat ignored the thought. All of it.

"Must have been before you started following me," she said. "And must have been a pretty quick transfer from here to the station considering she was here when I left, and not long after I caught sight of you."

"Figured that out, didn't ya?"

She gestured to his head. "Your hair. A bit of a giveaway."

"Yeah?"

He fingered some of the long locks. Even with the dusting of ash and soot it'd received, it still seemed to glow with some golden, inner light. The kind of blond that she knew many ladies would simply die over. That there was a head of hair that could've meant a way out for quite a few ladies she'd known.

Cat thought it best to keep the comment to herself.

"Well," Blake said, "it was me who brought Mrs. Allen in, and I tell you, it *was* fast. Hell of a lot faster than I was expecting, beg your pardon, ma'am."

She waved off the comment. Swearing was the least of her worries, though she appreciated the gesture even if not... quite trusting it. Or, him.

"Truth is," he said, "she wasn't surprised, either. Almost like she'd been expecting me."

Blake went on, telling Cat that it had been Jere Murphy's call to bring Mrs. Allen in for questioning. And when Cat asked further on *who* gave the initial order, whether it was Murphy or not, Blake didn't have a whole lot for her.

"It didn't come from Murphy, that much I know. That much I can swear to, if you'd believe me, of course. Truth is, Murphy doesn't know who put the word in, only that it came down from the chief himself."

And of course, when the police chief wanted something done, you did it. Butte might be a city, but it was still at its heart a Montana mining town. And like any good mining town, there were a few people up top who you listened to, regardless of your own opinions. It'd been that way in Miles City, and well, Cat's original home town, too. Which meant Jere Murphy, whether or not he'd liked the order of bringing in Mrs. Allen, hadn't really a choice. He did as he was told.

Still... there was something there...

"What were the reasons?" Cat asked. "For bringing in Mrs. Allen?"

Blake shook his head. A stray lock of dusted blond hair settled just above his eyes, drawing her attention right there and holding it.

She ignored that, too.

"Don't know for sure," he said. "Just know it had to do with your deceased friend."

"Norma's not my friend. I've never met her before."

"Maybe not, but you're the one been asking. You're the one who's kept this whole thing from sliding down into some forgotten mine shaft. Fact is, half the city knows it, too."

Cat frowned.

Sure, that had been the point. At least for Mrs. Allen and Dusty's plan, putting the rumor out there, letting everyone know Cat was curious about what had happened to Norma. And yet... she couldn't help but wonder...

Mrs. Allen *had* asked these questions earlier, had even gone to her contacts with the police, Murphy and Blake included. She'd gotten nowhere, which was why she'd even considered letting Cat on, all so Cat could help her find those answers. And yet, it'd been Cat, something about Cat's presence, her interest in Norma, that had shifted the balance.

A balance of what, exactly, she still didn't know. But she was starting to, starting to getting a feeling and where exactly she should go next.

"You're telling me," Cat said, "that all this movement that's happening now is because I'm asking questions."

He nodded. "Least, it is now. You've got someone nervous, Miss Justice."

"Please don't call me that."

"Seems a good enough name, if you've earned it." He paused, those blue eyes staring into hers. "Have you?"

"I don't care what people call me. Or think of me."

Which was a lie.

Especially when his tone told her *exactly* what he thought about her, which to be fair, she didn't disagree with. She also wasn't gonna argue with him either. Not when her mind was racing ahead and thinking hard, thinking about something that actually mattered.

Norma and her death, and the little bread crumbs she'd been gathering without quite realizing their significance.

She'd that feeling again, that tingling in her belly.

Had new evidence been discovered? Something that made the officer, the person or persons who'd initially declared Norma's death an accident, revise or even question that conclusion?

Maybe even the doctor himself coming forward?

What Cat felt right then was an awful bit like hope, and it was singing along her skin, carrying straight down into her belly and pretty much kicking those warning tingles aside. There *had* to be something else, something other than Cat's arrival that'd sparked this new interest, had pushed someone very important to do what they could and stop Mrs. Allen's gathering.

To keep Mrs. Allen herself from attending.

That someone was important enough to make the call to the chief of police in the first place. Blake was right. Cat had made someone nervous. Even the fact this whole mess *hadn't* gotten swept under some rug like it should have, all because of—

"Norma," Cat whispered.

It had been the woman herself. She was the reason why the curiosity, the interest, hadn't died, and it'd been Cat who'd rekindled that interest in a way that Mrs. Allen couldn't.

"Norma and her smiles," she said. "*That's* why this whole thing hasn't been forgotten."

"Beg pardon?"

Cat ignored him, focusing instead on everything she did know of the woman.

Norma, who'd touched lives, who'd clearly, at least at one point, charmed the pants right off of MacDonald. And yet... Cat had a feeling the real reason Norma's memory had stayed alive and well was because of those warm smiles, the kindness she gave just about everyone. Sure, it all might have been part of her cover, to appear so desirable the whole talk of the town was about her. It'd been a smart move if what she'd really wanted was getting out of this business.

Except there had been an after effect, something Norma probably hadn't understood herself:

Norma had genuinely touched people's lives.

First with Mrs. Allen and Dusty, both of whom had been willing to go outside the law, who'd wanted to find the truth in what happened the night Norma died. And then again in those individuals, like Mr. Rippi and Fat Jack, both who'd thought kindly of her even now... even after how far she'd fallen.

No longer the star of one of the biggest parlor houses, Grace's Gardens. Reduced to sad, lowly street walker, working the shadiest, dangerous saloons and gambling houses. Probably even having her own crib.

Of course, she'd have her own home.

Maybe even, if Cat was lucky, Norma still did.

But there was also MacDonald's claim to consider, which if it held true, no one really understood how that fall had happened.

Which was horseshit.

Cat was betting someone did. Either at the Gardens or maybe even living near Norma's home. Night ladies, in general, looked out for each other. That wasn't always the case, and it differed by house depending on the madams running it, but... this *was* a hard life. And everyone needed a kind face from time to time. Even Cat wasn't immune to that same need, of a friend, of someone to let into your life, even if only a little.

Cat had no doubt Norma had been that face.

If all these men had cared for her, still thought fondly of her, there was no question at least one woman did as well. Someone who Norma might even consider a friend. Not Mrs. Allen, though. She'd been in the dark of the happenings of Norma and her life, especially at the end, but that didn't mean there wasn't another.

The hope was back, and it was singing right along her skin.

She had a few places to start her search, even without the guidance of Mrs. Allen and Dusty... all because of the gathering today, because of how freely the man had spoken with her.

She had names and places to start looking further. That was a lot more than she had this morning, or, if she were honest, before Blake had snuck into the house.

Cat let out a sigh, feeling the lateness of the hour and just plain exhaustion slowly taking hold of her body. Her mind, though, it was as sharp as ever and it just wanted her to get off that chair, throw her leftover coffee into the fire and get going.

Course, that wasn't quite an option, certainly with Blake sitting across from her watching everything. He studied her with the same intensity as he had earlier, even if now he was chewing away on another bite of pie. The second piece, nearly gone.

Cat stamped down on the hope, forcing herself to focus on the man in front of her.

One piece of the puzzle at a time.

"There's something else," she said, "about Mrs. Allen that you haven't yet told me."

"Not a whole lot, to be honest, but I do know that your Mrs. Allen had the chance to leave, to make it back here in time for her gathering even, but whatever it was she and Murphy discussed—behind closed doors, I might add—she decided to stay."

Cat blinked. "Stay?"

"That's right. She asked if we didn't mind her staying at the station for awhile, letting you handle the... event she was hosting."

"But that doesn't make any sense. Not to mention the rumors..."

The rumors that had indeed swirled about her little home here, how the police were questioning her. And it were those same rumors and speculation that had nearly caused the whole gathering to leave in a great huff, with O'Neil himself leading the charge—

O'Neil?

Cat's eyes narrowed, her brows pulling down just a bit. Even at the time, it had felt like he'd known something. Maybe not a lot, but something more than he should have, anyway.

Blake cleaned off another forkful of apple pie before again

pointing the fork at her. "You see it, too, don't you? Something here not adding up, something—"

"That doesn't feel right."

He stared at her, mouth pressing into a tight line. He clearly hadn't liked that she'd had the same thought, same words even, as him.

"Mr. O'Neil seemed awfully informed of events, almost as if he'd been aware of them before the rest of us."

Although MacDonald hadn't seemed much surprised either; he'd just been better hiding his feelings.

"That's quite observant of you," Blake said.

Cat shrugged. "It was something I noticed, is all. Part of my job, noticing things."

"You seem quite good at it."

"I had to be."

They all did, in fact. Each and every woman who worked the line, and especially those who managed to keep on living. It was even more true for the ladies who'd lived that life the longest, when their beauty was fading and flaking away, the hard lines of this life taking its hard, hard toll on them.

A hardness that at least Blake seemed to understand in some manner because he was suddenly so stiff again, like his back was made out of the solid straightness of some ironing board. Though this time it wasn't... unkind.

Just not exactly tolerable, at least from what she could tell.

Cat didn't bother hiding her sigh. "I hoped we'd moved past this, Mr. Blake. As I said, you're welcome to leave, and you can even take the pie to your Jere Murphy as well."

Blake stayed right where he was.

"In that case," she said, "what of Mrs. Allen? I hope for her sake, and I'm speaking personally here, that she gave you a damn good reason for leaving me like that. I'd not even a warning of what to expect."

Cat unfortunately had thought it was part of Mrs. Allen's plan, leaving Cat alone to face the gathering. And maybe it had been, to a point. But getting summoned by the police was a stretch for even someone of Mrs. Allen's caliber of conspiracies. At least, so Cat assumed.

And apparently Blake agreed with her.

"I did ask her before Murphy sent me out to find you," he said. "It just didn't seem... right, her leaving you with those fellows, some— well, as you saw for yourself—are a bit high-esteemed and highbrow. But she said you were better off on your own, that she'd only 'get underfoot' of your investigation."

He was actually kind with the word 'investigation.' Which surprised her.

And why the heck wasn't Blake upset or distrustful about her doing exactly this, going around the law like she was? Unless it really *was* true what he'd said earlier, believing that someone else was pulling the strings. Powerful enough, too, to tie these officers' hands, even the honest ones.

But... to the point where justice couldn't be done? That the only way to have justice was if it came from another source all together, someone who just didn't fit into the law, who fit neither in the light or the dark.

Someone an awful lot like Cat.

And yet...

Why care? Why *did* Blake and this Jere Murphy put themselves in danger? Clearly, this included their livelihoods, their careers. Why risk it? And why for a woman like Norma?

Because that was the key right there. All of it just kept on circling back to Norma.

Cat leaned back in the chair.

Her hair, still unbraided, still an absolute, uncontrollable tangle, fell over her shoulders, getting in her way. She worked to shove the whole mess behind her again, all the while Blake watched her with those blue eyes of his. Eyes that stayed right there on her hands... and her bumbling attempt to reestablish control over her own hair.

If it wasn't so late in the night, it'd almost be embarrassing.

Blake said nothing though, which kind 'a made her feel like shoving him, too.

It was childish, certainly, but so was dealing with long hair when really, she'd just be better lopping the whole thing off if not for her silly women's vanity. That, and most folks could barely stand seeing her in jeans. Having hair cut as short as a man's? Her role as Miss Justice would be over before it had even started.

Course, Blake's hair wasn't short in the least and *his* seemed to be under complete control. Not a tangle in sight, even if there was more than a layer or two of Butte's legendary ash.

None of these feelings, certainly not her frustrations, were entirely Blake's fault. Hell, he was already telling her more than Mrs. Allen had. He also wasn't making any secret what he thought of her, even if he was being somewhat kind in this particular moment.

Truthfully, though, she was just grateful for the honesty.

Specially when her situation with Mrs. Allen just wasn't making any sense. And Dusty, too. The kid whom Cat just couldn't see exactly how he was fitting into this. Certainly to the point where a woman of Mrs. Allen's reputation, a woman who'd summoned some pretty wealthy men into her home, gave a way to a kid's request.

Shadow soul, indeed.

"Mrs. Allen brought me in," Cat said. "She let me stay and board here in exchange for me finding the truth out about her former friend. The problem is I learn from a kid that she went and did the opposite. She kept me in the dark, kept from doing that investigating you spoke of, all because this kid had asked her to."

Dusty, who was yet another damn mystery, a mystery that tied right back to Blake.

They both knew it, too.

Cat saw the look in his eye, that glint, before he glanced down. He carefully set his plate and fork on the table, just a little clinking as the silver shifted on porcelain. He'd left most of his second pie slice there on the plate.

Either he'd gotten full or lost his appetite.

Honestly, Cat was betting on the latter.

"I can't answer to that," he said.

Can't, or wouldn't?

As if sensing her thoughts, Blake did the honorable thing: he kept talking.

"I wasn't with Mrs. Allen long, didn't have time to ask specifics. But as for the luncheon, well, she seemed to think you'd be fine, especially because you did have the kid with you."

A kid who Blake clearly knew and had said nothing about.

"You mean Dusty."

He said nothing.

Well, so much for some upfront honesty.

But then, he wasn't looking away now, either.

Cat crossed her arms and gave him a level look. "Between Dusty and Mrs. Allen, they know a hell more about Norma and her past than me, not to mention what the hell's going on. Why don't you ask them? Why don't you get them to investigate this?"

"They hired you."

Which wasn't making a whole lot of sense, in all honesty. Fact, this whole situation wasn't. After all, she was sitting here, in the middle of the night, wearing her night robe and stockings, right across the table from a reputable officer of the law who was, more or less, giving his consent on her unlawful look into some justice for a dead harlot.

Right. Maybe she should have skipped the coffee and gone right with the hard stuff.

Cat's head was starting to hurt from it all. She rubbed at her temples, trying to keep herself and her focus clear.

"Look," she said, "forgetting about Mrs. Allen for a moment, it still doesn't explain your involvement in all this. Or why your boss wanted me followed."

"I told you, something's not adding up."

"None of this is."

Now it was Blake's turn to lean forward. "The story didn't seem right, even from the beginning. How she died, the witnesses, it wasn't adding up. And then, this happened today."

He gestured behind Cat at the dining room. The dining room with the doors closed up, looking like just some regular old doors in the home. And yet, he knew exactly where the luncheon had taken place.

"Both me and Murphy," he continued, "well, we don't trust the kind of requests that... that don't exactly have trails, and whoever asked the chief to about Mrs. Allen, they didn't leave a trail. And there's a lot of that going on lately. Lotta money moving hands, especially with Clark running for senator and Daly doing everything he can to stop him. It feels... feels like the two of them are leaving a lot of room in the middle for others to do some moving and shaking of their own."

"And that's what you don't like?"

"That's what we don't like."

Cat had that tingling feeling again, and this time when she looked right in Blake's eyes, got the sense that he wasn't actually trying to hide the truth from her.

If anything, he was trying to tell her.

Warn her.

Cat sat up straighter. Her hair, the tangled mess that it was, slipping over her shoulder and hanging dangerously over the leftover crumbs and sticky juice of her apple pie.

"You investigated it yourself, didn't you? Norma's death. You found something."

"It's what I didn't find."

She blinked at him. "What do you mean?"

"The name of the doctor. He was scrubbed clean of the record. No mention other than what you saw reported in the paper. Just nothing, not even if he was associated with a hospital or practicing on his own."

"But... the other officers. Surely they know the man's name."

"Officer. And yeah, sure he does. He's just not telling. Me or anyone else, for that matter."

Cat got a sudden, sickening feeling in her stomach, like just maybe she had too much apple pie. But that wasn't the case here.

This time, it was the sense of foreboding she got.

That same sense she'd had right before Alice's husband had slammed his fist on the door of her sister's bedroom where Cat was holding her, broken and bleeding, her eyes so bruised she doubted Alice could even see straight, let alone stand or walk. That fist, falling so heavy and hard on the wooden door, hard enough that dirt slipped free of the rafters above and clattered down to the floor.

She'd had the sense in that moment, a warning almost, telling her this time, this moment, wasn't gonna be like all the others.

This time would be the last.

The memory held on even when Cat blinked and found herself back in Mrs. Allen's home with all the lace and the curtains. Cold, too, the kind 'a cold that slipped right on past her stockings and coat and whatever warmth the fire had brought. Sitting there, right across from Officer Blake with those blue eyes of his, eyes that missed nothing. Eyes and brows which rose up, as if in question.

Cat shook her head, forced herself to be in the here and now, not haunted by the past.

"Why's that?" she asked. "Why won't he tell you?"

"Because," Blake said, "he's dead."

CHAPTER TWENTY-FIVE

Blake's words had stayed with Cat all through the night and into the next morning. Haunted her, more like, same as Alice.

Didn't matter that she'd finally taken her own advice, following common sense with where it'd led her, and strapped on her gun. She hadn't realized until its weight caused the holster to dip a bit against her hip how much she'd missed it. Just the feel of it. The certainty it brought her. A time and a place, from another life with her pa. His sure and steady hands as he'd taught her all he knew about using one, and even more importantly, the respect one gave it. Especially when it came to not using it.

Still, the feel of it, the gun's comforting weight, it did nothing to dispel the feelings Blake and his words had stirred in her.

Haunting was certainly the right word for it.

Cat's hands were tucked into her coat to keep what feeling she had left in them, even with the heavy gloves she wore. She'd already lost feeling in her toes, no matter how many stockings she'd stuffed her toes in, struggling as she'd done in the continual dark of her room.

The day already reaching noon and not a glance of sun in sight.

Just a bare lessening of the smoke and darkness, enough that she could see down the silent, unmoving street but not any further.

She'd only managed a few sparse hours of sleep after Blake had finally left taking the promised slice of pie to Jere Murphy, and when she'd woken it was still dark outside. She'd sat there for several minutes, quilts all tangled about her, sleep crust about gluing her eyes shut closed as she struggled to figure out if it was day or night.

The coffee that came drifting from the floorboards and under the door, though, that had helped straighten her senses.

Coffee that Chin had been kind enough to make and keep warm for her. Not that he'd been much of a conversationalist, certainly because of her midnight visitor. She'd say he gave her a dressing down before stomping away, 'cept she really hadn't caught a word he'd said. Other than the fact, of course, he was mad.

And of course, it wasn't like the warmth from the coffee had lasted long, either.

Not with the news Blake had brought, the mysterious and untimely death of his fellow officer. She'd tossed and turned during what little sleep her tired mind and body needed.

His words, staying with her, never leaving.

Soon as Cat's hands had left that mug, finishing the coffee in about two gulps, it felt like the cold had worked its way into her soul and then stayed there. Or maybe it'd gotten stuck there before she'd even gone to bed.

And could how could it not?

Blake hadn't known many more details for her, certainly not the hard kind of facts that courts and justice members like him usually appreciated. All he had right now was the same as she did: a hunch.

A feeling that something wasn't right.

His fellow officer, Patrick White, the man who'd responded at the scene of Norma's death, was also dead. No gunshot or wounds or anything that'd suggest murder. Just very much dead. He'd been found lying on the floor of his own sparse home by a friend just the day before. White was the reason, Blake admitted, that he and

Murphy had taken an interest in Cat and her... unique position. She suspected he was referring to her being outside the law and not some *other* reason.

As if two upstanding gentlemen would ever suggest otherwise.

Still, Blake had investigated Officer White, sent there by Jere Murphy, because both men didn't like the feeling or timing of White's death. Especially since it'd taken place right after word got round about Cat and the gathering Mrs. Allen was hosting.

Officer White, according to Blake, had been found lying in his sitting room fully clothed and with no signs of struggle. Eyes open, not moving, not breathing. Just very much dead. With no other evidence or sign that something untoward had taken place, Blake had suggested they bring in a doctor to examine the body, just to be sure. The big brass hadn't liked this so much—something about bad for the department—but with Murphy's pull, Blake got himself a doctor.

Who then preceded to do absolutely nothing except complicate matters.

The doctor, who had apparently looked like he was about to keel over himself, so ancient and crippled he seemed to be, just glanced at the body and wrote the whole thing off as failed health. More than likely, the doctor had guessed, due to a failure of the heart.

Horseshit.

Cat felt this certainty right to her toes, and she knew Blake had felt it, too. The hard glint in his eyes as he retold this piece of his investigation made it pretty darn obvious. For once, the hardness was not directed at or because of her.

As far as the official record was concerned, for all intents and purposes Officer White had suffered a natural death. Didn't matter that he'd been in fine health and not the kind 'a man who'd just fall down to a heart weakness or some other failure. And while Cat couldn't do much on that end, seeing how it was more a lead for Blake to dig into, it'd given Cat even more of a push and reason of where to start looking.

At least on her end.

Because no doubt about it, someone was clearly trying to cover their tracks. Tracks that she'd no doubt led right back to Norma.

So here she was, on the very ground Cat herself was familiar with. Maybe not personally, but her history sure was. Heck, even the busted-up boardwalk could have come straight from Miles City. As if someone had slapped it down on the ground in a half-hearted attempt to make the place seem decent and civilized. That any patron or client who wanted to venture up or down these particular streets of their own choice and free will had to make do with a board-walk that wasn't much different than the street itself. A boardwalk that came complete with mud and hardened, black smudges, the kind that'd probably send a person running back up the hill in warmer weather.

Those same boards that shook with every step, like they hadn't been nailed in correctly or maintained by the city in a least a decade.

If not longer.

Even a few were missing, like someone had gotten desperate enough and started snatching up what pieces she could to build herself a home away from this dark bit of hell.

Not that there was much of an escape.

Not from this kind 'a life.

Which after Cat's conversation last night with Blake was hitting a bit close to home. Hitting there and staying right where she could feel it. And try as she might right now, it wouldn't let go. Like it'd lodged in her heart and had no intention of ever leaving.

Certainly standing here, on the edge of Galena Street and Wyoming, it was a feeling she couldn't run from, couldn't escape, much as she wanted to. Not when the truth was staring right back at her, seeing her, for exactly what she was.

And who she was.

See, unlike the rest of Butte that had both sides of the same coin, light and dark, right there, right up front and center, this part of town was different. Cat didn't need to step one foot across that invisible border to know. All the other parts of the city, they'd found a way to work together, to co-exist. Not that the city founders and upright folks running the place necessarily wanted this arrangement.

Still, it worked.

And Cat had seen it firsthand. From those fellows who'd shown up to Mrs. Allen's gathering from all walks and pockets of life to the very street Mrs. Allen called home, with those fancy mansions and one-bedroom homes bundled up next to the other, and all the different shades in between.

But this place?

It was nothing but darkness.

Nothing but shadows and a heavy weight. And nothing at all that anyone, anywhere, could do to change it.

The building in front of her, some grand piece of architect and construct reaching up three whole stories, all brick and carefully placed windows like itself was some grand statement to anyone who laid eyes on it. And yet, it was a building that hadn't seen an ounce of sunlight. Even the brick, which should have been a welcoming rusty-red, the kind of color that invited you in, to come and cozy up by some fire. Instead, it was a dusty black that sucked your soul right in and refused to let it go.

All the windows, and there were a fair few, were closed. Looked, too, like they hadn't been opened since the building had last seen the sun.

But Cat knew, without a doubt, that each one of them rooms was rented out to a girl, and each one of those girls brought in a nice, sizable sum to whoever it was that owned the building. Just like the rest on this street that looked like they led straight into hell.

The red light district.

The very place where women went when they had nothing else, no other prospects, no other hope but to keep walking that knife's edge between living and dying.

The truly sad part was Cat was under no illusion, no grand dreams of her own, about saving this place.

It couldn't be saved. Because it was needed.

Needed to balance the kind 'a life that went with living here. And she'd a hunch it was more true of Butte than any other Montana town she'd visited thus far. A place of nonstop mines and drilling, of harsh whistles going off whenever an accident or fire struck. Dark and desolate, with morale running so low and as deep as those mine tunnels carved in the rock below right where she stood.

It was certainly true now, especially with the smoke clogging the air, making breathing alone a painful chore. Her eyes, burning and red to the point she wondered if they'd ever be the normal again.

Cat wasn't immune to the weight, either.

It had settled over her heart and stayed there the moment her boots crossed that invisible border. The kind 'a weight that would press a soul right down into that ground and bury them, then simply move on to the next person, hungry as that weight was, needing almost to find another soul and then another. Always moving, always feeding.

The feeling was familiar.

Too familiar.

Which was why she'd come here first before following up on any of the leads she'd learned from both Blake and the gathering. She needed to retrace Norma's life, but not at the beginning nor at the end. She needed to go right in the middle, right where her gut was telling her, and if she was lucky, might be able to find a clue or two.

She'd try and find Norma's home, if it was still vacant and standing, or at least a female friend who still thought kindly of Norma.

"I hope you're with me, Norma," Cat whispered. "I don't think I can do this alone."

Not with her own ghosts, and with Alice following so close behind.

Best that she could do was try.

CHAPTER TWENTY-SIX

Cat let instinct guide the way.

Not to mention movement helped keep out some of the cold, even if her toes and fingers were numb and there was no sight of them warming up any time soon. And sure, the wind was merely trickling down from those high-up mountains ringing the city in, with those peaks all but covered in snow and ice, but dear Lord did she sure feel it. That biting cold that just about laughed at her attempts to stay warm. It was like the worst of both worlds: just enough wind to freeze your ass off but not enough to actually push away all that choking smoke and ash that stung and burned her eyes.

What she wouldn't give for some of that sun's warmth about now. To just pierce right through the black haze and heat the earth here up a bit. Give her some kind a feeling of hope, maybe.

That... just maybe, there was some light in all this darkness.

Though to be fair, it *was* a lighter haze of smoke and blackness than when Cat had first arrived in Butte. So, who knew, maybe there was some light heading her way... she just couldn't see it yet.

Still, she tried her best to see through the haze as her boots stomped on the boardwalk avoiding the worst spots, the ones rotted through and through that'd probably split open and swallow her boot whole.

Or those black smudges even horses steered clear of. Not that there were many horses out and about, hacks or wagons or other such vehicles. And like the street, the boardwalk itself was quiet. No movement, no pounding of feet on the uneven surface.

Really not surprising, given the hour.

This part of town thrived in the shadows and the night. During the day was when the folks here slept as well as they could considering the life they were leading, especially the ladies. Most would be fast asleep, their minds dull and hazy as they slept off whatever alcohol or opium or other substance they'd indulged in to push away the pain and weight of this place.

Not everyone would be sleeping, though.

Some, those who still had their heads on straight, would be stirring, starting to go about their business because at the end of the day those who lived here were, in fact, people. Humans who needed to be fed and bathed (to a degree), who had toiletry needs.

The basics of humanity.

Then, of course, there were those whose eyes really never did sleep. Who noticed and saw everything, let not an inch of their domain slip by them unawares. And that included Cat, walking as she was, dressed in her heavy coat and jeans and the revolver shining at her hip.

It wasn't long neither before she got the sense of heads peeking out from behind those closed-up windows, a consciousness that stirred, like word was traveling just ahead of her, announcing her presence. She didn't see anyone, and yet she knew they were there.

She'd a hunch that Butte didn't only have tunnels for mines. That tunnels just might very well be alive here and well.

Another thought, idea, that teased against her consciousness. Worth following up on when she saw Dusty again.

Finally, just about when Cat hit the heart of the street called Galena, a door to her left creaked open. It was a narrow-sized door, barely big enough for the too-thin woman with her stringy dark hair and haggard face. She wasn't wearing any coat, just a night robe, and one that was barely cinched about her waist as if she either hadn't the time to do so properly or simply didn't care.

Either option seemed a reasonable conclusion.

Cat paused, taking in every inch of the woman—the lines that spidered out from her eyes, from her mouth, the hollowness of her face. She took in every detail in that single glance, then gave the woman a kindly smile and tipped her hat towards her.

"Mornin'."

The woman said nothing, just stared at Cat with those narrowed eyes. Dark eyes, too, and not the usual red-rimmed Cat was used to seeing on women who lived at this level of the red light. Nor were the woman's eyes hazy. Instead they were sharp and calculating, which was completely opposite to her appearance, world weary that it was, like she had hardly anything left in her. Yet despite all that, she retained the kind of intellect one needed here to survive here...

Even if, no doubt, surviving meant livin' in a crib.

From the doorway of that single, narrowed room, Cat could just make out the brass bedposts, the thin mattress and even thinner quilt. It was amazing the woman hadn't lost her toes and fingers due to frostbite. Sympathy stirred in Cat's gut and she couldn't help but close her eyes at the sight. She'd known many a woman who'd lived in such a place and worse ones as well.

Couldn't save them, though. Couldn't save even one. All she could do was save herself.

Maybe, too, keep her promise to Alice.

The woman watched all this without saying a word, no doubt not missing a beat as Cat worked through her own past and hauntings. In fact, she hadn't even moved despite the cold, despite that the woman's hands probably were turnin' blue about now.

"Can I help you?" Cat asked.

"Depends."

The woman's voice was rough and worn, just like the rest of her.

"On?" Cat asked.

"Your reason for being here."

The wind decided to pick up at just that moment, sweeping by with that snow-capped touch, so cold you couldn't help sucking in a big ol' breath right through your teeth. The woman, though—her teeth only chattered once. She was exuding quite a bit of control even for the early hour. Which meant this meeting here with Cat was important to her.

Again came that little stirring of hope. That just maybe she had a lead on Norma. That maybe she could find some answers.

Cat nodded towards the street. "I'm sure you've heard why I'm here—"

"I'd like you to confirm the rumor," the woman said.

"And which one is that?"

"The only one that matters: Are you, in fact, here about Norma?"

A breath whooshed out of Cat. Definitely feelin' a lot like hope.

"I am," Cat said.

The woman said nothing for a moment, just a tightening of her too-thin lips that were still stained, still smeared, by the red she must have painted on the night before.

"Did you know her?" Cat asked. "Was she your friend?"

Finally, the woman's bony shoulders sagged and she opened the door more.

"Come inside, Miss Justice."

Cat started at the name. Couldn't help the reaction or the fact that this woman saw it.

"That's not my—"

"I know," the woman cut her off. "It's a name that's got to be earned. Get inside if you want to know about Norma, before my common sense comes back."

There was no time to linger on her thoughts or feelings, swirling as they were round and round her gut, the kind of pressure Cat wasn't used to feeling because the very name actually *meant* something to her. Or was starting to.

That just maybe the name meant something to these people.

Justice.

Like this woman before her, who revealed the single room to be exactly what Cat had first thought. Thin, bare bed, quilt that didn't even quite reach from one side to the other. A small, tiny nightstand with a candle that flicked and gave only the dullest glow in the otherwise dark room. The single photo, framed, with a handful of faces staring back at her. Clearly family. The children standing about parents, parents whose faces looked grim and world-weary, as if they'd forgotten how to smile long, long ago. The black and white faces were already started to fade, like they were cracking along the edges the same way this woman was.

And yet, the wood frame was dull and worn as if it'd been touched continuously, almost like a talisman.

The room darkened even more when the woman closed the door behind them. What light the day had provided shuttered instantly with the click of the latch. The cold though, that followed them inside as if it was part of her like a second skin.

And Cat was grateful for it.

Grateful for the way her nose had closed off, her ability to smell dwindling to just about nothing except sniffles. She wouldn't want to be standing here in the middle of a hot summer's day.

No, sir.

In fact, it was just too hard to contemplate that this woman did live here, just as many others like her. Again, Cat tried not to let her feelings show. All the remorse and sadness swirling about, bringing up feelings she'd rather run from than confront. Except it was staring at her so nakedly in the face to the point where, much as she wanted, there was no running from this.

It was a truth that lived in every inch of this woman, in every line and trial that had been carved into her, molded to her. The truth lived, too, in the corner of this one-room home, if she even dared call it a 'home.' Regardless, it was a place that probably cost this woman almost her entire earnings just to keep it and never ever have a chance of escaping.

Cat may have gotten out of this life, but in a way she hadn't. And never could. Because in some ways, she *had* been this woman.

And in many ways, she still was.

The life touched you in a way that you could never shake off. Held onto you, bleeding your soul away until it left you dry, a shriveled husk of yourself without an ounce of shine or spark left.

Certainly, no light.

And yet...

Cat looked at the woman, wishing she could do more, offer more. Often times, it was hope that was the most dangerous weapon of all. She needed to remember that. Because that's the way it had been for her.

Cat couldn't offer this woman anything she didn't already have. Hell, if she'd even wanted Cat's help in the first place. But this woman clearly had what counted: the will to live, the determination to set your feet on the ground and do what was needed, and always looking for a way out or a way to better yourself... before your time ran out.

And yet...

Justice, Dusty had called her. Then Blake, and now this woman.

Maybe justice was its own kind 'a hope. And dangerous, too, because that's exactly what it was.

Hope.

CHAPTER TWENTY-SEVEN

Cat swept her hat off as she moved into the woman's living space, much as she could, anyway, bumping up against the small bed and even smaller nightstand. The candle that flickered and thankfully kept most of the room shrouded in safe shadows.

Dark corners really weren't meant to be seen.

"Thank you," Cat said, "for speaking with me."

The woman leaned against the door, though in truth the wood barely seemed strong enough to hold her upright, let alone keep out any strong gusts of wind or snow.

"I haven't said much."

"Yeah, I noticed. But you let me in. I understand the significance."

Which Cat did.

Still, the woman said nothing to this, simply crossed her arms as a show of strength as she leaned against that door, though Cat figured it also had to do with staying warm. Cat would have an easier time standing there, what with her warmer layers and coat, certainly compared to this woman and her threadbare night robe, especially now with how the cold all about seeped right through the wood like it wasn't even there.

"I know what you called me outside, but please, the name's Cat."

The woman's eyes narrowed at her. They were still two sunken pits with all those lines you'd imagine trailing off like spidery webs, and yet clear. The kind 'a clear that missed nothing. That noticed every detail and shade because it was necessary. Needed, even.

Whatever she was feeling inside, this woman was keeping it close to her chest. Still, she'd let Cat inside, and that really did count for a lot.

"You have a name?" Cat asked. "Or would you like to keep that to yourself."

The woman's mouth thinned, making the small lines around her lips, the stained-smear of red, stand out even more.

"Don't matter now," she said. "Whole street knows you're here, knows I'm talking with you. Knew it, too, before I let you in, God save me—if the bastard ever cared at all. Look. My name is Madeleine, and yeah, yeah... I knew Norma, least as much as any girl can know the other."

"I understand."

And she did.

Just as she knew that Madeleine wasn't this woman's real name. Though the picture on the nightstand, the only one there, probably was truth. Yet those names, those children with those stoic-looking parents, remained hidden.

Secrets, the personal kind, were always kept hidden.

They were kept close to the chest like the treasures that they were. Couldn't be taken away unless a girl let them go, like a butterfly caught in her hands. And if she did let them go? Then what happened?

Well, it all depended on just what kind of wind was blowing and how hard.

"Please, sit." Cat motioned to the bed. "I'm not here to put you out. I'd just like to ask a few questions is all."

"Questions? Oh, no. *You're* here to dig up secrets. Secrets that are better left buried."

"I'm starting to get the sense that Norma had a few," Cat said carefully.

Madeleine's bony hands dug into her night robe, nearly piercing through the sleeves of the thin fabric. She was clearly fighting within herself, struggling over something. Maybe even the need to let go some of those butterflies.

Or if it was best to keep silent.

"I'd like to help," Cat said. "Don't know how much I can do, honestly, but I'm aiming to try."

"Why?"

Cat let out a sigh. That seemed to be the one question everyone wanted to know. "Cause I've got my ghosts, my own atonement, if you will. Truth is, I just couldn't keep on living as I was, standing by doing nothing."

"So, you came here to find out about Norma."

"I did."

"Why?"

Madeleine didn't look away, not once. This was certainly more than any test of wills, as if there was a whole lot more at stake than Cat yet realized. Maybe... even more than Madeleine, herself, knew.

Cat felt this truth like it was a harp string being plucked and held within her.

So, she went with truth.

"Because," Cat said, not breaking the other woman's gaze, "I opened the newspaper and I read her story. Except it wasn't her story. I knew that immediately. Knew, too, that it felt wrong. Something about her... about the words, what the doctor thought and what the police reported, it just didn't feel right."

Madeleine's eyes shuttered closed. Cat couldn't help but wonder if Madeleine had seen Norma's body, or if she'd been anywhere near close by. Maybe even working the same saloon before Norma had stumbled out into the black and the cold until she'd come to the spot where she'd stumbled no further.

Cat let the thought drift off. Time enough to follow up. First, she needed to earn Madeleine's trust, and that sure was no easy feat.

"Truth is," Cat said, "that's why I came here. Came to Butte to find stories like hers, ones that weren't being told proper but just swept under the rug because they don't matter. People like us, we don't matter."

Madeleine snorted. "You ain't lookin' so bad, yourself."

"Different city, different story altogether. I've a feelin' Butte's a lot harder than most others."

Especially when Cat had more than her looks, charms, and desires to fall back on. Her daddy had made sure of that, and for her own truth, she'd loved it. Loved the riding and the wrangling. But those options? Not available in Butte, no sir.

Madeleine gave her sad, mournful smile. "You know, when I first got here I found another girl I knew. Back in Kansas City, and she told me straight out to save some money, money enough for a ticket out of this hellhole or I'd regret it."

Cat didn't bother asking if she regretted it or not. She wasn't about to insult the woman, not when the truth was as black as the day outside was.

"Course," Madeleine said, "I didn't listen. Thought I knew better, thought I knew how to navigate and survive this life."

She held out her hands, fingers splayed open as if showing off the great victories she'd heard by the home she now lived in.

She was, however, still living. It wasn't much, but, it was something.

More than Norma had.

"We've all got our stories," Cat said, "and we've got our pasts that brought us to this moment. Now, I can't say what Norma's story is yet, and it's sure turnin' out to be a right pain getting to the real truth, I tell you, but I will. I need to."

She paused, but Madeleine said nothing.

"I need your help, Madeleine."

"Why here? Why me?"

"Because this is where she died, or near enough. And I've learned it's also where she lived, least last few months of her life. And I'm really hoping that there's someone here, someone she may have trusted and opened up to."

Cat stepped forward an inch. Her toes, still about frozen cold tucked as they were in her boots, though that was nothing to the cold Madeleine must be feeling in her stockings and the whole half-dozen holes she could spot from here.

"Someone," Cat said, "like you."

Madeleine shivered and tugged her robe tighter about her body, though she didn't let loose that hard, piercing grip on her arms.

It was clear she still didn't trust Cat, but she didn't distrust her either. Or maybe it wasn't Cat she distrusted but whatever war of feelings she was havin' within herself.

The thought tugged at Cat and she let it.

"Honestly," Cat went on, "there are bits of Norma's life that no one's willing to give me a straight answer on, and I'm betting, or feeling more like, that how she died wasn't no accident."

Madeleine's shivers stopped instantly. As if everything about her suddenly got very, very still.

"How do you know?" Madeleine asked. "That it wasn't an accident."

"I don't know, not in the way of evidence or the like. Like I said, just a feeling and in my life, my line of work... feelings make the difference between livin' and dyin', especially if I choose to listen to them or not."

Madeleine looked away.

"I'm not the only, either," Cat said. "There are others, and they're lookin' into it, too. Something about all this, it just ain't adding up and it's making a few folks very nervous."

"It should."

The tingling came back, stronger than ever. But she needed to be focused now, intent on not losing what ground she was making with Madeleine. Time enough to ask questions of her own.

Trust in this life wasn't an easy thing to earn.

Cat didn't reveal Blake or his own boss, Officer Murphy. Too many lessons from living on the line had taught her just how valuable secrets were, which was also why Madeleine was being so reluctant to open up and share hers. And yet, they were *still* standing there in Madeleine's cold-touched, saddened crib. If she hadn't wanted the help, if she hadn't cared for Norma in some way or other, she'd never have opened that door.

"Think you can help me, Madeleine? Point me in the right direction? Maybe help me find just where Norma kept her secrets?"

"Secrets."

Madeleine gave a sad laugh, as if she were the one laughing at herself and her own foolishness. A tear fell down her haggard, wrinkled face... and there *were* wrinkles, more so than Cat had first realized. Or maybe it was this business of Norma that was bringing them to the light.

Truth had a way of doing that.

"Yeah," Madeleine said, "Norma had her secrets. Lots of 'em. And the dangerous kind, too, which is why lettin' you into my home is probably the most God damned foolish thing I've ever done, but that woman, *Norma*—"

Madeleine closed her eyes, face clenched in some kind of pain.

Then she opened her eyes and looked right at Cat.

"Yeah, she had secrets, and you *should* be nervous."

Madeleine took a step forward, finally dropping the death grip she had on her own arm, reached out and grabbed Cat's instead.

Cat saw the shift in Madeleine's body before she'd even moved, just as her daddy had taught her, but stayed where she was. She let the other woman grab onto her, press those fingers into her arms as if she needed this connection, needed Cat to truly understand.

And she did. A chill she felt right through her whole body, settling there, cold and hard, right in her gut at what Madeleine said next:

"It's those secrets, Miss Justice, that'll get a lot of us killed if you keep on digging."

CHAPTER TWENTY-EIGHT

Cat stiffened at Madeleine's words, but she didn't pull away either. Not even when Madeleine's nails were somehow pricking right through her heavy winter coat. This girl was certainly no wilting flower, and neither was she barely hanging onto life like so many of their sisters.

Her hat suddenly felt heavy and cumbersome in her hands. As if the hat, like the rest of her, suddenly carried the true weight of the words Madeleine had spoken and meant:

Justice.

Cat managed a breath, hopin' like hell it'd do some favor to slow her suddenly racing heart. The last thing she wanted was to see anyone, certainly not her fellow night sisters, harmed. But justice and hope, hell, they both came with a weighty price and dear Lord, did she know it. But she couldn't walk away now, not when it was finally feeling like she was getting closer to the truth.

She had to tread carefully, both with Madeleine's warning and the woman herself, getting her to open up, to trust. Though, to be fair, that was damn hard to do when she couldn't quite see what the ground looked like before she put her foot down. Lord, she wished she'd talked with Dusty more, gotten the truth out of him about Norma before coming here.

Couldn't be helped, though. Had to do her best, and do it carefully.

Cat tucked her hat between her arm and gently touched Madeleine's hands. Her thick gloves kindly rested on top of the other woman's bony, clawed ones.

"Are you in danger, Madeleine? Because of these secrets?"

Madeleine laughed. Again, not the funny kind, but sad and ironic. She slipped her hand free of Cat as if she couldn't bear to be touched... by kindness.

Again... came that tingle, and Cat knew she couldn't back away. Not now. Not when, clearly, there were others who needed help.

Carefully, though. Very, very carefully.

Madeleine gave a small shake of her head, her laughter fading. "You think any of them, any of my clients, would hesitate if they needed to silence me? Or any of the girls here?"

"It's... been my experience that most men still value human life, at least in the takin' of it."

Though Cat knew, too, it didn't usually go much past that.

"Most of my clients don't even know my name," Madeleine said. "And Norma's former clients? Those big men on the hill in their fancy dress and even fancier smells, the men who Norma had dazzled along her fingers like brightly jeweled rings? No, no, they'd never sully themselves with the likes of me."

Cat frowned, thinking. "Or hesitate to kill you if it was needed?"

"What do you think, Miss Justice?"

Madeleine waved her hand at her own hollowed eyes, gaunt face, then the small room with its even smaller bed. The quilt that didn't quite reach from one side to the other and had lost its stuffing a lifetime ago. The candle just barely flickering, giving off just enough light for Cat to see the room.

"Your answer," Madeleine said, "is no. Not that they'd do the deed themselves or even ask another outright. But suggest? Imply?

And for the right amount of money? Not a one of 'em would hesitate, especially if it meant keeping their great businesses and their wealth and their reputation. Oh, and I suppose keeping appearances for their family be important, too. So yeah, not a one would hesitate to silence me and every single one of us girls who took Norma in after she'd fallen so low. Those of us who didn't bat an eye when she'd asked for help, when she asked to get herself back on her feet. She'd smile just so and we'd all feel it and be completely helpless against it. All that warmth and kindness, like it was about radiating from the damn woman, like some fallen star would."

Again, Madeleine gripped herself round the middle, fingers digging into her arms. But Cat was starting to get the picture all right, of the true cunning of Norma, and yet despite all her smiles and charms, all the kindness that she'd purposefully given out to anybody she'd passed, her true cunning *had* been found out.

Definitely by Madeleine.

And.... by someone else? Someone powerful enough to cause this kind of trickle-down effect? From the silencing of Mrs. Allen, Officer White, and now, as Cat learned, a possible threat to other women. But Cat didn't understand the underworld enough in Butte to really know, to really understand how the thing ran and who was in charge, and how everything got fed back up to the top. The many, many pockets all the money the red light district brought in, and just whose pockets, exactly, got a bit more fuller. Cat imagined the mayor and city officials for sure, to some degree, anyway. Quite a few police officers and who knows, maybe even the police chief himself. Not to mention the folks who actually owned most of these businesses, even the run-down cribs Madeleine and her sisters paid a hefty, hefty price to rent.

Cat didn't know all the players and their names, but the forms and the roles they played, she'd a feeling they were the same as Miles City and any other town perched on the western frontier.

And yet with all these thoughts, the one that was still quite clear and one that, much as Madeleine might regret it, remained: Madeleine *was* still Norma's friend.

She still... cared.

Otherwise she'd never have opened the door to Cat. She'd have let the whole thing get swept up and never see the light of Butte's day again. Even if that same friend's eyes now burned bright, filled with both hurt and... remorse.

For herself.

"You blame... yourself," Cat whispered.

Madeleine wiped at the tears that slipped out from her eyes. "I should have seen it. Should have seen the truth. So yes, I blame myself. Still do, damn that woman."

Madeleine shoved her hands down, as if needing something, *anything*, to take out her anger on, and started yanking on her stringy hair. She seemed to come away with more strands than Cat thought exactly normal.

"Here I am," Madeleine went on, pulling and tugging at her hair, "letting you in. Knowing that the whole damn street knows it, too. Christ."

Cat needed to gently take control of the conversation before she lost Madeleine forever.

"Like I told you, Miss Madeleine, I'm here to help, that means you and anyone else who might be threatened, but I *can't* do that without knowing the truth."

Madeleine's shoulders slumped forward, and whatever spark that had hauled her out of bed at hearing of Cat's approach, standing there not shivering in that winter cold air while she assessed Cat before even letting her, it was dwindling away to about nothing.

"As if it were that simple," Madeleine said. "You know this life, Miss Justice, you know there's nothing simple about it."

Then Madeleine collapsed in on herself. Like one moment she'd been the strong girl glaring at Cat from the door, testing her with everything she had, unwilling to bend or trust willingly, and then she was sagging forward.

All her spark, all her defiance and energy, just gone.

Cat moved quick. One step and she was there, grabbing and holding onto Madeleine before the woman cracked her knees on the dusty, black-stained floor. The woman was light, too. Too light, like she was a feather just waiting to get blown off into that cold wind outside.

When Madeleine gripped Cat's arm, this time it wasn't hard or piercing. If anything, it was the exact opposite.

"You have no idea," she whispered, "no idea what I'm riskin' by talking with you."

"I don't. Not unless you tell me."

So, Cat listened and learned, much as she could, much as Madeleine herself knew. How it was that Norma had arrived on Galena Street, stumbling on the boardwalk, not a scratch on her but acting like she could barely move an inch more on her own. No luggage or mementos from her other life, living the grand life in the big parlor houses with all them dresses and jewels, all the fancy undergarments and toiletries, brushes and combs of the ivory hilt variety. All them things were required in the big houses, and yet Norma had nothing but the clothes on her back, the button-up shoes lacing her feet.

That, and her smile.

That even though she'd fallen so low, had shown such generosity to the girls here, as if she couldn't even compare herself to them and their struggles, let alone sit and live in their company. Yet, they'd insisted. Not only that, they'd given her what they could, set her up down here, a place of her own. All that, and in return the girls had asked for nothing.

Which meant... Cat couldn't expect to find any clues in Norma's belongings. Whatever remnants remained of her life, they weren't in tokens of affection or talismans carried from another life.

But the fact that Norma had arrived with... *nothing?*

That made no sense. Even for the big parlor houses, even if Norma had been in so great a debt—and with a client such as

MacDonald anything Norma needed he'd have gladly given to her—but Norma would have had something. Even if only the small items she'd originally arrived with.

That's how it worked.

And yet, the story was different for Norma.

Which seemed to be the running theme from Cat's perspective.

But Madeleine was quite clear: All them gowns and dresses, sparkling jewels and even her own personal maid, Norma had had them. Just not when she'd finally stumbled onto Galena Street, and regardless of how often Madeleine and the other girls asked, Norma would not explain their absence. She'd just flick her hair over her shoulder and give them her famous, kindly smile and tell them:

"The matter is settled. Let's leave it that way."

And the girls had let her be, of course, for privacy of the personal kind was one of the few treasures they had left to them.

As Cat listened, she slowly lowered the other woman to the bed and wrapped her up as good as she could in that quilt. Almost... like a young girl's quilt. A child's. One that a loving mother had made a lifetime ago and now, now the stitching was barely holding on, the stuffing nearly completely flattened. So very much like Madeleine as she lay there with her eyes closed and her hands clasped round her middle.

It was entirely possible she was suffering from something more than the worries Norma had brought into her life, the fear too that others, and her own, lives might be in danger. But again, just as they'd done with Norma, Cat didn't ask questions.

If Madeleine had wanted those answered, she'd have done so straight out.

But there was something Cat could easily give, even if it wasn't taking away this woman's pain or making her world, small as it was, right. Kindness. Much as Norma had used kindness for her own means, her own purpose, the woman had understood the power behind such a gesture, behind a simple, joyful smile.

Cat wrapped up Madeleine with what warmth there could be found in this room, tucking that thin quilt about her just so 'cause it was simply the right thing to do. Because Madeleine here was human, and she was a sister. One, too, that Cat suspected wouldn't live past the winter, whether from natural means or the threat which Madeleine had hinted at. Perhaps that reason alone was why it'd been worth it for her to open the door, to take a risk, a chance, on Cat. Because at the end of the day, she'd come to the end of her journey here.

An end for her, but maybe not those other girls who'd been kind to Norma. Who, in doing so, might have made themselves a target to whoever was orchestrating such a grand, powerful scheme.

When Madeleine finally spoke, her voice was barely above a whisper, as if whatever strength she'd once had was gone. As if... completely drained by fear and... acceptance.

"I'll tell you what I know," she said, "but you must promise me something."

Cat took off her gloves and sucked in a breath at the sudden, biting cold. Still, with numb, cold hands she gently touched Madeleine's forehead. It was something her ma had done a lifetime ago when she needed comfort and what Alice had also done once their ma had passed.

Love and comfort and again, kindness.

"I promise," Cat said.

"Find them. Find the ones who're doing this, and don't stop neither when they start hurting the others."

"The other girls? You need to tell me more, Madeleine. I can't do anything if I don't know. Who are they? Who's threatening you? Who killed Norma?"

Madeleine's hand gripped Cat's again, finally with some of the strength she'd had in her earlier. And her eyes, when she opened them they were still as sharp and determined. She wasn't gonna pass on just yet, clearly if she had anything to say 'bout it.

"They're not gonna stop," Madeleine said. "Not with Norma. Not with me. They'll keep on going, keep on hurting cause they can, and cause they know not even the police can stop them."

Madeleine's words brought a deep, heavy chill that raced straight to Cat's heart and stayed there. Because Madeleine was finally filling in those details Cat had needed... the politics, the undercurrents, the ebb and flow of life here in the shadow world. Those who lived in it, like Madeleine, who was doing her best to survive, and then there were those who owned it.

And profited from it.

The Stanchfields and their brothels, selling out and leaving for Helena while the Nadeaus, with their fancy Dumas which constantly rivaled the prestige of Grace's Gardens, stayed and bought up as much as they could. In fact, they were the ones who'd built that fancy building right on the edge of hell. The very one Cat had been admiring, with all them windows that had never been opened, that'd never seen an ounce of sunlight and never would.

But Madeleine's understanding of the world didn't stop there, either. In fact, she knew quite well of those living in the higher, crystal-like life of Butte's upper society. How the feud between two of the copper kings, Marcus Daly and William Clark, brought everyone in the shadow world a steady, steady profit. Those two kings, pouring as much money as they could onto both sides of the line, one hoping to keep Clark from reaching the senate, the other doing everything he could to make sure it was his bum, and his alone, that'd be warming Montana's vacant seat.

Madeleine laughed, then. It was a croaking, sick thing.

"Oh, you should have seen it, Miss Justice. The big ball William Clark himself threw and the feuds those two madams had trying to get him to pick one over the other. Madam Grace lost that battle and I wasn't sorry, not sorry in the least. And if Norma were here, she'd be smiling about it, too."

The smile Madeleine gave Cat wasn't a pleasant one, not with the colors or the amount missing. It was a sight that twisted her heart and made her listen to Madeleine's story all the harder.

She couldn't save everyone. She couldn't even save one.

But she could listen.

And it was through listening that Cat picked up on something else Madeleine wasn't quite keen on talking about at first, anyway. There was a big boom rocking through the red light here, but there was something else, too. An uncertainty. A slight... change in the winds, like they were shifting but it was so small, so minute you couldn't quite tell. When Cat asked for more details, Madeleine could only shrug. It was... an impression, more than anything. How certain owners, the businessmen like the Nadeaus, were putting down more claims, buying off many as they could, and on the other hand this sense that they were startin' to squeeze out some the others. Maybe even the Hotel Victoria and Grace's Gardens, even. The way Madeleine described it, it felt like a wave to Cat. The kind that you didn't notice until it was crashing down around you, sweeping you, your home, everything you ever loved until all of it was simply gone.

Gone forever.

It was a lot to process, and her mind was working overtime trying to catalogue and understand everything she heard. Hoping like hell she didn't miss even one small detail, The very one that could prove the answer she needed.

Finally, Cat shook her head. "It's... it's a lot to take in."

"Specially for someone just off the train."

"Aye." Cat rubbed at her face, feeling heavy from the little sleep she'd had. "Do you know why all this is changing now? Or how Norma found herself mixed up in all this?"

Madeleine shook her head. "She wouldn't tell me. Oh, I tried, Miss Justice, I tried to get her to tell me, convince her that it was safe, that she could. She wouldn't. Told me, 'no, it's not safe, Madeleine, and it won't ever be.' She kept saying that she'd already said too much."

Madeleine shook her head. "I didn't believe her, then. Do now, though."

"Did something... happen, then? To you."

"Not me. The officer. The one who found Norma."

A chill settled in Cat's gut. The kind that came from more than just cold. A certainty.

"You know him," she whispered.

Madeleine gave Cat a harsh, cracked smile. "All us ladies on this side of Galena *know* him."

And with halted breath, Madeleine revealed what she knew about Norma and about this Officer White, not that it was much, but it was still more pieces to the puzzle, more bread crumbs for Cat to follow. And the most important piece so far was Officer White himself. One of several assigned to walk this stretch of Galena Street, but he was the one, without fail, who shook down the ladies here for... fees.

Now, all the ladies paid fines to keep their establishments open, it was just another part of doing business. Fines helped stave off police raids, or when that wasn't possible, at least gave proper warning. Even the big parlor houses catering to the greatest and richest men, including those frequented by Daly and Clark, paid their share of the fees.

No one was excused in this.

No one was an exception.

It was almost like a special tax cities put on the red light, part of the whole 'everyone gets a little bit of something out of the deal.' The uptight folks didn't like the presence of night ladies, but the ladies brought in a tidy bit of profit, so as much as the uptight folks pushin' to get rid of them and their houses, the ladies stayed put. Again, lining all those important pockets, which was making Cat's task of finding out the real truth behind Norma's death all the more difficult.

Fact was, the city needed the money and the ladies needed the city. So mostly paying such a fine meant you went unmolested by the law.

Usually.

Yet, it was also well known, didn't matter which city you hailed from, that it wasn't *uncommon* for ladies to get shaken down for more than this fine. There were lots of folks willin' to step in and demand their share, lookin' to line more of their pockets or even enjoy the ladies' attention. Including corrupt cops.

Madeleine's shoulders shook a bit as she talked about Officer White. "He's not the only one, you know. Others share in it, too. But White... he wasn't a kind man. He was harsh and hard and took out all that harshness on whoever he choose for that evening's fee. It was a... standing rule that whoever got White for the night got a bit of extra helping the next day."

Madeleine met Cat's gaze and there was nothing soft or apologetic about it. "We take care of our own."

She nodded. "I believe you."

So why hadn't Blake mentioned this bit about White? Did he not know? Or was Blake covering up his own nightly visits, hiding it behind what he called truth and justice?

Cat felt her shoulders tensing at the thought and forced herself to relax, to keep on stroking Madeleine's forehead with slow gestures. To keeping on breathin' slow and easy, just as her daddy had taught her.

It wasn't easy, though.

Not when, for whatever reason, the thought of Officer Blake walking this here street, demanding favors or money, maybe even both, rocked through her like a hailstorm ripping down out of the sky.

Maybe cause she'd believed him to be honest. Not just believed, but had been so sure—

Cat shook her head. Her braid dangled across her shoulder, smacking her cheek like it'd been needed.

It was.

Even now, Butte was still handing her its surprises, unsettling her, keeping her off balance. She needed to let all this go, all these feelings that were doing nothing but unsettling her, and finally put 'em out to pasture or something.

Yet, much as she wanted to, it was darn, darn hard to do.

But she succeeded, or mostly, and was glad she did because it was getting real clear that Madeleine was about done with her visitor. Madeleine's energy was slipping away and falling fast into some slumber.

But Madeleine had enough energy for one last warning.

"Like I said, I don't know the name. All I know is Norma's secrets, her troubles, they came with her from the Gardens."

The Gardens. The one place Cat wasn't about to get into any time soon, certainly not for asking questions.

"Were you working with her that night?" Cat asked. "Did you see anything out of the ordinary? Someone who stuck out as not right?"

"I... was... working with her, for a time. Didn't see nothin', though."

Damn. Any kind of a hint, even the shape or size or impression of the man—or men—would have helped narrow her search down.

Madeleine reached up, gripped Cat's hands in her own. The hide gloves did little to keep the chill from slippin' right into Cat, like it was a living thing inside Madeleine and the touch alone meant it was now Cat's.

Part of her, too.

"That night, later, after we started our shift, something changed. Something happened again, like I was seeing that same girl who climbed up out of the tunnels. The girl with nothing, like her whole world was crashing down around her."

Madeleine's grip on Cat's hand tightened.

Cat didn't dare breathe, didn't dare break whatever strength Madeleine had found within herself.

"This time," she said, "I didn't leave it alone. Don't know why I didn't, like maybe I had some sense or other that she wasn't all right. So, I asked. She hadn't meant to tell me, but she did. She was upset and already... already had too much drink. I knew she'd answer and maybe that's part of the reason she got killed."

"I doubt it. Whatever Norma was in, she was in deep."

Course, one never knew just who was listening in when you thought you were safe. When you thought you were alone.

A feeling that Cat had, right at this moment. A prickling along the back of her neck...

And yet, there was nothing for it. Not when she didn't dare remind Madeleine of that danger she clearly believed in.

Cat squeezed Madeleine's hand, as if she could give a bit of her own strength. "What did Norma tell you?"

"The Lucky Horseshoe, that wasn't where she'd started the evenin', Miss Justice. Not that night. And it wasn't at any of the other saloons on Galena, either."

The saloons that *would* welcome a girl of Norma's standing.

"Where? Tell me."

Madeleine gave her a cracked smile, as if the red from her stained lips was bleeding along those same cracks. Goodness did Cat's heart call out for this woman and all the pain she'd lived through, all the pain she was still livin' through.

"You really are who they say, aren't you?" Madeleine asked.

"I doubt it."

"No. I think you deserve the name. I think we deserve a little of it, this justice. Norma, too, God help me."

Madeleine found some strength in her yet, enough to squeeze Cat's hand and even through the cold numbness, Cat felt the sharp prick of her fingers.

Just like the prickling she still had along her neck.

"She was at the California Saloon, Miss Justice. A place the likes of me had never once set foot in and never will, either."

Cat felt a real chill this time race right on through her. It slipped down her spine then came right back up again. She didn't know every saloon and gambling house in Butte—hell, probably no one did, there was just so many—but she did know that one.

Cause that one there, it was sitting tall, all regal like and important, right next to city hall.

CHAPTER TWENTY-NINE

It wasn't long after that Madeleine finally shuttered her eyes and fell into some kind of exhausted sleep. Cat stayed there a few minutes more, holding the woman's hand and stroking her forehead with the other. Didn't matter that she'd lost feeling in her fingers cause, truth was, she'd lost feeling all throughout her body at everything Madeleine had said. Almost as if the coldness was a living thing inside her now and had no intention of warming up any time soon.

Cat closed her own eyes. "Christ, Norma, what *did* you find yourself in?"

No one answered.

Not Madeleine, certainly not the ghost of Norma, whom Cat felt as if her ghost was as real as Alice's, as if the two ladies were grudgingly standing side by side, their hands resting on Cat's shoulders, imploring her to make good on her promises.

A chill she felt right to her very soul.

When Cat left Madeleine's home, closing the thin door behind her, the latch sticking with cold so she had to use her weight to slam it shut, not a whole lot had changed outside. It was still dark with all that ash and soot that lived in the air like they were some high and mighty birds circling the town. More foot and horse traffic, too, though most didn't pay her much mind.

It was, after all, still damn cold.

Cat tugged on her gloves but that did about nothing to relieve the numbness she felt sweeping through her whole body, nor did stomping and moving her feet on that uneven boardwalk. She was freezing, through and through, and the chill out here was only part of the problem. Madeleine's words kept on haunting her even as she started going through them, sorting them, piecing some together while letting others stand on their own. She was finally starting to understand a picture of Norma, even if there were many pieces still missing.

Norma's troubles though, they'd clearly started at the Gardens. Brought on, most likely, because of her kindly smile. After all, the smile had been the plan. It got her name on the tongues of many, spreading the legend of her kindness and generosity throughout town without her doing much work. And in turn, it brought her attention from all walks of life, including the most important men of this city. Maybe even from others as well, who came to visit her when they did their business in Butte.

Norma's kindness and smiles had hidden her intellect and cunning to the point that not a single one of those men from the gathering had even an inkling of who she was underneath. Or maybe that wasn't fully true because she *had* been found out.

Someone had learned the truth, had learned who Norma truly was.

After all, Madeleine had at some point as well. Even now, Madeleine was still clearly conflicted towards her friend, living in that between space of caring and disdain.

Cat didn't blame her.

As Madeleine had told her, she'd taken Norma in, given the woman what little she had and done so freely because... because

Madeleine had believed in that kindness. But it was a kindness that only went so deep. In truth, it'd been just another kind of face to show the world, that it wasn't as true and genuine as Madeleine had been led to believe. Then somewhere along the way, she'd also realized an even greater threat... that Norma *had* brought her problems with her. That whatever the reason caused her fall from one of the most prestigious parlor houses in Butte to crib-walker, it had come with her like a darkening shadow.

A shadow that soon touched Madeleine and the other girls who'd accepted Norma and her smiles into their fold.

Cat tugged her coat closer about her neck, trying to ward off a new, deeper chill.

If this was how a friend reacted, a fellow night sister, what about an ex-lover? Someone, perhaps, who'd thought themselves more important in Norma's affection? More than she was willing to give?

Jealously *was* quite common in the profession between clients, yes, but also professional jealousy among girls, which Cat knew first-hand. In fact, she knew quite a few ladies and their gentleman callers who'd gotten harmed or killed due to jealousy of the heart. It was a... hazard of their profession, for sure.

Could that be the reason?

Cat shifted her hat better, doing what she could to protect her ears from that chilling cold wind. Truth was, there were just too many questions, too many variables and not enough eliminations for her to make a proper guess, let alone an educated one.

Still, whoever was behind this, if there was a 'someone'—seeing how there was no evidence sayin' otherwise, other than her gut, of course—they'd be a powerful someone, indeed.

Yet why keep beating on the same bush?

Norma was dead.

Now so was this delightful fellow, this Officer White, the very man who'd found her and issued the official report. And yet... this powerful someone wasn't inclined to stop there. He—or they, truth be told—could very well be threatening Madeleine and the few friends Norma had made on Galena Street. Not to mention the summoning of Mrs. Allen for questioning.

Again, there went that tingling feeling racing along her spine, swirling there in her gut in just that way. She couldn't help get the sense that the reason it hadn't all died down had quietly been forgotten, as was usual, was because... of her.

Because Cat was digging.

Just like Madeleine had known she was.

That heavy feeling kept on rolling round in her gut, rolling and rolling, never for a moment settling.

A feeling she knew, clear as she knew her own name. It was surety, plain and simple. A truth, and one she couldn't very well deny, either. At least as she planned on living out her life a few more years.

Someone was clearly feeling threatened by Cat.

Cat glanced back at Madeleine's door, which was shaking and shivering from the gentle breeze that had come a-knocking. And hers wasn't the only one, either, that seemed unable or unwilling to last out another winter. All the cribs lining up and down this street were a similar style and temperament, having their age show clear as day from the peeling paint and the rusted-out locks and knobs. So many, too, that it was like lookin' at a sea of narrow doors pressed so close, as if one were on top of the other, that you couldn't so much as move and stretch without the ladies next door hearing the creaks from your bedsprings.

Such a desolate, heartsore place to live, and yet one that brought in so much money to the few who owned them. Buildings the girls rented out, barely much leftover for their own care, meaning... more than a few would be willing to selling what information they might have learned. To the business owners, to people like Dusty who thrived and traded on rumors and facts, and how they could be interchanged as necessity dictated.

Christ, what a mess.

The hairs on the back of Cat's neck rose. Just *who* was news of her visit here gonna get back to? And more important, how many of these ladies like Madeleine were gonna pay that price?

If Madeleine was right. If she'd been telling the truth.

Which Cat believed she had.

Much as she knew the truth to be, anyway.

Cat had a feeling, though, right along with that heavy tingle in her gut, that she'd have answers to all them questions and soon.

Still...

Cat found herself turning 'round, taking one last look at the street behind her with all those cribs and their thin, shaking doors as the wind, weak as it was, acted like it was gonna blow the things full-on over. She searched what she could see of the street, lookin' maybe for something else. Something that didn't belong...

Like a streak of blond standing out like sunlight in the ashy black.

Nothing.

No sign, least none that she could see.

Cat pushed back the brim of her hat a bit and squinted, not quite ready to give up. Course, that made her red eyes burn all the harder, tears lickin' at their sides. Maybe he'd taken their conversation last night to heart. Maybe he'd realized she wasn't quite the threat he'd first thought. That they really were on two sides—well, of not the same but a similar, coin.

Not that she was sure what she thought about *that*.

Nor the sudden feeling in her gut, like the bottom was dropping out, heavy and full of... disappointment. Which was a bit silly to feel considering all she'd learned about Officer White and his... taking advantage of the uniform he'd worn.

And she realized, too, that all these feelings coming together as they were, swirling and turning in her gut, made her skin tingle as she searched, the very anticipation of just... maybe... he was there. Well, all that? That was an awful bit like hope, and she knew, flat out knew what hope could and *would* get you.

Nothing good.

And something heck of a lot worse than the disappointment she was feeling, that the person doing the watching of her right at this moment was *not* Blake.

Which she was right.

Just as Cat turned to head down the boardwalk and follow Norma's footsteps the night she died, a door several doors down from Madeleine's creaked open.

A face appeared, looking in so many ways like the exact mirror to Madeleine. This woman, though, her eyes were dull and so rimmed with red Cat could barely make out the white. But even through the shock it was to her system, seeing a fellow sister so low, so barely hanging onto life, manners won out.

Cat tipped her hat to the woman. "Morning, ma'am."

The woman's eyes flicked to Cat's holster as if it was the only thing that mattered. This time it wasn't empty, and this time the lady's gaze flicked back up to Cat. There was no mistaking the warning in those red-rimmed eyes.

"You best keep on movin', Miss Justice."

A chill again raced right through her. Another person calling her by the name Dusty had given. Christ, it *had* to be a rumor he'd started.

Had to be.

"It's Cowboy Cat, actually."

"You ain't welcome here."

"Understood."

Cat tipped her hat yet again, but the woman merely scowled at her, then she simply slammed the door shut.

Warning delivered.

Cat didn't need telling twice.

A new kind of heaviness weighed about her, feeling quite like the shadow that she'd seen on Dusty back at Mrs. Allen's place... dear Lord, had it only been just yesterday? Yesterday, facing all them fellows, her having to decide to walk out on Mrs. Allen and this whole business with Norma or see it through to the end. Felt like so much had happened since then, or maybe it was her who was just doing all this changing. But make no mistake, Dusty's attitude had changed from when she'd very first met him, a new kind of fear, a real honest-to-God one when before he'd been nimble and quick and so confident. An untouchable lad, really.

Almost like her. Like she'd been, at least on the surface.

Cat reached up, fingered her fading pink scarf, that small piece of Alice she still carried with her... not counting her ghost, anyway.

Finally, she dropped her hand.

Curious how Dusty came to her mind just now. Dusty, and the shadow he carried. Dusty, who'd planted that name on her without so much as a by-your-leave from her.

Truth was, she hadn't the chance to question the kid proper, to really find his place in all this, or even *why* he'd gone and asked Mrs. Allen to *not* confide in Cat. Yet despite his deception, despite him workin' to keep Cat from doing this digging, he'd been earnest in his feelings. He'd wanted her to find the truth... no... *needed* her to.

Cat's steps quickened. Her boots thudding heavily on that uneven boardwalk, grateful that even though she was alone, and who knew the amount of people watchin' her from the shadows right now, she wasn't helpless.

Or unarmed.

No question 'bout it, a powerful person was behind this moving and shaking. Powerful enough to put a request in with the police chief himself to get one of the few honest cops tangled up with Mrs. Allen and this mess.

Now Cat had only met two of those kind 'a men so far, that she knew 'bout anyway. There *had* been a number of wealthy types at the gathering—they just hadn't drawn the kind of attention the way MacDonald and O'Neil had. And while both men were clearly hiding something, MacDonald with this almost hidden cold, despite his declaration of devotion. And O'Neil? Well, he was about the exact opposite of MacDonald in every way. But did they have the pull needed for something like this? They were rich men, sure, but did they have the necessary power to really put all these pieces into play, keep them on that game board and in only the way they wanted?

That part, she wasn't so sure 'bout. Least what she'd learned so far.

It didn't seem like they'd have the leverage needed to keep all them voices, all those people knowing all them little bits of the secret, silent.

Certainly not O'Neil who couldn't even keep himself quiet.

But MacDonald?

Maybe.

And it was quite possible, too, that there was yet another player she hadn't yet met. Maybe someone else pulling these strings in this elaborate game all because, for a moment, someone had lost control, that he'd fallen for a woman's kind smiles before knowing her true character underneath. Maybe he'd let something slip that was detrimental to him and his position in Butte society. Or maybe it was all just a house of cards that had just been waiting for the right, or wrong, kind 'a wind to blow and poor Norma, she'd been that wind. Or threatened to be.

Maybe it really all did come back to Norma and the choices she'd made.

Choices that Cat was still not yet clear on.

Again, mystery upon mystery, and those who might give her an answer or two, clarify a few points, were conveniently missing.

Or dead.

Something she needed to be more mindful of, even walking as she was, alone and in this black-hued day. If nothing more than the natural hazards of simply *walking*. Like how she hadn't been paying as close attention to where she stepped, her mind racing with all them possibilities, and that boardwalk taking advantage of her distraction by nearly swallowing her foot whole, boot and all.

A few times.

And she *was* distracted. Mostly because she felt more than just eyes on her back, and ones not coming from the blond streak of Officer Blake. But... it was like she could *feel* the very words traveling right underneath her feet. The news of her visiting the cribs, speaking with Madeleine, as if they'd the power to stay one step ahead of her regardless of how quickly she and her frozen limbs moved.

All the while her eyes kept on watching, kept noticing every bit and inch of detail street side. Noticing which windows had a thin hand pullin' back the curtains and a face glancin' quick before duckin' back inside. White faces, dark faces, pale ones, then that flutter as the curtain draped closed again.

Maybe she had been foolish leavin' the house unescorted, certainly after her... well, not unwelcome, but certainly not *welcome* midnight visitor. But who would she have taken with her? Chin? Dusty, the kid who couldn't be found?

No, she only had herself to rely on. Her, and her own wits. If she couldn't trust herself, couldn't keep herself safe, then she didn't deserve this name everyone was insisting on giving her...

Even though she was the exact opposite of it.

Regardless of word racing about the red light 'bout her being here, she wasn't truly alone. Not when the ghosts of both Alice and Norma nearly about stuck to her, keeping each side of her that same freezing cold. Almost like she had a god-damn matchin' set.

She couldn't help the strangled laugh that slipped out.

So be it.

After all, she *was* on a fool's errand. Coming to a place like Butte, allowin' people to call her Justice when she was anything but, when all she could do was dream of her own justice. And here she was spinnin' round in circles with more questions and answers, and still feelin' like she was no near closer to learnin' the truth than when she'd first opened up that darn newspaper.

And yet... she had to be honest.

She believed in justice, even if it didn't and couldn't look the same for the likes of them. She *had* to believe in it, that it existed.

This reason, and this one only, was why she hadn't yet run tail home. That, and stubbornness. Still, it was why she found herself at the very doors of the last place to reportedly have seen the Miss Norma alive:

The Lucky Horseshoe.

And from what she could tell, there was nothing lucky 'bout it.

CHAPTER THIRTY

From everything Cat could see standing outside in the chill air, bundled up as good as she was on a boardwalk that shifted like her weight alone was gonna cause the whole thing to buckle and fold, the Lucky Horseshoe was a far, far cry from the kind 'a place a lady—any lady, really—would be smiling about.

The peeling, faded paint alongside the building's front, with the gaping-like front teeth of where swinging doors might have stood once a time ago. Which, as she expected, meant the place was freezing when not pressed with bodies. All that heat and sweat of the unwashed, feeding off themselves, keeping them and the whole room warm in a kind 'a sweat lodge that'd make even the Fins envious of.

Sawdust and other bits of flaked wood caked the ground, most a dirty black kind 'a color as if they hadn't been swept or changed out in ages, like more had simply been dumped on top when the smell was gettin' a bit ripe even for this esteemed clientele.

At least it was cold, so Cat could skip that unpleasant part.

The floorboards shifted and groaned as she walked, 'bout as much as the walk outside had. The kind of creaking under boots that made her wonder how solid the foundation was, and just how many tunnels were runnin' underneath her feet. Possibly, too, just how many other activities were takin' place behind closed doors to rooms that neither the law could see or find. Boy, it'd be nice if she had more knowledge of this place, if Dusty were here to ask him what the hell kind 'a place she was walkin' into.

Alone.

Gun or no gun.

The weight of it, pulling and dragging her holster in just that way against her hip, didn't bring a whole lot of comfort simply because she had this feeling rolling in her gut. Of eyes watching her and assessing, curious and not, all at the same time. Wonderin' and guessin' just what she was gonna do next.

Not that she, herself, knew. She was taking this one step at a time, following her instincts, her feel of the place, and the man standing at that bar counter with a thick, bushy mustache that did nothing to hide the full-on scowl twisting along his mouth.

The kind 'a man who wasn't pleased, not in the least, to see her.

And there was certainly recognition in his dark, beady little eyes. No doubt he'd been warned of her coming, probably too before Cat herself knew this was the place her boots were bringing her. But this was a place she needed to see. Needed to see just where Norma had fallen with her own eyes, feel the desperation Norma might have experienced pushin' her along, squeezing her until she had nothing left but one final effort, one final try, to claw herself back out of her predicament...

Again, this feeling tingled along Cat's spine. Instinct, again, guiding her.

Common sense or no, this was the place she needed to be, this was where her investigation had taken her next, alone as she was.

At least, if one didn't count the ghosts that followed her.

Now, the kindly thing upon entering a new establishment would be for Cat to sweep on in, smile and all, taking off her hat and gloves, and sidle right on up to that bar counter. Completely, of course, ignoring those big 'ol stains along the counter, like someone had taken a raging-hot iron and started practicing their letters right on top.

See, putting on her charm *would* have been a natural enough choice in this situation, except for the fact that she was freezing. Except, too, for this feeling in her gut that wouldn't leave. A feeling that'd come peaking out from the moment she'd seen that second girl on Galena Street and hearing the warning she'd given Cat. But now, though, that feeling was hitting new highs, an almost nervous warning that being here was not in her best interest.

And a good thing, too, 'cause otherwise she'd surely be considering her time on this world was about up.

It was just *that* kind 'a place. Certainly with the bartender, his white apron tied so tight round his bulky frame it looked it was about to squeeze him in half. And the glare he was still sending her way, making no effort, none whatsoever, to hide it?

Oh yes, certainly far from the warm and welcoming type.

A hard man who ran a hard place. One who clearly didn't want her here.

Not that she wanted to be here either, and sure as heck didn't need to see the place in full rippin' and roarin'. She could tell, plain as day, the kind 'a folk who frequented a place like this. And truthfully, it wasn't at all surprising for someone of Madeleine's standing to be working here when not calling outside her front door, where all manner of creatures pawed at her. Cat remembered every line and wrinkle about the woman's face, and yeah, much as it broke her heart a bit, it made sense. But... for Norma? For a lady of her former standing, who'd been used to wearing all them jewels and dresses, living up in that big fancy parlor house? A woman who, somehow, had managed to survive a full couple months of living this low, distasteful light.

Most would have bet good money that she'd only have lasted one night, not several months.

That, too, told Cat just how strong a will Norma must have had, which in and of itself was just another piece of the story.

There were many, many others missing, certainly what the hell had actually happened to Norma that night, not to mention what caused her death, but an idea was starting to take shape. A story, maybe, of what had happened to the girl who'd first been banished from those golden, gilded halls to a place like this, and then only to be killed a few months later...

It was certainly no surprise why Norma had stopped smiling.

And when her smile *had* stopped, so too did all that warmth and charm and kindness, everything that had set her apart from the other working girls like Madeleine. She'd become just another harlot 'cause that's what she *was* at that point, not some high lady with dreams reachin' higher than those black clouds surroundin' the city.

But *how* had she done it? How had Norma survived, night after night, banished as she'd been from all the glitz and glamour because she'd gone and made the wrong person unhappy or wary? Had it been something more than determination? A seed of an idea, to use as her own little chip for bargaining, to pull herself back up and out of this life. Dusty had said that'd been her dream, that Norma had wanted out.

Cat couldn't see a way out.

The bartender, glaring at her in just that way, gave her the sense that Norma had moved beyond desperate. That maybe, just maybe, she'd done something far worse than desperate.

Something down right foolish.

Something that had caused her to go from simply banished, to dead.

Christ, Norma... what had you gotten yourself into?

Course, Norma's ghost, sittin' as it was on Cat's shoulder, chose not to answer. If anything, she pressed her cool hand harder on Cat's shoulder, making her shiver and her teeth chatter, and Cat felt a wave such remorse and revulsion for being here, standing here, it suddenly took all her control to not lose the little she'd eaten.

Which the bartender didn't miss, as his beady, little eyes somehow got even smaller. "You want somethin', Miz?"

Cat mustered a smile and introduced herself as Cowboy Cat, politely ignoring the yellow-stained glasses he was cleaning. And using a cloth dirtier than the bar itself to do it. Definitely a classy joint.

"Afternoon, sir. I was wonderin' if you wouldn't mind answering a few questions."

"D*a*pends."

The man's accent was so thick and rich it sounded like he'd come straight off some boat just two nights ago. Her knowledge of nationalities wasn't as keen as other areas, and she wasn't able to identify which coast or strip of Europe the man hailed from, just that he was from somewhere around those parts.

Still, he seemed a shrewd man. Not the kind that would accept kindness or polite manners as she'd used at Mrs. Allen's home to charm the gathering and learn what she could. This man was about near as opposite as you could get. A harsh man with a harsh view of the world, and he was making some pretty harsh opinions about her even as they stood there, her smiling or not.

She'd met plenty like him in the past, recognized him for who he was, and trusted her instincts. She'd go with the other trait she was quite darn good at, maybe even earn a small enough favor and get herself some answers:

Bluntness.

Cat reached the bar, pulled off her gloves, and slapping them down on that counter. "I'm here about a dead prostitute."

The man blinked. "You a here 'bout *Norma?*"

Cat straightened, unable to hide her shock. He knew immediately who she was asking about.

"I am," she said.

"What in the hell for?"

"Well, sir, she's dead."

He snorted. "Course she is."

Yet another damn shock to her system. This time she was prepared and didn't let it show. Much, anyway.

"Think you can tell me anything 'bout it?" she asked. "Anything you might know? I heard she was here the night she died; the last place, too."

He frowned at her, his eyes nearly getting lost in those heavy folds round his face. "Course she was here. Unhappy, drunkin' tart. Yeah, yeah, she was here, until I kicked her ass out and sent her home."

Cat felt a chill race through her body and this time it had nothing to do with Norma's presence or her touch.

This time it was all Cat, all instinct.

"You see something?"

He stood there considering her question, weighing and measuring her right from her wide-brimmed hat, which was most likely dusted in the same ashy crap as the rest of her, before his gaze trailed on down to her jeans, and finally, to the revolver at her hip. He turned then, reached up to the shelves behind him and grabbed an even filthier glass, if that were even possible. He filled it up with some amber-like liquid from the shelf that was already sagging with too many bottles of the same amber-like substance.

He shoved the drink at her.

Drops splayed out onto the bar counter and she swore she heard some sizzling.

He crossed his arms, one hand still holding that filthy cloth, making his white apron strain even more. His glare hadn't moved an ounce, either. Still right on her, waiting.

Cat, suppressed a sigh and took a sip.

To say the drink was disgusting would be an embarrassment to the word. So would fire. Yet, she sipped and kept control of every involuntary reaction her body *demanded* she react to—much as she could, anyway. Like choking. Like her whole face seizing up in disgust.

This was another survival... trait she'd learned working the line, though it'd been some time since she'd tested herself to *this* kind 'a extent. She managed though, taking her two healthy sips before lowering the glass and doing a little glarin' of her own.

"If this was the swill Norma was drinkin' it's no wonder she didn't keel over sooner."

"Good men pay good money for that swill."

"Good men pay good money to forget existing."

He frowned at her, then at her drink. "Ya didn't finish."

"I'm on the job."

Cat put the drink down, hard. Hard enough for a few drops to spill over the top. Yep. Definitely some sizzling. Either that, or the sound was now coming from her insides.

"Now," she said, "tell me 'bout Norma."

"Someone hire you? Someone actually care what happened to that harlot?"

Cat was finding it a bit hard to control her own temper, seein' at the constant disdain of the man. Seeing, too, it was most likely men like this, and circumstance of life which never took kindly to women, that had finally found Norma workin' here.

That, and the powerful man she'd somehow pissed off.

"Yeah," Cat said, leaning across that counter, ignoring the sizzling still going on. "Someone hired me. Her ghost."

The bartender kept on glaring as if he was lookin' for any little sign to tell him she was lyin'. But Cat had taken the blunt and honest approach with him and he must'a known it, too, because when he didn't find what he was looking for, his face softened. Not a whole lot, mind you, but the folds 'round his eyes receded to a normal kind 'a frown.

He huffed. "Yeah, yeah, she worked here. Not that she was good at her job or good for business. I had to toss her out that night. Too much drink. A complete disgrace to my hard-earning business."

The irony, indeed.

"You see anything?" Cat asked. "Someone she was with? Someone who stood out?"

"She was with a lot of 'em fellows that night, lady, what'd you expect?"

"Someone different. Someone who stood out. Didn't belong."

He twisted his lips until they were tight, thin things. "Yeah, yeah, I reckon she was. Fancy fellow, certainly not the... usual type we see 'round here. Great and fancy black coat and hat, wouldn't let us hang it up for him as if we'd damage it."

Stain or steal, more than likely the case.

But Cat felt that tingle again, slipping down her spine until it reached her belly. She glanced about the Lucky Horseshoe, with the high ceiling and rafters, the way the boards creaked and groaned as the wind did its blowing. She could almost picture what it might have looked like that night, with Norma hanging off that counter there amongst those childlike carvings of letters along its surface, all the men pressing in on all sides. Their very touch leaving dirt stains on her once creamy, always washed skin. Bottles and glasses of beer and whiskey and what-not being bought, all the while Norma being in the center of all that, that and her lined, wrinkled face. So desperate, so in need of a way out... how maybe she'd turned in just the right way and saw a familiar face, saw a man straight from her past, a ghost that wasn't really there and yet undeniably was there.

Coming to speak with her? Confront her, maybe?

Or both?

"You see what the man looked like?" Cat asked.

"I can do you one better, lady. I can tell you his name."

CHAPTER THIRTY-ONE

Seamus.

That had been the name that came whispering off Norma's lips when she'd turned away from the Lucky Horseshoe's owner. Her eyes wide, maybe full of hope that finally her luck was 'bout to turn around, that finally she was gonna be swept up and leave this dirty hellhole she'd found herself in. That small moment, balancing on the edge where everything could and would change, holding your breath because breathing would make the moment crash down around you and just maybe not in the direction you'd wanted.

As it had for Norma.

Cat was now back outside in that cold, ashy-black air, tugging her gloves back on and for once, not caring or wondering when the feeling would ever come back to her fingers. Didn't care 'cause her mind was a swirl with what she'd learned. Not that the owner had told her much more. Bluntness only earned a person like her so much favor, certainly when there was clearly someone powerful, someone watching from the shadows of Galena Street who didn't want her here.

Or more than a few someones.

Which made sense. Here she was, walking into a town with a name like Cowboy Cat while another, unofficial name seemed to dodge her heels, earning both trust and distrust in one fell swoop. There was simply no denying it—there were plenty of movers and shakers in the shadow world here that didn't want so much as a hint of the word *justice* to come creepin' along its surface.

And yet, the owner had spoken with Cat.

He'd told her that Norma had whispered the name "Seamus" and rushed after him. Not that he'd seen much of what happened next, just that Norma had grabbed onto the rich man's arm with those claws of hers and didn't seem the least bit interested in letting go. And the girls that immediately swarmed around their prey?

Norma had glared.

She'd spouted some venomous warning or threat, enough, too, that it made the other girls lean back in a bit of shock of their usual, sweet-mouthed Norma.

Which Cat found a bit curious as Madeleine hadn't mentioned neither this display from Norma nor the presence of the man. But then, that's usually about what happened when it came to trust in the shadow world. You never found yourself a straight and narrow, full-honest answer. Including the owner of this here Lucky Horseshoe.

He was holding something back, and make no mistake.

Sure, she pushed him a bit, got maybe more than he'd be willing to let go if he'd even been aware how much he was giving away. But that was Cat's talent, her way of leading the conversation like a wrangler riding herd. Moving and speaking to the point where the other person didn't see those gates slamming closed until you heard the actual clang and the latch sliding shut. And yet in other areas, try as she might, he was steering far, far clear from that gate. Cat knew there was no amount of pushing that was gonna let the rest of the story fall from this owner's lips.

Especially when it came to the rich man himself.

Yes, the owner was quite disdainful of Seamus O'Neil and his fancy dress and lordly like manner, but the owner also *knew* him.

The how and the why, all those fine details... well, he wasn't letting loose on those regardless how much wrangling and angling Cat was doing.

Now, she sure got the perception that the owner didn't know O'Neil personally. Maybe, too, that O'Neil had never stepped foot in the disgusting, unlucky Horseshoe before that night.

Which she was willing to believe.

It seemed his presence here had both been a glittering shock as well as downright offensive to everything the Lucky Horseshoe stood for. But no doubt 'bout it, the owner knew of him and he wasn't gonna budge on the how or why he was familiar with a rich banker man from clear the other side of town.

Justice, after all, only got you so far.

"Like I told you, that man never stepped foot in my establishment before that night." The owner had kept on glaring at Cat with those two beady eyes of his. "And what happened to Norma? She deserved it, and make no mistake."

"She deserved to be killed?"

"No one saying she was. Fell down dead of her own devices."

He wiped even harder at the glass, as if intent on making the whole thing spit-shine brown. Then he paused. Looked right at Cat.

"Anyone sayin' different?"

"Maybe I am."

His mouth twisted hard again before he got back to swiping and wiping, moving those dark smears over that cloudy glass.

"Maybe," he said, "there's somethin' to that. I knew she'd fallen on hard times. Harder than most, and she was takin' it harder than most, too."

"You remember what happened that night?"

"Maybe. Maybe I do."

Cat had kept herself good and calm, not letting lose her own swirl and rush of excitement. The tingling that told her she was inching closer to the truth.

Truth was this man didn't have to talk with her. She certainly wasn't holding no gun to his head, nor was she pulling out all the stops with her charms.

Yet he talked anyway.

He stood there, swiping at those glasses lining the shelves like they were some prized pieces and trophies. Swiping and wiping with a white cloth that just got dirtier with each swipe.

"I tell you, Miss Cowboy Cat, what I remembered most? Is that she smiled. *Smiled.* Sure, I'd heard tales of it, part of the reason I hired on the woman, letting her work her trade here 'cause there were still plenty of tales running 'round. But in the few months she'd worked for me, she was just another one of 'em tarts. Till that night. Till she set eyes on that Seamus fellow and smiled. Hell, she'd have done that before, I'd have kept her on for an eternity or more. Given her more share of the take, too."

Sure, he would have, the generous soul that he was. Especially since that smile would have lined his pockets with even more coin. Maybe even make enough extra to actually sweep out some of those dark wood shavings off that there floor.

Her smile, he'd said, well, it about lit up the whole room. Light and joy and warmth, and he was suddenly busy pouring more drinks than he had enough hands and arms for. Doing all he could just trying to keep up with those few fellows who had caught sight of that smile. It was like all they wanted in on some of that light, anything really, so long as they kept in her presence.

"Smile didn't last long, though," he said, "and that there's a real shame. That other fellow, Seamus, he said something to her that wiped her smile right clear off her face. Swear I thought the sun might'a disappeared, if it hadn't disappeared for a whole week now behind those black clouds. Look, Miss Cowboy, don't know what Norma had got herself into, but it's no good, I'm tellin' you. No good comes from servin' men like that. Promises them the moon, they do, with their fancy clothes and sweet smells. But the actual truth? Well, truth turns out to be nothing but lies and dust. Those girls wake up thinkin' they got the whole world comin' to them, but the pillow next to 'em is empty except for a bill laying there beside her, caressing her and laughing at her the whole way."

He'd pointed a meaty finger at Cat. "And *that's* the look Norma had on her when he'd said whatever it was he said."

The owner put down his uncleaned glass then and leaned over that counter, nodding at Cat. "At least my fellows here, they're honest folk. In what they do. In who they are. Something Norma apparently couldn't ever come to terms with."

"Yet your place is the last she walked out of alive."

He huffed. "If she overindulged, that there's on her."

But Norma was only a piece of this story, and Cat wasn't yet satisfied with all she'd heard. After all, there had been another who'd partaken in this conversation.

Mr. Seamus O'Neil.

The very man who'd shown nothing but contempt and disdain for Norma's memory, of Cat and others in her former profession. And yet he'd come down here to a place like the Lucky Horseshoe, clearly to speak with Norma. A place where the seamiest side of the shadow world lived in full, unashamed view.

"And what about Seamus?" Cat had asked. "What was he doing during this whole exchange?"

Cat could imagine the situation quite well. All those dirty ladies swarming and pawing at his nicely pressed, soft coat? Well, even if the owner knew of Seamus O'Neil, he still took quite the pleasure in telling Cat this little bit. How the other man's face got so darn red it looked a bit on the purple side, certainly when he started speaking with Norma. Though, when the purple look didn't seem to go away, the owner found himself getting a might bit nervous.

Which was understandable, really.

The last place an establishment like the Lucky Horseshoe needed was a high and mighty banker, a personal friend of the copper king Marcus Daly himself, keeling over from a failing heart. No doubt, it was a blame that would surely be put on the saloon and *not* the clearly over-lavish and over-indulgent lifestyle of the rich man.

The owner, well, he was about to go over and break up this little reunion between Norma and her former client, when after a few more heated words the two calmed. Now, he claimed not to have overheard this part of the exchange, which to Cat sounded a bit incredulous. After all, *she'd* been on the receiving end of Mr. Seamus O'Neil's angry barrage. It was almost downright impossible to *not* hear the man and that booming voice about bouncing and rolling like thunder off the walls.

Then again, it was possible, too, that the Lucky Horseshoe just became that kind 'a place at night, rowdy and rough and crowded.

Which Madeleine had described, more or less, in her own words. Enough that she'd lost sight of Norma easily throughout the night, getting focused on her own job and own coin to earn. Still, after the owner got to tending to his clients, there being a mighty sized group of thirsty fellows that night, and well, he looked up and next thing he knew Norma was standing by herself.

The gentleman was gone. No sight of that tall top hat or that neatly pressed coat. Just vanished, like he'd never been there at all. Nor, too, did any of the usual patrons of the Lucky Horseshoe see the man leaving, either. But all one had to do was glance at Norma and realize the whole thing hadn't been some strange aberration.

He'd been real, real flesh and blood, and make no mistake.

'Cause that's when she really got to drinking. Got quite a bit of attention, too, from those thirsty fellows who were more than willing to take advantage of her newly saddened state.

He didn't elaborate on this bit, and Cat didn't need him to. Those fellows probably bought themselves more than a few favors by just buying her a drink alone, with her either not knowing, or more likely no longer caring.

What conversation had exchanged between the Norma and O'Neil? What had pushed Norma from living on that knife's edge, walking and dancing on it, both excited and desperate when she saw him, to suddenly feel like she'd lost everything and nothing at all mattered no more? And besides that, why the heck had O'Neil come all the way to a place like the Lucky Horseshoe when, according to Madeleine, Norma had spent the earlier part of the night in O'Neil's neck of the woods?

Still, whatever the answer, Norma got to drinking hard, hard enough that the owner had asked her to leave.

"How did she seem?" Cat asked then. "Anything that didn't fit right?"

The owner's mouth had twisted at her again, his special version of a frown no doubt, and no doubt he was quite aware of the *real* question she was askin' without actually asking it.

Had something happened to her here? Something more than could be attributed to too much drink?

"Glassy eyed. Unsteady. Like the whole world had fallen out from under and she'd not anythin' left."

"Was that all?"

"Norma liked to drink heavy during those darker moments. I always knew when one of 'em was on her. Money stopped flowing in 'cause she stopped trying as hard. But even when I could tell her head was spinnin', she still kept it on pretty good, kept up a pretty good act, like it'd been bred into her or something. Never lost that sway to her hips or that slight smile she'd manage at a fellow. Never stumbled or bumped into folks, not Norma."

"And that night?"

"It's like I told you. Unsteady."

He'd glared at her then, as if defying Cat to push... to ask maybe why he hadn't cared enough for her safety, or called for a driver to bring her home safe.

She didn't, though. There was no need.

Instead, she tipped her hat to him in thanks and walked out of the Lucky Horseshoe, hoping like hell she'd never have to be back even as her boots trailed bits of those dark wood shavings after her like fallen, broken snow.

Cat understood where Norma fit in this life, and so, too, had Norma. She'd left for her one-room crib, heartbroken and heartsore, unescorted, inebriated, and quite possibly more. But then, she'd never made it home. Instead, dying on some rotting plank of the boardwalk, surrounded by the black and sulfur air, alone except for the arms of some doctor who'd appeared out of nowhere, trying his best to save her.

And failed.

Kind 'a like Cat was feeling now. Doing her best to investigate, to find out the truth. Getting only a bare few hints of an idea, of a story that surrounded Norma and the person she was, only to feel it slip by her once again.

It felt like she was runnin' about in circles, finding some answer only to be dragged by her tail in a completely other direction, with only one smidgeon of the true story coming out.

Truth was, she was feeling a bit raw about her allies, too, people she should be able to trust and yet still kept on holding out. Maybe this was a fool's errand. Maybe it was true that people like her, people like Norma and Madeleine, that none of them deserved any measure of justice, even if only the kind a person like Cat could hope to bring 'em.

So, she thought.

So, she was startin' to believe...

Until she stepped back out into the day that looked more like night, the smoky world and hell that was Butte, and nearly ran right over Dusty.

Dusty, who'd clearly been waiting for her.

CHAPTER THIRTY-TWO

Now, while Dusty might have been waiting for her, bouncing off one foot than the other, hands tucked deep in that thread-bare coat of his, doing his best to stay warm, he also clearly wasn't expecting her to come stomping out of that saloon in quite so fast a fashion.

He was mid-bounce when her boots thudded outside onto that uneven boardwalk and he jumped back a whole three steps at her sudden appearance. So shocked was he that his cap flew right off his head. Also, too, he found himself pinwheeling backwards.

His arms, well, they were still locked up in the deep folds of his coat so he was flailing with his elbows and body, doing everything possible to keep from not falling... falling off that short lip of the boardwalk and straight onto some black-like, frozen sludge that was called the street.

Cat reacted.

Didn't much think about what she was doing. Or that she was a bit annoyed with him and maybe he did deserve a dive right into some sludge. But either from her own personal code of honor or instinct, she moved. Simply reached out, grabbed a fistful of the boy's coat collar, and yanked him back down until both feet were planted firm—least as firm as one could be—on the uneven, rotting boardwalks.

"Miss, Miss Cat! I've been looking everywhere for—"

Oh, no. She wasn't about to have none of that.

"Where the *hell* have you been?" she cut in.

Cat was quite, quite done with pleasantries. Of dancing and dippin' round the subject and all them reasons why everyone was keeping her in the dark. Especially this kid. The same damn one who'd sent her on this wild goose chase in the first place, straight to that little blip in the paper about Norma and all the mysteries surroundin' her. And each time, before Cat got a chance to grill into him, he was gone. Disappeared without so much as a shadow being left behind.

Not this time, though.

She didn't give him a chance.

Cat grabbed him again by that collar just to be on the safe side, and hauled him into the first noodle house she could find.

Both noodle houses and the Chinese, well, they were good at keeping secrets. Mostly the rest of the city folk ignored them, pretending they didn't exist or worse, that their whole race were the equivalent of a dung heap at the bottom of their shoes. At least until they wanted some noodles or needed their laundry cleaned, at which point most folk didn't have no issue going to the Chinese's place of business.

Such was the life in western small towns, and so too, apparently, life in the bigger, glittering city that was Butte.

Now, about the only ones who *didn't* much mind the Chinese, how they dressed or them being a so-called threat to the jobs of all them working folk, were the night ladies. They liked to band together, these outcasts from the rest of the civilized world, and did just fine. The night ladies paid for laundry services and meals, both which were delivered prompt to their doorsteps, even offered with a bow, and the Chinese did what they did best: kept their opinions to themselves and their mouths shut tight.

Which was a reception that carried over as Cat hauled Dusty to the nearest noodle parlor, one with the red-painted door and some gold-like cat statue perched on the counter, with a grin that'd give even a full grown man nightmares. But hey, the Chinese here, glancing up from out in the kitchen area, with all them smoke and steam, didn't so much as blink when they got an eyeful of Cat with her blue jeans, boots and hat.

In fact, they took it all in stride as she came in trudging in, being sure to knock off as much of the dirt and bits of Butte stickin' to the bottom of her boots.

Though to be fair, her gun did draw out a few more stares.

But again, the Chinese were kind and knew their business. Instead of offering her scowls and glares such as the owner of the Lucky Horseshoe had done, they plopped down a porcelain bowl of steaming noodles and a small glass of something liquid and hot. One for her, one for Dusty. And oh boy, were they smelling something like heaven herself had created, making her stomach grumble and growl, but Cat didn't move, didn't reach for her chopsticks, either.

Not yet.

She had business to attend to first.

That also meant she wasn't lettin' go of that boy's collar, squiggling still as he was, until he gave her answers.

Finally, after a few hard shakes and a resounding sigh (though the noodles might have had something to do with his change of heart), Dusty gave in.

"All right, all right." He shook himself free of Cat's grip. "I'm not budging. Promise."

His promise wasn't exactly holding much weight with her, though the way he was eyeing that bowl of noodles was.

He'd stay put.

At least until the bowl had been scraped clean.

"You have quite a bit of answering to do," Cat said.

Dusty shifted in that uneven, wooden chair of his. It scraped on the hard, cool floor, drawing a few gazes of the Chinese to him, those working behind the register and in the back, before they got back to what they were doing. She and Dusty were the only ones there, taking up only one of three small, squished-in tables, but even with only those workin' here being present, Dusty couldn't seem to stop squirming.

Or looking over his shoulder and out the door they'd come in.

"You expectin' someone?" she asked.

"If I said no, would you believe me?"

Cat shook her head. "You've pretty much used up all the goodwill you'd made with me."

He rubbed along his collar. "Yeah, I noticed. Still don't make it not true."

That part, she believed, that he really was worried about someone following him.

Still, neither moved for a moment, not taking off their coats or gloves, not digging into that steaming bowl of noodles, neither.

Business first.

Cat put her elbows on the table and leaned closer. "Are you gonna tell me what the hell's going on, or do I need to do what I was promising just yesterday?"

That she'd take her bags and leave, walk away from the mystery of Norma and the circumstances surrounding her death, which Cat now knew for a fact weren't adding up.

Dusty bit his lip, face goin' a might bit pale.

He knew. He remembered.

"Even now," he said, "after everything you've heard 'bout Norma, 'bout her life, you'd still leave?"

"That's the problem. I don't know what I've learned. I don't know what's truth or not. All I've got are guesses, and those people I was hopin' to rely on, who wanted to see this here through, and they end up doing the opposite. Like disappearing. Or letting themselves get caught up with the police and staying the night there instead of returning home and shedding light on this whole mess."

Dusty flushed a bit at that.

'Cause yeah, the kid had probably figured out—or heard—that part for himself.

"So," she said, "you can see why I'm feeling not so trustful again. And yeah, I heard 'bout Mrs. Allen. Officer Blake made it a point of stopping by last night. Late. Or... maybe you knew that already."

He didn't meet her eyes.

Of course.

Cat sighed. "Yeah, that's what I thought. In fact, you probably knew he was gonna stop by before the man even got it in his own head to do so, but nah, you decided to keep all that to yourself. Did I get that right?"

Dusty shifted in his chair, which made the whole thing scrape even louder. Earned themselves a few more glances from their Chinese hosts.

"Thought so."

Cat crossed her arms, suddenly feeling more exhausted than she'd felt last night while sitting across from Blake in that mostly dark room, just the dull glow of lantern and the weight of Norma and her story heavy on her shoulders. Alice's story, too, and the promise Cat had made.

A promise that, try as she might, didn't seem like she'd be keeping any time soon.

But then... she thought of Norma. Thought of her smile and the way the Lucky Horseshoe's owner had described her, how O'Neil, with only a few words, had taken the sun that was Norma and flung it right back into the smoky-black hell that was Butte. No one but a few had cared what happened to Norma. Mrs. Allen, Dusty, Madeleine. Just those few, really. Not even Officer Blake or his boss, Murphy; they were more concerned about the corruption that might've led to the incident itself. But Norma? The woman she'd been before falling into this life? The woman who'd fallen so far as to take up residence in that single-roomed crib with no light at the tunnel's end, no chance of escaping?

No, they didn't care one bit.

And problem was, she did.

Dusty was right. She couldn't leave. Not until she got to the bottom of this.

"You're right, Green Eyes. I can't leave—"

He started to smile, prim and proud that he was, but Cat cut him straight off with a shake of her head.

"—no, you're gonna listen now, because that's not enough. You want me to stay, you want me to find justice, a name I'm hearin' from quite a few folks—more than I'm liking, too—well, then you're gonna be part of this. Right here. Right by my side. And you're gonna tell me the truth, straight-out. It's the only way this is gonna work. Only way we're gonna find what happened to Norma."

"...why?" He finally asked. "Why's that the only way it'll work?"

"Because there's someone powerful doin' their damnedest to keep what happened hidden. I can't fight both sides, kid. I can't fight the shadow world *and* the up-and-clean one, certainly not you. You understand?"

He said nothing, just gave a slow but firm nod.

Good enough.

She leaned across that table again, reached out and grabbed his arm. He was cold, colder than she'd first realized—probably 'cause she'd still been living on a bit of her own anger when she'd grabbed hold of him, keeping him from falling into the street—but she felt the cold now.

Felt it right through her own gloves and finally saw what'd been staring her in the face the whole time: the hidden toll all this was takin' on Dusty.

Cat took a good, long look at him, something she should have done when she'd first seen him, but damn it, she'd lost herself in everything she'd learned and heard at the Lucky Horseshoe, all those mysteries 'bout Norma and O'Neil, and then Dusty here, who seemed to leave his trace on *everything*. Everything from the pet name he'd given her to her being out and walking down Galena Street.

She'd been mad and frustrated from hitting on all those walls and dead ends, never seeming to really get her footing under her. But now, though, now she was seeing another side of Dusty...

In what he *hadn't* said.

How his eyes looked like bruised, sunken sockets, like he'd been up all night without a wink of sleep. So, too, with his nose, so red it looked maybe like he'd spent the night's vigil outside with nothing but this flimsy coat and his gloves, which were sportin' quite a few holes, and looked too like they were too small.

"Damn it," she whispered.

Cat hadn't seen any of it. Hadn't noticed, hadn't put the pieces together. All those things she was supposedly good at. Or had been until she'd come to Butte. Come here hoping and dreaming of doing some good. The kind good people like the two of them would no longer see, living in the shadow world as they did, but that they deserved nonetheless because damn it, they were human beings.

They *were* still people.

It were those thoughts that even now still touched her in the cold, dark places of her soul. Emotions that she couldn't seem to keep at bay.

And maybe, that there was the problem.

Cat leaned back. Finally making some sense of her problems and why she always seemed caught on her heels ever since she'd walked off that train and into the dark ashy world that was Butte.

She slapped off her gloves before pushing both her bowl of noodles and the hot liquid cup at Dusty.

"You need to get warm. Eat."

He glanced at both bowls, then at her. Whatever he was thinking, whatever desperation he was feeling towards food and warmth, the kid was so good he didn't let it show. And she noticed, too, that whatever darkness was still clutching at him, the fear that held him so tight yesterday while they met with the gathering in the missing Mrs. Allen's place, well, it wasn't as strong today.

Christ, had that only been yesterday?

Cat rubbed a hand at her eyes. Yeah, yeah, it was.

Still, whatever had happened since then, whatever had shocked Dusty's existence into acting as he had, into a more scared and unsure version of himself, he was clearly finding his way back.

After all, he hadn't bolted for the door yet.

Again, Cat nodded at the noodles. "Eat."

Still, he didn't move.

"Look," Cat said, "I'll be honest with you. I'm... I'm not at my best right now and to tell you rightly, I'm having a hard time coming to grips with it. And I'm sorry. Sorry I missed seeing what I should have seen right at the beginning."

She closed her eyes a moment, picturing and feeling Alice and her cold beside her. Easily seeing, too, Norma beside her sister.

All those failed promises.

Well, she hadn't failed them. Not yet, anyway.

"None of this is your fault," he said. "You just got off a train."

Cat opened her eyes.

It was true. She'd gotten off a train, but the reason had been one filled with hope and maybe too, that she'd be someone else's light at the end of the tunnel. And if not light exactly, at least a bright enough candle flame to lead all the right people to the truth.

Her included.

But truth, it cut both ways, and that's what she'd been missing, that's what she *hadn't* been seeing.

"Being here," Cat said, "everything that happened to Norma, how everyone thought of her, how they treated her... it hits close to home, Green Eyes. I'm having a hard time shaking it."

"Shaking what?"

"My past. My mistakes. Everything."

Herself.

Her truth.

Dusty stared at her a moment more, then peeled off one of his gloves. He grabbed some chopsticks, expertly clicking 'em together. But then, he pushed one of them bowls back at her.

"Me, too," he said. "Me, too."

CHAPTER THIRTY-THREE

Cat stared at Dusty a moment, then nodded at him. They both got to eating in a comfortable, safe silence. The warm noodles and broth filling their bellies and their souls, warming them in places that hadn't felt warm since their own demons took to haunting them years ago.

And when they were done, when they pushed their bowls aside with all them scrawling-blue script along the rim and the refills their Chinese hosts had provided without them asking, they finally got to talking. And Cat learned exactly why Dusty had been the way he'd been, sending Cat on this mysterious chase of the woman named Norma, only to later have Mrs. Allen keep Cat from finding out the very thing she needed.

Cat sat back, arms crossed over her belly, enjoying the warmth seeping into every bit of her. Enjoying, too, seeing Dusty's face get a nice, healthy-red look under all that ash and soot. His eyes, still lookin' sunken and black, like he hadn't slept in a month, but here's hoping that'd change once they found their answers. Already, though, the food and warmth were clearly reviving him in ways nothing else could.

Or maybe that was just this feeling...

Something that felt an awful bit like hope.

Cat very carefully stepped away from that thought lest it catch her in its snares. Much as she wanted to believe in it, live the way like such a feeling belonged right 'side her heart, she also knew how dangerous it could be. Best to keep a wary eye on the feeling, keep her distance, at least until she got a better grounding under her.

It was just the two of them sitting there, heads bowed together in a quiet acceptance of finally searching for the truth Dusty so desperately needed.

Her, too, she guessed. Her, too.

Cat let Dusty talk. Let him fill in all those details, putting what pieces he had with what she'd already learned for herself. Seeing what was missing, and seeing, too, if Dusty was trying to steer her wrong again.

This time, he wasn't.

This time, she believed him.

And from everything Cat was hearing, teasing out with what he hadn't yet said, it seemed like Dusty had known Norma longest of everyone she'd met so far, and from the sound of it, before Norma had even come to Butte. However, Cat noticed he was quite careful to stay away from anything too obvious or clear. All of which made her sit up a tad bit straighter, made her focus in on his words even more. The warmth he had for Norma, the confidence and surety with which he spoke about her. Not the way you'd talk about someone you'd only known for a few months or heck, even a year. It spoke, instead, of long-term association, and friendship.

And listening to him, hearing these pieces of Norma's story come together, damn it, but she couldn't quite tamp down on that feeling called hope. 'Specially the way it swirled in her belly like a pack of flitting butterflies.

Hope really did bring its own kind 'a danger, something shadow souls learned early on to be very, very careful of. Which was why it'd taken her this long, this many run-ins with Dusty before the kid actually told her the truth.

So, Cat stayed sitting and listening. Listening hard very hard, indeed.

Dusty finally finished his noodles, putting down his chopsticks with a soft clack as they hit the table. "I know what you're wondering, what the hell happened when Norma left the Gardens, but I don't know, I swear. She wouldn't talk to me. Past few months she stayed clear of me and anyone she knew I'd sent."

"You have an idea?"

"Yeah. Somethin' happened, somethin' bad. It *had* to be bad for how quick she found herself on the street."

"What did you hear exactly? She anger someone? The madam? Another girl? Client, maybe?"

Dusty shook his head. Bits of ash fell off the tips of his unruly, unkempt hair.

"Honestly?" he said. "I've heard nothin'. Not one bit about why she got tossed aside, and that's what got me worried most of all. Soon as I heard the news, I knew something was wrong. It was like one night Norma with her smile was the talk of the town, the lady every gent worth knowin' sought to have on their arm—well, I guess that's not entirely true, some of them really rich ones never seek out the ladies. Or not so rich ones, like your fellow, Blake, there—"

"—He's not my fellow—"

"—but the very next day? Norma was on the outs. No bag with her. No home. No nothing. And *everyone* knew 'bout it. Just not why."

"And no one was asking the 'why' question either?"

"That's right."

Cat thought about this and all them implications. How everyone had known who Norma was and yet... yet...

She felt a tingle right along with those butterflies, and honestly, it felt a heck of a lot like a spark of an idea. The tiniest bit of light before a flame engulfed a whole city.

"If everyone knew," she said, "why didn't *The Bystander* mention Norma by name?"

It'd been her experience that any chance to ruin a woman's name further was usually the taken course of action. Just not this time.

"'Cause someone asked it to be removed," Dusty said.

There was no denying the sparks Cat felt, striking hard on flint.

"How do you know?"

"I asked the guy who wrote it," Dusty said. "And no, he doesn't know where the original request came from. The editor was the one who made the change. Did it all himself, right before goin' to print, and no, I didn't get a chance to ask the guy why either."

Dusty paused, then it was his turn to lean across the table, voice dropping to a whisper. "He went out of town, all sudden like. Very next day, he got himself on a train to Anaconda, something about business, and he hasn't come back yet."

And Anaconda was only a short trip away. Easily able to return in a short bit of time.

If he'd wanted to.

Cat shook her head. "There's something else you have said that's not making sense. If everyone knew about Norma, knew she'd fallen overnight it seemed from the Gardens, how were there *no* rumors?"

"That's my point, Miss Cat. Nobody was *asking* why. It was like some unspoken agreement. From all those big bankers and rich folk, to the fellows workin' the mines who looked forward to their daily smiles. Everyone was keeping their mouth shut and I couldn't find one hint as to why. Sure, most were willing to talk about how they missed her, but not a one would speculate as to why. Not a thing. Not some rumor of a former lover, not some internal spat amongst the ladies. Nothing. Nothing at all."

And in a town like Butte? Place that ran on rumors and stories, anything to make the hard, dark existence here feel a little more like they actually had a bit of spark of life, maybe?

Quite unusual, indeed.

"Except you," she pointed out. "You were askin' questions."

"Yeah, yeah I was. And try as I might, and Mrs. Allen, too, we couldn't find out nothing. Not that Mrs. Allen was involved much, back then. She was runnin' her business and Norma hadn't gone and asked her for help. If she *had*..."

Dusty shook his head. "All she had to do was ask. But she wouldn't. So proud, like she had the whole world on her shoulders and by askin' she'd let her more than herself down. And Mrs. Allen, she was right there, right and willing to help her out—"

He cut himself off like his throat suddenly got closed off and he glanced away.

As if he didn't want to show Cat the way it was affecting him. The first glistening hints of tears in his eyes.

Finally, after rubbing his nose some, smearing the ash there further onto his cheeks which actually caused those green eyes of his to shine even more, he turned back to her.

"I went to Mrs. Allen for help. After she died, after I couldn't find any answers on my own."

Cat nodded. "So how did they know each other? From everything I've gathered, Mrs. Allen's been out of the business awhile."

"You know as well as anyone, you're never quite 'out of the business' and Mrs. Allen, she still helps out as she can. Like with the letters."

Cat remembered the stack of letters in the sitting room. Each of them addressed to a lady that wasn't Mrs. Allen.

Dusty shrugged. "But their meeting was in passing, really. I knew Mrs. Allen first. I did some runs for her, errands and such, and I kept doing it when she asked. I liked her. Liked her home. Liked her pie. Mostly, though, I was sending the right kind 'a folk her way when they got off the train. Like you. I mean, all us boys know the best boarding houses and where the right kind 'a folk should head, and Mrs. Allen's name usually came up amongst us often."

Cat's brows raised at this. "Even though I'm the only one staying there now?"

Dusty's face got dark, 'bout as dark as the ash hanging off his hair.

"Fallout, Miss Cat. You go askin' the wrong questions, the kind 'a questions someone big and important doesn't want asked, you start losin' business."

Cat let out a slow, slow breath.

Thinking, and thinking hard.

It wasn't that she was surprised. After all, she *was* the only boarder and it was clear from the gathering folk that Mrs. Allen was quite well known and regarded in town. She was practically kicking herself for not seeing it sooner. She'd had the hint of it, but her own past had muddled her thoughts.

Yet another thing she'd missed.

Well, all she could do now was keep looking forward.

"All those folk showed up at her gathering," Cat pointed out. "If Mrs. Allen was blacklisted, none of them should have been there."

"Course they showed up. Like I told you, she's got some famous pie there."

Cat raised her eyebrows. Didn't believe that was the reason for a second.

"All right... I don't know how many of them knew about Mrs. Allen and the police. Most of 'em seemed pretty shocked at the time, but a few knew, no doubt 'bout it. And I've a hunch that most showed up because they wanted to know... wanted answers to questions they'd been ordered not to ask."

Amazing that one person had such a reach.

Or maybe Cat was just looking at it wrong. Maybe it wasn't one person, per se. Maybe it was a lot of different, unique interests coming together in a common goal. And the loss of one unwanted prostitute meant a whole bunch of those interests were kept nice and safe.

Cat shook her head, yet again amazed at the level of depth Norma had gotten herself into.

"You know who it was?" Cat asked. "Who knew beforehand about the police?"

Dusty shook his head. "O'Neil for sure, but that was pretty obvious. I spent most yesterday night finding out what I could, but again, no one was answering my questions."

"How did you find out?"

"I heard from a friend, Tall Timmy, who sells near the station. He saw her going in and sent word to me and I rushed on over to the house. Not knowin' what the heck I was gonna do exactly, just needed to stop you from making a mess of her reputation by stomping in there in a hissy. You were her champion, after all, a pretty unhappy one, rightly so. But then, I guess none of that really mattered in the end cause those gents *were* surprised—by you."

"Me?"

Dusty grinned and Cat swore his eyes sparkled like emeralds. It was a happy grin, too, and she wondered when the last time was he'd had such a feeling.

Happiness.

"Yeah," he said. "Not a one of 'em saw you coming. Sure, they'd *heard* all about Cowboy Cat, walkin' 'round in her jeans and hat, but seeing first hand? How you went in there and wrangled them the way you did? I can promise, Miss Cat, you're quite the talk these days."

Cat had a distinctly different memory of the event, and that Dusty had not been so encouraging, or excited, about Cat's approach to the... situation. Still, it was no real surprise if what he was saying was true. Why news had later traveled the way it had when she'd visited Galena Street. News which had probably reached Dusty as well, probably from another friend, and why he'd known to wait outside the Lucky Horseshoe for her.

All this... all this for Norma...

And Mrs. Allen, still being in the custody from last she heard, with the police. Of her own free choice. A choice that her boarding house business surely couldn't survive even if her name was cleared. In the mouths of those doing the gossiping, it'd never be cleared.

Cat's braid had fallen over her shoulder, and she fingered some of the many lose strands. Bits of ash smaller than an eyelash floated down, catching onto the table or her jeans or just getting sucked down on the floor with all the rest of the dirt.

"That's a lot to risk," Cat said, "from Mrs. Allen. Sounds like she's putting her livelihood and everything else on the line, and for a woman she wasn't such great friends with. Why?"

Her gaze met Dusty's green one, and for a brief moment she thought she saw a bit of that shine again.

His lips twisted tight, as if the habit of silence was takin' hold again, so Cat just waited.

And waited.

Finally, Dusty let out a breath. "It started more cause of me, I think. Mrs. Allen liked me and she went out of her way to be kind to Norma. When they saw each other."

Which still didn't really answer her question, but then, Cat was again hearing what the kid wasn't saying. In the way he said Norma's name, the cadence of each letter, the emotion hinted there, just under the surface.

It was like the parts of Cat, who she'd been before coming to Butte, were slowly coming back to her. As if by accepting her own truth that she was emotionally invested in all this, she could finally see clear again. Like, she could see what she could before, hear what she could before. All them details, all those shapes and feelings and impressions, coming together in her mind and finally forming the story that was Norma.

It really helped, too, that she was finally learning exactly *who* Norma had been. Not just her renown or devotion or even her smile, but her as a person. A proud, independent person. One who held her head high, and despite all that, managed to keep a genuine amount of kindness still in her. Sure, she'd used that to her advantage, making her cunning and intelligent, meaning that Cat probably would have liked her if they'd ever a chance to meet.

Other than ghosts, that was.

Plus, she'd managed to not only touch a closed-off kid like Dusty, shadow soul that he was, but in turn touched a piece of Mrs. Allen.

Cat had no doubt that regardless of what Mrs. Allen had claimed that day in her sitting room drinking tea and eating her glorious, mouth-watering apple pie, she'd have more than liked to leave the past in the past. Including her own mistakes and sins.

But then you never really got the chance to forget, to leave all the bits and parts of yourself that you didn't like or enjoy in the past. Just not the way life was built.

And life liked to have a real good, hard life, when shit turned around on you like this. Hell, she could almost feel its chortling chuckle right now, as if it were rolling under her boots, right underneath the noodle house and all them crisscrossing mines and shadow tunnels.

No doubt life was laughing now.

Which also usually meant that Cat was on the right track. She had the right trail, the right hint of a path. Now it was all about following up on it... and trusting it...

Like Norma's sudden fall from grace.

"Is that common?" Cat asked. "That no one, nowhere, was telling you anything 'bout what happened?"

He snorted. "No, ma'am."

Which she believed.

Cat remembered Dusty on that train platform, standing there amongst all the other boys, him with all the different kinds of papers while the others had only sold just the one. Maybe two. And there was that bigger boy, too, bigger and beefy in all the ways that mattered, and he'd willingly let Dusty have that corner spot. Didn't challenge him for it, nothing.

So yeah... this probably wasn't something that had ever happened to him before. Yet it had. Right to a person.

Curious, indeed. It spoke of a long, long reach of someone—or many someones—and their intimate knowledge of the shadow world.

And knowing exactly the part that Dusty played in it. A very, very effective part that this someone had managed to silence.

"What about Jim MacDonald?" Cat asked. "You seemed pretty

darn stormy with him at the gathering. He also claimed to have been betrothed to Norma." Well, nearly so. "He claimed to have asked 'bout Norma, about where she'd gone and what happened to her, but no one would tell him. Said he'd never heard from her again."

Dusty huffed. "You really think a guy like him's gonna tell you straight?"

Cat raised her eyebrows. "As opposed to you?"

"I've got my reasons."

Which she was bettin' that Jim MacDonald had some good ones as well.

Dusty crossed his arms, making a whole slew of ash drop onto the table. They'd better remember to tip their hosts good—both for the mess and the silence. And as if sensing Cat's thoughts were on them, their hosts came back, bowing and not saying one word, at least not a word that Cat could understand, and refilled their cups. Hot steam and the sweet, spicy scent of tea filled the air between them.

Still, it was interesting hearing what Dusty told her next about MacDonald. That he wasn't nearly as sincere in his affection and devotion to Norma. That if it *had* been true, and seeing how Norma well and truly wanted out of this life, she'd have taken MacDonald up on his offer in a heartbeat. Now their romance, if he'd been sincere in the first place (which Cat also seriously doubted), most likely wouldn't have lasted long. But then, it didn't need to. Norma being a smart, shrewd woman—and for all intents and purposes, it sure seemed like Norma was—she'd have done just fine. All she'd needed was one foot out of that door and a chance.

Something a woman like Madeleine or her charming neighbor would never get.

Course, both those ladies were still alive and breathing.

Norma was dead.

"MacDonald liked Norma fine," Dusty said. "But never enough to marry her. She knew it, too. He wasn't the one she'd had her eye on."

Cat took a sip of tea, still hot, but not the kind of sting that burned the roof of her mouth. It was enough to ward off the growing chill that slowly filled the noodle house as the day creaked on. Her mind thinking and racing as she sipped.

So, there *had* been someone.

Her real chance, her real shot out of this life.

"But yeah," Dusty continued, "MacDonald was one of her suitors. He liked to claim her first before the others, liked to have her smile and her radiance on his arm, as if her presence made him even more important amongst his fellows."

"Oh? I got the distinct impression the man was pretty important."

In fact, at the gathering it'd seemed like there was an interesting back-and-forth between O'Neil and MacDonald, their little power struggle, and how it didn't really seem like one was on top of the other. And yet...

Yet she'd gotten the clear sense that it was MacDonald, with his cold, withdrawn nature, who kept his cards and his thoughts close to his chest, that held the real power.

"Well, he is a pretty powerful man, MacDonald," Dusty said. "Or he was. Hard to tell with them bankers. Keep their secrets locked up as tight as their vaults, they do, except of course for the ladies they like spendin' their time with. Funny thing that they seem to forget the ladies are people, too, and most of 'em have a good enough head on their shoulders. And a pretty darn good memory."

Cat had a hunch Norma was just that person... but... she clearly hadn't shared what she'd heard, either bed talk or from another night lady, with Dusty.

Or anyone, maybe?

Dusty went on, oblivious to Cat's distraction.

"See, MacDonald *is* a partner at Daly's Bank and Trust, but he *isn't* Marcus Daly's close and personal friend, if you know what I'm sayin'."

Like Seamus O'Neil was.

Dusty nodded, clearly seeing her understanding.

"So that's the power play I was seeing between them," Cat said.

"That's right. And I tell you, it kept on shifting depending on who'd managed to claim Norma for the night."

A real honest-to-God power tug-of-war over a night lady. Those situations never ended well—for the lady. The men just usually moved on and picked a new kind of fight. God help 'em all if it was a new lady.

"Hell of a mess," Cat whispered. "And poor Norma, stuck right in the middle."

With no way out... except her mysterious dreamer.

"Which means," Cat said, "either man could still be the reason she's dead. Both are good for it."

But did they have enough motivation?

Well, that depended on what the heck Norma had learned—and what she'd purposefully chosen to *not* share with Dusty. Including after she'd found herself on the streets, alone and with no luggage. A very strange way to go out of the limelight like that.

"You think it was either of them?" Cat asked. "Why she got booted from the Gardens?"

"Don't know."

"Cause no one's talkin' to you?"

"Yeah."

"What's your best guess?"

"That they had something to do with it."

'Course, having two gentleman fighting over a lady wasn't exactly bad for business, and if there was one kind 'a person living and breathing who knew how best to take advantage of a situation, it was the madams of the world. Cat was betting Madam Grace didn't mind the competition for Norma's attention, probably even allowed her to drive up the price for Norma's services, or at the least for the champagne and other such niceties. Unless, of course, the competition had started gettin' out of hand, though it seemed cordial enough at the gathering.

Still, it looked pretty darn clear that Grace's Gardens would be her next stop, though getting through the door would be a bit hard considering the state of her own reputation—and how it seemed to be two steps ahead of her.

Not to mention whoever it was who *wouldn't* want her askin' the kind 'a questions she was gonna be asking.

She eyed Dusty and thought about how word had traveled ahead of her... right under her feet, in fact.

Cat smiled.

Dusty's eyebrows went up. "What is it?"

"Oh, just an idea, one we'll get to right enough. First though, I had one other question I need to be askin' of you."

Dusty squirmed, causing the chair to scrape hard again. This time their Chinese hosts didn't pay them no mind.

"Yeah? What's that?"

"You ready to tell me?" Cat asked. "Tell me who Norma was to you?"

For a moment, Cat watched as those dark shutters closed tight up on his green eyes. Like the light there suddenly got snuffed out or the curtains were pulled tight fast. And too, she thought she'd glimpsed the shadow that'd been hanging off him, the darkness that he'd worn like a second skin at Mrs. Allen's home. She saw the fear creep back in him...

And then, slowly, creep away.

"Yeah," he said. "I guess it doesn't matter so much now."

"I think it matters more than ever."

"Yeah, maybe."

Dusty took a deep breath, causing them bits of floating ash to stir, especially as he blew it right back out.

"She was my sister, Miss Justice. The only one I had left."

CHAPTER THIRTY-FOUR

S oon as the words were out of Dusty's mouth, Cat had this feeling settling 'round her, heavy but not in an uncomfortable kind 'a way. Instead like she got another piece of that puzzle she'd been missing.

And realized, too, that she wasn't surprised.

She easily recalled the protectiveness Dusty had felt towards Norma, especially how he'd acted at the gathering, surrounded by all those men who'd known her or were acquainted with her. Even before Cat had stepped off the train, Dusty had wanted to find the truth about Norma. He'd gone to the one person he could trust and asked for her help—Mrs. Allen. But then not long after sending Cat to Mrs. Allen, something had shifted and a heavy, dark shadow had followed him. It had nearly turned him almost completely from wanting to find what he so desperately needed. But somehow he'd struggled his way back and was sitting here now with Cat, and yet...

He was clearly still struggling with parts of the story he hadn't yet shared.

Cat brushed a stray strand of hair tickling at her cheek, giving them both some moments of silence and quiet.

Letting the pieces keep on falling together, just so.

They were still the only two in the noodle house except for the Chinese themselves. Though from the sounds coming from the kitchen, all them pots banging, sizzling oils reaching a sharp crescendo, they were about gearing up for the dinner rush.

Cat glanced out the window, saw the outside world still just as dark and black as they'd left it, probably colder, too. Still looked the same, but her sense of time definitely told her they'd passed quite a bit of it in here. It had taken that long just to get the real heart of the truth. The very reason why Dusty was so invested in this, putting so much of himself, possibly risking his own life, too, into discovering what had really happened to Norma.

His sister.

And what was it that Madeleine had said? That her and the others, the ones who'd taken Norma in, would pay the price if Cat kept on digging...

Cat let out a breath, slow like.

But Madeleine hadn't just been talking about the girls, whether she'd known it or not.

Another piece of the puzzle starting spinning in her mind, rotating.

She felt the tingle again, right along her spine and down to her belly, like it was tap dancing the whole way, tapping harder and harder as this puzzle piece kept on twirling and twirling, and finally settled down.

Fell into place.

Of course.

The shadow that had suddenly followed Dusty, him asking Mrs. Allen to *not* tell Cat about Norma, especially to not reveal his ties with her... Dusty had been threatened, too. Or maybe not him directly but someone he cared about, and seeing how Norma was dead, meant there was only one other—

Mrs. Allen.

Cat swore softly.

"Why didn't you tell me, Green Eyes?"

"I figured it's no one's business but mine that we were related, and we swore long before coming to Butte to not tell anyone—"

Cat shook her head. "Not that, but I'll tell you now someone else clearly knows 'bout you two. Probably had learned from Norma herself."

"She'd never have told—"

"You'd be surprised what a woman will say when the dream she so desperately wants is close."

"Never."

"Someone knows."

"Well, it ain't her clients. She kept her personal life clear of *them*."

"Even if she was getting close to her dream?" Cat asked. "Of getting out?"

Dusty thought it over a moment, then shook his head. "Certainly not MacDonald or O'Neil. She put up with them, accepted their attention, but she'd never have told the likes of them. Not about me."

Cat took another slow slip of her tea. Again doing her thinking. Letting her mind plick and pluck through this new information. Thinking about what she did know of the two men...

"No," she agreed. "Not them. Someone else, maybe? Someone who really *was* important to her, and somehow they slipped through her fingers? Or maybe I got that wrong and she found herself tied in theirs."

"She was careful," Dusty said again.

Cat thought about herself, her own life... Alice and her husband, Stan.

"You'd be surprised," Cat whispered, "the mistakes we make for our dreams."

Or the hope of a dream.

Or maybe they were both wrong. Maybe someone else entirely had been watching Norma enough, long enough to notice the two together. Maybe similar mannerisms, similar tone or look. Maybe even a similar smile, though she doubted Dusty smiled often. Or at all. Certainly not since Norma's death. But still, it was possible that someone saw a resemblance and put two and two together. Cat probably would have. She tended to notice those little kinds of details. Who's to say she wasn't the only one.

Cat shook her head. It was too easy to get lost in guesses and what ifs.

"Either way," she said, "that's not what I'm talking about. I'm talking about you, and *you* being threatened."

Dusty blinked, as if a bit shocked that she had picked up on what he'd purposefully left out. Probably figured it had flown right on by her without her ever noticing or questioning. But she had.

So now, she waited.

He went pale. Real pale. For a moment she saw his stark white skin underneath that near painting of ash and soot dusting all along his cheeks, his nose, almost like he was a ghost underneath those black spatterings.

Cat watched him close. Watched again how his eyes flicked to the doors.

She didn't bother with swearing quietly this time. This time she swore loudly.

"Damn it to hell, Dusty. What do you think I can do when you won't be goddamn honest with me?"

"I am."

"Bullshit!"

Cat slapped her hands on the table. Her slender tea cup teetered but didn't fall. Their hosts didn't dare glancing up either—they either recognized this was a conversation they wanted no part of, or they were just too darn busy workin' their asses off for the hungry folks about ready to be heading their way. Which Cat was bettin' Dusty knew damn well was gonna be happening soon and *that* would put an end to this little bit of conversation right fast.

"I told you," Cat warned. "I told you I'd leave if you weren't gonna be straight with me."

"I have been."

"Then why the hell haven't you told me it was Mrs. Allen who was being threatened?"

Dusty swallowed.

Again those green eyes of his flicked to the doors, and she really, really wanted to deck the son-of-a-bitch who'd taken this strong kid, surviving on these streets as he'd had been for years most likely, a straight-up shadow soul, and overnight it seemed like, changed him into this. Someone who really was scared of his own shadow—

Because the one person he had left in this world, the one person he cared about, was being threatened. The one person who showed him kindness and warmth and probably the first place in a decade that felt like home. A person who was quite well known in Butte society. Who had a few favors to call in to... keep herself safe, if needed.

Again, there was the tingle and the hard heel-press of its tap dancing was starting to feel a might-bit uncomfortable.

Still, another piece fell into place.

"That's why Mrs. Allen stayed with the police," Cat said. "That's why she didn't come home that night and that's why Officer Blake came by. It wasn't just to check on me. It was to check on the house."

A house he'd easily entered into because neither Mrs. Allen or Chin had locked the door.

They hadn't yet known to.

Damn it.

Dusty worked his bottom lip with his top teeth, an unconscious kind 'a movement probably drummed up from his childhood. One of those small ticks you'd seek comfort in and half the time not even being aware you were doing it.

"He was glad, you know, Officer Blake," Dusty said. "That you were there with Chin, keeping an eye on things."

Blake? A strange person to bring up now in just this way.

"Why's that?" she asked.

Again, Dusty squirmed in his chair, as if maybe he hadn't meant to mention the other officer.

"Dusty." She gave him a hard glare to go along with the warning tone in her voice.

"Look," he said, "it's not my secret to tell, all right? They're just families, is all."

Cat's eyes shuttered. Of course.

Yet another damn piece of the puzzle she'd missed—but no, she wasn't gonna shame or guilt herself for missing it. She'd seen the details, the clues, she just hadn't known how they all pieced together because all the players had been working real, real hard on keeping their pasts a secret.

Something she knew herself damn well, too.

But Blake had known Chin was a light sleeper. He'd known all about that front door, too, knew just how to close it, in just a certain way, to keep the loud slam from announcing he'd entered.

Cat sighed. "Please tell me he's not her son."

Dusty blinked. Slow like, as if in shock. "Oh, no. Not her son. Just her nephew."

Oh, great. This just kept getting better and better.

And considering this was a boarding house and most were usually run by the family or relatives, chances were high that Blake had not only worked there as a lad, but he'd lived there, too.

She groaned, letting out the sound before she could stop it. What a hell of mess this was, including her own very clear annoyance at the man. After all, *he'd* been judging *her* when his very aunt had not only been in the business, but had in fact done quite well—something he'd probably grown up living with his whole life and even now carried that resentment with him.

Except he'd gone to the house.

He'd checked on the house and on Cat.

"Officer Blake ain't important now." Or ever. "But Dusty, I swear, you *will* be telling me all you know about this threat, about who's doing it—"

Dusty's hands flew up in defense. "I don't know, I swear. I just got a note is all, delivered by another newsboy who knows me well. And he was sportin' two black eyes and a busted out nose as part of the warning."

Christ.

But Dusty wasn't done yet, though. "I admit, I was taken aback. It happened quick, too. Not long after I sent you to Mrs. Allen's, before I'd even a chance to talk with her."

Cat thought back to the day, just a few days ago... dear lord it felt like a lifetime. She remembered the way the ghost of Alice had been following right beside her, cold and unyielding, her eyes that'd stared at Cat like they'd never know an ounce of peace again... and then Cat had spoken with Dusty. Suddenly, this idea she'd had of coming to Butte, working some change for those who had nothing, this dream... well, it'd started to take shape. Unfold. Like it *could* be a real thing. And before she'd a chance to ask Dusty about the newspaper article, he was gone.

But she and Dusty had talked.

Sure, it'd been cryptic, but if a person knew who Dusty was, knew the kid had been asking questions... apparently the *wrong* kind of questions... It would be real easy to figure out what was being said.

Which, clearly, someone had.

They'd overheard that conversation and must have quickly followed up at Mrs. Allen's. Real quick cause Fat Jack certainly made those turns through town at a breakneck pace. But then, the shadow world could and did move that fast. When there was a need. And clearly, someone may have overheard her conversation with Mrs. Allen... though... it could have been over tea, maybe even while they'd been sitting at that window. Or maybe it was the front through the front door. Cat couldn't remember if it'd been closed all the way; she didn't remember that heavy thud. But then she'd just assumed Chin had done his job in closing the door proper.

But it was clear someone *had* overheard the conversation and they'd then taken measures to keep this very conversation right here from happening.

The real truth of who Norma was.

Which meant someone right from the beginning, before Cat had even stepped foot off that whistling, horn-blowing train, had been watching the kid.

Why?

Because he'd been asking those questions? Because he wasn't willing to believe the only story being told about his sister's death, the very one wrote up in the paper?

No police investigation. No successful inquiries from him or Mrs. Allen. No rumors.

And what would happen now that she and Dusty finally cleared the air?

Nothing good.

Cat felt the tingle again, but this time instead of its hard, tap dancing number, it was a cold chill. The kind 'a chill that slipped through your clothes, past your skin, and lingered there right in your soul. It was a cold that had nothing to do with the winter weather outside or the snow-touched wind that kept on rolling down those nearby mountains.

One thing was for sure, whoever had wanted to keep her and Dusty from talking, that person or persons would definitely be hearing about this meeting.

And soon.

She hoped like hell that Madeleine had been wrong, wrong about the other girls paying the price when Cat kept on digging. Because she'd no doubt that she would, and unlike Mrs. Allen, who was safe in the custody of the police, and her nephew, those girls didn't have the law.

All they had was Cat.

CHAPTER THIRTY-FIVE

T ime to get going."

Cat pushed away from their table at the noodle house. Her chair scraped on that ash and dirt stained floor and Dusty followed her. He was stuffing his hands into those hole-strewn gloves of his while she placed her hat back on, adjusting it just so to achieve the greatest protection for her ears from that never-ending cold.

Not that it'd do a whole heap of good, not with evening quickly approaching and the temperatures dropping like mad.

They might not be able to see the sun, but apparently the earth still felt her presence cause there was a definite difference when it was day and when it was night, when the sun was hidden behind those black clouds and when she was done and sleeping for the day.

Definite difference. The kind of sudden cold that caused you to suck in a breath, hard and sharp and shrill, right through your teeth.

Cat heard the whistles sounding off up and down the hill. The mines giving off their shrill warning that miners were about to be descending down, either heading home or other such places to wet their thirsts and fill their bellies. Or even just quench other forms of appetites.

Truth was they needed to be going if she was gonna catch her next appointment. Otherwise, they'd have to wait another day.

If the big parlor houses kept any kind of regular schedule, certainly like the few in Miles City had, it meant the girls there were just settling down to a light meal before their evenings started. Maybe a few even getting painted up or having their hair done or their maids pulling on them dresses and tightening those corsets closed.

It was a small window of time, but hopefully enough of one.

There came that feeling again, of hope.

Still, Cat knew waiting wasn't a good idea. Certainly with the sense that home, which she was clearly starting to think of Mrs. Allen's place as home, wasn't safe anymore.

Cat paid the bill, leaving a hefty tip for silence and discretion. She walked outside, sucking in a breath through her teeth because of that sudden and sharp bite of cold, especially after the kitchen-heated noodle house. She took two steps, boots smacking hard on the uneven boardwalk, almost stepping into a hole from some missing plank, only to 'bout run over none other than a man she knew.

A face she'd spoken with at great length at Mrs. Allen's gathering. A person who'd been openly fond of Norma and her gleaming smile, who even after her fall and subsequent passing, still thought kindly of her.

Mr. Rippi.

Cat sensed more than saw the man. Just this slight stir of air, like the space she was walking into was no longer open but filled. That was all.

She glanced up, tearing her gaze away from the unsteady board-walk, and it seemed like the man appeared out of nowhere. His thin, shadow-like body stepping right out of them black, smoking clouds. Dark overalls, dark coat, grease stain down the length of chin like he'd just come up some chute and didn't bother washing or cleaning himself before heading down the hill and to home or wherever else he was going.

Which clearly was the space that Cat herself was heading to.

Cat stopped just in time. Her hands flying up to keep from colliding, gently pressing into the other man's arms—hard and lean, despite his thin nature. Which made sense, working down in the mines and under all that rock. A profession that called for brute strength and lots of it. Truthfully, she didn't know about a miner's life other than it was hard and wore a person down until they hadn't much left but threadbare shreds of their soul hanging on like tattered rags.

All those thoughts, all those impressions and ideas, all that happened in an instant.

Mr. Rippi in turn, as if sensing her as well, somehow caught Cat by the arms, juggling his lunch pail as he was, and steadied her. Her smaller, slighter frame must have been quite obvious even compared to his, though she was no small and delicate woman by a long shot. And yet it must have been this reason, this touch alone, or maybe some similar sense, for he instantly seemed to realize she was a woman.

And one he'd nearly run over.

He apologized again and again in his native Finnish language. At least, she assumed it was an apology. His hands roamed up once and then down her arms, as if to assure himself that she was indeed all right.

Then he finally got a good look at her face or realized the woman in front of him was not wearing yards and yards of thick, heavy cloth but blue jeans. His eyes about lit up and out of his face when he realized who she was.

"Cowboy Cat! By the grace, what a treasure and joy it is running to you here."

He was still smiling and holding onto her.

Cat smiled warmly back at him, instantly falling back into the gracious hostess she'd played at the gathering, kind and attentive, like she remembered him quite well. Which she did. But it was all in the look itself. The kind of a look that made the man, himself, realize that all this attention and focus was on him and him alone. And she did it all in a single smile, as well as slipping free of him.

The movement was one of grace, yes, but also one that didn't draw attention to the fact that she was, in fact, moving away. Putting space between them, switching to a more defensible position. As she did, she noticed the grease stains his fingers had left on her coat, then paid it little mind, focusing instead on keeping Dusty behind her. It was a purposeful act, especially since the man's attention was on her and only her, *not* the boy who could either step in to offer aid or run for help if needed. Now, if she'd been escorted by another, certainly one of Blake's stature, Rippi would have instantly noticed him. Dusty, on the other hand, was ignored.

And which, true to form, Mr. Rippi noticed none of this.

"Why, Mr. Rippi," she said. "Fancy running into you here. Have you just gotten off shift? Are you on your way home?"

"I have, indeed, Miss Cat. On my way home fer the evenin'. I like stopping by this here shop, filling my belly with their great noodles. Nothin' like me mother made, of course, nothing like from the home country, but then that's part of life, yes?"

"I suppose so."

He gestured to the door she and Dusty had just left. "Can I tempt you in for a bite? I love to share your company, yes? Perhaps even share a tale or two of Norma with you?"

Cat shook her head. "Sadly, I've just finished eating. But I'm comforted to know I chose a place that has such high praise from you."

He frowned at first at her dismissal, but then he seemed to rally behind the good cheer she remembered from the gathering.

"I hope it met with your approval."

"It did."

"Norma, she liked eatin' here, too, yes. When she moved from the big house to here."

Mr. Rippi grinned at her. His grin was the same as before, dark as the air outside, except for that one shiny gold tooth. It practically glinted at her, like a trick of the light, maybe.

"Is that right? I'll keep it in mind."

She nodded again at him, taking another step back as if to continue on her way, when he saw Dusty behind her, standing so close to the shadows he about looked like one again.

It was a look that both relieved her and saddened her.

"Ah!" Rippi's eyes widened. "I recognize you, yes? From the gathering? Yes, yes. Young lad that was with you, Miss Cat. You are good friends, then?"

"Just here on business, Mr. Rippi," she answered. "The lad has been showing me around town."

"But, *these* parts Miss Cat? Surely they're not where a lady like you should be seen."

Cat's eyebrows raised. "I was thinking my attire would probably be more acceptable here than uptown."

Rippi's smile waivered, but only a bit. Just enough that the gold got another snickering glint at her. "Yes, well, quite right I guess. Just don't be out wandering late, though I see you've armed yourself again. Good. Never too careful. Never know who's stumbling home and at all hours, too. Certainly no place for a lady, even one as familiar with a gun as you are, Miss Cat."

Rippi lingered a moment more, as if wanting to ask her something, maybe about Norma, maybe about herself, but Cat easily ended the conversation before it had a chance to strike up again. She bid him good evening, wishing him well, then continued on. This time leaving the boardwalk all together. Something told her dodging the hacks and wagons and carriages, and all the necessary droppings that came with them, was a better choice at the moment.

Still, the tingling from earlier, from her and Dusty's conversation about Norma, about them being related, all of it stayed with her. It was a cold kind 'a feeling, one that this snow-touched wind had nothing on. A sense that more than just eyes were following them, watching every step they took. Never once wavering. Never once willing to simply... let go. And how yet another person, in their own way, had warned Cat to take care.

Now, maybe she was putting her own spin on things, seeing what she wanted to see, but she didn't think so. Not after what had happened to Norma. Not after the belief she'd seen staring straight back at her from Madeleine's eyes, lying down on that bed as she'd been, believing her and the others would be next. Not to mention Mrs. Allen herself, who was hiding out with her nephew, a police officer.

Cat's right hand dropped down to her hip. She felt the cool metal of her revolver even with her glove on. Or maybe not, maybe it was all just in her head.

But again, she didn't think so.

She knew it as well as she knew every wrinkle and scar on her hands. Knew when it wasn't working right, when the chambers needed extra cleaning, extra oil. Even knew when the aim was a tad off target. Had to. It 's how one kept living in this shadow life.

Just like she was feeling the tightening in her shoulders. A tension that raced on up her neck and right to her temples.

She was glad for the weapon, even gladder that she'd found Dusty—well, he'd found her—before the other party did. Yes, definitely safer this way.

Because someone very soon indeed would be hearing about her and Dusty. About them being together and the conversation they'd shared, a long one, too, at the noodle house.

Which meant they needed to reach Grace's Gardens and fast.

CHAPTER THIRTY-SIX

Thankfully, Dusty knew all about fast.

Knew all about the underground tunnels that lived and breathed right underneath Galena Street and her neighboring counterparts makin' up the Red Light.

Cramped and dusty and dark, and smelling the kind 'a foul that old ladies would make the sign of the cross at while their younger counterparts would just faint-dead away because ladies were no longer made of the stern stuff one needed to survive on a homestead or riding range. That, or they just couldn't much breathe, what with them bone-ribbing corsets stealing all that God-giving, life-breathing air that allowed for those sterner kind 'a ladies.

Not that her ma would approve.

Of stern ladies, that was.

Nor of Cat, come to think of it. Certainly if she could see her youngest daughter now.

Which, her ma couldn't... unless you believed in God-the-almighty and heaven and hell. Which, as Cat found herself ducking into yet another narrow passage, the thick, black slime smearing onto her coat and jeans, easily obscuring the grease stain provided by Mr.

Rippi earlier, she rightly decided that there was no way God or heaven could exist. No great force, man or woman or being, not in their great wisdom or oh-so loving care, would ever create a place like this.

Hell, on the other hand, Cat was quite sure it existed.

She was, after all, walking through it.

She'd been right earlier, walking down Galena Street, when she'd practically felt the gossip and news of her arrival traveling like wildfire through the Red Light... and how it had traveled, right underneath her feet. It was also no surprise really that Dusty had known exactly where to go. In fact, soon as she'd mentioned it, he led her straight away to the nearest entrance.

One that also happened to behind the very noodle house they'd eaten at. After making sure no one was looking their way best as they could tell, especially the way those thick, smoky clouds started rolling in again, obscuring just about everything but the whole five feet in front of you, they'd shifted aside a manhole cover and got to climbing. Truly, the ladder, not much more than a coiled rope with the ends twisted together in a few spots, led straight down into these black depths that Cat was sure had only existed in her worst nightmares.

Dusty had a few candles on him but promised they wouldn't be needed. Which proved true enough. About right when you hit that edge of light, where the fading yellow would've been swallowed by darkness, a darkness so black and complete it looked like hell really *was* about to swallow you whole—just at that point when you were sure the darkness was thinkin' about eating you, there was another faint glow of light. Not a lot, but enough to get you through that gap, through the edge of the knife when you really were feeling fearful of the dark.

Hanging overhead, low enough to clock you right in the forehead if you were Cat's size—which did happen once or twice with the ones that weren't working no more—were light bulbs. Each of them naked and yet somehow swinging in that still air, as if the darkness alone wasn't scary enough. Most worked either by gas or electricity or a combination of the two, and the ones that didn't... well, she found those right quick. Until she learned to duck a bit better.

Still, it was a wonder those lights did their job. Especially down here.

In hell.

And it wasn't like she and Dusty had much of choice, either. The only way to get into Grace's Gardens without being shown the door immediately upon arrival was coming in from underneath. In the tunnels. The one place where the Madam Grace wouldn't expecting be them.

Or anyone, really.

Least, not for a few hours.

Including the gentleman who usually guarded such entrances, making sure only the... right kind of men were allowed entrance.

"Right now, though," Dusty had said, "runners like me will use 'em. That's why no one guards them. Only people who use them are the ones that have business there."

Like him, she was guessing. No point asking either how he knew. Norma had been his sister, one he clearly still cared about, and he'd have made it a point to gain the house's trust. Gain the trust, then gain access to his sister for a few quiet, stolen moments. And if that didn't work out, hell, at least they'd be able to see each other, even if only from across the room.

Sometimes that's all one needed.

She could only imagine what he must be thinking and feeling now, going back to that house and knowing his sister would never be there, never standing across the halls, probably giving him his own special kind of smile.

Sibling love.

Cat's chest tightened, and for a moment skipped a few breaths. She let it, too. Let herself feel the sorrow like it was just as much a part of her as her hand or her gun, then she regained control and got back to business, ducking just in time to avoid her forehead getting smacked with yet another dead light bulb.

"And what about the ladies who work in the Gardens?" Cat asked. "Any rivals I should know about? Friends who might be willing to talk?"

"Last I heard, it was an okay kind 'a acceptance. Norma never talked a whole lot about her life there or the girls. But yeah, she said they all got along well enough. Sure, there might be some disagreements about the johns and some unkind words exchanged—in private, of course, but's all I've ever heard... Actually, come to think of it..."

Dusty pulled his cap off his head, causing the dark hair there to spring up in all kinds of directions. He rubbed his hair, as if thinking hard, then put the cap back on.

"Actually, no. I haven't heard much about the Gardens at all. Not since Norma, that is."

Curious, indeed.

She nodded towards the hand-carved walls of the tunnels. "What about the rest? The shadow world? You heard anything recent about that?"

Dusty shrugged. "Plenty of talk. Plenty of people moving in, some taking over more, others leaving. It's the usual. More so now, too, because of the copper kings going to war, as it were. Lots of extra money flooding into the place."

Just not to the girls doing the actual work.

Still, something Madeleine had said tickled at Cat's thoughts. The sudden pulling back of water moments before a giant tidal wave crashed down around you.

"You hear anything," she asked, "anything at all about some kind of change?"

"There's *always* change, Miss Cat. You know that."

Fair enough.

Still though, the thought nagged at her...

All the while, they kept moving on through the dark tunnels, following one turn, only to have a naked light bulb just about appear right in front of her face.

Cat ducked, right quick. Barely missed a trip to the doctor herself for some unpleasant stitches.

Next time she'd remember to bring some of those candles the miners likened to use when all the other lights went out.

"You think they'd talk with me?" Cat asked. "The girls?"

Dusty rubbed at his chin. "Maybe. Maybe if we can get to Abigail. She might. And if she'd talk with anyone, it'd be you, Miss Cat."

Which meant it was worth the risk. And the trip.

Which in of itself was quite the education.

There *was* quite the extensive underground underneath all those streets, parlor houses, and cribs. How it seemed that every manhole could potentially lead one down into a dark and dank system where the lowest of the low, those who were barely human anymore, lived.

'Least, if you could call such an existence living.

Because the tunnels didn't just take a person from one parlor house to the next, one brothel to the next. They, in fact, had multiple purposes, depending, of course, on who you were. And where you entered from.

Now there were certain kids of people who used the tunnels, make no mistake. Those who didn't want to be seen by the outside world in any way, shape, or form. They'd rather press their delicate, white handkerchiefs to their mouths, hold their noses, and rush through the tunnels as fast as they could. Anything at all to avoid being seen by someone who might take it upon themselves to ruin their reputation.

In fact, this was most likely how Seamus O'Neil had gotten into the Lucky Horseshoe without being seen, and then again when he disappeared. Either he knew, or someone else did, of the entrance in to and out of that place, and the owner... well, he just didn't see fit to reveal those kind 'a details to Cat. But certainly *that* wasn't the kind of establishment a man of O'Neil's stature would dare be seen at.

But again, the tunnels were for many people. Rich ones, runners like Dusty had been, and... well, the others.

Like this particular stretch here from the noodle house on Galena Street to Mercury where both Grace's Gardens and the Dumas resided in their great brick brilliance, two-stories high to the rest of the world. These tunnels, however, were used for more than just a passageway, more than just a way to get a person from one side of the street to the next.

These particular ones were occupied.

Carved straight out of the rock, like they'd been done so by a pick or axes wielded by the Mr. Rippis of the world, were more cribs. If you could call the carved-out hollows cribs. If Cat had thought Madeleine's home caused a searching ache, one she felt right to her soul, that was nothing compared to this.

She took only one glance, just one, and it was enough. Enough to make her want to pound her hands bloody into the harsh rock surrounding them and cry her eyes right out. There were no doors along these carved-out... rooms. Just an opening. And a bed. Maybe a lantern. And the creatures who existed in them?

Cat closed her eyes at the thought, the memory, even now still burning inside her. But she *had* looked. She owed it to those girls, to acknowledge their existence even if there was nothing she could do, even if they no longer looked like girls.

Or even human.

Cat didn't bother wiping away the few tears that fell. Her gloves were covered in the disgusting sludge and it'd only smear along her face, which was not the right kind of look she'd need to convince the flower Abigail living in the Gardens to help her out. So, she let the tears dry where they fell, though it felt more like freezing than drying. The air was so cold it puffed out white in front of her—when there was enough light to even see clearly, that was.

The journey was so low and cramped she'd shoved her hat as far down as she could and the thing still kept getting caught in outcroppings of rock, like the shaper hadn't bothered to finish one wall before going onto the next. At least the wide brim gave her some amount of warning before she walked right into one.

Dusty only looked back at Cat once. His green eyes, they cut right through that darkness and held there, steady on hers for a moment, then another. She waited, meeting his gaze, not knowing what he was seeing in her and hoping it'd be enough. It was like he needed reassurance... that she was seeing the horror here, seeing it and feeling it.

Maybe they both needed it.

Cat reached out, touched his arm, squeezing it once, then urged him on.

"We can't do nothing for them," she whispered.

She meant it, but she still felt the horror, like it was marking itself on her soul. And she had no doubt that it was.

Even though it felt like a lifetime, it wasn't long at all before Dusty made another turn, coming up to another tunnel and taking the left there—how he even knew which way to go was a small miracle, really. He kept making the turns, clearly comfortable, clearly capable and not at all lost—like she'd have been. As far as she could see even with her instincts, even with her strange gift of mapping out a place, she saw nothing. No markers, no indicators about which ladder led up to which building, which turn here brought you to which house. Or just led you deeper into the city.

Yet somehow, she knew they were getting closer to Grace's Gardens...

And they must have because before long it got a bit lighter. Not like as in sun or windows, but more light bulbs. They hung from the ceiling, swinging and creaking in that air that wasn't moving, and they were closer together too, in closer intervals. More were actually working as well. Also, the cribs were gone, and while the tunnels here were a slight bit wider and a slight bit... well, cleaner wasn't the word, but it certainly didn't give the feeling that your soul was now covered in the same grime that covered the walls.

Dusty didn't bother waving at her to follow. He just expected that she would, and together they finally reached some ladder and climbed up. This one was newer and didn't contain near the amount of dirt and grease as the first, but it was still clearly used. The threading was smooth, not coarse or harsh, and as Cat pushed up that final leg, she found herself in the underbelly of Grace's Gardens.

She got to her feet and immediately rested a hand on her gun. Making sure it was there, needing its reassuring presence. In some ways, deep down she'd been expecting what she saw in those tunnels and the poor creatures who somehow still existed down there. But the Gardens?

All she'd heard were tales of dazzling light and glitz and jewels, and no one had made mention otherwise. And yet, it was silly that she *hadn't* realized this place, this underbelly, existed.

After all, it was just good business to have their own version of the cribs. A place to toss the ladies who'd gone so far into debt and who'd lost their shine, no longer able (or willing) to lure in those rich gentleman of the world. They'd need a place to go, and well, there was space to earn a few more coins.

The hall itself was narrow, if you'd dare call it a hall to start with. Regardless, the narrow stretch of room was surrounded on either side by cribs. Narrow and also one room, just like Madeleine's had been. The light here was a bare shade brighter than the light down in those tunnels, and the air was touched with the same kind 'a chill that no amount of sun or heat could ever warm. It was the cold touch of despair, one that Cat had felt herself breathing in down in those tunnels without ever realizing what it was.

Here, though, here it was more obvious.

How could it not be when up above another world existed? She could hear it, taste it. A few delicate notes of a piano drifted down from the ceiling above, as if slipping in between those hastily-placed rafters, taunting you with their sweetness, their touch of civility and upper gentry. The first continued tapping out a few chords, as if slowly waking up their fingers to play and play through the whole night long...

Cat swallowed.

She didn't want to look in those cribs, and didn't consider herself a lesser woman for not wanting to. There was just only so much despair a soul could take before wanting to curl up in a little ball.

And yet, that's why she was here. Because her soul *couldn't* take any more, couldn't keep on breathing and living without acting, without being different, without... being herself.

Her true.

So, she turned and she did look.

And felt tears filling her eyes once again because again, those girls there were her. Or they could have been. They were trapped, and she'd found herself another way, another path. They, like Madeleine, had nothing and no one and nowhere else to go but continue on spiraling down.

And yes, she could see each of them clear enough. Each one of these cribs had a door which was blessedly shut, giving the girls an illusion of privacy. And it was an illusion. Because right next to the door was a glass-paned window.

A tear slipped down her cheek.

Dusty saw, but he said nothing.

Windows were there so clients could wander up and down the hall, taking their time, studying and sampling the wares before deciding which one suited their tastes more. And there were ladies in each and every room. They were lying on their beds and not a one was stirring. They were just... dark shapes who couldn't find the energy or the heart to move. It was approaching time to begin their evening and yet they were there, lying down. Perhaps down here in the true heart of the Gardens, life didn't work the same or move the same as it did upstairs. The ladies didn't need to get pampered or strung into their dresses or iron their hair.

Here, they just rolled up out of bed and got to work.

Another tear fell.

Again, she didn't wipe it away.

"I didn't know this place existed."

Cat kept her voice low, hushed. She didn't want to disturb these ladies in what little sleep and peace and comfort they found here in the silence, in the cold. A cold she felt straight to her soul.

"This," Dusty said, "this is where Norma *should* have gone. It's where all the cast-offs of the Gardens go. At first, anyway, until they can't even meet those standards."

His fists clenched at his sides.

"But they didn't even send Norma here. Don't you see, Miss Cat? They didn't even send her out to Galena Street first."

Cat blinked, unsure exactly what he was talking about. "But she *did* have a room on Galena. Madeleine said as much."

"Yeah, but not a first, and only cause of Madeleine, after I... after I asked. I called in favors, many as I could, and yeah, we got her a place on Galena. Wouldn't have mattered much if those girls hadn't helped, but they did. But that's not my point. At first, they sent her to the tunnels. That's where I found her."

His voice broke. Now it was his turn to let a tear slip, and then another.

"I found her there, Cat. *My* sister. She was down there and I found her."

CHAPTER THIRTY-SEVEN

And now she was dead.

Which living in the tunnels or lying cold in the ground somewhere in some small, scrunched-up pine box, didn't matter. They pretty much equaled the same thing.

Except Dusty *had* gotten her out, had done everything in his power, and others had as well. Others who had barely more than Norma, yet helped anyway.

Didn't have to, but they did.

Because it'd been the right thing to do.

The women living down here on these creaking cots and with lighting so dim you could barely see down to the edge of that hall, they had nothing but each other. They didn't have justice, they couldn't go after the ones who did this to them, the ones who kept pushing them lower to the ground all the while denying them that kind and helping hand to pull them up and out of the muck, out of the darkness.

But they could help. They could offer anything they had to give, even when they had nothing left.

At least they weren't alone.

And neither was Norma. Much as she had tried to distance herself, to shove away all those who wanted to be close with her, who cared what happened or who just wanted to live a smidgeon more in the light, in the end she wasn't alone.

And she hadn't died alone either.

Cat closed her eyes, breathing in all the cold air, so filled with despair it could snuff a person's light right out if they weren't careful.

Norma.... hadn't died alone. There *had* been a doctor there, and something in the writer's words, the person who wrote the article, made it seem... like maybe... he'd known her. Or known enough to believe her death was caused by some other means than what the police had ruled in their report.

Or what Officer White had ruled.

Cat opened her eyes, again taking in this underbelly of the gardens and the delicate cords being played on the piano above them. She could almost see the beautiful glow of light slipping in between those rafters, like gold dust and notes floating in that very light. At least until it touched the dim darkness of this place. The despair that hung in the air, that clung to you and refused to let go.

Norma hadn't been sent here. And she would have been, unless she'd made some serious transgression with Madam Grace or one of those very important clients. If what Dusty'd said was true, and oh yes, she believed him, then someone really and truly had been trying to take Norma out without actually killing her.

They'd expected... well, nature, to take its natural course.

That's what happened down in the tunnels.

But then Dusty had found her. Maybe by some off chance or lucky roll of the dice. Or maybe someone had given him enough hints that's where she was without ever realizing he'd been steered in this direction. This might be one piece of the mystery she never got to solving, whether her leaving the tunnels had been a lucky chance or on purpose.

Still, it wasn't hard to assume that for a woman like Norma, one who appeared as golden as those dust bits floating in the air, whoever had demanded her banishment would never have expected her to last long. Maybe she wouldn't have. Or maybe she would have. Norma was, no question, a resilient woman. Smart and intelligent. She'd have found a way out of those tunnels to at least scrape a living up at the surface. She had a way with people, including working her way right into the hearts of those ladies like Madeleine. Ladies who'd wanted kindness and a smile, and Norma had used every bit of it, every bit of herself and what she had left to her advantage. And with no luggage, no nothing to her name except that smile...

It was a wonder she'd survived as long as she had.

But then, she *was* a resilient woman, and one with friends. Whoever had sent her sprawling to finish out her life in the tunnels clearly hadn't known her well. Or if they had, they'd underestimated her.

If it were a man, Cat had no doubt that was the case.

But even so, even with everything Norma had gained for herself —finding new homes and friends, even a small amount of protection for herself—despair *had* eventually found Norma. Everything Cat had learned at the Lucky Horseshoe said as much.

Norma had gotten desperate. She couldn't handle the life anymore, so she'd reached out to her old one. Used whatever information she had to claw her way out—

And whoever had her banished from the lovely Gardens had clearly had enough. Probably sent O'Neil to tell her so. Then they'd finished the job. Finished whatever threat Norma had represented.

And yet... something was missing.

Cat couldn't put her finger on what or how or even what direction she should be looking in. Just knew that it was there. The kind 'a feeling that nagged you, like when you just discovered a newly chipped tooth. And the more she thought, picking through what she knew, examining the details with a fine focus, it still kept slipping away. Like the harder she concentrated, the more fuzzy the whole thing became.

Cat let out a breath.

There was no point wasting any more time. She wasn't about to learn the answers standing here in the cold and despair. She might as well get a glimpse of what Norma's life had been like before the streets and why she was willing to risk her very life to get it back.

"Come on, Dusty."

She gently touched his arm, pulling his coat as if to pull him back to the present, as if he too was seeing ghosts.

"Let's go speak with this Abigail."

Dusty nodded once, then led the way. There was a narrow staircase leading out of the hell hole, creaking and dust floated down with every step of her boots, regardless of how light she tried stepping. He paused at the top, at the space between one world and the next where light flowed on down and the piano notes, too, grew in a tone and cadence, the kind of loudness that vibrated in the air as if those notes, and they alone, owned it.

He checked left and right, holding his hand up indicating she should wait.

Cat did.

Heard nothing, no nearby shuffling of feet, the telltale creak of a wooden board warning of another's approach. Nothing but... soft voices drifting among the house. Female voices clearly, but quiet. Almost as if they, too, weren't ready to break the calmness of the house, reluctant to be the one to get the ball rolling, to ring that bell signaling the start of another evening, another many hours and hours of entertainment and captivation.

The walls were white and well cleaned, as if the ash and smoke that lived outside in the air didn't dare come in here. Or when they did, were immediately scrubbed clean until they gleamed in the golden light of those light bulbs. The walls themselves were even adorned with some special-like styles, carved right there into the plaster itself, like a master artist had been right alongside those builders or whoever was responsible for putting up the wall, and he went and made all these shapes and angles and designs. And they were beautiful, too. The kind of adornment Cat would have expected to see on the really big and fancy houses on Mrs. Allen's street. Certainly in those grand mansions where the copper kings lived, like Daly or Clark.

All of which were a pretty sharp contrast to the grime and darkness living under their feet.

No one ventured down the hall.

Cat assumed the hall broke off into a handful of individual rooms for the girls, while most of the space here was for the ballroom and dining room. She guessed, if word on the street was to believed about the Gardens, that in fact the room partitioned depending on demand, opening and closing, changing from a small, intimate parlor into a grand ballroom which the likes of those copper kings themselves attended. Probably, too, where that great piano now sat, heavy and fat, as it played those notes.

There were also telltale sounds coming from the nearby kitchen, conveniently located in the back of the building well away from the grand entrance and the twinkling chandelier she could just barely catch glimpses of from where she crouched. Pots and other heavy metal pans were being moved and banged about a bit, as if the meal for the evening was well on its way.

"The cook is preparing the meal," he whispered.

Which meant the girls would be coming out soon enough. She and Dusty needed to be long gone before that happened.

"Let's go," she said.

Cat followed right at his heels, stepping only where Dusty stepped, making sure the heels of her own boots didn't give them away on that finely polished wood floor.

They didn't.

Nor did they see anyone either.

They followed a new set of stairs and made their way up to this second story, and these stairs... oh, were they a real work of beauty. A white and black marble kind that seemed to curl up to that second level, slow and languishing with each step. And even there in the ceiling up above was a kind of crystal skylight, ready to capture and hold and dazzle whatever sunlight dared peaked through all that smoke and darkness. And even though it was black as any night Cat had ever seen, it was still breathtaking. She could almost imagine Norma leaving her room, the golden sunlight falling about her shoulders, glinting off her hair.

It was the perfect backdrop to capture the hearts and souls of some of the wealthiest men living in Butte.

Because right here, no doubt, was where the real beauties lived. The true rare and beautiful flowers in the gardens, including Norma with her smile, the legend of her kindness that still lived and thrived in this desolate city...

Right alongside Madam Grace, herself.

Oh, yes, the madam would live right up here as well, keeping a careful, watchful eye on her most promising flowers.

Which Dusty's manners confirmed.

He was keeping a real sharp eye out and his gaze kept flicking back to one spot in particular. He'd pause after a few steps, whole body going still, and he'd stare right there, right at that spot in front of this beautifully curling brass railing. A spot that was simply perfect to stand at, to look down and gaze cold and calculating, taking in all of her domain.

And behind this spot was another room and this delicately scripted word *One* written across it.

There was no window here, of course. Windows were only to peer in at the girls on display and not for the one woman who owned them all.

Madam Grace's room and no doubt the place where Madam Grace stood, gazing over all, seeing everything, missing nothing. She would have a perfect view, making sure all her ladies were playing their parts and playing them well. The madam would be able to see more than just the few rooms up, too... two, three... no four, in total. She could also see the ones below. The ones where Cat had heard the soft voices coming from, hushed as if they didn't dare draw the gaze of that stern eye who usually stood there.

Truly a perfect view.

A perfect way to ensure all was moving according to the way it should.

The thought alone made Cat's stomach tighten.

But then, each of them really did have their place in this world and the madams, as cruel as they sometimes could be, were needed. Necessary, just as the clients who came through those heavy, oak-carved doors upfront. Or crawled up those rope ladders from down below. The madams were the ones with the shrewd minds, shrewd and sharp enough to not only raise themselves from the status of a regular old working girl, but had also found a way to control it, to profit from it.

Even if it was at the expense of other girls.

Of course, that was all depending if the madams themselves managed to survive the traps and pitfalls, the addicting pleasures one needed to ease the heart and mind while living so far down in the darkness. The color and gleam of money and coins didn't change the color of darkness. Couldn't. Alcohol, gambling, all of it was fair game, all of it a noose waiting to tighten on the unsuspecting madam who thought herself above her girls.

And, as Cat was suspecting, holding the title of madam was most likely a role Mrs. Allen had played once upon a time. The thought niggled at Cat, and she wondered in the back of her mind if that was why Blake was so disdainful of this profession, of the very house he'd more than likely grown up in.

Cat gently pushed the thought aside. It wasn't her concern or her business.

Regardless, Mrs. Allen had gotten herself out of the life fully and completely, with the one exception of holding a soft heart for those still in it—or a heavy one, depending on the way you looked at it. Madam Grace, however, was another story altogether, and how exactly she'd played a hand in Norma's eventual death.

Perhaps Cat would even find answers. Course, here's hoping that such questioning didn't draw the attention of the madam herself.

Dusty led Cat upstairs, slow and quiet like, moving in a way that told her he really did know the inner workings of this place. She stepped where he stepped, paused where he paused. If there was a squeaky board on that upper floor, they didn't step on it. If Madam Grace knew how well Dusty seemed to know this place, she'd probably be quite frightened.

As she should be.

Cat paused a moment, risking a glance at the door labeled *One*. She almost wished there'd been a window, if just so she could see if Madam Grace was about to take her place or if she were ready to head on down for a last meal before the evening's... festivities.

She heard nothing and saw nothing from Madam Grace's door, but from the one nearest to her came the unmistakable sound of soft shoes, like slippers, walking over an even softer carpet. The creaking of a small, wooden door opening, like to a closet or a chest, then the rustle of silk as a dress was taken out, examined, then shoved aside as if deemed unworthy.

She could picture Norma doing this every evening, looking over her fancy dresses with a critical, practiced eye, knowing that each evening was as vital to the next, and nothing ever taken for granted.

The risk was simply too great.

Dusty tugged on Cat's coat again, bringing her back to the present, and they kept moving.

They passed by one window with a girl inside.

The girl who'd been sorting through her wardrobe, which was nearly as tall as Cat. Cat didn't pause long, just long enough to discern that the girl wasn't looking right at them nor into her mirror, which would have given her a clear view of the two sneaking where they shouldn't be. Cat glimpsed cascading, long red hair falling over pale, narrow shoulders. A corset, already bound and tightened.

Shit.

They must be here a lot later than she'd first thought. Or maybe the ladies here prepared themselves earlier than other parlor houses she'd known.

Dusty seemed to sense her concern because he moved again, shoes still quiet but at a faster pace, pausing long enough to make sure the coast was clear. He stopped in front of a door with the single number *Two* written in delicate script above it. He reached out to open it, then froze.

As he should.

For just at that moment, there was another sound.

It wasn't the quiet cadence of female voices that slowly drifted up from the floor below them. It wasn't the piano, either, though it was still playing completely unaware of anyone but itself, as if in its own world, practicing and working out the kinks before the evening's performance.

The sound they heard was another.

And unmistakable.

It was a lock being turned.

Madam's Grace's room.

The very room right beside them.

CHAPTER THIRTY-EIGHT

The sound was unmistakable. One she and Dusty both recognized instantly. The not-so-quiet knob twisting as if there were older working mechanisms inside and it was taking a bit longer to get going, to get moving and turning. And which, once the knob was turned and the door actually opened, it would reveal the whole upper balcony with that twisting brass railing. Also the individual exiting would easily peer down at the girls in the rooms below. Girls who were stirring and dressing and brushing out long, lengthy hair until it gleaned with unmistakable softness.

But those rooms weren't the only things to be seen as the door slowly creaked opened.

The light fixture hanging from the ceiling, this blue ornate thing, which Cat couldn't tell if it was a working electricity variety or a gas one—heck, maybe even both. Regardless of its power source, it was working just fine and it gave off enough glow to completely and totally illuminate the two strangers crouched right outside door number *Two*.

There was no time to think, really. No time to ponder what decisions one had in front of you, to look them over carefully and thoroughly, as if sorting through and then discarding the ones, along with their accompanying outcomes, that simply weren't appealing.

There was, in fact, no time.

All Cat had time for was instinct. To follow, to trust, to act.

Which was what she did.

She grabbed Dusty by the collar yet again and opened the door leading to room number Two. She shoved first him through, then herself. Boots sliding a whole six inches on that smooth, polished floor. She slammed her heels down before she found herself cata-pulted right onto that monstrous bed of pink and white and lace. She turned, quick as body and movement would allow, and shut the door behind them both.

Quickly and quietly.

At least, as quietly as possible.

Just beyond the door, Cat heard the unmistakable final turn of that ancient knob, the creak of hinges being forced open, then... nothing.

No sign or acknowledgement that something, indeed, was amiss in her parlor house. No calling out or question. No yelling for assistance, either.

Which, Cat considered, was quite the successful sneak in.

Until she heard the startled, strangled sound coming from behind her. In fact, inside this very room itself.

Damn it.

Of course it hadn't been empty, and she'd been too focused on avoiding Madam Grace to really take stock of someone who, Dusty claimed, might be willing to help them.

So for the second time in the space of about five seconds, Cat again simply acted. She *moved*. Just one movement, nothing wasted or silted. One second she was the facing the door, in the next she was turning, spinning. Heels easily sliding on that polished floor, hand instinctively going towards her gun.

Gloves made the action bulky. Awkward. The heavy winter

gloves made it harder to grip, harder to control. But she was there and ready. Threatening, too, if need be.

The gloves didn't matter.

She trusted herself, trusted her reaction, trusted in all those things that existed in this world, the ones she couldn't see or touch but felt and sensed nonetheless. All those minute things that added together had kept her alive and breathing when faith and prayers and believing in the good will of others had failed her—

Cat finished the turn. Her gaze swung to the source of the sound —a sob that sounded as if it was tearing right from a woman's throat—

Which it was.

The woman in question, half-dressed in her silk lingerie with the white ribbons of a corset hanging open at her back as if waiting patiently for a maid or servant or other girl to come in and dutifully assist her. Long, golden hair cascading around her like a shimmering halo. Perfect in every way as if imagined for some dream, even the look of surprise was perfect. How her eyes widened until they about reached her brows. Eyes which, even from here, were bluer than any sky Cat had glimpsed above Miles City or even her home town. Even on those calm early spring mornings just before dawn, when the air was so crisp and clear, when you could see your breath coiling out your mouth, even those perfect moments couldn't come close to the woman Cat was now gazing at.

Perfect, yes, but Cat's hands were still resting on her gun.

She was no fool.

The woman didn't notice Cat, though. Her eyes were totally and completely on Dusty. In fact, her hands flew right to her mouth, stifling another shocked sound Cat was sure—instead of calling for help, which most other girls would have done the second an intruder barged in on their room.

Not this woman, though.

In fact, she did something Cat didn't expect at all.

She threw herself at Dusty.

That's right. There one moment, standing straight and frightened and well... shocked beside that pink thing of a bed. And the next, she had her arms around the boy and was hugging him. Tight. As if she were trying to hold him tighter than any rib-crushing corset. Which *was* impressive.

And she didn't stop there, neither.

Hell, she about lifted the kid right off his feet, right then and there. Even with that half strung-up corset, Cat had no idea how she'd done it. Had no idea, in fact, how the woman still managed to breathe.

Maybe she could get a few pointers of her own for those times when she was forced to stuff herself into one of them things.

"Dusty!"

The woman cried out, completely breathless and very much still whispering.

"A-Abigail—"

Dusty tried talked again, but Abigail—since that's clearly who this was—just kept on squeezing. Whatever he'd been about to say got muffled in all those long, flowing locks.

"*Where* have you been?" Abigail asked. "And how dare you leave without so much as a goodbye. How dare you leave at all!"

Now, while there was a great deal on intensity in Abigail's words, make no mistake, the girl was smart. She might be all focused on Dusty and the hugs that seemed about determined to break his spine, but she *was* being quiet.

Her voice, still barely reaching above a whisper. Clearly, Abigail didn't forget the real danger a short distance down that hall.

Then Cat found herself blinking and trying to make sense of what the heck was going on. Hugs were one things, but then Abigail went and planted three big, wet kisses on Dusty's cheek.

First one, then the other.

Then back to the first again.

Just in case he'd missed it the first time.

Well, alrighty then...

Cat's hand dropped away from her gun, feeling yet again a bit off with her footing. Well, this time the surprise wasn't on her for missing some important detail or other. This one was on Dusty. *He* should have warned her. Hell, *he* should have expected Abigail's warmed... joy at seeing him.

Though judging by his pained expression, he *hadn't* seen this one coming.

Cat crossed her arms and watched them for another breath, then another. Letting Dusty have his pained moment in the arms of a very beautiful woman, all the while she shook her own head.

Seriously? Dusty had thought that *Cat* was gonna get Abigail talking?

Well, clearly he was dead wrong about that.

Dusty glanced at Cat, giving her one of those strangled, puppy-dog looks, practically *begging* her to come and save him.

Cat merely sighed. Yes, it was probably about time she intervened, if just to make sure the boy suffered no permanent damage and could still walk. She did need him to guide her through those tunnels, after all. And... she'd a feeling Norma's ghost would be pretty unhappy if Cat allowed lasting harm to befall the boy. Even if harm came from such a... beautiful woman.

Cat made an appropriate kind of sound in her throat, you know—the throat-clearing kind to politely demand attention.

Which worked just fine.

Abigail about dumped Dusty flat on his ass, letting up a whole new slew of dust and ash into the air, like one small dark cloud suddenly burst. Abigail clearly realized there was someone else here and suddenly blushed all the way from her cheeks down to her chest. Which was where her white, untied corset clung to her, hugging her ribs like it'd been made just for her. All that white and perfect skin, almost a perfect camouflage between the two, if one didn't look too closely.

Clearly this girl wasn't the riding-under-the-sun kind 'a girl.

And her hair? Dear lord, it was the kind that Cat only dreamed of. Silky smooth blond, the kind that never needed to be brushed, just never. It simply *glowed* with its own warmth like it was the sun and the rest of them were just basking in its glory. Nothing at all like Cat's tattered braid, strands and wisps jumping out in every way they pleased, not to mention the accompanying grime and dirt that undoubtedly she'd collected from their trip down in those tunnels.

Needless to say, it was quite the gulf that separated the two of them.

Cat had the feeling again... that slight stirring in her gut. The swirling of a thought. A slight tingle along her skin, especially at the back of her neck.

This was probably the very thing Norma had seen herself. Maybe even seeing that difference in person, just as Cat now was.

Perhaps she'd come across Abigail while walking or eating at the noodle house. Or maybe Abigail was one of those ladies who liked to rent a horse and just ride about town, letting the wind stream itself through those golden locks, just not under the open sun.

Yes, Cat could see it and see it clearly.

Could see how the two ladies would stop and stare at each other, because how could they not? They were drawn to each other still, almost like a sick fascination with what was, with what could be, and with what would never be again. At least for Norma. For Abigail? Cat guessed Abigail had seen her future, clear as day. Well, as clear as it ever got in Butte. But it *would* be Abigail's future if she didn't find some way out, if she didn't recognize the trap and the prison for what it was.

And for Norma... well, it would have been just that push she needed. The determination to do whatever was necessary, whatever risk was demanded, just to get back to this beautiful, sun-kissed life. It didn't matter that Norma knew the truth of this life. She knew that these shiny, clear windows, the twisting brass railing, that monstrous bed with the kind of thick, warm quilts that Madeleine could only dream of, was all a lie.

Grace's Gardens was a prison, through and through, but all the lace and glitz and glitter worked better than any prison bars ever could.

Norma had wanted back in.

Not to escape, as Dusty first guessed. At least not anymore, anyway. Because when she hit rock bottom, when she found herself staring into those sky-blue eyes of Abigail's and her acres of perfect, silken blond hair, she wanted back in. Would do anything to get it, too.

Even Cat herself could see the temptation and understand it. Perhaps if she'd been a different person with a different purpose and life, the truth was she'd have felt it, too, same as Norma.

Easily.

She didn't, though.

And Dusty, as if knowing what she was thinkin', looked right at Cat. He had this look in his green eyes, the kind of look that shone and cut right through the darkness. He saw the differences in Cat and Abigail. He knew it, felt it, the same way she now did. But it was more than that, too. She saw relief in his eyes, shining so bright and true, and it was in that moment she finally released a breath she hadn't realized she'd been holding.

Relief that he was showing and sharing with her.

For her.

All that, it just took place in a heartbeat. Maybe two.

Okay, three, if she was feeling generous.

But then the world went on moving again, as if it all clicked back into place. Which was also when the girl, Abigail, actually got a good look at Cat.

Her eyes, and oh yes they were *blue*—no doubt about it, life really was just so good to some people. Well, Abigail's baby blues widened so much they about reached her forehead. And her delicately painted mouth? Well, it *had* been painted all nice and straight... until she'd gotten to planting those kisses...

Which were now clearly all over Dusty's cheeks.

He blushed when he noticed Cat looking. Which was fine, 'cause now he matched Abigail.

Cat, though, kept on ignoring him. Right now her attention was on Abigail and if she was gonna give them up to the madam who, even now, Cat heard heels clicking delicately on that smooth, wooden floor—

"*You!*"

It was Abigail. Again, her voice breathy and hushed, a skill no doubt she'd practiced a thousand or more times. She was whispering, though, because again this gilded cage *was* a cage and there was no such thing as being safe.

Even if Abigail wasn't fully aware of the madam clicking her heels on the floor just a few feet away, her subconscious knew it.

"You're her," she said. "You're Cowboy Cat."

Cat blinked.

Was she really becoming the most famous person in town or what? This was getting about ridiculous just how many people knew her on sight, though at least this time she knew it wasn't because of Dusty and his rumors. At least, not directly.

Thank goodness Abigail hadn't used the other name.

Yet, anyway.

There were only so many surprises she could take.

Like Madam Grace and her heels, tapping right along that floor and then stopping...

Stopping right in front of the door. The one labeled *Two*, and then knocking.

Gently.

"Abigail? Are you all right in there, dear?"

CHAPTER THIRTY-NINE

C at wanted to swear.

Like really, really swear.

She didn't, though. That would have given them away for sure. But for heaven's sake—could they just *not* catch a break here?

It wasn't just about Madam Grace having them thrown out on their asses, which was an absolute certainty. In fact, after watching Abigail interact with Dusty she was damn sure that Abigail would hunt them down regardless of where they went—Galena Street or Miss Allen's boarding house, didn't matter, she'd find them. Cat would get the answers she'd come here for, make no mistake, but that's not what had her blood running cold.

Ice cold.

It was the person, or persons, who had issued the order to banish Norma in the first place. Norma who had been, up until recently, the girl who'd probably lived in the Number *Two* bedroom at Grace's Gardens, the girl who'd brought in all that money. The shining star of the garden.

Yet Madam Grace had thrown Norma and her smile all away without so much as a hesitation or backward glance. Cat would be an utter fool to believe the madam was no longer in contact with those certain individuals, and right now neither she nor Dusty could afford that news gettin' back to them.

Just yet, anyway.

Madam Grace knocked again. "Abigail? I thought I heard something. Are you all right?"

All right?

Cat highly doubted *that* was the madam's motivating concern. The more likely pressing concern would be: Were you entertaining an unknown gentleman in this very bedroom? *Especially* a non-paying one.

Once again, Cat didn't wait or think.

She acted.

She yanked off her hat and pressed herself so tight against the wall, right where the door would open towards, would press itself against that wall. Just enough space for her. If she didn't breathe.

Meanwhile Dusty dove for the bed... that monstrosity with the kind of lace and drapings that her ma would about faint dead over. And thankfully, so heavy and voluminous it was, along with the unmade bedspread, that it was easy enough to hide a boy's form from unwelcoming eyes. Especially since Abigail—or her maid, most likely—hadn't yet gotten to straightening the linens for the evening's entertainment.

Meanwhile, Abigail switched from excited young woman with pure joy living in about her every feature, to reserved. Cautious. Aware. One who was completely in control of her emotions... which was quite important as Madam Grace opened the door at that moment and saw Abigail.

Not that Cat was surprised the madam simply helped herself into the bedroom. And she doubted Dusty or Abigail, herself, were surprised either.

Cat couldn't see Madam Grace. This was a good thing because if she could see the madam, well... the madam could see her. Instead, Cat got herself a side full of doorknob and sucked her own breath in the same way those damn corsets did, anything and everything to make herself as small as possible. And while she wasn't a large woman, she also wasn't a small one by any stretch of the imagination. She'd earned her muscles, every one of them, and was paying the price for it now, not being some wilting flower and all like Alice.

Then again, she wouldn't exactly be in this situation if she had been.

"Madam Grace."

Abigail spoke with complete dignity and grace, something that came through mighty fine even though Cat was getting an eyeful of door at the moment.

"Can I help you?" Abigail asked.

Grace said nothing for a moment, and Cat easily imagined her eyes roaming about the room, particularly staying on Abigail for one moment... then another and another. Most likely seeing that smear of her lipstick, thanks to the kissing she'd applied to Dusty's cheeks, and the madam's thoughts... well, they'd be wondering and turning about just *who* Abigail had been kissing.

Not knowing the person was still in that very room, a boy huddled against that monstrous bed.

Still, Cat had no issue praying that the madam wouldn't enter, that she would stay right where she was. Although, if need be, she figured Dusty was small enough to slide underneath the bed and without anyone being the wiser.

Cat, on the other hand, was having a hard, hard time staying still, not moving an inch.

Or breathing.

"I thought I heard something," Grace finally said. "A... someone, perhaps."

"I've heard nothing. Perhaps Elizabeth would know better? Or Miss Olga? You know she's up before all the girls. I've... only just risen myself."

Cat imagined Abigail gesturing to her bed. Imagined because all she could see was the door about a half breath away from her nose, but her imagination was pretty good. Especially with what she'd seen of that slept in, rumpled bed.

"Hmm... perhaps I will," Grace said.

Except Grace didn't move from her spot by the door.

Cat would have heard if she had. Some shift of those heels on the floorboards, perhaps a squeak even as the weight shifted to a spot that was feeling its age a bit more than the rest, as if it was nailed in nearly as tight at the others. But Grace stayed right there as if truly lording over her domain, inspecting it all without taking that final step inside... as if her presence there was more than enough of a reminder.

That this room was hers and hers alone.

That even though Abigail lived here now, her stay here was temporary. She would be gone, soon enough. When her looks faltered, when the rich men with their deep pockets were no longer interested in silken, gold hair with those sky blue eyes. And when that happened, another would take her place.

It was that simple.

And still knowing this truth as she must, Abigail waited, waited with all that grace and dignity. She truly was a master of the art, completely at ease under such intense scrutiny and hiding any shred of discomfort or unease. Because while Grace stayed where she was, so too, did Abigail.

Cat heard no rustling of her undergarments, no swishing of those corset ribbons still waiting to be tied—

Shit.

Cat could practically picture Madam Grace's attention narrowing on those ribbons, perhaps the thought to offer and tie them herself, if just to give herself an excuse to come in. Kindly though it was, the truth would be quite obvious. It *was* an excuse to enter, and how could Abigail deny the very woman who allowed her to stay here? To sell her wares when she, beautiful as she was, was still replaceable.

But through it all, Cat didn't hear one nervous shifting of feet from Abigail. It was like nerves didn't stand a chance with this young woman, and finally, it seemed Grace agreed.

"Yes, well, perhaps I will ask downstairs," Grace said. "Soon enough, I think. You will be joining us, yes?"

"I will. After I'm dressed for the evening."

Again there was that pause, and Cat held her breath even though her face felt like it was gonna start turning blue.

Please, anything but askin' about those laces—

"Do you need assistance?" Madam Grace asked.

Shit.

"No need, Miss Grace. I've sent for Miss Laura."

Another pause, this one longer than the others by far. Finally, when Cat was about ready to turn blue and fall over, she could almost see Madam Grace finally nodding her head in agreement. Not a comical kind, mind you, but perhaps only once, short and curt and clearly final.

It certainly seemed to fit with the woman's no nonsense voice.

"Very well," Madam Grace said. "I will expect you down for the evening's meal—"

"Actually, I'll be down even later today."

Cat nearly passed out right there, Abigail practically inviting in the sudden, more intense scrutiny from the madam. Not to mention it was getting a bit warm in here seeing as how this room was comfortably heated—Abigail was only wearing undergarments, after all— while Cat still wore her winter coat and gloves. Sweat lined her forehead and dripped off her nose, tickling it the whole way down, too, and mixing in with the dirt and grime she'd picked up from the streets outside and the even darker tunnels below.

Still, the very last thing they needed was Grace on the scent of what actually *was* going on in this very room.

"I have no desire to see you exhausted before the evening even begins," Grace said. "Especially, from all accounts, it appears we will have quite the gathering tonight. Maybe a few unusual but important visitors joining us."

Abigail's breath seemed to catch in her chest, but it was slight, and Cat hoped Madam Grace didn't hear it as well.

"You are sure?" Grace asked. "You don't wish to have a fuller meal?"

"No."

"May I inquire as to why?"

Again, Cat could imagine Abigail shrugging, that smooth, curved shoulder of hers rising once and then falling.

"Honestly, I'm still exhausted. My sleep was not very restful and I'm not hungry at the moment."

"Hmm..." Grace said, like she was smiling the way a cat on the prowl does. "Yes, well, you had quite the lengthy visit with Mr. MacDonald—"

Cat sucked in breath to keep from moving, from making a sudden noise.

"—last evening," Madam Grace continued. "Understandable, really, that you'd like some more... personal time."

Abigail said nothing.

Cat sure as heck wanted to say something. MacDonald, *here?* And last night of all nights, right after the gathering where Cat had dragged out this business with Norma, shoved it right onto center stage so not a single man in that room could deny it, could deny her. *Norma.* And there'd been Mr. MacDonald, even then declaring his continued affection for her—

Cat really, really wanted to deck the man.

Madam Grace was apparently appeased with Abigail's answer, at least enough because she started closing the door. This meant their little hiding ruse had worked. Cat was just starting to relax, breath in a few times, when she heard Abigail step forward.

It was Abigail, for sure, because it was the soft shuffle of slippers on smooth floor and not the hard click-click of Madam Grace's heels.

"Do you... do you think Mr. MacDonald will return tonight?"

"My dear, I truly hope so. He seems to have taken a shine to you, though I must say, I'm surprised it took him so long to select your, or anyone else's... company. To think he's been here nearly every night for these past few months and done nothing but enjoy the drink and food. A disappointment, really, a terrible one, one that we could scarce afford to continue."

Abigail straightened. "What, what do you mean—?"

"And one I'm glad to see it well behind us. But then I suppose I should be grateful he didn't just leave for the Dumas when all that *unfortunate* business transpired."

"You mean his affection for Norma."

"You know my rules, Abigail. Do not speak her name."

"Why not? He does."

"He has no need anymore. Not with you. Which I'm sure you reminded him of quite often last night, and if not then that falls squarely on you, young lady, and you, I know, are quite aware of what those consequences can and will be."

"Yes, Madam Grace."

"Thankfully, Mr. MacDonald seemed quite satisfied with your attention, at least, that's what Miss Ogla informed me when she checked on you this morning. Or... was she misinformed?"

It was a warning, no mistake. And Abigail, smart girl that she was, clearly choosing her words very, very carefully.

"No, not at all," Abigail finally said. "Mr. MacDonald was... quite charmed with our hospitality."

"Good," Grace said. Her tone was one of complete finality. "Then let's leave this, this business with Norma in the past where it belongs. And more importantly, perhaps tonight *will* be a repeat visit by Mr. MacDonald. Or maybe Mr. O'Neil will claim you first, yes? After all, I'm sure news will have reached him that his good friend has finally chosen another to dote his attention on."

"But he doesn't, I mean, he's not—"

"Now, there, there. Such good-natured rivalry is always best for business," Madam Grace said, rolling right on over Abigail. "And business is not always a guarantee in these times we live in. Steps must of course be taken to ensure, well, that *others* do not take our place. Now, I will allow you your personal time. Ring me if you need assistance on dressing, or preparing, or anything else you might... require. In fact, I demand it."

Then Grace closed the door and Cat found herself finally breathing again, except she wasn't breathing quite so well.

The heat was one issue, for sure, but not the only one.

Cat's mind was spiraling, heading so far down it was gonna pull her right along with it if she didn't get her feet under herself.

The very last thing she'd expected was to hear those two names: MacDonald and O'Neil. Especially seeing as how MacDonald was here last night... probably at the very same time when Cat had found herself awake by candlelight, staring out that front window of Mrs. Allen's home, while Blake let himself in. Then the two of them sitting together, eating what was left of Mrs. Allen's apple pie, discussing the very mystery practically living in the walls surrounding Cat right now...

But one thing she couldn't refute or deny: MacDonald *hadn't* moved on from Norma.

At least, not entirely.

Norma, who fallen from her place in the Gardens, fallen so low that she'd been destined for the tunnels, would have, too, if not for Dusty. And yet, MacDonald hadn't moved on. He'd been waiting for her... waiting, even after she'd been found dead on Galena Street. Had that been because of the affection he still felt for her? Or something else? Perhaps atonement for the part he may have played in her predicament? Whatever the reason, it'd kept him from truly moving on, from sweeping this whole business up under the rug as Madam Grace seemed wont to do. But then Cat had arrived and changed the game. She'd gone digging, and everyone, from all those men at the gathering to poor Madeleine who would be lucky to see the summer, knew exactly what Cat had been digging for.

Norma and the truth surrounding her death. A suspicious one that even the police were investigating, albeit unofficially.

Another piece of the puzzle was settling into place.

It didn't quite fit, though, not yet. Not when the story was still taking place in her mind...

Cat could almost imagine that night in question, Norma's last night here when it felt like she had the whole world at her fingertips. The night when it all changed. Forever.

Norma with her smile, who'd probably worn some rich, lengthy gown that had been shipped straight over from Paris. Maybe pearls adorning her bodice and a few dozen sewn right onto the skirt. Then, of course, the sparkly jewels in her ears and another matching set circling round her neck. All the while having both men right at her elbows, MacDonald and O'Neil, while a half dozen others watched on, perhaps wishing they might have a shot at dancing with her this evening.

No question about it, certainly with her smile, Norma really would have been the beauty of the evening. Perhaps even leaning against the shining, black piano, the very one that was still working out its chords and melodies for the coming evening's entertainment.

Funny enough, the notes felt just as trapped and strained up here, in the much coveted room Number *Two*, as they had been down below in those cribs. Here the notes were just... more sparkles and comfort. But the sound, the heaviness, it felt the same.

And what about that night? Would the notes have felt the same as they did now?

Perhaps Norma had even noticed them, noticed the truth of this place right before it all shifted. Changed. Perhaps when she went upstairs with her full, heavy dress, the one made from the finest silks European dressmakers had to offer as it dragged on the steps behind her, maybe the expensive silk catching on some uneven floorboard and tugging, ripping even. And then once she was closeted away with the evening's winner, her world simply fell away right underneath her.

Just like that, this life Norma had built for herself, the name she'd created—gone. Just gone. Snuffed out, like blowing out a candle.

Cat stared at Abigail who had raised her chin in just that way, and Cat wondered if that defiance was something she'd learned from Norma or if it'd already come bred in her...

Abigail had answers.

She may not know it, but she did. She understood Norma's life here, her place in all this. Maybe the girl even knew who Norma had spoken with that fateful evening when everything she loved had changed forever. Maybe even Abigail remembered which gentleman Norma had gone upstairs with that night.

More than likely, though, Abigail wouldn't know the whole truth. Just as Madeleine hadn't.

Norma had been too smart for that; she'd have known the consequences, just like she'd known them with Dusty. He'd been the one person she could truly trust, and the one person she would have wanted to keep safe.

She hadn't told him.

But someone, though, someone had known.

Whatever it was that Norma had learned, someone had indeed known about it as well and wanted her out of the picture. Not completely.

At least, not at first.

So the first step to tracing Norma's life here in Butte, to understanding what she might have found herself in, Cat needed the answer to one simple and not so simple question:

What the hell happened that night?

Not that she could ask; not yet. Not when the threat of being found out was still very real, indeed.

Because Madam Grace, sly lady that she was, hadn't yet moved from her spot by the door.

Which meant they all stood there or hid, holding their breaths and waiting. One second, then another. Including Abigail, with her chin still tilted up, wearing her undergarments and unbound corset. Those ribbons and that cascading hair hanging off her in all the right places, looking perfect in every way, and also lost.

Alone.

Though not completely alone.

Cat continued to wait. Heard nothing.

Another heartbeat passed.

She couldn't help thinking they were wrong, that the ruse hadn't worked. Any moment Madam Grace would burst back in and demand explanations. She'd already snuffed out Norma's existence; losing another girl would not be an issue. After all, she'd already declared as much.

So they waited.

Another heartbeat.

Then another.

Meanwhile sweat kept on sliding down the side of Cat's face and falling off her jawline.

Then finally there was the unmistakable click of heels on that polished floor, heels that were finally stepping away from the closed door leading to room number *Two*.

Madam Grace was leaving.

First passing by that window, then slowly making her way downstairs... Not that Cat could still see the woman herself. Again, risking a peek meant risking herself and Cat was just fine if she never met the callous businesswoman in person.

Or at least face to face.

There was a hushed silence about the room, like each of them were still holding their breath as those heels clicked on down the short hall, following along the balcony, pausing every once in awhile as if the madam now checked on each window of her girls' upstairs before finally, blessedly, going down those damn stairs.

Leaving them in peace.

If you considered peace to look and feel like dynamite that had just fallen onto her lap.

Cat's insides tingled so much it felt like she had her own piano concert going on. Especially with the warning of Madam's Grace words still echoing in the comfortable-sized bedroom.

Taking steps to make sure that others didn't take her place.

To take or most likely ruin her business.

That was what a woman like Madam Grace cared about. Her business. Her reputation, and that of the Gardens. A place that wealthy and powerful men visited, came to each night to enjoy the company one could find here and nowhere else, certainly not with their rivals down the street in that ragtag brick building, the Dumas.

Cat swiped at her forehead with her arm.

Well, there wasn't much question about it now. Whatever Norma had discovered, it was enough to threaten Madam Grace and her thriving business. Could be a direct threat or an indirect one, like if it was a client demanding that Norma had to go.

And while all this was certainly starting to feel like dynamite, especially when you went and added in MacDonald and O'Neil's clear interest in Norma and their fighting amongst each other over her, the real spark, the light that was feeling dangerously close to that fuse, was because even with Norma gone, Madam Grace didn't allow the girls to speak her name. And that, well, that only meant one thing:

It wasn't safe here.

Whoever Norma had gotten herself tangled up with was still a threat, including to Madam Grace and her well-regarded parlor house.

Which meant for Cat and for Dusty, this place was nothing but trouble.

Big trouble.

And everyone they needed to avoid, to sneak off right back into those tunnels and disappear the way they'd came... well, they were all downstairs.

Between them and their way out.

CHAPTER FORTY

Cat sagged against the wall, breathing hard and deep. She pulled off one glove, then another, and wiped the sweat from her brow. Even shrugged out of her coat and dropped the whole dirty thing onto the floor.

Thankfully, that alone made the air feel much cooler and lighter, and her head... well, it stopped spinning. Mostly, anyway.

Amazing, really, that she hadn't passed out yet. Hell, if she'd tried doing all that in a tight gown and corset, she'd have fainted about five seconds in, before Madam Grace had even turned that damn door knob.

Dusty poked his head up from underneath the bed where he'd clearly crawled under, and Abigail relaxed. Her bare shoulders started shaking and tears, unmistakable ones at that, filled her eyes.

Which wasn't at all what Cat had expected.

But Abigail still stayed right where she was. She lifted her head, those blue eyes gleaming like the whole world was about to open up and weep, and then she met Cat's gaze—

And the girl didn't back down either, even with all them tears.

"Is it true?" she asked. "What they're saying about you?"

"I don't know. These days, they're saying a lot."

"That you want to help. You want to find out what happened to Norma."

"I do."

Abigail's bottom lip quivered. "How can I trust you? How can I trust what you say? Do you have any idea how many people come here, how they say one thing and with their actions, then do the opposite?"

"A lot, I reckon."

"So... then why? How?"

"I could say I'm just like you, that I lived that life, so I know what it's like. But I also know, too, that a whole lot of girls don't care about the others, don't want to help or lessen the load or the burden. They're only looking out for themselves and their interests."

Cat nodded towards the door. "Like your great lady, there."

Dusty pulled himself up and straightened out his shirt, as if he needed to fully separate himself from the lace, like he couldn't stand any of it touching him.

"It's all right, Miss Abigail. You can trust her."

Abigail laughed. It wasn't a funny kind of laugh, but so sad and so alone. "Your sister taught me to never trust anyone."

Dusty froze, those green eyes of his going so wide.

Again, Abigail laughed. "You think I didn't notice? That I was just, just some silly farm girl from Kansas City? Both of you. Your eyes, if nothing else, gave it away. Especially when you stood there, right next to each other. It was unmistakable that you were related."

Cat felt a cold chill slid down her back.

Clearly Abigail hadn't been the only one to put two and two together.

Abigail reached up and wiped at her face, leaving a smear of black under her eyes from makeup she'd not fully wiped off the night before. The kind of smear that'd take some delicate scrubbing to make go away again. And if Madam Grace heard about it... hell, there *would* be hell to pay—for Abigail.

"Look," Cat said, "I can't demand that you trust me and you've got no reason to. But I gave my word and I know it doesn't mean anything to you, but it does to him." She nodded at Dusty. "I promised I'd see this through, that I'd find the truth."

She'd also promised Mrs. Allen.

Madeline.

Not to mention the two ghosts that followed her. And Norma's... which seemed to grow colder by the moment, as if being here, being in this room was too much for her. Most likely, it really had been hers. And all those memories here, probably even those sparkling jewels peaking out from their boxes by the mirror, that'd probably been hers, too.

Yeah, Cat imagined it would be a sight too much to handle, even for a ghost. All those reminders of the life she'd had and lost.

Twice.

Cat could picture Norma with her green eyes though, looking just like Dusty, so bright and true, like they just went and cut through that darkness like it was nothing.

No wonder the tales of her kindness had spread amongst the town, no wonder at all.

Abigail though, she was shaking her head and her lips twisted into a small, tight line. "You're right, that's not good enough."

"And what would be?"

"Nothing, nothing, I suppose."

Dusty stepped forward. "But Abigail, she's—"

Abigail waved her hand at Dusty, and surprisingly he stopped.

"I'm trapped here," Abigail said, "trapped in this life. Neither of you can get me out, and I can't get myself out."

Cat shook her head. "Then why didn't you tell her? Madam Grace was right here, all you had to do was let her know. You'd be even more in favor, more secure in your position here, and we'd probably be riding that Black Maria all the way to the town's prison—"

"You'd never make it. Not to the prison, which is my point."

"I don't really follow."

Abigail took a deep breath, the kind a woman could only take while her ribs were still free and unbound. It'd probably be one of her last deep breaths of the evening.

"That's because you don't live here, and no, Dusty, don't go telling me you know all about it. You don't. Hell, I didn't and I lived here for two months. But I was under Norma's wing and she kept me from the worst of it. She kept me safe and ignorant, but after that night?"

A tear slid down Abigail's cheeks, making that black stain go a bit further.

"After that night, I knew. I finally knew and I wished to God I could—could just go back to not knowing. To thinking this place was some great fairy tale and I got to live in it. And Norma, she did me no favors keeping me from the truth. Now all I want is to go back to being that sweet little girl from Kansas City, but wishes? They don't come true, no matter how hard you wish for 'em."

Tears kept on falling from Abigail's eyes, but she met Cat's gaze and didn't look away. Didn't flinch or blink.

"But you know, don't you?" Abigail whispered. "You can never go back."

"No, no you can't."

There were more tears now, and Cat's instincts were pushing hard, practically bowling her over to get to the truth of the matter, to stop this dancing round and round. But there was another instinct in her, too, and it was the one that just wanted to wrap her arms around this young girl's shoulders, pull her close and help her feel safe.

Even if only for a moment.

Abigail was strong, stronger than even she knew. Nothing at all like Alice, who instead of fighting back, instead of finding a new way, a new path, she'd just given in to life and circumstance, and that was that.

But Abigail...

She was the reason Cat was here. Not just because of Norma and the ghosts. It was this right here, doing something, even something small, to help another. And it was why even now Cat couldn't help but come closer, couldn't help but feel every ache that Abigail was now feeling right to her soul.

She reached out and gently touched Abigail's cold, bare shoulder.

"You're not alone, Abigail. I know it feels like it, but you aren't."

Abigail wiped at her eyes again, but this time there was just no stopping or slowing them things. Whatever it was she had worked up inside her, keeping it hidden and locked away so none of her clients or the other girls and especially Madam Grace, would see. Would know the depth of hurt she was now feeling.

"Abigail," Dusty whispered. "Do you know? Do you know what happened to her?"

"You weren't there that night, Dusty. Why... why weren't you there? But if you'd been, it, it wouldn't have mattered. You wouldn't have *understood*. Don't you see? He looked, he looked like all the others. Everything about him was money and privilege, and he expected you to dote on him and cater to his every need before he even knew them himself. More champagne and the like. The song for you to sing next. Always a demand, never a request, like... like we were some product and not people."

Abigail's shoulders were shaking something fierce and her makeup was about all over her face, smeared and making her look so much older than she was, as if she'd gained years on her when it had only been a few months since Norma had been banished from the Gardens.

"But," Abigail continued, "while he looked the same as all the others, he wasn't. I... I didn't see it at first. Didn't see it until too late or what it meant. But, I do now."

"And Norma, did she know?"

"She knew. I took one look at her at... at some point in the evening, when she was watching him, and... she knew. And, and she was scared, too."

Like Abigail now was.

Cat was reaching out for Abigail. Unable to help herself, unable to stop from feeling all Abigail was feeling. It was like she was getting lost in both their emotions, the life they'd both led that brought them here, brought them to this moment.

She wanted to push, to ask nothing but this mysterious man, who he was, what exactly transpired that night that changed Norma's life forever.

But she didn't.

Not yet.

"I'm sorry, Abigail," Cat said. "I'm sorry you've been alone."

Cat lifted her hand from Abigail shoulders and gently touched the younger girl's hand. Then held her own there. The simple touch, such a small act of kindness, the same gentle nature she'd shared earlier with Madeleine. It wasn't much—hell, it was nothing compared to what this girl had already been through in life—and what Cat was offering just now, it was nothing.

Nothing but kindness.

But then in the end, that's all Abigail really needed.

Kindness and connection. And more than anything, the knowing that she wasn't alone.

Abigail about flung herself into Cat's arms. Her entire body shaking and wracking with sobs that Cat swore the whole house could feel. And she was worried that someone would come rushing upstairs, and her and Dusty would really be up a creek.

But no one did.

And it turned out to be a good thing that Abigail had gone and excused herself from the early meal. Perhaps deep down, she'd known she needed this. Needed someone to cry to, someone who would simply hold her and she could trust. So that's what Cat did. She held her and let herself be the person Abigail needed, someone to listen and hear.

Someone to trust in.

And Abigail did.

In between the tears and the choking sobs, Abigail told Cat what she knew of that night. Not that she knew all of it, because Abigail had in fact been working hard to gain the favor of the exceptionally wealthy men there that night, though she finally accepted the short straw she'd been given and went upstairs with Seamus O'Neil instead.

Cat bit her tongue to keep from asking why *he* was considered the lowest of available partners, but Abigail seemed to sense her unease and explained, as if it were no matter at all, that O'Neil's emotions ran... higher than most men. Not that he was unkind, Abigail was quick to add, but he was a rather touchy patron. And that night he'd been feeling... well, quite sensitive.

All of which meant Abigail missed much of what transpired below afterwards.

Cat's breath was a bare whisper as it brushed over the top of Abigail's golden locks, who she still held and comforted like a sister.

"And MacDonald? Do you know who he spent the night with?"

"No one," Abigail said. "Only reason I know is because *all* the girls were furious. That's all they talked about the next morning, at least until we all found out about Norma. They'd finally had their chance to dance him away, steal his attention from her, and he'd refused them all. Including me."

Abigail shrugged. "At least back then."

An affection that had changed the previous night... because of Cat, of her and her gathering and all those questions she'd asked about Norma.

Cat's eyes closed for a brief moment.

Pieces slipping into place. Still not quite fitting, but again there was that sense. That tingling along her skin.

Getting closer to the truth, no doubt about it.

Norma hadn't spent her last night at the Gardens with either O'Neil *or* MacDonald. So, who then?

Who had she been with?

And Abigail didn't know the answer either, because by the time she'd come down the next day, all the girls were in a tizzy. At first it'd been all about MacDonald, but then Madam Grace appeared and told them that Norma was gone.

Norma's room, this one right here, still contained all the dazzling dresses and jewels, all those gifts from suitors and from MacDonald, in particular. It was all there, all present and accountable.

Except empty of Norma.

Of any reminder of the girl who'd lived there for nearly a year. What little pieces and belongings that had been hers, simply gone.

Like she'd never been.

Madam Grace answered none of their questions, either, and there were a fair few, including from Abigail herself. Madam Grace simply said that Norma was no longer a boarder of the Gardens, that she was seeking opportunity elsewhere, and that was that.

They were not to speak her name again.

Not ever.

"Except," Cat said, quietly, "MacDonald still did. And he spoke of her to you."

Abigail moved away from Cat, sitting up on the bed there of her own willpower. Her tears mostly gone but had clearly left a mark.

"Jim knew we were friends, is all. He's good like that, his memory. He even remembered that first day I'd met him, when Norma was kind enough to introduce us. I was awkward and shy and doing just about everything wrong, but Norma was kind and so was he."

"What did he say? About Norma."

Abigail blushed and it went from her face and right down to her neck, making Cat wonder just what he'd been saying and what they'd been doing at the time this particular conversation was taking place.

Which wasn't her business at all.

She just hoped Abigail had gotten a decent shake of the profit from Madam Grace with all that wine and champagne Abigail must have convinced MacDonald to... indulge in. But from the sense Cat got of Madam Grace, that woman was a hard penny pincher. Hell, everything about her had seemed hard and cold.

Abigail tucked a lock of her silky blond hair behind her ear. It curled there, still perfect like even though her face was red and blotched with smeared makeup.

"He said he missed her, and that he was real, real sorry for what happened."

"Anything else?"

Abigail shook her head. "Just that he hoped I understood. I told you, it was nothing much."

Cat sighed. So much for hoping that MacDonald had made her job easier, tying up this big ol' puzzle in some nice ribbon or something.

"Alrighty, then, what about the man? The one who came in that night?"

Abigail lifted her head. Eyes red and the circles under her eyes, not just from the smear of black make-up, but shadows, as if the girl hadn't slept since this terrible nightmare had started.

"I thought you knew?"

Cat shook her head, and so, too, did Dusty.

"It was Marcus Daly *and* Joseph Nadeau."

CHAPTER FORTY-ONE

Two men that night, not one.

Cat felt the breath leave her lungs in one giant sweep. She saw Dusty in his thin, hole-filled coat do the same. He accidently brushed up against the glass window, causing a loud knocking sound.

Thankfully, no one upstairs or downstairs seemed to hear.

Which was good cause Cat wouldn't bet on her reaction right at that moment.

"I think.... I think you need to start over, from the beginning this time."

Her mind was doing quite a few flips of its own, working hard at rearranging the puzzle she'd been putting together, the story that was Norma's life. The last thing she'd expected was to hear that a well-known brothel owner *and* a copper king had stepped foot in the Gardens that night. The very night Norma's life got turned upside down and tossed out the backdoor.

It couldn't be a coincidence.

Only fools and drunks believed in coincidence, and that was mostly because they hadn't been paying attention in the first place.

Which, truth be told, Cat was feeling a bit now as she hadn't seen this one coming, not in the slightest.

Such was the story of her stay in Butte so far.

She shook her head, tossed those critical thoughts aside as best she could, and really listened to what Abigail had to say. Not just the facts, but the impressions. Abigail knew more than she thought, had seen more than she thought.

All Cat needed her to do was tell her.

Every little detail...

Like how dazzling Norma had been, standing there in her deep midnight blue gown as she leaned up against the piano. She'd apparently liked to do this, even sitting in for a spell because she used to play when she was a child, and that's when it had happened. In between her dazzling the men with her beautiful music and then charming them all with her smile, those two had entered the Gardens.

Marcus Daly, as Cat learned, almost never visited a brothel outside of the one he owned. So his appearance was quite the to do. Sure, the Gardens regularly got visits from the other two, Clark and Augustus Heinz, the newest self-declared copper king, but Daly? Never.

His presence alone would have been the talk of the evening if not for the man he'd entered with.

Nadeau.

A name that Cat had heard mentioned a few times since she'd come here. A wealthy businessman whose business was this one right here, the flesh trade. A man and his family, all of them involved in the business, who also owned their own big time parlor house, the Dumas.

Cat's eyes closed.

A new picture was taking shape, one she didn't begin to see or fully understand and couldn't. Not with all the tunnels running right under their feet. Branching off this way and that. Some heading right on up the hill, to take you towards city hall and perhaps even a stop at the California Saloon. Others, well they just stand down there in the tunnels. Reaching, infecting, and darkening anything and everything they touched.

How in the world had Norma gotten herself tangled up in all this?

Too bad her ghost wasn't in no position to answer, and neither was Abigail. She didn't know the answer to that question, and Cat certainly wasn't going to put her in a position to ask. Not when these two clearly powerful men were involved.

Cat's hip felt heavy then, as if her gun and holster were suddenly weighing her down, the kind of weight she hadn't felt since that moment with Alice, her sister looking her clear in the eyes and telling her to leave, never come back. Didn't matter that Cat had saved both their lives. Alice's husband, Stan, was dead. Because of her.

It felt like someone had taken a whole bucket of lead and poured it right into her holster, then right into her heart.

Not lead, though.

Copper.

"Shit," Cat whispered.

Abigail nodded. "This... this is why I didn't want to tell you, why I didn't... know if I could trust you."

Cat certainly didn't blame the girl. Certainly hoped she had enough money for a ticket to take her right back to her family in Kansas City and damn the consequences. But then, that was something neither of them could do.

Running.

Or Dusty for that matter, who was still standing guard at the window, his back so ramrod straight but she saw those little shivers, those little movements for what they were...

Tears.

He, above all, understood the powers Norma had gotten herself mixed up in. Maybe it'd been an accident at first. Maybe she'd heard some tidbit from O'Neil or MacDonald, but her with that sharp mind of hers probably broke the one law none of the girls were ever supposed to break.

She'd tried doing something with that information.

Cat let out a breath.

So instead of asking Abigail to hightail it and run, Cat asked about that night and about those two men.

"He... he had this look about him. Carried this... presence. The kind that just made the whole room go still. Quiet. Even those beautiful notes, coming right off that piano, they simply disappeared, right then and there, just dissolving into nothing."

"Which one?"

"Nadeau."

Cat didn't know if that was a good thing or not. Didn't know which man was the more dangerous to tangle with—Nadeau or the well-to-do and well-liked copper king, Marcus Daly.

"There was this look in his eyes." Abigail shivered. Pulled up some shawl from the bedposts and wrapped it tight about her shoulders.

The shivering didn't stop, though.

"I didn't know then," she said, "what it was I was seeing, but I do now. And honest to God, if he ever looks at me the way he looked at Norma..." Abigail closed her eyes tight, and kept 'em closed. "He smiled, Miss Justice. Looked right at Norma and smiled... like he'd finally found her."

———

It was by luck alone that Cat and Dusty managed to sneak back on out the Gardens without being seen. Course, having Abigail enter ahead of them, once again the well-dressed lady with all signs of stained and smeared makeup carefully hidden and reapplied. She made sure all eyes and attention were on her as she waltzed into that dining room. It was certainly a gift, one that all star boarders had.

Abigail certainly had it. Her help went a long way ensuring their luck held, for no one was looking at the back door to the tunnels.

At least no one that mattered, anyway.

There was the colored cook, who'd turned just at that point, her hands heavy with some giant pot, steam slipping up and around that cover, carrying with it the lingering smells of roast meat and garlic. The kind that made your stomach grumble with just one whiff. If, of course, you weren't so nervous exiting a place of establishment you technically had no business being in.

Well, the cook, she just looked at them, gazing through that steam. Caused Cat's breath to hitch a bit, especially as the cook's eyes widened. Then her gaze slid to Dusty and all look of alarm floated away with all that steam. She simply nodded at him, then turned and got back to her work and that was all.

If anyone else saw them, Cat didn't know.

Her senses were on high alert as they descended that ladder down into the underbelly of the Gardens and from there to the hidden tunnels underneath. Tunnels which, according to Abigail's account, neither Daly or Nadeau had used the night in question. They'd gone in through the front door as if they hadn't minded the whole world knowing who they were and just where they were going.

Cat's hand crept towards her gun. It felt like the space here was a bit darker than the first time, a little more closed in. A kind of tension that the brain itself couldn't sense but some deeper part, one from long, long ago, still remembered what it was to be hunted.

To be watched.

Followed.

And maybe it was her imagination, but it sure seemed like a light bulb or two had gone out. Or gotten smashed.

Truth was, everything Abigail had told them was still fresh in Cat's mind. The threats, the possibilities, the very powerful people who just might be in play. Madeleine had said whoever was behind this wouldn't hesitate to take out her or the other girls who'd been friends with Norma. Cat certainly believed her. Especially as they moved through those shadowy, dank tunnels. All this thick darkness, thinking just how easily they could be waylaid down here. Not knowing a danger until it jumped right out at them.

Word had to have reached whoever at this point that she and Dusty had traveled this way. It'd be an easy thing really, especially if they'd known where she and Dusty had gone and where they might be heading now.

But no danger jumped out at them.

Not this time, anyway.

They made their way back through the tunnels, passing by the girls there—if one could still call them girls—who were stirring and getting themselves ready for the evening rush. Finally, after what felt like ages of crawling through that dark underworld, picking up more grime than the first time 'round, Dusty led them out and into a world that was just as black as below.

And yet all the ash and soot was somehow a relief to what she'd felt down there.

Cat tugged her gloves up higher and wrapped her coat closer about her as the cool air hit her with the kind of force that'd steal the breath right out of you. The temperature had sure dropped like mad since full dark took affect, not that they could see the difference, themselves. But the cold? Oh, she could sure tell the sun was long, long gone.

What she needed, though, was home. And one glance at Dusty told her he needed it, too.

"Come on, Green Eyes, let's go home."

Dusty closed those piercing green eyes for a moment, as if the very word home brought up feelings and emotions he didn't dare feel.

Cat understood.

The kid who'd just found out more about his sister than was fair for a living soul. And to think they hadn't even reached the end of this game yet.

She wrapped an arm around his shoulders and together they started walking. Neither saying a word, just taking what they could in each other's company, poor as it was, with all that weight they both held.

Funny enough, it was Fat Jack who came upon them. Pulled right on up in his hack, nearly running them off the side of the boardwalk as he quickly veered his team up to them, making those poor horses stop on a dime. Jack lifted up the brim of his tall black hat and peered at her.

Cat wasn't sure, but the man looked more like a skeleton than when she'd seen him those couple days ago.

"Need a lift, Miss Cat?"

She merely nodded, her heart heavy just by looking at the man who'd brought her to Mrs. Allen's. She'd been a different girl then, with this lofty ideal of finding justice for those folk like her who had nothing left in the world but the breath in their bodies. She'd been a fool and this driver had grinned at her the whole way, most likely knowing the rattlesnake nest she was about to go tromping through... and had done taken her to Mrs. Allen anyway, without one word or peep of warning.

Still, it was a ride and she was tired and heartsore and in desperate need for something to warm her soul. Coffee would do. Or perhaps whiskey.

So she and Dusty got in. They settled on those hard cushioned seats, her gun butting up against the side of the door, which caused Jack to look down at her sharply, though again he said nothing. Yet it triggered the memory of her first day in Butte and this very ride with Jack, and how he'd mentioned he'd driven all kinds in his hack, from the ladies like her...

To those copper kings.

Like Marcus Daly.

Cat was too darn tired for finesse and word play, not to mention she was settling on mad about now and decided the best course of action was one where she wasn't likely to reach for her gun and shoot the man.

So she decided to be blunt.

"You knew, didn't you?"

"Heading to Mrs. Allen's, I presume?"

"About Norma. About how she tangled with some pretty powerful individuals."

Dusty looked at Cat, his head snapping up.

Fat Jack picked up his whip from where he'd rested it on his lap. "Well now, Mrs. Allen's it is, though word is she's not in residence at the moment."

This time, it was Dusty who spoke....

"Jack."

But Fat Jack didn't pause or give Dusty the time of day, just lifted up his whip, ready to crack down on those horses to getup—

When Dusty reached out and snatched that whip right from Jack's hand.

The tall, thin man just about spun around. "Why! You boy—"

"She was my *sister*, Jack, and she's dead. Dead."

"And I am sorry 'bout what happened to Norma. Nice lady. Kind. Not nearly enough like her in this town, though it seems we might be hitting right back at one again—"

"Then tell us what you know."

"And follow her to the grave?"

There was no fear in Jack's voice nor any trace of it on his face. Just this kind of surety that he felt with his whole being, and Cat, being who she was, saw it all. Felt it, too.

He believed that statement with his whole being.

Dusty shook his head. "Ain't gonna happen."

"Why the hell not?"

"You're a fixture in this town. *You* can't be swept up under a rug like some trash everyone else rather 'd forget. *You* can't just be forgotten."

"Not the kind of gambling I likenin' to make, kid."

Except Fat Jack's mouth twisted into a tight line, and his gaze flicked all around them, as if he could see right through those billowing clouds of smoke and black. As if he knew there were eyes already watching, ears already listening.

Probably was, too.

Cat was thinking of skipping the coffee and going right to whiskey.

"Give me my whip, Dusty, and I'll keep on driving."

And talking. Cat clearly heard the unspoken statement, and when Dusty hesitated, Cat took the choice from him. She slipped the whip free and handed it to Jack.

Then she looked right at Dusty. "You've trusted me this far."

"That's before we knew... knew about you know who."

"We don't know anything, not yet. Just ideas. Just thoughts. Nothing at all we can act on."

If they ever could.

Cat looked at Jack. "Well? You gonna take us home or what?"

And Jack did.

Just like true to his unspoken agreement, Jack told them all about those rumors and rumblings that had so far been kept from Dusty's keen ears and his network in the underground. Rumors that, as Cat had first guessed, were as numerous as those tunnels and mine shafts snaking under the ground they now rode on. Everything interconnected, everything shifted and turned all dependent on who you were, who you owed money to, and who caught you doing the kind of things you weren't supposed to be doing.

Cat leaned into the hard cushion of the hack's seat, her gun pressing hard into her hip. She tipped her hat further back so she could get a better view of the city, not there was much to see. Both lanterns and lights glowed in this hazy yellow color in the darkness, not beacons lighting you home but there, nonetheless. She maybe glimpsed what looked like a gallows frame marking the entrance to some mine shafts. Wondered if that one there was owned by Daly or Clark, and just how much money that one mine was making in the copper it was hauling up to the surface.

Through this all, she listened to Jack. He had quite the gift really for remembering just about everything he heard, from small details to the grand sweeping gestures that made you feel like you were there and heard it yourself firsthand.

It turned out that Madam Grace's little slip-up with Abigail and the financial side of the Gardens was indeed, correct. Cat had picked up on this detail, but it was only now that she began seeing the real significance of it.

Madam Grace was not as financially stable as she'd led her girls to believe. She'd recently found herself in the gambling halls and unwilling to break free of the joy and rush of winning as her number was called out. So she'd taken to charging her clients more as well as bringing in new girls, like Abigail.

All the while the other big houses only housed four girls each.

Cat closed her eyes for a moment, doing the math, running the numbers and what she knew of maintaining one of those big parlor houses. And the big expenses needed to maintain one. Always current with the fashion, dazzling and sparkling, hosting balls and whatnots. Didn't matter that the girls would pay a hefty sum for their own room and board, the math simply wasn't adding in Grace's favor.

Not when with only four girls, you got to charge a premium for their use.

Jack brought her to the present. "See, from what I heard, it wasn't enough for Grace, all those new changes she'd gone and made. Real problem was she'd started borrowing money to keep her 'lifestyle' going."

"And fell into debt with the wrong people," Cat answered. "You know who it was? Daly? Nadeau?"

Jack snorted at her. "Miss Cat, I drive on rumors here. Your guess'd be as good as mine. But I can tell you this, no man smart enough to deal with those two men dare speak of it. Not even in the back of my hack, here."

"But Norma did. She told *you.*"

Dusty started at this and Jack laughed. Laughed so loud and hard Cat thought he'd seriously choke on all that smoke living in the air.

"Now that, my girl, that's why I like driving you. Hope to keep on doing it, too, for a long, long time. Unless you're not careful just where you stick your boots."

He winked at her and she found herself forgiving him, if only a little.

She really did enjoy his laugh.

And he wasn't wrong, neither.

Cat was in trouble. It was the kind she felt crawling up the back of her neck. This sense, almost like an itch, that she should reach for her gun and keep her hand right there, right there at the ready.

Her breath puffed out her mouth, white at first, then disappearing right into that smoke and black.

"And what did Norma tell you?"

Jack sighed, then adjusted his tall black hat before giving the horses another encouraging whip. She tried not to wince, wishin' he'd just let them be at the pace they wanted.

"That she was in trouble and it was coming for her. Did she give me a name? Nah, but then, she knew better."

Cat sat up, her bum right on the edge of that hard, hard seat. "When was this? When did you drive her last?"

"The night she died. See, I was the one who picked up from the California Saloon. Mighty surprised to see her there, too, you know she'd didn't fit the... sort of lady that was allowed there now."

Cat let out a breath.

Norma had risked everything, at least what she had left, her life for certain, to go into that saloon that was frequented by the biggest movers and shakers in town. Hopin' for... what, exactly, Cat didn't know. But she guessed the only risk worth taking was one that got out her out of the life she was living. Maybe to convince a former lover to run away with her—but Cat doubted this. More than likely she'd tried to use what information she had as a bargaining chip, putting her hand of cards on the table and just seeing what card the dealer pulled up next. And she'd failed. Whatever cards she played, she'd come walking out of that fancy saloon knowing she'd come up dry. She was in trouble and there was nothing she could do about it.

Fat Jack confirmed this.

And for Cat? For Dusty?

Trouble, indeed, was coming.

And Jack... well, he knew it, too.

They all did.

CHAPTER FORTY-TWO

When they finally reached home, pulling open that creaking door and then shutting it closed, Cat had secretly been hoping that Jack was wrong about Mrs. Allen. That she would come bounding out of that kitchen, flour dusting her dress, sprinkled in her hair and on her face, and wave some ladle spoon at them for being home so late and missing supper.

No such luck.

Instead it was Officer Blake who was there, sitting comfortable in the same spot he'd occupied just last night. They'd sat across from each other, and each enjoying their slices of apple pie. A slice that was indeed in front of him right now, resting there all nice and neat on that slim dish of china... along with two others plates, each with their own slice of pie.

One for her.

One for Dusty.

Blake didn't bother rising like a gentleman might have when a lady entered a room. But he did study them good and hard, noticing every detail, every inch and speck of grime.

She didn't mind. She was quite the sight, after all.

Besides, she was doing the same to him.

Blake looked cleaned and well kept. Clearly he hadn't been crawling in the underbelly of Butte all afternoon. Though, he looked a bit bit rounder in the middle, as if he'd suffered through his aunt's cooking for the day and yet still couldn't pass up on another slice of pie. Truthfully, he looked the same as last night, or early this morning depending on how you looked at it. Still hard and cold, as if those eyes only knew one state of being...

A hardness that made her sigh in regret, though she didn't dare look to closely at what that meant.

Certainly when he lifted his own blue eyes and met hers.

For a moment, she thought she saw a softening and perhaps... relief. Relief that she was here, alive, and safe.

Which meant she was a lot more tired—emotionally, physically— than she'd first thought. Because a man like Blake, his ideals, his faith... well, it was like the sun. Rose in the east, set in the west, and left nothing else in between. Blake wasn't about to worry himself over a woman like her. So yes, she was clearly imagining his brief look of concern... of relief.

Then the look was gone, and he opened his mouth:

"I'd ask where you've been, but then it's pretty obvious."

Cat shrugged. "You go where the information takes you. You know that."

Blake nodded at Dusty. "Glad to see you're okay, kid. Mrs. Allen will be happy to know it, too."

Dusty, who'd been so much open earlier when he'd climbed up out of those tunnels, body shaking with the kinds of emotions no kid should ever have to feel, certainly not alone. But all that? It was gone. He was back to being that kid she'd met at the train tracks, letting nothing at all show; he couldn't afford to.

"We'll get ourselves decent," Cat said, "before heading back down. We've got a lot to share."

"Me as well."

It didn't take long to make herself presentable, to actual resemble a human being and not some creature who'd come crawling out of the dark. Her hair needed a good washing, but that wasn't gonna happen tonight, so Cat gave it the best brushing she could. She braided it all back together, tossed the annoying thing over her shoulders, and set off downstairs.

Unlike last night when she'd been wearing nothing but her sleep robe and warm stockings, she was now sporting a clean shirt and jeans, and a warm coat as well, seeing as how the boarding house wasn't kept near as warm as Abigail's room. And Cat kept her gun right where it was.

Blake certainly didn't miss that, either.

"You know the laws on firearms in town, right?"

"I do."

And then Blake nodded.

Which was how, once again, Cat found herself sitting down with Officer Blake, a man she'd never expected to eat with once, let alone twice. To apple pie and coffee, again.

Yes, coffee.

Chin had actually refused to give her the whiskey straight off, practically insisting she drink the damn coffee. All of which was fairly impressive seeing as how she still couldn't understand a thing the man said. He'd also gone and got a good size fire going, heating the place right up. And between the cozy fire, all them lace and curtains, it really did feel like home.

Company included.

Cat took a grateful sip of the very hot brew, feeling it slide down her throat and warming her insides the whole way down.

So, perhaps Chin did know the best way to warm a soul.

Then this brief moment of pleasure passed. Cat set her cup down and got right to business.

"So, Officer Blake. Lots to share, but first I'd like to clear the air here and ask you to be honest with me."

Blake picked up his own cup and took a long, lingering sip, before lowering it. "Depends on the question."

"How's your aunt?"

Blake's blue eyes widened a tad, but then he just shook his head and gave Dusty a long look. "Couldn't help but tell her, huh?"

Dusty shrugged. "She figured it out most on her own. Miss Cat *is* good at that, you know."

Blake sighed; it was a long one and resigned. "That's what I been hearing. Yeah, Mrs. Allen's my aunt. Moved right on in when she first opened the place, me and my ma. I grew up here, helped out."

She nodded. With his intimate knowledge of the boarding house, with Chin, and that especially temperamental front door, she'd expected nothing less.

Blake was shaking his head, that blond hair of his lookin' like it was swaying in the firelight.

"Don't know how you do it," he said, "but I've been hearing nothing but tales of your visits all afternoon."

"Really?" she said. "So *you're* keeping tabs on me as well?"

"Bet your britches, I am. And everyone else who's been watching you as well. Or trying to, anyway."

Blake ran a hand through his hair, that long, glorious mane of his. And now that she thought of it, probably would have caused even Abigail to take a second look.

It sure must be nice to not go crawling through the underbellies of hell and come out lookin' like you were ready to move in.

"I sensed I was being followed," Cat said, "pretty much everywhere I went. Didn't see anyone, though."

And no blazing streak of blond either.

"Yeah, you wouldn't have," Blake said. "And no, I wasn't following you."

Today anyway.

"And truth be told," he said, "you wouldn't have seen all the eyes following you. Not even you, Dusty."

Dusty, who'd been priming his fork to dig right into that apple pie, shot Blake a dirty look. "Hey. I'm good at what I do."

"Yeah, but you can't do much when the whole damn town is watching."

Which was also the sense that Cat had gotten.

All those eyes, all those ears, each going their own separate ways to report. One network or another, didn't mater. It meant the same in the end. She'd been followed and someone—lots of someones, including Blake here—had known about her comings and goings. Probably even who'd she'd been talking with, when and where, though hopefully not the details inside the Garden. Hopefully ones that didn't lead right to Abigail...

Christ, if it did, she couldn't ever forgive herself.

Not again.

Not another innocent soul.

Cat noticed Dusty was staring at his plate as if thinking the same, or maybe just thinking back to the Gardens or even those tunnels underneath, the same place where he'd found his sister and helped her back up to the light.

What a mess.

Cat leaned towards him and bumped his shoulder with hers. "Eat up, Green Eyes. You know darn well the chance might not come again."

Eat when you can. Rest when you can.

It was a damn good motto to live by.

Blake was watching all this with that way of his, so focused, nothing at all slipping past him, except... he had almost this uncertainly in his eyes right then. Like maybe he really didn't know what to make of her.

Which was just fine.

And then Cat ignored him, too, and while she wasn't taking her own advice and eating plenty, her stomach still revolting from what she'd seen and experienced (and smelled), she did take comfort in that coffee.

Her soul really did need an uplift after her time today, even if she only found it in this warm, soothing drink and the strange but comfortable company she was passing the evening with.

She certainly could do a lot worse, even if one was a police officer who didn't think too kindly of girls who'd worked on the line.

While the boys ate, Cat explained what she'd learned. How she and Dusty had spoken with Abigail, and the sudden appearance of Marcus Daly and Joseph Nadeau onto the scene. From Madeleine, too, how she believed her and the others girls' lives were at stake, and that Officer White's death was a reminder that no one was safe.

At this which point, Cat did put down her fork and gave Blake a hard, hard look.

She didn't ask a question. Didn't need to.

The look was enough.

And the one he gave her in return, just as hard and just as unyielding.

"My aunt," he said, "a woman I love with my whole heart, is a former brothel owner. A madam, and one with quite the renown. You really think I'd be found anywhere in those cribs or any house for that matter?"

The fire cracked in the corner just at that moment, and sparks flittered and fluttered in the air before finally fizzling out. Dusty didn't move, didn't say anything. He was no fool.

And Cat waited and watched, not sure why his answer was so important and not daring to question herself, either. She studied every line and inch of the man, every emotion he might be trying to hide—

Except he wasn't hiding any.

And she believed him.

"I know you wouldn't," she finally said, "but I know, too, quite a few officers find their way there."

Blake nodded. "You're not wrong. It's an angle I've been looking into, but everyone on the force knows I'm one of those 'honest cops' and they ain't willing to talk with me, not even about rumors."

Dusty perked up. "I can help with that."

Cat didn't like it. Didn't like putting Dusty in the way of some dirty cops who certainly wouldn't care about doing away with some kid from the shadow world if they felt threatened.

She sighed and nodded, just as Blake was shaking his head—

"No."

Cat blinked at him. So did Dusty.

"Why the hell not?" Dusty asked.

"Because my aunt would never forgive me if anything happened to you." Blake poured himself another serving of coffee. "Damn woman wouldn't stop needling and worrying about you all night. Barely got any sleep at all."

Cat gave him a pointed look. So did Dusty. *They* knew he'd been up half the night talking with Cat.

"Look," Blake said, ignoring their pointed looks, "What I *can* tell you is that Officer White was taking bribes. My sources admitted that he was in the pay of at least the Nadeaus. For Clark or Daly?" Blake shook his head. "They couldn't say for sure. Probably was at some point. A guy like him doesn't mind how many masters he has, so long as he gets paid."

Dusty, not bothering to put his best manners forward, was chewing around a mouthful of apple pie. "Most of them cribs are owned by the Nadeau family. I saw their oldest son often enough when I was visiting Norma. Ovila. Unfriendly fellow he is."

Blake nodded. "Ovila helps his father run their red-light operations, least as much as I can tell."

Which translated to: no real evidence.

Not that the Nadeaus needed to hide their operations. It wasn't like prostitution was illegal. Far from it. As Nadeau and Daly and Clark had discovered themselves, the brothels were quite the booming business.

Even if... there was the changing tide coming.

The thought tugged at Cat.

"You think Nadeau would have hired White to 'keep an eye' on things?" she asked Blake.

"Aye." Blake's mouth twisted into a tight grimace. "White would have, too, and did. Every spare moment he had, from what I found out, anyway."

Dusty agreed.

Cat sat back in her chair. "We know White's connected to Norma because he's the officer who found her first."

"And because he's assigned patrol on Galena Street," Blake said. "For sure, he would have known her."

"There's also the matter of the report he filed, making sure that her death looked like nothing special, even bringing on a doctor who could confirm that."

"Not to mention," Dusty piped in, "*he's* the only one who knew the name of the real doctor who'd tried to save her."

Cat nodded.

The doctor who hadn't agreed with the police and who had told the newspaper differently...

She looked at Dusty, but he was already shaking his head.

"Sorry, Cat. I asked the writer, but he didn't know either."

"Then how...?"

Dusty shrugged, then went to scraping the last of his apple juices off the plate. "Probably the same way I do. Probably heard some rumor, especially considering who Norma used to be, living in the big house and all, and thought, why not? Why not write about it? Makes good headlines for the paper, and makes our job selling 'em easier, too."

"And White," Blake said, "regardless what he'd been paid to do, not even he could stop the rumors or people from talking."

"That's right," Cat whispered.

Another thought... tickled at her.

It was one of those fluttering kinds that if you started chasing it you'd only drive it off, cause it to hide back in the depths of your subconscious. So Cat didn't. She simply sat there in the comfortable chair, the worn cushions forming perfectly against her back, her hips. And that thought continued to flutter and flitter.

Her fingers started playing with the ends of her braids as if completely of their own desire, and she let them.

Dusty was peering at her like she just might have gone crazy. "What are you—"

Blake put a hand on his shoulder.

She nodded her thanks, or thought she did.

Something about what they'd said... about White... and the doctor.

Cat's fingers paused on her braid and her gaze focused on Blake. "You were there when White's body was found."

"I was the officer tasked with the investigation."

"Describe it to me."

"The report—"

She waved at him. "Was probably changed, and you know it. I want to hear it from you. Everything. Every little detail, don't matter how small or insignificant. Tell me what you saw."

"I already did."

Cat shook her head, causing her braid to flop to the other shoulder. "You told me how he was found, how he looked, but I'm asking you for more. I'm asking you for the kinds of details that'd be easy to overlook, especially when you didn't know what we know now."

"We don't know anything," he said.

"We have an *idea*," Cat countered, "and that's something. We know your Officer White—"

"He's not my officer—"

"Was tied to Nadeau. And Madeline, and all them girls, pay rent to the Nadeau family, which also included Norma while she lived there."

Dusty pointed his licked-clean fork at her. "Also, White was the first officer there when she died. He knew even before I did."

Which was saying a lot.

Cat nodded. "It also meant he got to control the narrative. He put on the record how she died and made sure no other opinions differing from his were mentioned."

But Blake still didn't look happy, and truth be told, it was still a lot of rumors and guessing and connecting stories that didn't have no concrete evidence.

And yet, it felt right.

"You said it yourself," she said, looking at Blake, "something didn't feel right. So I'm asking you again to think, to remember. What did you miss that day? What didn't you see when you responded to Officer White's death?"

Now, Blake could have kept arguing. Truthfully, she wouldn't have been at all surprised if he had. That was usually the default position most men took, especially when she was dealing with them. Something about her blue jeans and revolver not quite fitting within their accepted worldviews.

But Blake surprised her.

He thought a moment, eyes getting a distant look to them, like he wasn't looking at Mrs. Allen's room anymore.

"I could still move his body," Blake said. "So I know White hadn't been dead long, but not recent either. He was damn cold to the touch, but then the whole house had been freezing, like he'd forgotten to throw some logs on the fire before sitting down, enjoying himself a glass of whiskey or something. Two glasses, in fact, one empty, the other full, like he had company over. But it wasn't just the cold that surprised me, though. He was pale, real pale, like he'd been out for stroll for hours wearing nothing but his boots."

Blake let out a breath and crossed his arms. "There was some vomit, too, though not much. Looked like what might have been dinner, maybe too, the drink he'd finished it down with. Or that maybe as his heart was giving out, his body couldn't take what it had it in it anymore and let it all back up again."

Which had probably given the examining doctor, the one that Blake had sent for, the perfect excuse to write off the death as natural —as in 'the natural course of events.'

But... usually when a person died in such a manner, most doctors wrote it as accident. So why hadn't this doctor?

"And you're right about the doctor," Blake said, as if reading Cat's thoughts.

Which was mildly disconcerting if he could actually do so.

"I checked the reports again," he said. "The same doctor examined both Norma and White. Doctor Stan Edgar."

Cat couldn't help the flinch at the man's name. Stan. Even after all these years, just the sound of the name caused the hairs on her arms to rise, her heart to race, while her gaze darted to the nearest door... stairs... windows. Checking if anyone she didn't recognized was approaching.

And like always, there was no one.

No Stan.

Blake noticed this shift and frowned at her, his attention shifting to the door, then the window.

"Something wrong?"

"No."

Just more ghosts.

Cat worked hard on calming herself, smoothing out her face and all the tension she suddenly felt pulsing through her. This was one ghost she hoped to drop down some hole and never let see the light of day again.

"We know anything about him?" she asked. "Edgar?"

"He works with the police, quite often, too," Blake said.

Dusty shook his head. "I haven't heard nothing about him, but that could be as planned."

Then Dusty went back scraping off that pie from his plate until he gave up, seeing as how he got every lick of juice and speck of cinnamon, then eyed Cat's as of yet untouched slice.

She sighed and pushed it to him.

So much for the easier answer. If a doctor who the police often used in their investigations had ties to the underworld, that was the kind of information that would be kept under close, close wraps. By both parties.

"Well," Cat said, "I think we can assume this Dr. Edgar has ties to the person trying to make Norma go away."

"Agreed," said Blake.

See, doctors were an interesting bunch who almost lived in this sort of gray area. They were respected members of society—important members, even—but they worked both sides of the line. Although the respectable side often choose to openly ignore this part. In fact, most houses usually employed a doctor to examine their girls on a regular basis, or to offer the treatments necessary for the hazards of their profession. And those doctors, along with their names, were kept secret. Generally they were the younger doctors, just out of school or starting a new family, who needed the extra money and well, there was sure a lot of extra money to be found in the Red Light district. But if word ever got out he was treating fallen women... well, none of his regular clients would be having none of his services no more.

Again, they lived in that gray area.

Just like her, just like Dusty.

Cat let out a sigh. There was nothing for it. They didn't have much else to go on with this angle, so Blake would need to talk with Dr. Edgar. Maybe some hard questioning would reveal just how he was connected to all this...

She paused in her thoughts.

Blake's attention had shifted from her to the fire near them and stayed there. He simply... gazed at it. Like he himself was now watching some fluttering thought circle round and round his brain. Then, he looked at the table between them, her plate with the apple pie Dusty was clearly enjoying, while the other two were empty and scraped clean.

Then that hard blue gaze, the kind she felt right to her toes, looked right at her. And stayed there.

"You're right," he said. "There was one thing I missed."

She kept herself still. Not wanting to move when he was looking at her so intently.

"And?" she asked.

"Almonds. Bitter almonds, like... like the one time my aunt tried baking some new dish. Cookies, I think. She had to roast those almonds, except I was helping out in the kitchen and had two left feet and two right arms. I was such a mess back then that I knocked over a whole bag of flour. It dusted everything and she needing to finish up with the noon day meal and get all those pails ready for the waitin' men..."

Cat didn't dare breathe.

Blake was, though. Breathing and still looking... right at her.

"She forgot all about those almonds, Miss Justice. The kind of smell unlike any other. And it was there that night at White's house. Faint, yes, but it was there.

"Cyanide." He scowled. "And I missed it."

Cat didn't bother soothing his feelings; he was a big enough man to do that all on his own. She was just glad she hadn't bothered with her slice of pie because a kind of numbing, cold chill swept through her.

Not that the details themselves were overly disturbing. Cat had seen plenty of disturbing sights during her short life, as had Blake and Dusty, she was sure. But in this, in what Blake had remembered, was the implication that caused her blood to chill, her breath to almost still in her lungs.

It didn't though, and she said enough breath to say the words she and Blake were both thinking:

"Officer White was poisoned."

CHAPTER FORTY-THREE

Dusty's face turned green as he swallowed, looking at Cat and then back at Blake. "You're... you're sure?"

Cat shook her head, causing her braid to flop back around and nearly smack her in the chin. "No, we can't be sure. We need a doctor to examine the body, a reliable doctor this time. Not someone already on someone's take."

"And... my sister?" Dusty asked.

"Sorry, kid," Blake said this time. "We don't know."

Couldn't know, either, not without talking to the doctor. The one who'd found her. The one who'd told the police, and Officer White in particular, that his report was wrong.

Cat swore quietly.

Blake grunted. "I thought ladies weren't allowed to swear."

"I thought we'd already established I wasn't a lady."

He nodded in agreement.

Cat didn't know if she wanted to smack him for either complimenting her or degrading her. Or if she just wanted to smack the table in frustration. She was so damn close to finding answers, and every time she thought she was gettin' close, something kept her from the truth.

Now it was this missing doctor.

"We could search for him," Blake offered, as if reading her mind. Again.

Cat shook her head. "A needle in a haystack and you know it. And the chances of him admitting it was him that tried to save a *prostitute?*"

It was a hard word. A cold one. And one that included both her and Norma, and heck, even Mrs. Allen. Both Dusty and Blake looked at her in stunned silence.

"I know she's your sister," Cat said, "but to the rest of the world? A respectable doctor? He's not gonna reveal his part in this, not for helping a fallen lady, a prostitute."

"He stopped to help her," Dusty whispered.

"In the moment, yeah, he did. But he's kept his name hidden all this time. And if those rumors and what the *Bystander* reported, that he believed she died of some other means? He hasn't come forward yet."

And probably wouldn't. Unless his hand was forced.

He might have been a good Samaritan in the moment, but now? In the light of day? Cat greatly doubted he was the kind of soul who actually cared about such silly ideals like truth and justice.

As it was, they had no idea who this doctor was. No one but White knew, except for perhaps Norma, and neither would be much help seeing as how they were both dead. And even with Norma's ghost, her presence so close, so cold that she was making Cat's breath turn white right as they slipped out her lips, regardless of the heat coming off of that there fire.

All the while Norma, of course, said nothing.

Dusty stopped eating the pie and was looking at Cat with those green eyes of his, heavy and seeing everything as they always did.

"So, is that it, then?" he asked. "We just stop? Give up? Is that what you're saying?" Emotions flicked across Dusty's face. "But we can assume she was poisoned."

"Yeah. I'd say that's a safe bet."

She looked at Dusty. Really looked at him, letting her own emotions shine and the weight of the words to fall between them.

His sister had been murdered.

"I'm sorry, Green Eyes."

His mouth tightened. "Yeah, well, this whole time I was the one believing someone did her in. Just... just didn't think..."

That she had died in such a painful, frightening way as poisoning. If she'd even known what was happening to her body as it was shutting down. Maybe she couldn't move in the end or breathe, Cat didn't know. It all depended on the poison used—not that they'd know or even guess at, without a doctor lookin' at her body.

But Cat knew a small bit of poisoning, the pain it wrecked over a person's body. Not like she'd seen a whole lot back in Miles City, but the few... well, it hadn't been pretty. Mostly, too, because there hadn't been a thing she or anyone else could do about. Not even the doctor they'd sent for. Too long, he'd told them when he'd finally arrived; the poison had been in the girl's system too long, nothing to do now but make her as comfortable as possible and pray it'd take her quickly.

It hadn't.

Or maybe it had, and it just had seemed like an eternity.

Course, in each case she'd seen and been a part of, holding the girls' hands... Johanna and Rosaline... as their bodies passed away, inch by agonizing inch. Well, it'd been a toss up if the girls had dosed themselves, desperate to end their existence, or if it'd been the cause some former, jealous lover. Not that the law in Miles City had cared either way.

It hadn't.

But she had, just as she did right now.

Cat reached over and gripped Dusty's hand. Gave it a firm squeeze, and she saw his mask slip a bit, all the depth of what he was feeling shining right at her in that single moment. A moment Blake couldn't have missed, yet he said nothing.

Then the moment passed and she watched as Dusty withdrew into himself, keeping himself safe as best he knew how.

Then the kid kept on eating.

Actually, he went after her slice of pie with renewed gusto, and she welcomed him to it. Meanwhile Blake was watching Cat again, his gaze intent on her hands that had once again found themselves tangled and fiddling with that braid of hers without her even being the wiser.

She purposefully let go.

And to distract herself from the swirling and tingling going on in her stomach, from the intensity in his gaze, as if he was somehow seeing those moments she'd shared with the other poor girls, maybe even something more, regardless these were the kinds of tingles that weren't appropriate now. Certainly when talk of poison was floating around the table, which was when she noticed Mrs. Allen's letters sitting by the table.

There they were, resting oh so quietly on the little end table, right beside a reading lamp just waiting to be flicked on. Cat had first noticed the letters upon entering Mrs. Allen's home those three days ago, and they were exactly where she'd last seen them. Those neat scripts addressed to girls hailing from all over the country, and not a one of them for Mrs. Allen.

It had been one of Cat's first clues that Mrs. Allen's wasn't a typical boarding house, but a woman who carried her own open past... and still couldn't fully let go of her old one.

"We're gonna need some more options," Blake was saying, "before we go talking with Daly or Nadeau, or it won't just be my job we're risking here."

She nodded, but there was something about those letters...

Cat picked up the stack and thumbed through, reading the names, seeing the places these girls came from, the snippets of the lives they'd each left behind, either because they no longer had a choice or were hoping to make a better life for these families. It was quite the stack, really, as if Mrs. Allen hadn't had time over these past few weeks to get to them. Well, probably not seeing as she'd been busy trying to help out Dusty and save his sister. Mrs. Allen really had taken a liking to him. Probably because she thought he reminded her a lot of Blake at his age.

Probably.

Cat couldn't keep the smile that was pulling at her lips, especially when she imagined Dusty standing there in all that flour instead of the ash and soot, all that fine white coating him in about every inch possible and the smell of roasting, bitter almonds...

Cat turned over a letter, this one stiff and coarse like it'd been made from the cheapest paper a person could find... and froze.

Abigail.

A letter addressed to Abigail.

But it wasn't just the letter itself that had her wondering, had her thinking... she'd come inside Mrs. Allen's home three days ago, and had seen this very stack of letters. She'd glanced at the names and realized what it had meant: Mrs. Allen was tied, in some way, to the Red Light. But the letters, in and of themselves, were not evidence exactly. Their presence didn't *mean* that Mrs. Allen herself had walked that life, that she wasn't a former madam (although she was). All the letters had meant was... a possibility. A short little note in the narrative of Mrs. Allen's life, and her home here, and maybe that was what she needed.

Not direct evidence tying Norma to any of those men who may have been involved in her death. Yet maybe all those ties, just as she and Dusty and Blake had discussed over coffee and pie, maybe they were enough. Enough, certainly, to ask questions. And simply the questioning was a danger all in itself.

For Cat, for the other night ladies like Madeleine.

Abigail's letter felt heavy in Cat's hand, but the script was clear enough, and she wondered if it had been a loving hand that had done the writing.

She closed her eyes a moment, then came to a decision. The truth of the matter was you couldn't get anywhere in life without taking risks. And if she let this matter lie as it was, there was no telling just how many other girls would fall victim to it. This way, at least, coming right and just doing the asking... well, it'd be her that'd have the target on her back.

Not Madeleine, not Abigail.

Her.

That had to be enough because she'd come too far, too close to the truth, to give up now. Heaven help her if the cards didn't land in her favor.

"You find something?" Blake asked.

Cat lifted the letter so both boys could see. "What do you think an official visit to Grace's Gardens would yield, hmm?"

Blake shook his head, making that blond hair just about shine in the firelight. "It's not gonna get you far. Madam Grace might let you in, but if she's really in debt to Nadeau or Daly, she won't say anything."

Dusty nodded.

Cat, just shrugged, her mind... already thinking, already working through the possibilities, the chances she was thinkin' about taking.

Was it enough? Was it worth it?

She could almost feel Norma right beside her, as if she was reaching out that one delicate hand of hers and touching Cat lightly on her shoulder.

She shivered.

Both Blake and Dusty saw, though neither said nothing about it. Maybe they also believed in ghosts.

"Maybe," Cat finally said, "or maybe I'll just have to convince her I'm the sort of girl worth knowing."

A girl with just enough information to be dangerous. Just enough to set the town's gossip mill on fire. The kind 'a talk that carried straight back to those big men living large on this rich hill. The kind they couldn't ignore, just like they couldn't ignore her, either. Or get rid of her. They also didn't have the option of stomping her down so low into the ground like she was speck of dirt on their boots as Norma had been.

And Cat wasn't alone, either.

She had Dusty and Mrs. Allen, Chin, too, as his job seemed to keep her going and on her feet. Then there was Blake. Somehow, someway, he'd ended up on her side.

Certainly not friends, but definitely allies.

Which, honestly, wasn't a feeling she was used to. She'd distanced herself from that, from needing others, ever since Alice.

Course, it wasn't like Cat was gonna find answers tonight. It was starting to get on in the evening, although the Gardens wouldn't be shutting anytime soon. Still, this certainly wasn't the kind 'a visit to rush. She was better off going over with a plan, with a clear head and not with the horrors of those tunnels, of Madeleine and those haunted eyes of hers, still so very, very fresh in Cat's mind.

As if she'd manage to sleep tonight. Unlikely.

Or maybe... maybe she should just go. Go to those Gardens, fling open those big, fancy doors that their fancy guests (who didn't mind being seen using them) and stride right on in. After all, wasn't that the reaction that they'd been hoping of her with Mrs. Allen? To get so mad, so frustrated that in just one move she ruined her biggest ally, biggest supporter? Fair play, and all that, so maybe she *should* just go on over and shake things up. And if she got lucky, they might not even recognize who she was until the truth, or the threat of the truth, was staring right down their throats.

For once *she'd* be putting *them* off balance.

Not a bad idea.

Cat let that thought roll 'round in her mind as she stood from her chair, stretching out her back, then patting down her blouse. Bits of crumbs bounced off and she gave Dusty a look, who just grinned at her with the sheepish look only a boy could achieve. She set Abigail's letter down on the table with the small lamp, right on top of the others.

Maybe that was something else she could do when all this was done. Simply go out for a walk and deliver all these letters. See that minuscule hope in the ladies' eyes as they got word from home, from their families, friends, loved ones. Share with them, even in this small way, what that might feel like.

Cat turned slightly towards the window, which revealed the darkness of the world outside and those few flickering, hazy yellow globes of light fighting to light the city regardless of all that soot and ash. She was ready to tell the boys she'd made up her mind, that she was gonna head on over to the Gardens and turn their worlds upside down for once, when Cat noticed something out of the corner of her eye...

Movement...

The quick kind. The kind you never really had a chance to think about, to register, just... sensed, more like.

And she sensed it. The danger.

Almost too late.

CHAPTER FORTY-FOUR

Cat turned slightly.

There.

She glimpsed—orange and yellow, then—burning and bright—as the flickering hurled through the darkness. All that ash and soot, trying its best to conceal the light, like that had been its whole purpose, each of these long, dark-filled days, all leading to this moment right here...

And the darkness failed.

At least enough, anyway. Enough for her to see what it was.

Flames.

Not that her mind was fully registering what was going on. Too fast. Faster even than an eye-blink.

One moment, a glimpse of angry, orange flames.

Then Cat moved. Not much, just... enough.

Her jeans rubbing against each other, against the soft fabric of Mrs. Allen's chairs. Her body, her whole presence sensing the true depth of the threat, while her mind was still workin' on catching up.

Didn't matter.

All that mattered: reaction.

Every hair on her arms, her neck, rising. Standing straight up. All her senses tingling. Pushing her to act, to *move*.

She wasn't the only one either. Blake pushed to his feet and reached—for Cat.

He'd seen it, too, the danger.

Or sensed it.

Then the half-eye blink passed and time caught up with them.

Blake's hand clamped down on Cat's arm hard, determined, just as she reached for Dusty. Grabbed his collar and yanked him towards her—

Dusty fell to the ground, tumbling right off his chair. What was left of the pie fell to the ground with a quiet thump.

Cat stumbled from the movement, from the force of shoving Dusty to safety.

Glass shattered. The window just beside her, breaking into a thousand pieces. Maybe more. Probably more, it was a good-size window, one that Chin had diligently kept clean and free of the ash and soot that about lived in the air here, but now that window was gone. Or at least a good portion of it.

Cat felt the hot touch of flames licking at her cheeks—

And then Blake was yanking her. She would have fallen right down, too, if not for him and that hard grip he had on her arm.

The flames, the rock, passed by her. Instead of pummeling into her head, which was right where she'd been standing, it gouged a deep hole in the plaster of Mrs. Allen's walls. The wallpaper burning black round where it touched, before bouncing down and rolling on the floor. A rock the size of Blake's fist that was still burning, thanks to the oil-soaked rag tied about it. Oil that she could smell, no problem.

Blake's arms had wrapped around her. Held her there tight for a moment, as if neither his fingers or hands had actually realized just how close she'd come to ending up just like Norma. But then in all fairness, Cat found herself standing there in her own moment of shock.

Just a blink, mind you.

A blink that lasted a lifetime.

Like how she hadn't realized he was even there, nor even that she didn't actually mind so much—she didn't. Which was certainly a bit of shock as well. She'd been quite frustrated and ticked-off with him just last night, and now, now she wasn't minding that he'd gone and saved her. Truth was, it felt *good* to be alive and breathing. Good, too, that he'd apparently cared enough to do so. And another thing she knew for sure—his arms were heating her right through the warmth of her coat, light as it was. It was still the kind 'a warmth she wasn't likely to forget anytime soon.

Even if it was brief.

Cause it was.

Just an eye blink, remember.

Then Cat was leaping out of his arms. She grabbed one of Mrs. Allen's quilts, hoped like hell it wasn't some family heirloom, that it hadn't been sewn or knitted by anyone special, like Blake's mom, because then Cat was stomping on it and the flaming rock.

Blake left her to it, trusting her.

He'd moved to the window, revolver drawn, and peered out through the darkness and ash, with only the few handfuls of glowing bulbs to reveal their assailant. Then Dusty was jumping up to help her. He grabbed the pot of coffee (at least the half she hadn't managed to finish) and quick as a flash, dumped the whole lot at that stubborn flaming rock. And thank God, they managed to snuff out the flames, causing quite the sizzling sound and cloud of suffocating smoke which came out from underneath that poor quilt, and managed to *not* burn down Mrs. Allen's home.

Then Cat was right beside Blake, her own gun drawn, crouched down low right beside him. The ends of her coat trailing along that once polished floor but now littered with glass that crunched beneath her boots. She peered out into that darkness and saw...

Nothing.

Nothing at all but darkness.

For a few moments, anyway. The darkness part was changing real fast. Even as they watched, lights flickered on from the nearby homes, even in those big, fancy mansions. Windows creaking open, doors, too. Flaming rocks crashing into windows probably wasn't the kind 'a noise that went unnoticed in this part of town.

It was the kind of sound that called attention, that called everyone to come rushing out of their beds, their own weapons at the ready. Butte was a civilized city, but she was still very much part of Montana.

Course, what that meant was whoever had done the throwing was long, long gone. They'd have known they couldn't have hung round waiting to see what kind a damage they'd inflicted, that they couldn't just go and 'blend in' with the crowd.

Her tingles were going crazy, and not just because her blood was boiling and her finger was itching on the trigger.

"See anything?" she asked Blake.

"Someone running. Fast. Dark clothes. Couldn't get a better look."

He swore softly but stayed right where he was. Waiting as if he had all the waiting and all the patience in the world. She certainly didn't. She was really starting to just feel like shooting somebody.

Preferably the guy who'd just thrown that flaming, oil-soaked rock at her.

"Whoever it was," Blake said, "he knew how to get away quick and not be seen."

No kidding.

"Think it was a man?" she asked.

He glanced at her, eyebrows raised.

"I'm being thorough."

"You could probably make the throw, 'specially too with enough force to break that window. Anyone else? Unlikely."

And they didn't exactly have a whole lot of female suspects. Mrs. Allen... well, that just didn't make sense why she would want to trash her own place. And Madam Grace... well, she'd be busy entertaining her guests.

In fact, now that she thought about it, it wasn't a throw that could have been made just by anyone. If they'd been closer, like on the boardwalk, or even if they'd tried sneakin' around the fence, she would have seen them. Blake, too.

So, that rock had been thrown from farther away. Especially because they *hadn't* glimpsed the flames until it was actually coming right at them.

Which meant it was a throw that a man like Daly and probably Nadeau couldn't have made. Not that she'd met them yet and examined their muscular levels, but based on what she knew of men like them and the kind like MacDonald or O'Neil, *none* of them could have made that throw. Well, perhaps MacDonald—from what she'd seen he'd been the trim enough sort, and age and overindulgence hadn't caught up with him as it had O'Neil. So MacDonald... definitely a possibility.

She said as much to Blake, who nodded, though it was Dusty who pointed out they could just as well have paid the right type of guy to do the rock throwing.

Which was also true.

True, too, that it was the kind 'a trail that those big and powerful men wouldn't want leading back to them. Reputation, after all, was everything.

Everything.

A thought tugged at her, and Cat's senses got to tingling again, but not this time from danger...

Well, at least until Blake holstered his weapon and looked at her. Really looked at her.

"You okay?"

Well, if that wasn't a loaded question, she didn't know what was, especially with the smoking, coffee-soaked quilt a mere foot away. A rock that, while it may not have been meant for her, almost had been.

"I am," she said, "thanks to you."

"Maybe you're not all bad."

"For a fallen lady?"

"Yeah."

His gaze held hers for just a moment more. Again, there came that softening she'd thought she'd imagined earlier... except this time she knew she hadn't. Knew, too, that there was indeed another kind of tingling that had nothing to do with finding the truth about Norma's death or the danger they'd found themselves in. It was a tingling in her stomach that had nothing to do with any of that.

And she hadn't a clue what to do with it.

Which made it quite helpful—and distracting—when Chin came running out of his room right at that moment. Chattering and jabbering as he was, especially the way he was gesturing back and forth with his hands at the ruined floor and the smoldering quilt, then back at Blake. As if clearly this had all been Blake's fault.

And wow was she even more surprised when Blake, the hard, determined police officer that he was, actually started blushing.

Cat lifted her eyebrows and meet Dusty's gaze, who just grinned at her. She felt a grin of her own answering in return.

Sure, someone had thrown a flaming rock through the window, nearly clobbered her silly, but apparently there was still something funny about imagining Blake as a kid Dusty's age... and just what the hell kind 'a grief he'd put poor Chin through.

Chin immediately took to cleaning and straightening, sweeping up the glass—and there was a sure lot of it—while the rest of them dutifully backed away. The Chinaman was a bit furious with that broom, after all.

Meanwhile, Cat shook her head, not needing such thoughts and feelings about Blake, even those about him as a boy. Certainly not after someone had tried to kill her. Or maybe that'd been them hoping they'd get lucky. Maybe someone had just wanted to warn her off, scare her, even. And maybe, too, they hadn't known there was a police officer inside, the very nephew of the boarding house's owner.

As usual, she had a heck of a lot more questions than answers, and it was high time she went and did something about it.

"I think it's safe to say," she said, "that someone really wants us to stop looking into Norma's death."

"That," Blake said, "I can agree with."

"You know I'm not gonna stop, right?"

Blake looked right at her, and there wasn't an inch of softness in that look, either.

"Can I talk you out of it?"

Why would he want to? But instead, she said:

"No."

"Yeah. Thought as much."

Which meant if they were gonna find out the truth and do it before any of them got hurt—or worse—she was gonna do the very thing she hated most.

She was gonna put on one of those damn corsets.

CHAPTER FORTY-FIVE

Part of her had been hoping the necessary parts and pieces involved in dressing up for the evening—those specialty kind of gowns and undergarments, along with the torturous device known as a corset (something she'd personally sworn to never wear again after walking away from her life on the line)—would be impossible to find at such short notice. Which, of course, would make going out also impossible.

But then she'd forgotten just *whose* boarding house she was staying at.

Mrs. Allen might no longer be in the profession, might have given it up a good twenty or more years ago, but she was still quite aware of the fashion and seemed to take pride in it. Not that she'd been picking out the latest and greatest from overseas, or that the dress Chin had pulled out of her closet compared to the five dozen that had resided in Abigail's, it was still more than enough to pass muster.

The delicate pink fabric, likening to satin or something equally soft, that shimmered even in the dim lantern light of her room. All those ruffles and lace fallin' in all the right places, with most of it hanging just off the shoulders or resting in a nice, delicate arc right at the chest. Not to mention the trim waistline and the way the dress simply *flared* out at the hips, like she was walking into her very own fairy princess tale.

If such fairies or princesses or tales even existed.

Which they didn't.

And right now Cat didn't need them to exist, either. She just needed to swallow her own discomfort, and her breath, and get the damn thing on—and leave her jeans, boots, and hat behind.

Somehow, with just her luck, Cat also happened to be a similar size to Mrs. Allen. Or maybe the woman had taken some calculated precautions and seen fit to have at least one dress that fit Cat for such occasions when jeans weren't appropriate. (Not that Cat didn't have a dress of her own; she did, it was just much... simpler than this pink, fairy-tale thing. Also, she could breath in hers, too.)

And Chin, bless the man (if Cat was feeling in a blessing mood, which she currently wasn't), he had known exactly where everything was... including how to get her into that Goddamn, breath-stealing instrument of destruction. He pulled and tugged on those ribbons, which caused the bones of the corset to dig unbelievably painfully into her ribs, making her *really* second guess her need to find out about the truth dear Norma had found herself in.

Cat grabbed at her waist at another expert tug, and saw black spots appearing in her eyes.

Chin kept on chittering, possibly asking if that was too tight, but she seriously doubted it.

Clearly, the man knew his way around a corset, as if he'd been helping Mrs. Allen off and on over the years, regardless of what was proper or not. Then again, Mrs. Allen was a former madam and what was considered proper for most ladies didn't exactly apply to her.

Or to Cat.

Dusty, though, he was waiting outside like the good gentleman-in-training he was, had even left her room and closed the door before she'd asked. Though he wasn't too much of gentleman, training or not, because he stood on the other side of that door and snickered like crazy at Cat's struggles to keep on breathing.

An exercise that, when she got enough breath back in her lungs, was followed closely with an awful lot of swearing that she was sure, if Blake was nearby and heard, would be blushing like mad at her foul tongue.

Cat didn't care.

She *hurt*, Goddamn it.

"Wow!" Dusty called to her from the other side of the door. "I didn't actually think you were gonna do this, put on that pretty pink dress and all. Guess that means I win the bet."

She glared at the closed door, knowing exactly *who* he'd been making that bet with.

Chin had finished with her corset and was now helping her strap on and tie on that shimmering pink dress, which, if she were feeling a generable mood, would have admitted she hadn't worn anything quite so fine and lovely back in Miles City. And maybe, if just a smidgeon, was a bit glad to put it on.

Minus the corset, of course.

Cat got her hair done up in some complex knots and piled the whole thing on her head, Chin handing her the necessary pins when she asked, mumbling under his breath as he did so. She figured he was unhappy to be leaving the room downstairs in such a state to come up here and help make Cat... presentable.

And she wasn't the only one either.

Blake was getting himself darned up in something equally nice and fancy, thanks to Jere Murphy, who'd come right down when he got the news about the whole flaming-rock-through-a-window incident. Murphy hadn't been too pleased about the situation, especially seeing what they were gonna do next, but Mrs. Allen hadn't been wrong about him. He was an honest man and an honest cop, a combination Cat didn't see together too often.

Truth was, Murphy couldn't exactly bless what they were about to do, stomping into the Gardens where some of the wealthiest men in Butte spent their evenings, including at least one copper king, not to mention how the police chief himself was somehow tied up in all this.

It was a right political rattlesnake's nest, and Murphy couldn't be allowing anything official going on.

He'd been pretty clear and upfront with Blake about that. What Blake was doing here, it was on his own free will as a civilian and not an officer of the law. There were too many balances to be maintained, and Butte just couldn't handle the kind of upset she and Blake were looking to make.

And yet even so, Murphy had understood the need and wished them luck.

In truth, whatever they found out tonight, it wouldn't be the kind of thing they could use in a court of law. Also, there was the matter that Norma's official case as started by Officer White was closed. It'd been ruled an accident, and with no evidence, no autopsy stating otherwise, that maybe she'd indeed been poisoned like White had, it was gonna stayed closed. For better or worse.

But then, considering all the players involved in this scheme, these quite rich, powerful men compared to the death of a prostitute, Cat had never been under any illusion. Evidence or not, poisoned or not, this wasn't ever gonna get settled in the courts.

Otherwise... well, Cat wouldn't have been needed in the first place.

Murphy was sending officers over, trusted ones he'd promised, to watch the house and keep an eye on things while they were gone. It was all he could do, but really, it was enough. It'd be a comfort knowing their home would be safe, and Chin and Dusty (who was still furious he was being left behind and all), but at least they'd be safe.

Even if Cat and Blake wouldn't be.

And, safe or not, truth was Cat was looking forward to finally picking up that puzzle board, the one all those rich and powerful men had controlled right from the start, and tossing the whole thing upside down and seeing what the hell shook out.

She'd do what she could, even if it only amounted, in some small way, to justice for Norma.

It had to be enough.

From down below Cat heard the front door open and then slam shut, causing her upstairs window to shake. Blake apparently had returned. All darned up and ready to go... while she wasn't even ready yet. Figured.

Still, with Chin's help she made pretty good time. Cat managed to finish making herself just enough on the presentable side that she'd be allowed admittance into the Gardens. And with Blake looking equally respectable as her chaperone for the evening, they would not be turned away. And just in case, she had the letter to Abigail. Not that the evening entertainment was the time and place for such deliveries, but hell, why not?

So, Cat opened the door from her bedroom and headed downstairs where Dusty and Blake waited. She was watching her footing, getting the feel for the new restrictions her body was placed under. Breathing, unable to walk more than a half inch or two it seemed, also that constant lightheadedness one felt when not being able to breathe properly.

Which really was the worst part of all.

She needed her thoughts clear and focused if she was to do this tonight, certainly if she expected answers. Regardless of how beautiful she might look or how fine and delicate the dress fit her—which apparently it did, if Blake's and Dusty's reactions were any indication.

Cat made it down the stairs without tripping or falling or blacking out and stepped right into the sitting room where they waited. The skirt of the dress swaying about her, fitting to her hips in just the right way, while the longer train almost curled about her lean legs as she stopped at the base of the stairs.

Both men had stopped talking, turned, and now simply stared.

It certainly wasn't the usual reaction when she went and put on a dress.

Dusty managed a whistle and Blake... well, he just continued to stare at her.

Which was only fair seeing as she was doing quite a bit of staring at him and how... fine he looked right now.

The matching three-piece suit, dark of course, best to hide all the bits of ash that seemed to land on everything in Butte. Neither too lose nor too tight, but still feeling like it'd been tailored just for him. Then there was the crisp, white shirt underneath and what looked to be a silk tie about his neck, expertly placed and knotted, it seemed.

Blake must have noticed her gaze because he glanced down and said, "My aunt."

"Of course."

"She umm..." He cleared his throat. "She's sorry to have missed this, but we both thought it best if she kept staying at my place, and just stayed away. For another night."

"Considering what just happened, I'd say that's a safe call."

"Yes, well, it took some convincing for her to agree. She was more interested in grabbing my shotgun and riding hard on Fat Jack's hack to get here when she heard about the window."

A smile tugged at his lips, just about lighting his whole face up. Apparently, he had quite a few memories of Mrs. Allen in such a manner, and Cat found she'd likened to see some of them herself. Certainly Mrs. Allen wasn't the type she'd picture wearing this pink, silken dress while totting a shotgun, fully cocked and loaded.

Which caused her to smile in turn until she realized they were just standing there, smiling at the other... while Dusty just kept on grinning, as if seeing her all trussed up in such a fine dress was the greatest amusement of his life.

Cat really wanted to smack the kid but restrained herself. She'd need the energy to get through the evening alone as it was. Not to mention it was a darn good thing she'd skipped on the apple pie, though hopefully she had enough in her to keep going before she needed to eat again—eating and corsets were not a combination that worked.

The fire continued to glow in the corner, casting a comforting, yellow-orange light about the room. And despite the obvious broken window and smells of oil and burned quilt lingering there, not to mention the ash and soot that had followed the newly opened airway inside and already was settling on all of Mrs. Allen's nice things, including the pile of letters, this place... well, it still felt like home.

And home, it was certainly worth defending. Worth protecting.

"So," Dusty said, looking her up and down carefully, "if someone tries to kill you again, what the hell are you gonna do? Faint?"

"Probably," Cat growled.

Chin, who'd followed Cat downstairs, held up her gun and holster.

She raised her eyebrows at him. "That ain't exactly gonna fit in my handbag."

It certainly wasn't about to go with her dress.

Chin shook his head, then headed down the hall, tutting off words she didn't understand, but Blake clearly did because he was now grinning ear to ear, the kind 'a grin she'd never seen on him yet.

One that looked... good. Relaxed and comfortable.

Cat shook her head, causing one of her curls to unfurl and dangle at her cheek. She shoved the annoying, unruly thing behind her ear. It felt like just about everyone, her hair included, were having quite of a laugh at her expense.

Chin returned and came back with a much smaller, more appropriate gun. A derringer. A single pistol. It wasn't exactly gonna win her any gun fights, but keeping her alive when running away certainly wasn't an option.

It was perfect.

"*That* will fit."

Then she smiled at Chin, the first true real smile she'd had since coming to this hell of a town. She might be wearing a dress, might not be able to breathe worth a damn, but she wasn't going in defenseless (even if the derringer wasn't exactly gonna be easy to get to, strapped to her thigh as she was planning, but hell, it was something). And she wasn't going in alone.

Blake held out his arm for her, and she took it.

Off to the rattlesnakes' nest they went, and to see just what kind 'a trouble they could kick up.

CHAPTER FORTY-SIX

Turned out they could pick up quite a lot of trouble, even if that trouble didn't exactly notice them. At least, not at first.

Not that this was the *usual* kind of trouble, either.

Nothing like the trouble Cat had felt earlier moving down in those tunnels, where the walls were so close and dark, and the whole time she was thanking God for it being so cold she couldn't actually smell much. Down there, where trouble meant someone sneaking up behind you and pressing a knife hard and fast right into you, and you not knowing it until your body went and hit the ground.

This current trouble was a different sort altogether.

Beautiful.

Dazzling.

The piano notes she and Dusty had heard earlier, which had sounded almost sad and mournful, now played with such a lovely, swaying beat that you wanted to grab the partner standing next to you—in this case, Blake—and simply dance. *Dance* to your very heart's content. Twirl and move, dip and laugh, and simply find the joy in living. Something Cat hadn't done in a lifetime and didn't realize, until that very moment, how much she missed it.

Like the smile she couldn't seem to help or the way her grip on Blake's arm tightened, just a tad, almost like a longing.

He glanced down at her, quick and curious-like, and she found that she wasn't the only one smiling.

Maybe it'd been a while since Blake had danced, too.

"You like dancing?" he asked, his voice a bare whisper, as if speaking any louder would bring the attention of the few gentleman still lingering about in the hallway.

"Once upon a time," she said.

"Me, too."

Well... maybe the rich and mighty weren't the only ones in Butte who liked to dance and maybe, after all this was over, she could go and find herself a place where feeling this kind of joy was more appropriate. And where wearing a corset wasn't a requirement, of course.

Maybe.

Cat tightened her grip on Blake's hand once more, deliberate this time, communicating what she didn't dare to aloud.

He simply nodded.

No words were needed. They'd come here for Norma, for Madeleine and all those girls like her, and for Dusty. All in the hopes of tossing over that table and shaking things up.

It was time.

Time for her to get to work.

Nor was she alone, either. Blake was right beside her, someone she'd known for not even twenty-four hours yet trusted him here above all others. And Norma, her ghost, she was here as well. But instead of her deathly cold grip on Cat's shoulder, it was like she needed space, needed this last moment to gaze back on her life and how worthless it all had become.

If only her ghost could talk, could tell them all what had happened here, what had changed and what had caused her to end up in tunnels.

And maybe they'd never find out that piece of the truth. Maybe they'd find nothing at all.

At least, they were trying.

Cat breathed in, deep as she dared, as much as that painful contraption wrapped around her ribs would let her, before slowly letting it out again.

And felt her focus sharpen.

As if sensing his cue, Blake touched the top of her hand with his and led her straight into the heart of Grace's Gardens, into the very ballroom itself.

The sight was nothing short of breathtaking even for Cat, even knowing the true cost of this place.

Beauty truly was deceiving.

All those dazzling lights, the way they glinted off the giant, hanging chandler right in the middle of the huge room with the even taller, canopy-like ceiling. All those crystals which seemed to shift and sway with the music, catching both notes and light before retracting them in a whole other direction.

Even though Cat was prepared for the sight, having glimpsed the elegance of the Gardens when she'd snuck up those stairs with Dusty to Abigail's room, she still found herself a bit taken aback. Or perhaps that was more a difficulty with breathing.

Still, the place was still nothing less than perfection and even in that perfection, a thousand details she didn't dare miss. Too much at stake.

It was quite easy to understand why these men came here. Outside, a dark, unforgiving world. The side of Butte that didn't hide who she was and all the ugly she had going on, and didn't care neither what you thought. The richest hill on the earth. The ugliest hill on the earth. Butte embraced both.

But those rich and powerful men? They didn't. Instead, they came to places like this to forget that truth. Here where the world was nothing but light and beauty. Here where not even a speck of shadows existed.

If only you looked close enough...

If you looked at the girls themselves, and the light that was slowly, slowly dying from their eyes.

Fading. Just as they were.

Those girls with their dying eyes, so many of whom were already turning to other substances as a means to cope, to survive, to give them some small spark of happiness, even if the happiness was an illusion. Just like they were. Here, right now—illusions.

Each of them were these bright, shining, dazzling jewels, who to a one were just as carefully arranged as the Gardens. Cheeks and lips as red as any rose Cat had seen. Hairs curled and done up in such styles it would have taken Cat a week and still not gotten right.

The girls were, indeed, quite a sight, even with the light fading out of them. While the men, on the other hand, were another story altogether and who Cat focused her attention on.

One breath, then another.

Slow, deliberate, just like the steps she took as Blake led her further into the ballroom until they finally stood right in the center, right underneath that crystal chandelier.

Those men, they didn't carry the same quality of 'beauty' as the ladies did. They didn't need to. Their worth came from the money they owned, which they wore just as obvious as if they were the ones wearing rubies and sapphires. Really, by one look alone you could just know who was the wealthiest and who had... well, just enough to be here. Then there was Blake, who immediately upon entry into the ballroom had every single female glancing his way—and their gaze staying there.

Blake who had each of them girls were wondering: just what was *his* worth?

He was not flaunting or obvious about his wealth, nor was his manner one of disdain towards all other living things, a common trait Cat had noticed in the more wealthy individuals. Instead, Blake was hiding it all—including his own wonderment of the place.

And his loathing of it.

Cat saw a glimpse of this, and that was all.

Just a glimpse, one she only recognized because it was the way he'd first looked... at her. And how much that look had hurt and infuriated her. One that... she wasn't seeing now, certainly not when his gaze briefly landed on her.

No, it wasn't there. At least, not towards her.

Not anymore.

Then the moment passed. All of it. Back to whatever depth Blake hid himself and his emotions, safe where they were out of reach from them all, her included, and it was for the best.

Certainly now.

And while the girls didn't know who Blake was, all the men, they knew who *Cat* was.

Well, not exactly.

They didn't know she was Cowboy Cat, but they knew she was a fallen woman... even if she was on the arm of another man. The only women who'd ever set foot in this kind of establishment, high class or not, was a woman of ill repute. And those men were sizing her up as well.

A new girl.

Someone... different. Was this the kind of different they were interested in? Or should they not bother at all?

And because they were staring so openly at her, Cat put on her best, most charming smile, hoping that Norma's ghost would feel a small measure of pride at the display, and openly gazed right back at them.

One breath, then another. Slow-like.

Seeing everything, hopefully missing nothing.

Because underneath all this wealth, they really looked about the same.

Ugly.

Sad.

Their souls decaying.

Each of them older, with their graying hair, perhaps overweight as well, or maybe no hair and overweight as was the case with Seamus O'Neil who was even now standing over by the bar, if one could call *that* a bar—nothing like the Unlucky Horseshoe where it'd looked like someone had practiced etching their letters there.

All of this Cat saw in an instant.

That momentary... pause... between breaths.

With Blake's hand still on hers, he gave her a slow twirl about the room, allowing her to see all... to take it all in...

Everything.

O'Neil, who stood by himself in the corner. No lady hanging off of him, trying her best to charm him into another glass of champagne or some other form of entertainment, though it didn't seem he needed charming as far as the drinks were concerned. He held a small shot glass in his hand, full with amber liquid, and another empty one beside him on the counter, with the bartender immediately slipping away as if sensing the scrutiny. O'Neil with that glower on his face as if he alone were holding all them shadows the lights had cast aside, one that turned almost murderous as his gaze flicked across the room...

And right to Jim MacDonald.

Yes, MacDonald was there as well, sitting in some great armchair with none other than Abigail, more elegant than all the others in her deep, midnight blue dress, and somehow kept her whole self perched there on that arm rest. She was giving MacDonald this charming smile, the kind that, thanks to her golden hair, made it look like she was some sort of angel.

And MacDonald? He was bathing in that warmth. As if... desperate for it.

Then Abigail's attention, like all the other girls, shifted direction, taking some of that warmth with it. Enough for Cat to notice a sudden change in MacDonald, as if he couldn't bare to part from that warmth.

His eyes looking sunken and hollow. Dark circles that she could see even from this distance, as if he hadn't slept at all. And no, it wasn't sleep loss from a long, rowdy night in silken bed sheets but a deeper kind of loss... the kind that touched the soul and allowed one no moment of peace.

Cat knew that look. She'd seen it in Alice the very last time she was with her sister, and then she saw it in herself. In the mirror, staring back at her every day until... until she'd decided to come here.

Another breath.

She could have forced herself to concentrate on the task at hand, but that was the old her. The one who buried her hurts and pretended like they didn't matter none. But she knew differently now. They mattered.

So, Cat let herself feel all that sorry and sadness, let it live inside her chest and fill her heart until it almost felt like she could be crying.

She didn't, though.

Feeling was more than enough, apparently, for Alice and her ghost, for Cat didn't cry. Instead, she felt her focus, her senses become so clear it felt like she herself was a knife that could cut the very air.

There... there by herself was Madam Grace. Sitting on her throne right in the center of the room. A simple wooden chair but right there facing the whole room. Her neck—hell, her whole body—was bound up in the strictest kind of clothing you'd expect from the matrons who spent their Sundays in church or going to city hall and making sure the founding fathers were doing their good works for the day. Hard eyes, hard mouth, the kind that hadn't smiled in a century. All of her attention was on the two newcomers and not trusting a thing she was seeing.

Cat moved on again.

Felt time starting to catch up with her.

They hadn't come for Grace or O'Neil or MacDonald.

They'd come here for Marcus Daly and Joseph Nadeau... the

people who, deep down, she was hoping were those 'unusual visitors'
Madam Grace had commented to Abigail about. Except...

"You see them?" Blake asked her.

Cat closed her eyes a moment. Opened them again.

Nothing had changed. No one new had arrived.

"No," she whispered. "They're not here."

CHAPTER FORTY-SEVEN

D*amn* it.

Everything they'd been hoping for had hinged on the presence of either those two men. The only ones who, Cat could see, held the power to move pawns across the board like they had. From the editor of *The Bystander*, while not exactly impressive to bribe or blackmail, the chief of police, on the other hand, was. Then there was the necessary doctor needed to write off the two deaths as natural causes, and that kind a pull wasn't easy to come by.

It required money and balls.

And a lot of both.

It was the music that came back first, cluing Cat in that her awareness, this pause between breaths, was slipping. Time was moving back into place, settling in and carrying on, regardless if she was ready for it or not. O'Neil, who huffed after a moment of staring at her, immediately downed his drink then clinked the glass back down on the counter, a clear signal for *more*. MacDonald, on the other hand, he was taking his time assessing Cat, as if something about her, something in his memory, tugged at him... familiar maybe... but no, couldn't possibly be...

This curiosity was slowly replaced by another kind of look in his eyes. A coldness. Not one of recognition, but... of calculation. As if she were a mere object to be weighed and examined, to be owned for a short while and simply tossed aside.

Cat was careful to not meet his gaze, not knowing why but following her instincts. Trusting in them. Instead her gaze settled just beyond him, at Abigail, and she saw the other girl's slight stiffening at this change in MacDonald. Her back going a tad bit straighter.

As if... she knew what this look meant.

Or perhaps it was simply because she was the only person in the room who recognized Cat.

Again, it was just a moment. Abigail's baby blue eyes, bluer than any Montana sky Cat had ever seen, widened as Abigail's gaze met Cat's. Then a small smile, really more of a smirk, that pulled at her lips. Followed by a little nod.

A promise shared. Made from one girl to another.

And Cat was upholding her end of the bargain, even if it didn't look like much would come of it because neither Nadeau or Daly were present. There had to be something she could do—

Then MacDonald grabbed a glass of champagne and shoved it into Abigail's hand. Shoved it hard enough that a few drops spilled on that beautiful dress of hers, causing Abigail's face to flush deeper than her red lips. And MacDonald didn't care, either. Instead, he grabbed her by the arm. and pulled her after him. And she, with so little say in the matter, followed. She didn't glance back at Cat, as if she didn't dare. The two left through those ornately carved doors in the back heading to Lord knows where. Her rooms? Perhaps a private sitting room for just such occasions? Or... somewhere else entirely?

Cat didn't know, but she wasn't the only one to see the exchange. Blake had, and more importantly, O'Neil had as well.

O'Neil's frown deepened to the point that it looked like his face had become nothing but folds and wrinkles, and red as all get out. Especially as he went and downed yet another glass of the amber liquid. The clink of that glass smacking on the counter cut right through the fine notes coming from the piano.

All of which didn't still or calm the sudden panicked feeling in Cat's heart. What if... what if she was wrong? What if this whole time, it hadn't been about Daly or Nadeau, but the charm of a snake's tongue standing right in front of her? She'd always suspected something off about MacDonald, something that didn't quite fit with the picture he'd portrayed. And what if it was Abigail who was now in danger—?

"You're worrying."

Blake's voice.

A whisper, right against her ear. So close she felt the unruly, loose strand of her hair blow against her cheek. And a tingle, too. One that didn't stop. In fact, it raced right down her spine and to her boots... if she'd been wearing boots. And dear Lord was she missing her boots about now. Her revolver. Not this silly little derringer strapped to her thigh, as if she could possibly reach it in a moment of crisis when all those damn layers and yards of silk and fabric separated her and her only weapon.

"Keep breathing," Blake said.

"Trying."

Except she was really feeling out of place all of a sudden, like she was actually standing there naked and not in this fine silken dress. Maybe it was 'cause of how very little she was in control here, and the very little she could do if it was needed if... if Abigail needed her.

"She's fine," Blake said.

Somehow he'd known she'd been worrying about Abigail. In her heart, she blessed him for that.

"I wish I could believe that," Cat whispered back.

"You'll have to, or at least lie to yourself and worry about it later because Madam Grace is heading this way."

And she was.

The madam herself, sliding off her simple yet very deliberate throne chair, and heading straight towards Cat and Blake. No... not

Blake. Just Cat. Those gray eyes of hers, as hard and as cold as the darkness outside, were on Cat and Cat alone. As if the gentleman beside her was of no consequence, but the girl who was now threatening the success of her own girls... well, that was something indeed.

Madam Grace's gray eyes didn't leave Cat, not once, not even as she maneuvered around the few couples who danced about the room under that glinting light of the chandelier high above. Grace's eyes, which matched perfectly with the silken, gray dress she wore. The only spark of coloring she had on came from the silver hanging off her ears and the silver brooch clasped about her throat about the size of Cat's fist.

Madam Grace looked exactly as Cat had pictured her.

And just as cold and unwelcoming as well.

Blake, clearly reading the signals, excused himself. He'd known, just as she had, that Madam Grace wasn't interested in him. At least not until she took care of Cat and opened the way for one of her girls to find herself a new beau for the evening.

Cat smiled.

The anxiety she felt a moment ago, the worry and panic in her chest for Abigail, disappeared. Not completely—oh no, it was still there—but it was gone from this moment. All her focus, all her attention was on the threat in front of her. Because there was no question 'bout the threat, either.

And both ladies knew it.

Madam Grace slid up beside Cat, giving her a long, slow measure from the tips of Cat's slippers to her coiled-up hair. Calculating, assessing, and along with the definite look of someone who found the woman before wanting.

Cat merely smiled, charming and graceful, which in its own way said *I don't give a shit, lady.*

"I am the madam of this establishment, Grace, as the name implies. I don't believe we've had the occasion to meet before."

"We haven't," Cat said. "Not officially, anyway."

"Oh? Then, unofficially?"

"Passed by, I believe."

"Hmm..." Grace's gaze again took a long, measuring look at Cat. "Well, I'm ashamed to say I don't remember this 'passing by.' I certainly wouldn't have forgotten a lady of your quality."

Grace held out her hand for Cat to take in welcoming, and held it out so delicate-like, as if she were some great flower the entire world must indeed pay homage to, and not the lady who was secretly raking up her own fair share of gambling debts and fallin' in deep with Nadeau or Daly or someone who saw fit to pay her bills.

But then, seeing as how this was *her* house, Cat didn't mind being polite.

She reached out, took Grace's hand, and shook it. A good up and down pump, the kind that a person felt whether they wanted to or not, and while not a *hard* grip—she wasn't tryin' to break the lady's hand or anything—she was trying to make a point.

A very good one.

She wasn't dainty or delicate. She was different than any girl Grace had ever met.

In fact, Cat's hands were hard and calloused, and were unforgiving in that they *weren't* soft. These were hands that had seen and welcomed a harder life. One that she was proud of, too.

And instead of a charming smile, the kind that curled about the face, taunting and teasing and enticing all at once, the kind of smile the girls here had mastered their first evening on the job, Cat merely grinned.

Grace's eyes widened.

She would have stepped back, probably in alarm or in horror, except Cat was still holding her hand.

"Actually," Cat said, "while we haven't had the chance to officially meet and all, you do know who I am."

Grace glanced at their hands. And the fine lady that she was... well, she gave no indication at all that she was ruffled by this whole situation. Now *she* was quite the master of her craft.

"Is that... is that so? As I said, I would have remembered—"

"You do. Remember, that is. In fact, you probably learned quite a lot about me just tonight."

"I assure you—"

"My name, Madam Grace, is Cowboy Cat, and I'm here about Norma. Think we can talk?"

CHAPTER FORTY-EIGHT

Y*ou."*

It was a whisper, nothing more, that slipped out from between Madam Grace's lips. A whisper that carried shock and disbelief, and maybe something else...

For a moment, it seemed the world around them slowed to a stop. Simply... halted in its movements, its breath. Like what was happening here was too important to miss even a single glance, a single shift of the body on that polished, gleaming floor underfoot of their too-soft heels.

"You're right," Grace said, so softly it was nearly impossible for Cat to hear over the notes of the piano. "I have heard of you. You've been... quite the talk of the town since you arrived. What are you doing here?"

This last was said with a hard, demanding bite.

To which Cat simply shrugged, a movement that was not befitting the elegant, ruffled dress she now wore.

"Keeping a promise."

"To whom?"

"Does it matter?"

"Always. In fact, promises and those who were are indebted to are the people who matter most of all. They hold our strings."

"In that case, a couple people have an interest in my strings," Cat said. "Not sure how interested they are in pulling them, though. Or, I guess more to the point, they had an initial interest in Norma's strings and I was the only one who came along and was willing to look into it. Or maybe this had about nothing to do with strings and debts and promises. Maybe they were just mighty sad to see Norma thrown out of here when it seemed she'd done nothing wrong, certainly nothing to warrant getting tossed down into those tunnels—"

"It was a deserved course of action."

"And a complete waste of resources, as you well know. You'd have been better off tossing her in the cribs under this place, and yeah, I know 'bout those, too. She'd have worked out just fine right there for you. Probably draw in quite the crowd, maybe help pay off some of those strings you're so concerned about. Probably would have worked, too, seeing as her smile was near legendary with the working men."

"Her removal was a necessary decision."

"Course it was. Just like it was necessary when she wanted back in this life and started stirring up trouble, that she had to go and die."

"To which I had no part of. It was a fate of Norma's own making—"

Cat, who still held Grace's hand, gripped it harder, cutting off what else the madam was gonna say.

"She was poisoned, did you know?"

Grace's face paled. "That, that's not...

"Possible? Sure it is. Especially since the officer who found her, who made sure any investigation into her demise was neat and orderly and quickly closed, also died of poisoning."

Grace got so pale then that Cat could see the red powder applied to her cheeks, as if sticking right to those pores and wrinkles for all the world to see. She swayed a bit and Cat, moving quickly and gracefully, both which were barely possible considering the way the bone ribs of her corsets just about dug themselves a new cozy spot in her ribcage (and not sway herself at the sudden movement), caught Grace about the wrist. She kept the other woman upright in a manner that betrayed nothing.

Nothing at all was going on here, just a conversation between ladies, to which the entire ballroom seemed smart enough, or aware enough, to give them their space.

Cat met Blake's gaze just for a moment. Not sure why but knowing she needed to, if just to say that she was all right.

And she was, mostly. Just a bit caught off guard.

Because this wasn't exactly what Cat had expected of Grace, certainly not the cold and hard madam she'd heard ordering Abigail about in her rooms earlier. Still, Cat wasn't one to miss an opportunity.

All her instincts, all her tingling—hell, even the hairs on the back of her neck raising. All of it focused on Madam Grace.

Piecing together the clues before her, the mannerisms, the shock, the almost desperate need to reach out to Cat for something...

Something that felt an awful bit like hope.

Regardless, it was a chance to get some answers, to bring some small manner of justice to Norma, even if that justice was only truth.

Sometimes truth was more than enough.

Had to be.

Cat continued to hold Madam Grace, letting the woman rest against her strength while she offered freely. Well, mostly freely. She did want answers, after all.

"I know you're not involved," Cat said, being sure to keep her words quiet. "At least not directly. But see, I do know that you have a place in all this. Why, if it wasn't for you, Norma would still be here. If you hadn't sent her off...."

Grace looked away.

"Yeah, that's what I thought. Probably why you didn't want your girls talking about her, reminding you of your part in all of this."

"How? How did you...?"

"You think you're the only one with ears in the shadows around here?"

Grace got a bit of color back in her cheeks, enough to hide the obvious tint of painted red there. Cat gestured for a server to bring a glass of champagne, which he did and promptly, too. Yet, even though the cool, slim flute was in Grace's hands, she didn't drink. She just... stared about the room, but distant like, like she wasn't actually seeing what was going on here. Or... maybe she was seeing what had taken place that night, after Abigail had retired for the evening with Seamus O'Neil when it was just Norma and those two powerful men, Daly and Nadeau, and with Nadeau's obvious attention on her.

"You think the answer is so easy?" Grace asked. "That it can all be nice and neat and tied up with a bow. Just blame one person and then Norma can finally rest in peace?"

"No."

Grace looked at her and blinked.

"I lived this life," Cat said. "Nice and neat doesn't exist. And the more you believe it, the quicker you'll fall. Not to mention, I don't think Norma's ghost is gonna find peace any time soon."

Not when she was still right beside Cat. Her cold presence keeping away all the heat from the dozens of lights.

Grace let out a breath that was almost, but not quite, a laugh. Or a sigh. "Would I have learned that sooner. And Norma, too."

"Why? What did she know? What put her in the middle of all this?"

"You already know the answer, Miss Cowboy Cat. Too much. Too much... desires, ambitions, foolishness. Put whatever word you like on it, but she forgot herself, she forgot her place, and she paid the price."

"How exactly?"

"She heard the wrong... *tale* from a partner's bedside pillow and forgot the number one rule."

"She tried to use it."

"Yes. She did, and the real mistake was not realizing who those people were. Didn't matter that they... had never been her original intent. The end result was the same."

Because... it was like Madam Grace had said... this was not something that could easily be tied up with a bow. Something that could not be tied to just one person. Which meant whomever Norma had heard those tales from... it had eventually worked its way back to those who'd be made most vulnerable by them. Not the lover, but the person in control of the lover. And maybe not that direct controller, but the one above him. And then above, and so on until it worked its way to the very top. To the very two people whom Cat had wanted to meet tonight.

Yes, the story of Norma, what happened here, what happened to her, was nearly complete.

Nearly, but not quite.

"Yes," Grace said, as if seeing Cat's thoughts and their final conclusion. "Exactly. So, when you ask if I played a part in what happened to her? Then yes, I did. But then so did she."

Which... made Cat wonder all the more...

"Why are you telling me this? Why are you speaking with me, risking that same wrath?"

The very one that Madeleine and all those girls on Galena Street, the ones who'd been friends with Norma, were afraid of.

"Or why haven't I simply thrown you out? Believe me, the thought *did* cross my mind. But then, you like a good mystery, yes, Miss Cat? Or should I call you Miss Justice?"

"I'll answer to either."

Grace gave her a small, sad smirk. "A lesson you should have learned sooner, especially if you believe yourself so wise. I'll leave you to figure out my motives, but I can tell you honestly, there is no justice for the likes of us. And you being here? You asking about Norma? You think that will bring her justice? You think that will cause anything but harm and pain to the other girls who walk this life?"

Cat shook her head. "I'm no fool. I know it will, I know it has already."

"And yet, you came here."

"I came here because I was asked to, and because I made a promise."

"Then they, and you, are all fools. There is no *one* player in this city, Miss Cat. They are *all* players, and each one of them owns us. Including you. You just don't know it yet."

"I am my own person."

"You care about them, those girls. That means you belong to them. You *belong* to us."

Grace tapped Cat's chest with a single finger, one of the fingers holding the untouched champagne, right below all those beautiful ruffles, which Grace seemed to notice.

"The dress really does suit you. Even after all this time, Mrs. Allen still has a fine taste. Though perhaps next time, you'll call on me as yourself and not someone else in disguise."

"Aren't we all in disguise? Playing the parts demanded of us?"

"Spoken like a lady who's walked in the shadows."

"I'm still living in them, just... a different kind of shadow than the ones you're used to."

To which Cat gave a long, pointed look about this elegant, glorious room, all the shining and all the light, and not a single shadow to be seen...

Except for what the ladies themselves carried.

Including Madam Grace.

"I can't help you," Grace said.

"You already have."

"You wanted answers."

"I still do."

"Then you just might get them. Your answers. If they mean that much to you..."

Grace glanced away from Cat at that moment, her gray eyes widening, losing some of that hardness, which was instead replaced by something else entirely. Something that Cat hadn't ever expected to see in a woman like Madam Grace.

Fear.

And not any fear that was directed at Cat, per se, but at who was coming up behind her.

CHAPTER FORTY-NINE

A person whom Cat hadn't sensed.

She'd been so focused on Grace, on reaching through to other woman, in trying to understand her, to read all that swirl of emotions in her manners and in her voice, that Cat had completely missed the person who'd entered the ballroom. The person who even now *compelled* the attention of every individual there. As if his presence—and yes, Cat was sure it was a him—was simply to great to be ignored.

She felt him now, though.

His presence.

Quiet but intense and... cold.

Very, very cold.

It was in the way he walked, too. Deliberate. Purposeful. Clicking those hard shoes on that equally hard, polished floor. Shoes that had probably been polished to an inch of their life, ones too, that probably hadn't been worn more than twice before a new pair was called for.

Shoes that were clearly heading right towards her.

Part of Cat wished it was Blake beside her right now. The

comfort and trust they shared, from when or even how how it had started, she didn't know herself, only that it was there. And even though he couldn't do much given the situation, given his civilian status, he was here. In this very room.

Meaning one important thing: Cat wasn't alone.

It was no longer just her and Alice anymore, huddled together in that tiny bedroom with the walls and ceiling shaking so hard under Stan's purposeful thumps. As thatched pieces of roof and dirt rained down on them, getting into their hair, their eyes. Alone. Terrified. With only one option remaining, and the very one that had torn Alice from her forever.

But Cat was no longer that girl.

No longer... alone.

Plus, there was Norma to consider. A presence Cat felt all the clearer in this moment. Her cold touch, one that now rested on Cat's shoulders as if she also meant to reassure, to promise that they were in this together. Even to the end.

She hoped it wouldn't come to that, though.

Because Norma and all those girls like her, like Madeleine and Abigail, each of them, were the real reason why Cat had dared come here, why she was willing to face down one of the richest men in Butte.

And it was enough.

Madam Grace, whom Cat was still holding, seeming to sense this shift in her because just as she was reaching for Cat, as if begging her to leave it and Norma alone, Cat instead gave her a comforting squeeze and then let go.

Let go, and faced one of the very men she'd been looking for.

Joseph Nadeau.

There was no denying who he was, even though she'd never seen a picture or any description of him 'sides what Abigail had given her. And yet, there was no mistake 'bout it.

Nadeau looked exactly as his presence felt.

His face white like snow, as if there weren't an ounce of warmth or love left inside him, as if this very business, or just business in general, required him to bleed every last drop of caring and laughter and love right on out of him. After all, it was the only way to get to where he was now in that fancy dark suit. Dark pants, dark jacket, which made him look all the starker. There was that sophisticated black tie, one that tightened all the way up to the tip of his chin, as if the higher it went, the straighter he would walk. And the straighter and taller he walked, the higher he'd be above the rest of them. Especially seeing as how *he* was the gentleman of standing here.

But worst of all, really, was the way he looked at everyone...

Like they were all worthless.

Pieces of property. Items and objects to be used and exploited and profited from. Nothing more. Just balances and numbers and worths on a spreadsheet.

Not human. Not even living beings.

That's how beneath far him they all were, and something Cat saw in that single breath as she looked at him.

Then his gaze finally fell on her and stayed there. He did not dismiss her in the way he did the others. Oh, no. For her, there was much more. Contempt, coldness, and a ruthless determination to do whatever it was that needed doing. He wanted to squash her, this annoying gnat that she'd become, buzzing and flying around him just so, probably even causing him to come down here to a parlor house he despised but one he held a considerable stake in, especially if their guesses were correct about Madam Grace being indebted to him.

Still, that look he sent her...

It was enough to make her wish for her revolver and not the tiny derringer strapped so far down on her hip, hidden by all that damn fabric, making the whole thing just about worthless.

As if sensing her thoughts, Grace tried again and this time got a good hold of Cat's arm, keeping her there, keeping her from moving or reacting. Or more than likely, going for her gun.

And yet within that single movement, Grace made a great show of giving a small curtsy, spreading out her dress in one hand, a hand somehow still holding that champagne flute, and holding Cat with the other.

Except despite the grace and flourish, the flute was now shaking. A single drop slipped over the side and slid down. It plopped right onto the polished floor, completely unseen by the rest of the party, completely insignificant.

Just as Cat was to this man.

An annoyance, a disturbance, but nothing more.

"Mister... Mr. Nadeau," Grace said, "I did not realize you were coming."

"Did you not receive my message, Madam Grace? I promised to come by this evening to... discuss recent events."

Nadeau's gaze landed on Cat and stayed there.

"But then, I see no reason when the very object of those discussions is standing right here before us."

It was lucky Cat didn't have the champagne because she was pretty darn sure she'd have lost her balance right at that moment, appropriately so given the heels she wasn't used to wearing, and dumped the whole glass right down his elegant, expensive suit.

His shocked expression alone would have made it worth it. But she contained herself.

If barely.

"I must say," Nadeau continued, "that you are indeed a lovely specimen, Miss Cat. Nothing at like the rumors I've heard."

Then he smiled at her.

A curling kind of smile, patient and dangerous. The same way a snake coiled up tight before it leapt right at you, striking. This was clearly a man who knew exactly what he was doing and exactly how to get what he wanted.

Cat had, in fact, been quite wrong about being gnat. Oh no, she was something much, much worse. Probably a cockroach or some vile pest he detested above all others. And while she just might be a gnat or a cockroach to him, she also had quite a few teeth of her own. Which she wasn't afraid to use, either.

And she showed him just that by smiling and looking right into those cold, hard eyes of his.

"Mr. Nadeau. I've been expecting you."

"Indeed? Well, isn't that quite a surprise. Did this, Madam Grace, to be expecting our guest here?"

Cat heard the inflection 'our' in there, which further confirmed her theory that Madam Grace was indebted to Nadeau.

Somehow, anyway.

This whole business had become one giant tangle of ribbons with poor Norma being the casualty right in the center.

Grace shook her head. "No, sir. I was quite surprised, actually. In fact, I didn't even recognize Miss Cat here as the famous 'Cowboy Cat' we've all been hearing about. Not even Mr. MacDonald or Mr. O'Neil gave her the proper credit, I'm afraid, and I was caught... quite unawares."

"Hmm, not a good place to be given your line of work, madam, though I say this as a friendly reminder, of course. But yes, perhaps I should have a talk with both gentleman about the proper telling of events..."

Nadeau glanced around the room and immediately looked at O'Neil, as if O'Neil was exactly where Nadeau had expected him to be—and O'Neil, for his part, didn't hesitate in finishing off yet another glass of whatever the dutiful bartender was surviving him.

Nadeau gave a nod at O'Neil, whose face flushed a deeper red, going from that bald top right down his thick neck.

"And... Mr. MacDonald?" Nadeau asked.

"I believe he's retired for the evening, sir."

"So soon? A shame. I was hoping to speak with him regarding another matter. You'll send a message for him, yes?"

Madam Grace blinked. "You mean now, sir?"

His cold gaze narrowed on her. "I believe that's what I said."

Cat, knowing exactly how to put her foot in, said: "Actually, it's what you implied. The immediacy of the matter... well, you left that part out, especially since we here all know how he's going to be *engaged* at the moment."

Nadeau merely looked at her, as if surprised she was not only still standing there but that she was actually speaking. As if her form came with a voice and a tongue and all that nonsense.

Madam Grace, however, paled.

"Well yes, then," Grace said. "I can certainly send a message to him."

"His earliest convenience, of course, seeing as how he's engaged at the moment."

This last he said to Cat.

Except Madam Grace didn't yet leave. She lingered there, as if terrified to leave Cat alone with the man.

As she had every right to be.

There was only so much restraint a person, especially one getting as fired up as Cat, was capable of, and both ladies knew it.

Nadeau was studying her again, taking in the style of her dress, how her hair was done up, as if sizing every little inch and detail of her and putting some number, same value on what he saw.

"You've been staying at Mrs. Allen's boarding home, if my sources are correct."

"I am."

"Hmm. I wasn't aware she was still in business. A matter we may have to rectify, I think."

Cat bristled, biting her tongue hard to keep from really saying something that'd guarantee getting her thrown out on her ass—not yet, anyway, not until they got answers. But she was sure damn glad that Blake *wasn't* by her side. While he didn't seem the type to grab a man by the head and slam it into whatever surface seemed handy, she had no doubt that he loved his aunt. Not only loved her, but would do just about anything to protect her, and his, home.

No wonder why Murphy hadn't been keen on the two of them coming here. There were too many pitfalls, too many traps that'd be so easy to get sucked into. Especially when, in general, they had so very little and these rich men... well, they used all that little to their advantage.

And that they weren't above playing dirty, either. After all, there'd been a reason they'd gotten themselves nice and rich in the first place.

Which was why the dig at Mrs. Allen and her livelihood stung so badly, and why Cat was glad it was Grace beside her and not Blake.

Grace's grip on Cat's arm tightened to a fairly considerable amount.

Silence, she instructed Cat.

Her grip was, in fact, much harder than Cat had thought possible for the aging woman. Maybe she wasn't ready to simply lay down and curl up to her new financial overlord.

Still, Grace's advice was sound and so Cat kept her anger in check and held her tongue.

For now.

Nadeau, on the other hand, didn't. He didn't need to.

After all, he, being who he was—rich and powerful, with any number of men and ranked officials neatly tucked in his back pocket —had no reason or concern to hold his tongue. When you ran one of the most successful parlor houses, not to mention many of the lesser ones all throughout the Red Light district... well, it was one of the perks of the job. You got to say what was on your mind and damn the consequences.

It was especially when said officials were also clients who wanted to remain anonymous. Something a man like Nadeau wouldn't hesitate to use to his advantage in all his... business dealings.

"I thought," Nadeau said to Cat, "that your tastes ran to the well... how shall we say, the *simple* side of life? Such as my property on Galena Street, which I heard you passed by. What did you think, hmm? Did it compare to your Miles City some, or was that even more upscale than you're used to? And how about my soon-to-be-famous Copper Block? I have no doubt it will put the rest of the... unsavory establishments out of business."

Cat kept on breathing, much as she could given the constraints put on her by the dress and that horrible corset.

"You mean," she said, "the building several stories high? Big? Fancy?"

"That's the one, and I must say—"

"Just to clarify, you *also* mean the building that didn't have a single open window, not a single shine of light, as if it had never seen the sun? The same building that was so downright depressing and horrifying it made me think twice before even crossing the street? Yes, yes, I did see it, Mr. Nadeau. Quite impressive. I'm sure you're proud of the *brisk* business you do there. And the tidy profit you make off those girls, stealing about all they earn just to make yourself richer."

Nadeau's smile slipped ever so much, which made Cat's grin grow even wider.

Yes, she highly doubted he was used to his... pets standing before him like this, telling him exactly what they thought of him and his business, and not making a single Goddamn apology for it.

Cat leaned in closer, her smile curving up to let him know just how dangerous she was—even without her gun.

"Yes, Mr. Nadeau, I know who you are and I know what you've done. I know about Norma, too, and I damn well intend to tell the rest of the world."

Nadeau's thin, pale lips pressed together. "You think very highly of yourself."

"And you don't think enough of me. Especially if you think I'm bluffing."

"That's the thing, Miss Cat, I don't believe you are. A boldness that even a man like me can appreciate."

Nadeau turned and gestured to the piano player. It was some simple motion of his hand, one that meant absolutely nothing to Cat but clearly meant something to the other guy, because he got to playing. And it made Cat wonder, had this same event happened to Norma on her last evening in the Gardens? As

Abigail went upstairs with O'Neil, leaving Norma alone, to face Nadeau?

Probably.

Norma, for all her faults and mistakes, hadn't been a fool. She'd have known when she'd misstepped. Probably knew, too, it was a mistake she couldn't take back.

Except she'd tried to.

Tried to change the course of events, to get back to this life of dazzling lights and beauty, and *that* had gotten her killed.

The music changed tunes to a softer, slower piece, bringing Cat back to the present. The music was of the kind that invited the slowest kind of dance, close and intimate, the two individuals all bound up tightly together until it seemed they were one.

To which Nadeau turned to her and offered his hand.

It was both offer and command.

Cat stared at his pale, outstretched hand. Her senses pushing outward, seeing everything in just that one breath, then another. The heads of the other guests turning towards them, and the ladies, too. Each looking their way and staying there. In surprise certainly, and perhaps even a bit of shock as if Nadeau, on the rare occasions he visited the Gardens, never danced. Perhaps even in his own establishment, the Dumas, it was well known by the patrons that he simply did not dance. Yet even with all the additional attention, there was one who Cat saw immediately. O'Neil still by the bar counter, all by himself, whose face was now turning such a bright red that it was already moving in the direction of concern...

Anger.

Seamus O'Neil was angry. At Nadeau.

And that thought... it tugged at Cat. Held there right during her pause between breaths, and she wondered and questioned... everything. Everything she and Blake and Dusty had thought they'd known because there was still something... something they were missing. Madam Grace had hinted that there was more than one player—had, in fact, warned Cat otherwise. What part *did* Nadeau play in all this? From what she'd learned, both O'Neil and MacDonald were in Marcus Daly's court. Both worked at Daly Bank and Trust, yet it was O'Neil who clearly appeared on the lowest rung of this ladder. Even though O'Neil was the close and personal friend to the copper king himself, not MacDonald. And with two men tied directly to Daly, what the hell was Nadeau doing here? Nadeau giving the orders, issuing the commands, and all the others following meekly at his heels.

Which he was now asking her to do.

Well, there was one thing she could do, something that no one had ever thought about doing, had even considered a possibility. Her included. Cat could plain and simply ask. Ask what part Nadeau played in all this. After all, she'd come here to find answers, to overturn that table and for once throw the rest of these gentleman off balance. And for as smooth as Nadeau was attempting to be, Cat knew she had.

She could see it.

Could see that tightening of skin around his eyes. The way the wrinkles there had become more pronounced the longer he stood near her, the longer he was forced to swallow his distaste and disgust at her daring behavior, at very her presence. And Nadeau's coldness had only grown. As if it wasn't caused by additional control or restraint but the opposite. The coldness *was* his way of displaying anger, compared to O'Neil who just went and turned a dangerous shade of purple.

And if the chill and the white puffs of air coming from her breath and Grace's were any indication, Nadeau was furious with her.

Furious and all the while still waiting patiently with that outstretched of his. A hand that had never seen a day's hard work in his life.

From the corner of her eye, she caught sight of Blake. His blond hair unmistakable even amongst this crowd. Not to mention his presence alone, which about shone as bright as the sun in this place where shadows hid in each of the girls' eyes.

For the briefest of moments, their gazes met.

Not long, certainly not long enough to draw attention or have others question their connection and real reason for being there. But then just for that one moment, it was enough. Enough to convey the very clear warning he sent to her.

That she, under no circumstances, was to accept Nadeau's hands.

Joseph Nadeau, one of the richest, coldest men in all of Butte. A combination that made him one of the most dangerous. And Blake, being an officer of the law, probably knew each and every rumor, every sordid detail by memory and not a solid slip of evidence to do anything about it.

Cat looked away first.

She had to, much as it twisted her insides to do so. She'd come here to fulfill a promise, after all. She might not be able to keep it, might not find any kind of justice for Norma, but she had to try. She owed it to Norma and Dusty and Madeleine.

And she owed to it herself.

So instead of turning away, of leaving with Blake and playing the hand that meant she stayed safe, Cat did the opposite. She reached out, accepted Nadeau's hand, and began dancing.

CHAPTER FIFTY

Now being rich didn't make one dangerous. Rich, cold, and ruthless, on the other hand... well, you better be wary and watchful. But when that individual also had a secret? Or more than likely, secrets?

That made them truly dangerous.

Like a wounded animal caught with its back against a sheer rock cliff and no other means of escaping. That right there was when the real danger appeared. When you were better off lifting your rifle and taking the shot from a good distance away. Certainly not running on in, charging with nothing more than a small-ass kitchen knife.

Or a tiny-ass derringer.

And yet here Cat was, dancing with this very dangerous man.

But sometimes principles, the real foundations of a person, were worth risking your life over.

She certainly hoped so. Certainly believed so.

Because Nadeau's entire world, the businesses his wealth was built on, involved both secrets and legitimacy. Everyone knew prostitution was legal in Butte, yes. For how long... well, that remained to be seen, especially as the west started settling down, bringing more families in, then raising those families and sending 'em to good churches and schools, becoming the kinds of places where the rough and rowdy weren't so much welcome no more. But for now, owning property where transactions of the flesh took place was legal. And quite profitable. But then, here's the thing: business in the shadow world was a slippery slope. You might be standing on one side of the law one moment, but then after you started walking into that gray, you might suddenly glance around and realize you're standing in muck up to your elbows.

All that muck... well, that there were secrets a person like Nadeau couldn't risk getting out.

And he had secrets, no doubt about it. And clearly Norma had found out. Perhaps she hadn't even known at the time they were *his* secrets, a mistake Cat had no intention of making. She knew they were his secrets, or at least tied to him in some way, and she, right to his face, was telling him so.

Publicly.

And threatening to go even more public if she didn't get what she was after.

Which, although Cat might still be an annoying gnat in his eyes, it made her a dangerous one. 'Cause in many ways, especially thanks to the flaming rock thrown right at her head, her own back was up against that wall and she was done playin' around.

Done dancing to his tune... even if they were for all intents and purposes dancing.

And it was no surprise really that the man was a fine dancer, either. After all, Nadeau was a well known, upstanding gentleman and business owner, not to mention him being married and all, so dancing was simply one of those activities he needed to know. And needed to be competent at. He was.

One hand gently holding hers, the other right at the curve of her waist. Both, perfectly placed, applying the perfect amount of pressure and guidance to get her where he wanted to go. And both leaving a coldness she felt right to her soul.

Though it had nothing on the two ghosts following her, following her and saying nothing.

The very last thing in the world Cat wanted was to dance with this man, and yet that was where he'd called her to come. If she wanted answers.

She did.

So, she allowed it.

Nadeau spun her once, causing her fine pink dress to twirl about her just so and the bones of her corset to dig even tighter into her ribcage. She tried sucking in as much air in as she could, as if she were saving some for later, but that didn't help much. Problem was, she wasn't like Abigail or the rest of the girls here, who at least were used to the restricted movement. For Cat, it felt like being bodily bound, gagged, and hog-tied all at once, especially when her vision got a bit spotty and her head a bit fuzzy from lack of adequate air supply.

Nadeau, as if sensing her discomfort, went and twirled her again. It was like he wanted to prove that he was the one in control and he was merely appeasing her.

Cat barely kept from stomping on his feet just to prove him wrong.

"Is something the matter, Miss Cat? Are you perhaps having a little difficulty keeping pace?"

"Not at all. It's the company I don't enjoy."

"The feeling then is indeed mutual."

He smiled at her, like it was some joke only the two of them shared, and then he twirled her again before gracefully pulling her back towards him.

Cat swallowed both grimace and dizziness. She absolutely refused to give him the satisfaction.

"You are," Nadeau said, "exactly what everyone said you were. It's refreshing, really, if it weren't my business you were entangling your-self with."

"My business is Norma."

"Norma." Nadeau's mouth twisted in distaste, as if he'd caught a scent of something right foul. "I will warn you once. You're better off leaving this business with her alone."

"Or what? You'll threaten the other girls? The ones who were kind to her? Toss them out as you did her?"

Cat lifted a hand and shook her finger at him, scolding.

"Oh, I know, you will. You'll toss them out of their pitiful homes and down into those tunnels where they have absolutely no chance of ever seeing the sun again simply because you can."

"You do like your suns."

Nadeau kept his tone light and teasing, quiet still, so no one else in the room could hear, but his eyes told a different story. A darker one.

"And," he said, "I see you've worked out some of Norma's story but not all, though."

"Not all of it," Cat agreed. "There are a few pieces that aren't fitting just right."

"A few, indeed, if you're here now threatening me. Because clearly you believe I am the villain in this little story."

"Aren't you?"

"Oh, I am certainly. Depending on who you ask, I am indeed the great evil villain. But in *this* particular story?"

Nadeau dipped her back just then, slow like, and Cat, if she hadn't been her, if she hadn't been watching him so close and saw that tiny, initial movement in his upper body and arms, it would have completely caught her off guard. She may have gasped aloud at the sudden, digging pain into her sides, then gasped again just because she would have needed even more effort. Perhaps her vision would have gotten worse, her head, even more fuzzy. And then... then he really would have the upper hand, if simply because of their genders and their stations.

He could have handed her off then, a woman ready to faint, to someone else to take charge of and walked away leaving Cat with no other means of getting her answers.

But then, she was her and she did see that slight movement.

She wasn't caught off balance, wasn't caught by surprise like he'd intended. And there was certainly a disappointment in those cold eyes of his when she didn't follow the narrative he'd written.

Though it still hurt like a damn.

All the while to those guests watching them—except for Blake near the far front of the room and Madam Grace near her throne, who lingered there with her untouched champagne, as if uncertain about leaving and sending the message to MacDonald as Nadeau had instructed—this whole dance appeared to be one of complete grace.

Two partners, somehow perfectly matched, perfectly in balance and in tune. And yet, this was very far from the actual truth.

In fact, it was Cat who always seemed at the disadvantage. Dancing, after all, called for a man to lead in the steps, and her dress alone gave him the upper edge. *He* could breathe whenever the hell he wanted to. And no surprise, being the type of man he was, Nadeau was using every tool at his disposal to control this narrative, and as if to prove this point, he brought her so close their noses were inches from the other.

Cat stayed right there, not moving. Watching everything.

"So," Cat said, "you're not the villain."

"Not *her* villain. You believe that Norma had some unpleasant information, which in turn led back to me. And me, feeling vulnerable over the word of some harlot, as if she could actually harm myself or my businesses, I then ordered her gone from this pathetic place she called home. That I had her tossed out like the worthless trash she was, wasting what little use she had because of this silly notion that she was worth more than life had given her."

This last felt like a punch to the gut because it was both true, and not.

Norma was worth more.

But at the same time, in Nadeau's eyes she was worth nothing.

It was the very paradox of this shadow world, the one Cat had clawed her way out of only to turn back around, walk right in, and demand justice for those who didn't have the means of getting themselves out.

"From where I'm standing," Cat said, "that doesn't make you the good guy."

"Of course not, because as a proper villain, why would I stop there? Your poor, deceased friend could have gone on to live a... well, if not full life, a longer one. But she couldn't let matters be. Oh, no. She had to rise up and try to reclaim her lost legacy and in doing so, sealed her fate. And I'm sure you believe that it was I who ordered her demise as well, yes?"

He didn't wait for her answer.

He should have.

Nadeau slowed their dance even further until they were simply standing still. But standing so close. His hands still on her when she'd rather him be sprawled out on the floor clutching his bloody, broken nose because she'd gone and grabbed Madam Grace's champagne flute and smashed it into his face.

And yet the trade off was worth it.

Because she missed nothing.

And Nadeau, like the proper, elegant villain he was, he just kept right on talking.

"You see, Miss Cat, I don't care about her. Your... *Norma*. You see? Her name has no hold over me. No power over me. I don't even care about her death except as it now seems to be interfering with my business, and that, my dear, I cannot stand for."

"Because... my digging—hell, even my being here—is threatening your business."

Not... directly, but sideways.

Yes, she could see it. Could feel how it *felt* right for this story. And like that, another piece fit into place. One of those pieces that had never quite fit right to begin with.

Nadeau waved a hand at her nicely done-up hair and then her dress. "Your whole presence... well, it's quite unprecedented and I'm afraid it will give my renters the wrong impression, and I would hate for any of them to learn an... incorrect lesson. You see, I am not one to make threats, certainly not lightly, but I am feeling very... uneasy regarding your association and interest in the deceased's harlot's affairs.

"You," Nadeau continued, "who are also a night lady, daring to voice your opinion against my good name and thinking... thinking I might actually be threatened by, by all this."

He gestured to the ballroom while Cat stayed where she was.

Watchful. Seeing those who glanced their way and those like O'Neil and Blake—no, she couldn't look closely at him, but he was still there, right there if she needed him. But O'Neil, too, it seemed his gaze couldn't break away from Nadeau. As if... held there. As if... compelled.

Another breath slipped from Cat's lips.

Another piece of the puzzle, shifting this time and turning, and then... fitting into place.

"Do you," Nadeau asked, as he leaned in closer again, "do you honestly believe that you, you of all people, could harm me?"

He gently touched her hair, the strand that had slipped free from behind her ear while they'd danced. The same hair that always refused to do as it was told.

He tucked it back where it belonged and took his time doing it, too. And he trailed a finger across her cheek to make a point. Both as a taunt and a promise.

"I'm sure," he said, "you understand my meaning. You, just like Norma, are nothing. Nothing at all. Simply a... a pest that must be attended to."

Cat didn't move.

Nadeau smiled then, thinking he'd won. Thinking that the matter was settled and he'd significantly put her in her place and would never have to concern himself with this upstart Cowboy Cat, again.

But then, that was her name now.

Cowboy Cat.

And Justice.

The room around her faded to nothing. No dazzling lights. No swaying music, compelling one to dance.

There was only one breath, then another.

He was wrong, of course. On all accounts.

They were not worthless. They had never been, even if their lives had seemed to be. And just as important, the dead certainly didn't see themselves as worthless.

And the dead... well, they saw everything.

Nadeau didn't know that Norma was beside Cat right now. The coldness of her presence, one which seeped right through that thin, beautiful silk dress Cat wore and left her skin standing straight on end. A kind of coldness, sharper and deeper, than Nadeau had ever felt, had ever known, and wouldn't know until his black heart finally stopped beating and the dead, all those lives he'd ruined, all the suffering he'd caused, finally reached up and claimed him.

He also didn't know Alice was there as well.

Alice, who haunted Cat. Who wouldn't let her rest nor give up. Who pushed her to be here even now, facing down a man like him because, despite his threats and all the terrible things he believed he could do, it was nothing compared to the guilt already shadowing Cat's heart.

Alice, with her faded blond hair and the dim eyes that had once, a long time ago, known joy. Eyes that in their final moments had looked at Cat with such sorrow and sadness, with rejection and loathing, because she'd gone and kept them safe. She'd ended that worthless life of Stan's so Alice would continue to have hers.

But now, at least for this moment, that look was gone.

Alice reached out and touched the back of Cat's hand. Alice, who wouldn't let her turn away. Alice, who even in death somehow believed in Cat.

It was enough. It would always be enough.

Fool that he was, with all his money and businesses and investments, he'd forgotten one powerful detail:

The dead and their hold over the living was mighty strong, indeed.

Cat slowly took Nadeau's hand off her cheek and dropped it.

His eyes widened.

She knew why.

He'd felt the coldness in her. The ice. The frozen touch of the dead. Because right now, in this moment, she had become their justice. Even if it wasn't an equal justice. Not a life for a life, not even a ruin to what he held most dear—his businesses—because she couldn't grant Norma that. Butte and her courts and her laws wouldn't allow for that.

But there was still another form of justice.

Truth.

And that was what Cat was after. This whole time, ever since she'd opened that newspaper and flipped to the short snippet of a tale, Cat had been weaving together Norma's life.

Her truth, as it were.

And all this time, without Nadeau being the wiser, Cat's awareness had filled her whole being and then more. It reached out from deep inside her and then into his, diving deep, then deeper still. He had no idea how far she could see, how much she could see. All those seemingly insignificant details and how very much they revealed.

The bare shadow under his eyes, like a little smudge of black paint.

But no, not paint.

Worry.

Worry that had kept him from sleeping well last night. She could see him lying in that great bed beside his wife, if they even shared a room. Tossing aside those layers of heavy, warm quilts because they had a stranglehold on him. Tightening round and round like a coiling noose.

Cat breathed in.

Then out again.

Felt each of these truths like they were her own.

"You didn't sleep last night," she whispered. "Barely a wink. And you were in a sweat the whole time, to the point that your dear wife asked after your health in the morning, isn't that right?"

Nadeau's curling, cruel smile slipped. A muscle there, right at his too-white cheek, as if he'd never seen the sun, twitched. Once, twice. Then a third time.

"I'm guessing," she said, "it was because you heard about my activities, specifically the gathering. How successful it turned out, especially when you'd failed at discrediting Mrs. Allen."

Nadeau would have been wise to look away.

He didn't.

Because the dead missed nothing. And with Alice and Norma beside her, touching her, and she in turn fulfilling a promise, Cat missed nothing.

Another piece of the story opened up like a flower slowly unfurling its delicate petals.

"Yes..." Cat said, seeing the truth even as he tried to hide it, conceal it. "It was you. You who called the chief of police and requested that Mrs. Allen be brought in."

"I haven't the faintest idea of what you're talking about, young lady."

Not a harlot anymore.

A lady.

She watched as his left eyebrow twitched. His eyes, growing colder. Fury and something more swirling up inside him, and it was all he could do to contain it...

Fear.

Cat breathed in again as deep as she could, ignoring the black spots circling around her when she did so, her corset protesting such a silly movement as breathing.

But the dead weren't done. They wanted more.

They wanted the full truth.

"The doctor," Cat said, "he was yours, too. Not the mysterious one who tried to save poor Norma, but the other. The one who lied, the one who said both her and Officer White's deaths were of natural causes."

Nadeau tried pulling away from her then, but he couldn't. Couldn't because Cat was suddenly there, holding his arm in place. She'd moved before his brain had even requested the action and now her grip was dead on his.

Strong, too.

Hell, she had to be in order to ride herd with all those other cowboys, as her daddy had taught her.

"But that's not all, is it?"

Cat pressed her fingers into his arm, gripping him even harder, as if her grip alone could impress upon him the real person she was and not the being he believed her to be.

"But," she said, "that's not where this story ends or even... where it began, is it?"

Because the real question was *why?*

Why had Nadeau done all this? Why had he gone and meddled in the affairs of someone like Norma? He, himself, had said that she hadn't mattered to him.

And then as if asking the question was enough, Cat began to see those puzzle pieces in whole new kinds of shapes. Curves and edges that had been hidden from her beforehand.

There was nothing Nadeau could do to stop it, to keep her from seeing. Not now, not ever again...

The truth which whooshed out of her chest was like someone had gone and kicked her right in the gut.

Nadeau had said it himself.

Norma *hadn't* mattered. Not to him.

She never had, never would, at least not until Cat came along and pressed the issue, forcing him to become more and more involved. And because Cat hadn't allowed the others to forget either, to move on... but then, Norma and her smile hadn't let them either.

Norma, who'd been haunting them, each and every one, Nadeau included, even if the man hadn't known it.

Except Nadeau hadn't been lying.

"Norma," she whispered.

Then she looked right over Nadeau's pale face to his shoulder and then right past him.

Looked right... at Seamus O'Neil.

Another piece of Norma's story took shape, a shape she hadn't realized or known before. Couldn't because she'd never been part of this world, of *his* world. She'd never been in the position of this gentleman standing here, someone who lived on the other side of the line, taking in all the profits and none of the risks, none of the dirt or muck. And she'd never realized just how tied in all this business he was, all those who he needed to line up, all the information he needed to turn that profit and keep it turning, keep it steady and even better, keep it rising.

And it wasn't just Nadeau, either.

It was all of them. All the businessmen like Nadeau and the bank owners, and then there were the three big names themselves, the self-declared Copper Kings of Butte: Heinz and Clark and Daly.

Not a one of their hands were clean.

And she was willing to bet that each and every hand somehow led back to the other.

Cat's gaze returned to Nadeau and those cold eyes of his were swimming again, filled with an emotion he'd probably never felt in his life before but now, now was learning about it plenty.

"Norma never had *your* secrets."

Cat felt this truth the way she felt her own name.

O'Neil.

The ties, all those ribbons with Norma dead in the center, they all wound back to O'Neil. And from O'Neil...

Cat hadn't released Nadeau and didn't intend to, either. Instead, she pulled him closer to her as if she were the mighty, unmovable mountain of control and poise and he... he was the weightless feather who had no say in which way the wind decided to blow.

"They weren't your secrets," she said again. "So why do it? Why toss her aside? Why bring Mrs. Allen—hell, even the doctor in? Why... if they were never yours to begin with?"

Nadeau watched her now with a wariness he'd never shown before. Uncertain. Shaken. He didn't know what she was or what to make of her. She simply didn't... fit into his world view anymore.

But then he shrugged. And that emotion Cat had sensed early, that swell of fear that perhaps she really could harm him, it too, shrugged away. As if the matter now was a moot point and he was simply tossing in the towel without a care, or a thought, in the world.

The slow, curling smile he gave Cat felt very much like a rattlesnake coiling, but not to attack. No. This time, it felt like the smile came from pure amusement, as if that rarely happened anymore.

"Because," Nadeau said, "a friend asked me to."

CHAPTER FIFTY-ONE

A friend.

Of course. Such a simple thing, such a simple request, and yet... all those ribbons, all those ties, each one heading in a new direction, each one somehow tied to the other. One man goes down, so the rest, too, will follow. Unless proper precautions were taken, and even then... as Cat had said to Blake and Dusty earlier that evening, the very threat to Mrs. Allen's reputation, of Cat and the police, the very idea of it would have been enough to ruin her.

Because here in this world where light and dark literally lived side by side, reputation was everything.

That, and money.

Cat could still see Seamus O'Neil over Nadeau's shoulder. That bald head of his shining and sleek under all those brilliant, bright lights. The sweat glistening off him. And his face... she'd originally mistaken that deep red for fury when, in fact, it was a whole other emotion all together.

Embarrassment.

Shame.

Cat stepped away from Nadeau, her dress flowing about her in one graceful sweep.

The pieces coming together right then, including the ones that yet hadn't fit right. Not all of 'em, but they were, and they were coming in fast.

Cat glanced back at Nadeau, looked right into those suddenly amused, cold eyes. "You mean Marcus Daly."

She did not ask it as a question.

Nor did he take it as one.

He nodded at her. "If I were wearing my hat right now, I'd take it off to you. You really are quite the detective. Perhaps there is something to you and this... this whole ideal you're trying to lead, justice and all that. It's really quite charming. Mostly."

This time she didn't have the urge to fling any champagne at him or stomp on his foot. Not even to reach for that tiny little gun strapped to her upper thigh.

'Cause right now he meant nothing.

Nothing... not when the bigger picture was taking shape and that other piece of her, being her instinct, was warning her, pinging hard trying to get her attention, get her to see beyond the surface to what was there and—what wasn't. Something, some piece, that she was still missing, still not seeing just right.

O'Neil had been enamored with Norma regardless of that big show he'd put on at the gathering. He'd been dazzled with Norma just as MacDonald had been.

Except... O'Neil was the close and personal friend of Marcus Daly, *not* MacDonald. He'd said so himself back at the gathering, which meant O'Neil would have heard ideas and thoughts, and perhaps certain actions. from his dear friend. The kind of actions that were meant to stay in close confidences because it was quite possible that they'd get him in some trouble if the truth ever got out.

O'Neil, however, felt emotions with such a passion the man couldn't hide them even if he were dying. And O'Neil... well, he wasn't nearly the man that MacDonald was and knew it, too. Both men who'd been vying for the affection of one particular lady, one who had a smile that could light the whole room with sun and generosity and kindness. The kind of smile that drew you in and asked you to trust it, trust in her...

But even there, O'Neil knew he'd drawn the short end of that stick. He couldn't stand beside MacDonald and win Norma's favor. So sure, it made perfect sense for him to share such gossip with the lady, hoping to win her favor, to prove that he did trust her above all others. Perhaps to even run away with her because again, he *was* enamored. And why not tell her all this? What harm could come of it? After all, it was only O'Neil's friendship with Daly that gave him the upper hand over MacDonald and this—this right here—it would *prove* his devotion and trust in Norma.

Except... Norma's smile had deceived him.

She wasn't just that little girl from Kansas City or wherever the hell she and Dusty came from, a girl looking to get out of the life. In that Dusty had been wrong. Perhaps before they'd ever come to Butte, sure, she'd wanted out. Wanted back to her home and her family. But after? Oh, no. Norma had wanted this life. She wanted to keep it... all the dresses, the jewels, the dazzling parties... but keep all of it on *her* terms.

Not Madam Grace's or some other madam's.

Hers.

And that was where both Norma and O'Neil had made the mistake, one, that it seemed, cost them both everything.

Because either through O'Neil's own admission or MacDonald, word had traveled back to Marcus Daly.

And as Cat knew well, there were no clear lines in the shadow world. Clear legal lines and the... not-so-legal ones. So whatever it was that O'Neil had shared with Norma had been a big deal, the kind that could take a precious commodity like reputation and destroy it utterly.

Hell, all Cat had to do was look around at the current political climate and get a real good idea what that mighta been. Not that she knew a whole lot personally, as she'd been running errands around town for Mrs. Allen before she the started hunting up and down Galena Street and the tunnels underneath. Yet even still Cat had heard talk and rumors, the kinds of stuff that one would be a fool to not pay attention to. How one king went and had his big ol' party over there, and another having one over there, buying rounds on the house all day, all night. Getting the word out, getting folks of Butte promising to vote one way or another.

Butte was literally shifting and sliding right on her foundations as Daly waged a statewide war against his bitter rival, William Clark. Marcus Daly, who was doing his damnedest to keep Clark from reaching the Senate, while Clark... well, he went and did the same to get himself there.

What the hell had Norma learned—

No.

It didn't matter, not to Cat. Because that wasn't part of Norma's story, not really. All that mattered was that she'd tried to use this information and it had gotten her tossed from the Gardens and then later killed.

Daly couldn't risk sullying his hands, so he'd turned to another in this venture. Someone who did walk closer to that shadow world, who could lean on policemen and their bosses, on doctors to get results achieved, at least with a lot more freedom and hands clean than someone like Daly could (especially considering the big political battle going on).

Of course, there was more to it than that, but really, that wasn't part of Norma's story, either.

Nadeau had acted as such because a friend had requested it and because it would give him the kind of blackmail he needed to make money and to stay on top, no question about it. Because again, with these two copper kings shooting it out, why the hell not? More room for others to start shoving their way up top; might as well take advantage while one could.

Cat breathed in.

Because someone... had taken advantage. Had seen an opportunity...

She felt the world around her go still. Everyone else, all those dancers in their glorious dresses, Blake who was moving towards her but seemed as if he were trudging his way through some thick bog—even Nadeau faded until he no longer existed.

But just for a moment.

Just for this one breath.

Because right at the moment, who finally looked up and met her gaze was O'Neil.

O'Neil who—between that stilled bit of time from one breath to the next—showed her his truth. A truth that was filled with such longing and self-loathing and... guilt.

He'd cared for Norma.

Truly.

Cat saw it all as if it mirrored right back at her through his eyes.

It hadn't been him. *He* hadn't told Daly about Norma, hadn't revealed what she knew and what she'd tried to do with.

O'Neil had kept her secret. Even now, he still did.

Even though... even though O'Neil *had* gone to her the night she died, just as the owner of the Unlucky Horseshoe had said. O'Neil had gone probably trying to reason with Norma from using such information, that there was no way she could ever get back into this life. Perhaps... he'd even tried to convince her of a different life and yet...

It hadn't been enough, had it?

Cat felt the ghost of Norma beside her. Could imagine the other woman shaking her head back sadly, not at Cat, but at O'Neil...

For Norma was also the one who'd missed opportunities and chances. She could have had a life with the passionate, hot-tempered Seamus O'Neil, could have gotten away from *this* life, leaving behind all the glitz and glamor and it could have been worth it. Except... she'd wanted more.

She wanted to have all of it.

And that got her killed.

O'Neil pulled Cat back to the present, back to the ballroom with the piano and those slow, deep notes filling the room, reaching and rising to that chandelier that caught all the light and music, hopes and dreams, and held them there, all trapped by that beauty.

He nodded at her, and she had the sense that he knew exactly who she was.

O'Neil, who saw past the beautiful dress with all the frills and lace, the dainty necklace clasped right at her throat, even the damn piece of hair that Nadeau had dared touch and had somehow at some time once again slipped free.

He saw her and nodded, and then looked away.

A nod and a look that carried nothing but loss.

Another piece turned and fit into the puzzle. Nearly complete now. Almost.

A shiver ripped through Cat. The hairs on the back of her neck rising. And again, the tingling she felt running all up and down her insides, telling her, warning her, that there was something else, some piece she hadn't yet seen... not, completely...

She sensed Blake, too, coming closer as if he knew something wasn't right, something was wrong.

It was.

Desperately.

Because it *hadn't* been O'Neil. Not him. He hadn't harmed Norma.

Cat breathed in then out again, and time, it seemed to speed up as if making up for those earlier lost moments, as if desperate to keep her from learning anything more, from putting that one final piece or two together.

So close.

An idea, one that tickled the back of her thoughts but just, just out of sight, like catching a faint glimmer of flames out of the corner of your eye, moving so fast in that darkness and then, then it was too late—

Cat's gaze shot towards the back door of the ballroom where she'd last seen Abigail, where *Norma* had last seen Abigail...

Abigail—long gone, of course, as she'd gone upstairs to retire early for the evening, but not Madam Grace. She was there and even now pushing her way towards Cat and Nadeau, all elegant and graceful, of course, slipping in between her guests, somehow not spilling a drop of that full flute of champagne, though she carried it around as if completely forgotten. Yet she moved with the kind of hurry and worry that Cat instantly recognized.

Instantly felt.

Madam Grace, who looked right at Cat even though her words were for Nadeau.

"I'm... I'm terribly sorry, Mr. Nadeau, but the message, the one you wanted delivered—"

Cold shot through Cat.

Her breath caught in her throat but her focus, her clarity, became sharper than ever. She saw the large man standing just outside those ballroom doors. A large, burly kind of man establishments like this one employed to keep access limited to only those who had the money to afford it. The kind of man who would have stood guard over the back door making sure she and Dusty and all the usual sorts who prowled the ally behind the house or ventured down below in the cribs didn't get inside.

A guard who had no reason for being right here. Right inside.

Nadeau slid away from Cat as if dismissing her. And Grace. He took his damn-ass time, too, straightening his tie as he did, like he had all the time in the world. And the bastard was completely at ease. Completely uncaring about the worry striking hot through Madam Grace, and now through Cat.

"And?" he asked. "Where is Mr. MacDonald? I do not have all night, you understand."

"That's the thing, sir. He's not here. He's not... anywhere."

Which was why the burly man guarding the back wasn't where he should have been. Madam Grace had called for him, called to check if MacDonald had left that way—he hadn't. Clearly. Nor had he left out the front. Grace would have checked there first.

Ice ran through Cat's veins, or perhaps that was just both ghosts gripping her so hard, practically flinging her at Grace as if demanding Cat to act, to *move*. To do something, *anything*.

She did.

She grabbed Grace's arm. Hard, letting that woman feel the cold fury of the ghosts behind her, the ones calling on her to bring justice.

"And Abigail? What about her? Where is *she*?"

Madam Grace's eyes went wide, just for a moment, and gave Cat the kind of look that filled her whole being with such dread that Cat knew no matter what happened, nothing good would come from this.

Nothing.

Which was exactly what everyone had warned her, from Madeleine to Nadeau, to even Grace herself. They'd all warned a price would be paid for Cat seeking this truth.

"She's... she's gone," Madam Grace said. "She's gone, too."

The final piece fell into place.

And Cat had missed it.

CHAPTER FIFTY-TWO

Cat didn't wait for Blake. Couldn't.

Already MacDonald had gotten a head start on her, and she had no idea where he'd have gone, where he'd have taken Abigail, but there was only one place he could go. Not out the front, not out the back, which left only one option.

The tunnels.

And with the piano dinging out its perfect notes and tunes, inviting the whole ballroom to join in in one elaborate, extravagant dance, Cat in all her finery, her simple jewels and done-up hair and frilly pink dress, shoved right past Madam Grace. And she wasn't kind about it, neither. Or graceful. In fact, Cat pushed so hard she knocked right into the other woman and at such an angle, the perfect kind, that right smacked into her elbows and hands... one hand which still held that untouched flute of champagne. And wouldn't you know, the whole thing tipped right on over and straight down the front of Nadeau's shirt.

And damned if Cat couldn't stop and enjoy the moment.

She couldn't, though it was enough to pull the tiniest smile on her face. Especially when she heard Nadeau's shocked gasp of outrage.

But that was all she had time for.

All that she could spare, even this one thought of Grace and Nadeau, that high and mighty lord who was even now demanding like a petulant child to haul Grace away in chains. As if that was even done anymore.

But... Cat had one breath, one single moment to glance back...

And saw Blake.

That blond streak of his which just about lit him up in the room, drawing her gaze right to him. And his gaze, which was hard and intense, met hers. Demanding, almost, that she stop and wait for him—

She couldn't.

Certainly not when he then got tripped up behind Nadeau, who seemed to know he was an officer and started demanding that Blake do something about his ruined wardrobe. Blake opened his mouth, probably yelling out her name, demanding that she stop.

And then it didn't matter.

Cat was out the ballroom and passing right by that burly guard who really should have gone back to guarding his assigned door, but he wasn't. Instead, he was just standing there blinking as if he couldn't believe the sight of Nadeau yelling or whatnot. Hell, the guard didn't even spare Cat a blink and he damn well should have, especially since she wasn't one of the ladies allowed in the heart of the house.

Cat just kept on moving.

She saw everything in a blur, her mind cataloging and stripping out each detail, each little bit and shade of relevance. All the while she was just trying to keep from fainting.

Her head spun, the room getting a bit tilty as her chest and lungs worked overtime, trying to get in enough air in to continue this sudden, foolish flight. It was foolish, considering what she was wearing. Her bound chest and ribcage pushed against those piercing bones of the corset, and she wished like hell she'd skipped the gun and gone for a nice, sharp knife. The kind that would slice right through the ribbons keeping this vile contraption on her. But she had no knife. And no time to stop in the kitchen and borrow one from the cook who hadn't told on her earlier.

The cook who was suddenly there filling the hallway with her dark skin, dark eyes. No steaming pot this time, but her feet were planted on that polished wood floor and her hands were planted right there on her hips, and the look she was giving Cat, it was like she was lookin' into a mirror, all menace and just a good ol' righteous anger.

"He took her, that friend a Norma's." The cook glared at her. "Norma was a good girl. Abby, even better one."

"I believe you're right."

"You gonna do somethin' 'bout it?"

"I am."

"Good." The cook pointed down towards the crib stairs. "They went that way."

Cat gave a nod, then rushed down those stairs as fast as she could. Rickety, creaking things that they were. Each step sounded like it was gonna break right clean through, taking her with it. And she, swearing as she tripped on the goddamn lace of her dress and all the ridiculous layers and extras some great gentleman thought would be quite fetching on a woman, completely forgetting all about the need to actually move in the darn thing.

Her whole body, trapped in pain, trying to breathe, and knowing she couldn't stop. Knowing that no matter what, she just had to get to Abigail.

Had to—

Cat's heels landed hard on the floorboards below. Bending and protesting. Dust and dirt shot up into the air, stinging her eyes, burning them. The rest of her body followed, including all those layers of dress and underclothes, as gravity took hold, as it were. And she crouched there, squinting in the sudden darkness down here. Nothing at all like the dazzling bright lights of the ballroom above, the lights that got themselves captured in all the hanging crystals that glinted down at them like little sparkling, trapped, jewels.

Not here, though.

Definitely not.

Her eyes still burned from the sudden kick of dust and dirt, and she strained to see through the dimness.

Cat kept shoving aside her dress, how much of it she hadn't a clue until she *finally* found the small holster strapped to her upper thigh.

She felt the comfortable, warm metal of the derringer, now heated from being so close to her body. It wasn't her usual gun, the revolver she knew how to use with her eyes closed, but it was *a* gun, and that's what mattered now. She might be wearing a dress and bound up tight like a roped-up calf, but she was armed.

Cat got the derringer free of its holster, free of her dress, and finally, after feeling like an eternity, her eyesight adjusted.

She took everything in, every little scrap of detail that she could see, even as her vision continued to swim with those black dots and the world remained just as fuzzy as her body fought for oxygen, as her heart hammered hard in her chest, as if it, too, wanted to break free of the contraption holding it in place.

Overhead, she saw those hanging, naked light bulbs. Hanging there and just creaking while the mournful notes from the piano leaked on down from the rafters, the real bars of this prison under the palace. Then the narrow, dank hallway of the cribs, and those sad ladies she'd seen earlier in their beds were now standing at the windows there. Each of them looking at her in some kind of amazement, shock, and curiosity, all of it rolled into one. Their fingers outstretched and frozen as if her appearance had happened in the middle of a tap-tap-tap on the glass and now they didn't know exactly what to do.

Or what to make of her.

Except... why had they been tapping? There were no clients here, at least none Cat could see, but not only that... where was the guard? The bouncer stationed down here watching the tunnels as Dusty said they did, least during business hours...

A tingling along the back of her neck.

MacDonald, probably. Paid the man off so he could sneak out with Abigail, but... but why? It didn't make sense.

The girls were mostly watching Cat, though a few glanced to the crib at the far end. Too far, too sharp an angle for Cat to see into the window, but there was no girl stationed there, no girl looking back out at Cat as the others were doing.

Cat turned to the girl nearest her, trapped in the small room with the even smaller window and narrow doorway. The girl with her thin, stringy black hair and black eyes that looked so lost they were nearly soulless. Those eyes which met Cat's once, just a flick and real quick, too, before they darted away again.

Eyes that had seen something.

Abigail.

"Abigail," Cat said. "I'm looking for Abigail."

Those eyes met hers once more, and Cat realized they might be soulless, might have lost every inch of light left in her... except for this one small glimmer, this one small spark because the girl, she nodded her head once.

And even though her eyes were nearly lifeless, had nearly given everything that she had to the shadow world, she also wasn't blind.

Because the girl's dark eyes suddenly flicked away from Cat... and purposefully looked... right behind her.

The cribs here—the underbelly of the Gardens—they weren't entirely empty, not like Cat had first believed.

She sensed the movement first.

Again felt the tingling along the back of her neck, like a slight tickle of wind when before, up until now, there'd been none. Everything here so still, just the dirt and dust hanging right there where she was crouched not moving, just the slight stir of her breath, and then it wasn't so still no more.

Cat's instincts came on fire. Warning her to get up, to move, to defend—

To *live.*

A shadow suddenly detached itself from where he had waited by the stairs in the heavy, dark shadows there. A person who'd waited so patiently for this moment, as if they were invisible. As if the girls hadn't truly cared because this person here simply didn't matter, not really, as if he weren't worthy of being noticed. As if... he weren't enough to earn the night's coin so was therefore ignored.

And then forgotten.

A shadow, it seemed, that hadn't liked being forgotten because he bounded out so fast from where he hid that Cat barely glimpsed him —tall, lean, thin—and that was all, though clear enough a man. A man who moved so fast and with such a fury it was like he knew damn well where his place was in all this and resented every bit of it.

A resentment which he demonstrated by the force of his swing.

A long-ass piece of wood, thick and heavy, lifted high over his head and then cut right on through the air, so hard and fast, and right at Cat's head.

Her head, which was still spinning from the lack of oxygen. The black spots that seemed to have clouded her sight like heavy rain until it seemed like it was just gonna blot out the sky entirely. But she didn't need to see to move. Didn't need to see to do what her whole being was telling her, demanding of her, to survive.

Cat didn't question, simply *moved*.

Reacted.

She rolled as best she could to the side. Out of the way. Far from the reach of that heavy board as it came swinging down, right at her head—

It helped that she'd already been crouching, already been near to the ground.

It hadn't helped that she was wearing the corset and the dress, both which almost instantly halted her movement like they were some great net suddenly thrown over her head, yanking her back to the ground.

Cat thudded right into that door of the poor girl and it crashed halfway open. And the man from the shadows, he was right behind her. He swung that heavy wood again, moving with such a force it was as if his entire being, his existence, depended on this moment, on crushing her skull right in.

Except he missed.

At least her head, anyway.

Twice in one night she'd been saved an early grave from a blow to the head, but this time there was no Blake to yank her aside. This time, her luck didn't hold far enough because the wood still hit, and hit hard. It smacked into her shoulder, followed by a loud, defining crack.

Something broken. Something at the least fractured.

She doubted it was the wood. And she was damn sure it wasn't the corset.

The gun flew right out 'a her hands, small thing that it was, and ended up somewhere in the shadows.

Too far to reach for sure, even if she could see right.

Which she couldn't.

Too far to reach even if she could move in the dress, scrambling on all fours.

Which she couldn't.

And the pain, it was something else entirely. The kind of pain that made her cry out all 'a sudden, as if the sound couldn't be stopped because it was simply part of living. Simply part of knowing that you still breathed and there were things like your heartbeat and breathing and pain reactions that you *couldn't* control. And that pain, well, it took you right to your core, to your soul if you still believed in such things, which Cat wasn't so sure about—though she did believe in ghosts.

Her vision got to swimming even more and her head spinning, too, and it was suddenly real hard to see which way was up and which way was down. The amount of dirt and dust flung up into the air really wasn't helping, either.

Then there were the tears which filled her eyes and spilled on down, also as immediate and reactionary as her cry had been.

Nothing she could do to stop it.

Part of her wished she could just hang up her hat and say she was done doin' her part for the evening. She'd tried, tried real hard, too, to find out the truth about Norma, to bring her ghost—unhelpful thing that it was—some measure of peace. Clearly though, not justice. Clearly Cat wasn't cut out so well for that job. Cause truly, part of her would have liked to sit back and let her own shining, white knight take over like in those stories. Her white knight riding in to save the day—but Cat had no idea if Blake knew she was down here, if the cook was still there and if she'd even tell him where they'd all gone.

And it wasn't like Dusty was here, either, and she was real sorry she'd ordered him to stay at Mrs. Allen's. It was just her and the girls down here, and each of them trapped.

But... at least Dusty was safe, even if Cat wasn't. Even if... Abigail wasn't.

Abigail.

Cat blinked and blinked some more. Wiped away tears and dirt and did her best to roll over onto her side. Pushing, doing everything she could to rise, to stand, to move.

Except there was nothing she could do, not when the man stepped in front of her and pointed that awful piece of wood right at her.

The wood, which was as common around town as the hacks and their horses and all them droppings they left behind. Wood used for fuel, wood used for blacksmithing and building and things, probably as common down below in those mines as the rocks they brought on up to the surface. And this piece right here, a good foot long or so with black markings running up and down its side, was simply an everyday kind 'a item, the kind that could have been picked up anywhere at anytime. Hell, even the Gardens probably had its own stockpile in the back just for lighting up fires and fixin' up broken boards when things got a little out 'a hand among their gentleman guests.

All this man had to do was make a short little stop, anywhere really, then stand here in the shadows where even the girls living here had immediately forgotten him. And then simply wait for Cat to show up, to follow after Abigail as he'd known she would.

Abigail.

Cat couldn't leave her. Couldn't give up on her.

She struggled to sit up and bit back another cry as that wood lifted and pushed her back down, pressing hard right on her injured shoulder.

Somehow through the pain, through the tears, Cat noticed the other girl. The one with the stringy black hair and her dark, soulless eyes. She now hid in the shadows, much as she could, huddled there in that corner between bed and nightstand. Her bare legs pressed against her chest, clutching them so hard it was like her nails were gonna pierce right on through the skin.

But this time the girl with the stringy, black hair, her eyes weren't soulless. Not entirely. Instead, they were alive and seeing everything, seeing Cat there on the ground, and maybe, just maybe, there was even a little bit of anger in her, too.

A bit, anyway.

And Cat remembered what Madam Grace had said to her... that because Cat cared about the girls here she could never be free. They belonged to her... and she to them.

But then, that was all she had time to see, time to think, because that wood slab with its black ribbing was back and pressing into her shoulder, demanding her attention.

And she gave it, too.

Had no choice, really. Because it was then that the man finally stopped hiding in the shadows. He took another step forward into the cloud of dust and dirt, and Cat blinked, trying to see as much as she could.

Saw the toes of his boots... just inches from her nose.

Cat breathed in.

It wasn't easy finding the clarity, remembering her pa and what he'd taught her a lifetime ago. How the time slowly came to a stop and the rest of the world opened up so you could see everything. But this wasn't like standing out in the field, hiding behind trees with a rifle's sights becoming level.

This time there was pain and her spinning head and she couldn't tell up from down. Yet somehow, she was still breathing... still seeing all those details.

As if... thoughts of Abigail were enough. Knowing that Abigail was out there alone, just like Madeleine in her bed with that quilt some loving parent had made, and even this girl here with her stringy hair and dark eyes crouching in her corner...

It was enough.

All of it.

Enough to keep her mind working hard, doing everything it could to keep her alive, to keep piecing all the little bits and story parts together because once she did that, she would know the story, and knowing the story meant she'd find a way out of this.

The boots... mud-splattered and covered in thick layers of dust... sturdy. Real sturdy. Made from the heavy kind 'a thick leather she'd only seen on the men trudging up the hill for work each day with their shoulders bowed as if the heaviness of the world above was already pressing in on them. Pressing them down. Trying to crush them. Those men who carried their dented tin pails which swung in time at their sides, the food within their only little piece of comfort they'd share down in that darkness below, down in that heat.

Cat could practically hear the creak of tin, of the metal shifting and swaying and... jostling.

A memory right there, right at her fingertips.

Just like Cat knew, first hand certainly, seeing as how her shoulder had an opinion on the matter (which it did) that the man who'd done the swinging was strong. Real strong. Not the kind who counted his coins and his bills, who smoked fancy cigars and waited patiently in parlor rooms where news would eventually reach him with the simple explanation that 'the deed was done.'

Instead, this was the kind of man the working girls here *would* have forgotten. And did.

Because this man, this one right here, was a working man.

A miner.

Also a nobody.

The kind of person you saw and then you forgot. As if your mind simply wanted to skip right on over him because you knew without really thinking, without really questioning, that he was of no consequence or importance.

Including Cat.

Because she'd seen those boots not just once but twice, and both times had dismissed him just as these girls here had.

Mr. Rippi crouched down beside her. "Why, Miss Cowboy Cat," he said with a grin. "What a treasure and a joy running into you here."

The light from the bulbs swinging overhead, finally cutting through enough of the dirt and dust so she could see, and finally she did.

She saw him for who he really was.

The man who'd killed Norma.

CHAPTER FIFTY-THREE

Mr. Rippi grinned at her from where he crouched, the heavy wood held easily in his hands, comfortable too, as if it were as much a part of him as her own revolver was. And he was strong, too, strong enough to do the deed. Clearly strong enough to send her sprawling to the ground, chewing on dirt and whatnot, but also strong enough to throw a flaming rock clear across the street outside Mrs. Allen's. To break that window with one shot just as the oil from the rag splattered about the room.

They'd been lucky. Real lucky.

Cat saw that now, especially staring into the eyes of the man who'd done the throwing, who'd known exactly what he'd been doing. How to tie the rag just so, borrowing the oil they used down in the mines to soak it with, probably even more powerful stuff, too. It would have been so easy for the flames to spread if they all hadn't reacted so quickly...

Which they wouldn't have if Blake hadn't yanked Cat to the side just in time. They'd all have stood there staring down in shock at Cat's lifeless body, losin' those precious few seconds needed to douse the flames before fire engulfed the whole house. Or more.

Real lucky.

Cat breathed again.

It was hard to focus, what with the haze clouding her mind, the pain that thudded like it was a drum smacking into her head. Especially when Rippi went and pressed that wood slab harder into her shoulder, making her cry out, making the black spots swarm her vision.

Still she breathed.

Couldn't give in...

Not yet. Not ever.

Because Cat wasn't alone in this, wasn't the only one down here in the dark with no help, no allies. Others depended on her. Like Madeleine. Like Abigail.

"I must say, Miss Cat, I was mighty lookin' forward to this. To you seein' the truth. Seeing the lies hiding behind the smile."

Mr. Rippi wore the same dark coveralls she'd seen him in earlier. They were still coated in mud and grime and grease, also the same as earlier, as if ... as if he'd never gone home to begin with. Because... because someone had told him...

About Cat and her being on Galena Street asking questions. Rippi, who'd gotten off shift and came right down lookin' for her. And then followed her.

Cat closed her eyes a moment, remembering. Breathing still. Putting together all those little details she hadn't fully seen before.

She and Dusty had run into him right after the shift ended, when those whistles had pierced through the evening. And in Cat's case she'd almost literally ran right into him. In fact, her coat back home, hanging where Chin had left it, still bore the grease stains from Rippi's hands, from where he'd gripped her, steadying her on her feet.

And... the strength she'd felt as she'd steadied herself in return.

Another detail falling into place.

Then another.

His interest in the noodle house, making a point of telling Cat how it was Norma's favorite place to go after she'd fallen from the big parlor house. And Cat couldn't help but wonder... *had* he asked Norma to join him as well? Had he asked... and been turned down?

The answer was simple.

Yes.

Cat breathed in, much as she could with her lungs screaming, her head swimming, and that non-stop pain caused he'd done a right good number on her shoulder.

She opened her eyes and looked right at Rippi.

There were certain things she couldn't know, like how exactly Norma had looked when she'd been found, but then Cat didn't need the details. As she'd told Dusty and Blake earlier, sometimes guesses were enough. Sometimes, especially when someone's reputation was on the line, guesses were all you needed.

And it just didn't apply to reputations either, but pride.

Pride.

Because that was what she saw in Mr. Rippi's grin, the way it twisted up as if finally, *finally* it was his turn to stand in the light. And his eyes, too, they took in about every inch of her, soaking up the sight of her sprawled out as she was in the dirt and dust.

A proud man who'd been rejected by the woman who'd been too good for him, even after she'd fallen from heaven and right onto his doorstop, so it had seemed.

This was far, far from the friendly grin she'd seen at the gathering, with his dark teeth and his one gold one. Because... that had been an act, one she had missed... or maybe not. Maybe he'd taken a page out of Norma's book, after having devoted so much to her, studying her, watching her, that he'd turned that smile on Cat and kept the truth hidden.

Just as Norma had done with him. Just as Norma had done with MacDonald and O'Neil and Abigail.

And like O'Neil and the others had learned, so, too, had Mr. Rippi.

Norma had been more than her smile.

Norma, whom Cat felt even now beside her. The cold touch of

her hands grabbing onto Cat's elbows as if her ghostly form was gonna haul her ass up whether or not Cat liked it. Or was gonna pass out from the effort.

Still...

Norma wasn't wrong. Cat *had* to get up. Couldn't just lay there, waiting for the end to come. Hell, she *hated* waiting.

Cat sucked in a breath, squeezed her eyes closed, and got her legs underneath her. Not that Rippi was about to let her stand, not with that wood slab right pressing into her injured shoulder again so hard all Cat saw was pain. The kind of pain that just begged you to lay yourself down and close your eyes, just end it all with cool darkness and oblivion.

She ignored it. Had to.

Had to be ready, though for what, she wasn't so sure.

And while she didn't have a gun, and couldn't breathe worth a damn, she had everything she needed. Her mind, her wits, her words. And she wasn't alone here, either.

There was Norma to consider and the other girls... the ones whom Madam Grace had warned that Cat belonged to them.

It was enough.

Enough for Cat to reach up, grab that goddamn wood pressing into her shoulder, and shove it aside. Hell, she might be a girl but she was a damn strong one. And she was pissed as all get out.

"Mr. Rippi. A little space, if you please."

Something cold and unyielding flashed in his eyes. Then it was gone as if it'd never been.

But Cat had seen it. Seen it and known exactly the kind a person she was dealing with.

And chances were Norma had, too.

Cat swallowed and forced herself to keep on breathing, keep talking. Keep... living.

One breath at a time.

"I'd ask what you're doing here," she said, her tone a tad bit softer, "but I believe that's fairly obvious. What isn't, though, is how you afforded your way past the door, even the underbelly one."

Rippi's grin, the not-nice-one, got even bigger.

"Is like I told you, Miss Cat, always dreamed of being here in the big house, seeing all them fancy girls in person and not just through the window. Uncaring. Staring down at us as they always were like we were nothin'."

Again, the coldness was back in his eyes and it didn't run or hide, neither. It stared right back at her, and Cat was grateful that Abigail wasn't here, wasn't anywhere near this man who'd wanted and coveted Norma. No telling what he would do if he got hold of one of the few true friends Norma had had.

The very man who'd done Norma in.

At that moment, the piano got to playing again, a lively tune, the kind that called one to dance and join hands. Rippi gestured to the rafters above as if trying to catch the floating music with his hard, bare hands.

"You see? Fate has smiled on me, poor man that I am. The house welcomes me as I knew it would. I am poor man still, but is thanks to my benefactor that I am here now. He understands what I set out to do."

"You mean Mr. MacDonald? The man who profited from your work?"

"That is not kind thing to say, Miss Cat, specially seein' as you still don't know the whole story."

Cat tried moving again, but Rippi was right there, pushing that wood slab back into her shoulder. It made her want to reach out and scratch the man's eyes out.

Or damn it all, find where the hell that gun had gotten to.

Except... no amount of sideways glances and searches revealed where the derringer had fallen. Too many shadows, too many nooks such a small gun could have got to.

She had to keep him talking. Had to keep him from thinking how easy it'd be to take one final swing at her and this time not miss. Mr.

Rippi wasn't a dumb man, not by an stretch of the imagination. His English might need some work but there was a calculating, angry mind staring back at her.

And as if to reminder her of this, Norma's own grip on Cat's shoulder tightened. A touch that should have sent her teeth chattering and her skin standing straight up on end, but didn't. Cat no longer felt the coldness, which wasn't a good thing considering the situation.

But then Norma's presence was enough.

Not alone.

"But you're gonna tell me, right?" Cat asked. "About Norma, about how she died."

Cat spoke louder, making sure her voice was enough to fill the whole narrow hallway. Hoping, praying she could reach the other girls here and that Madam Grace hadn't been wrong.

"You're gonna tell me your story," she said, "and then Norma's, 'cause otherwise, how will I know? How will I know she got what she deserved, that it really was all you and not some gentleman like MacDonald behind the scenes doing all the work, all without ever once getting his hands dirty?"

"All this was cause of me."

"So tell me."

Rippi removed the wood from Cat's wounded shoulder, considering her words.

"Tell me about Norma," Cat pushed, "about how she made you feel."

He closed his eyes as if... remembering. As if... savoring the memory.

Which one, exactly, Cat really didn't want to know.

"I tell you," Rippi said, "she was a mighty fine lady. Went and brought kindness and smiled not just to me, but so many. She was our light, and we to a man, we appreciated her. Brought us such joy when we had none left."

He opened his eyes and Cat saw nothing but hurt and pain, the kind that went so deep it was all a man like him *could* see anymore.

"I never lied about any of that. What I told you at your gathering, it was truth. Truth. But then I learned *her* truth, that none of it were real. I'd been blinded by her until I learned with my own eyes and saw what needed to be done."

"You're not the only one, you know, who loved her. And you're not the only one she fooled."

Cat moved her body slightly, shifting it inch by inch. Her knees under her, then her feet. Ready to act, ready to move.

Rippi didn't see, didn't notice.

He was too focused, too caught up in the past, in his emotions and feelings for Norma. He'd probably tried to contain them, trap them deep down as Cat had been doing with Alice ever since that night she'd killed Alice's husband, saving both their lives, and yet somehow losing Alice anyway.

And maybe... maybe a part of her had been Rippi. Not enough, not fully lost, but getting there. Every day reaching closer to that place of darkness and oblivion because that's all that was left when the anger wouldn't leave you.

No wonder Alice's ghost had stayed, why she'd pushed Cat, haunting her so, never letting up until finally, finally Cat had the silly notion of leaving her life in Miles City and coming here to do something as foolhardy as starin' down a crazy man who'd killed at least one person, perhaps more, while she wore nothing more than a dress and corset.

And with no damn gun in sight.

Cat glimpsed movement to the side... the girl with the thin hair. She'd shifted from her corner and was now pressing her back against the rickety bed... her bare, bruised arm stretched out underneath it and reaching...

Reaching.

Rippi noticed Cat's attention had shifted.

He glanced towards the girl and Cat pushed to her knees.

The whole hallway tilted like it was gonna topple right on over, but Cat ignored it. Ignored the pain as it just about barreled into her, trying so hard to knock her back down. Instead, she followed her instincts and said the one word she knew still had power.

Maybe not much left, but enough, enough for this...

"Norma."

And just like at the gathering, Norma's name seemed to echo in the air. It bounced off those rafters as if vibrating, as if strengthened by their presence because this, this right here had been her home.

Rippi paled and backed up a step as if he couldn't stand to hear the name, the power living behind it and the anger it held for him. As if... Norma's ghost and all the girls here were fueling it, keeping her and her name alive.

And they had been.

This whole time, they had been.

Cat got all the way to her feet. Slow and unsteady and gripping the side of that broken doorframe, but she was standing and she wasn't falling over, either.

All the pieces were coming together now so fast she almost couldn't keep up with the story. She didn't fight it, though, and didn't question it, neither. She just... believed. Just trusted her instincts to guide her true, just as her pa had taught her, staring down the barrel of her rifle where that chill wind nipped at her fingers, her cheeks, doing everything it could to distract her.

She held in that breath, the magic that it was, for a moment longer then let it out.

Felt her own power fill her.

"You saw Norma at the noodle house," Cat said. "After she was sent away from here and you recognized her. You approached her."

Rippi's face darkened, like every light in him, what little he'd left, blinked right on out. Whatever hold Norma had had on him, the power in her name, was fading now. Like it was being squeezed so tight there was nothing left, as if straight up swallowed by all the darkness staring right out Rippi's eyes.

"That's right." He took a step closer to Cat, but his eyes saw something else, or someone else. "I saw her there, though she seemed smaller, maybe. Not as bright or lovely, but I recognized her smile instantly and I was so pleased, so overjoyed to see her, is like blessing from on high. She was *here*. Here! And now she was one of us. Like, like me."

"But she didn't herself that way, did she? As one of you. She wanted back into that life, and so she rejected you."

Cat's words hummed about the small, narrow hallway, as if trapped there and held right up against each of those crib windows. And all their eyes, all the girls who standing, watching, all eyes on her and fully so.

Along with the sparks Cat saw in them. Each one lighting up slowly, tentative, unsure, but *there*. Small sparks of light, of living, coming back. Still faint but growing.

None of them were alone, not anymore.

"Norma thought she was better than you," Cat said. "But you let her leave that day. Unharmed."

"I am man of honor, but not a forgetful one. I honored her for the woman she'd been but I no forget the whore she became."

"You didn't," Cat agreed. "So you followed her. You learned everything there was to know about her. Who she spoke with, where she lived, *who* her brother was. All of that, you learned."

"I am intuitive man."

"More than intuitive, I think."

For as much wealth and control and power as the others had been tossing around—MacDonald, Nadeau, even Marcus Daly himself—the real threat came from this man here. Madeleine had been wrong. It hadn't been the others that they needed to fear, but Mr. Rippi. The average working miner from a country across the Atlantic who'd come here looking for a better life and having found none, started making up one of his own. His own dreams. His own little world where Norma and her smile stood at the center. And when he'd realized that dream was just an illusion, he'd taken action. And more than that, he'd planned and he'd studied. He'd learned all of Norma's comings and goings, her intent, probably even before she herself knew.

But eventually Norma had learned. Maybe she'd glimpsed him enough around Galena Street, always following at her heels, always waiting on corners when she came out of the noodle shop or picked goods from the store. She'd seen him enough, sensed him enough, to know the truth. He'd been the real threat, and it wasn't one that had followed from the Gardens. No, it'd been here this whole time and finally, finally he got his opportunity to approach her.

Even if Norma hadn't recognized him in the end, on her last night on this earth as she drowned her sorrows and her failed, shriveled dreams in alcohol and the darkness of the shadow world. Which was a most likely case.

No proof, of course, what she'd been thinking, but then Cat didn't exactly need any.

And it just might be enough...

Because she wasn't sure how much longer she had. Her body was hurting and shaking, too. The effort to stand, to pull strength from God knows where, it was taking its toll.

Sweat beaded along Cat's forehead and a drop slid down off her chin. She didn't dare move, didn't dare break the gaze of a man who'd lost what little hold he'd had over his soul.

"You are an intuitive man," Cat said. "You realized Norma was trying to blackmail O'Neil, and through him, Marcus Daly. And that's how *you* found Mr. MacDonald, am I right? You saw a kindred soul, so you approached him, you explained your disappointment in Norma and he... he ignored this relationship, didn't he?"

Rippi grinned again. "You are quite good at this. My friend, MacDonald, he told me so. But then I got to see a bit of it firsthand myself."

"Because you followed us. Dusty and me. You saw us go into the tunnels from the noodle house. It was you I felt in the shadows."

"Right again, my lady Cat, right again. Is too bad you will not live long enough to make this a profession, but then fallen girls no need someone lookin' after them. They just aren't worth it."

"Everyone is worth it."

Cat heard the girl with the stringy hair behind her. She didn't dare turn, didn't dare look. But... it was there. The unmistakable shift of a body inching along the floorboard, not much sound 'cause she was such a light thing, so tiny and thin like she hadn't a real meal in months.

Cat stayed right where she was, right in the center of the doorway. She used her body and her dirty yet still extravagant dress to block Rippi's view. But then Rippi didn't notice because the girl in the crib, even he who was a working man, didn't see the girl behind Cat as a real person. Certainly not a threat.

Cat, though, was.

She'd risen in his eyes. She was worth more.

Besides, Rippi was enjoying this, enjoying his little moment. After all, Cat was telling him exactly what he wanted to hear, her acknowledging that it really had been him.

"It was you this whole time," she said, "hidden in the shadows, controlling everything, everyone. And not a one of them were the wiser. Not Nadeau, not MacDonald. All this was orchestrated by you."

Rippi grinned at her, his dark teeth and the gold one catching just right in the naked, dim light from the bulbs overhead.

There was a faint cry from further down the hallway, and then the voice suddenly muffled.

It was one Cat recognized.

Her heat thundered in her chest, and as much as she wanted to race on over, she stayed exactly where she was, stayed focused on Rippi.

"What finally changed?" she asked. "All that time you'd left Norma alone. So what happened? What happened that night in the Lucky Horseshoe?"

She needed to know, needed this final truth for Norma and to bring her ghost what justice she could, even if it was only in the knowing. And truth be told, all the girls had a right to know.

Norma was theirs, after all. She was the one who really belonged to them. They deserved the truth of their lost friend.

"You... you are good." Rippi shook his wood slab at her. "Yes, yes I was there that night. I was sad and forlorn, but then she was there and then *he* was there. Seamus O'Neil. And he told her then, that O'Neil, told her her life was done. She'd never get it back, not dresses nor jewels, not him because it was not allowed. The great Marcus Daly, he declared it so and shameful O'Neil could not shame him again. Oh, I saw it all. I thought here, here it is, the moment to bring my heart great joy. But then... I saw her light fade. Her smile die. All her hopes and dreams, they shattered at his words."

Rippi shook his head once. The grease stain on his chin caught in the dim light and for a moment looked like a streak of shining black dust.

"But I did not feel great joy at this. There was... no joy, only loss."

Cat heard the shifting boards again, louder this time.

Rippi didn't hear. Still too lost in time, lost in the emotions swirling through him, ones that she could feel crawling along her skin, itching to get inside her, too. To live there and consume her.

She didn't let them.

"It made you angry," she said. "You wanted that light and you never got to have her."

Rippi turned his cold gaze to her and blinked... as if still seeing the past... but then his focus cleared and she knew he was looking at her again.

At her and not the sounds creaking on the floorboards behind her, heading slowly towards the window.

"It surprised me," he said, "this sadness. This... this anger. But then, I think maybe I always knew."

"You mean, you were ready."

"I had to have her then, or I'd never get to. She was dying, yes, her smile dying before I even got to have her. It was not kind of fate to do so to me and I couldn't let him take her, destroy her, before I saw my own justice."

"Justice," Cat whispered. "That's a funny word seeing how you killed her."

"She injured me."

"She exercised her own choice and said no."

"Fallen ladies no longer have choice."

Cat clenched her fists at her side, digging her nails into her skin as hard as she dared. Hoping each of the sparks in the girls' eyes were growing as big and bright and furious as she was now feeling.

But they all needed to know.

The whole story, the whole truth about Norma.

"You were ready with the cyanide," Cat said. "You'd probably carried it with you since that day at the noodle house, just waiting for the right moment. And you found it. You already knew Norma had gone to the California Saloon and that she'd spoken with O'Neil. In fact, it was MacDonald who told you, warned you what was happening—and that O'Neil was going to tell her later in person that it was over."

Cat inched closer to him. Her heels shifting on the uneven floorboards below. Dust and dirt still hanging over her head like a dark cloud.

"No one ever suspected you, nor would they. After all, why would they? Especially when Norma's former lover confronts her in the shadiest saloon in all of Butte. Not a man there would ever point the finger at you because not a man there would *remember* you."

"*She* remembered me." Rippi thrust his wooden weapon at her, shaking it like the deadly club it was. "Every time she saw me around town, every time she looked in the shadows and saw me, she remembered. In the end, her last breaths, she remembered. And she knew it was I who ended her."

"Are you so sure? So sure that she looked you in the eyes and recognized *you*, Mr. Rippi? You, who always hid in the shadows, who followed her but never approached her again, never spoke or offered to help when she carried her bags across the street? No. No, you never did. So I can promise, sir, she didn't remember *you*. Only your shadow."

Rippi's grin thinned until it became a scowl so ferocious she was nearly convinced he was going to lunge at her, right then and there.

But he didn't.

He maintained his composure, breathing hard, struggling to keep those feelings from spilling over him and drowning him completely.

Struggling... because...

He didn't want to let those feelings out, not like he'd had with Norma, with that last moment he had with her, using her for all she was worth like the whore she was. Probably showing her his true colors, and she'd... she'd probably been so far gone from the poison she hadn't even noticed.

But now, however, he wasn't entirely alone and it wasn't safe to let such feelings live when there were witnesses.

Not her or the other girls, but someone who actually mattered.

MacDonald.

"She was not the great lady I thought," Rippi said. "And it was quick death."

"A painful one and nothing quick about it."

Cat pushed away from the doorframe then. Didn't care that Rippi was still there, his grip tightening ever so slightly on the wood slab. Didn't care because in this, the truth mattered more.

The truth... the only justice girls like her would ever get down here in the dark.

"So you poisoned her," Cat said, " right before you paid for her services, too. And what about after? Did you follow her? Follow as she stumbled down that boardwalk all alone, her world coming undone from the inside out. Did you watch, hoping and praying and knowing that it was all thanks to you? Did you rejoice in what you saw, in taking away any other chance she had to smile?"

"Is better this way. No other man get hurt."

"Until I came along, right?"

Cat turned her attention to the hallway, to the very last crib, the one with no girl in the window, no girl watching the drama unfolding. The drama that felt like it'd been going on for hours and yet was mere minutes.

If even that long.

"And what about you, Mr. MacDonald? What do you have to say for your part in all this?"

CHAPTER FIFTY-FOUR

In truth, while it felt like she and Rippi had been engaged in a debate that took hours, it was truly only a few minutes.

Maybe no more than one.

Time was a funny thing when the blood got pumping, when pain edged out ahead, making it all feel like an eternity when really, only a few breaths had passed. Not enough for anyone to come crashing down those stairs to save her, but then Cat didn't need saving.

Abigail, however, did.

Abigail, who MacDonald shoved out of that crib. She tripped on the hem of her deep blue dress. It was torn now along the shoulders and falling so low it revealed her own undergarments and corset, and her hair, once sunny gold, was now coated in dirt and grime as if MacDonald had shoved her headfirst down those stairs.

The bruise sportin' on her cheek and her eyes told Cat it was likely.

Abigail lunged towards Cat but MacDonald was right there, grabbing her arm, gripping it so hard Abigail cried out.

MacDonald held no weapon, not even a gun, as if such things were beneath him. His wavy dark hair was still perfect, his clothes neither tarnished nor smudged. Nothing like Abigail's. His eyes, however, were the same brown she'd seen at the gathering though now they carried nothing but coldness. She'd glimpsed it that day, but this time that's all there was. Like Rippi, he was finally showing her his own truth.

And his eyes... well, they were just as cold and fierce as Rippi's, though not as calculating. Yet it was no wonder they'd found each other.

Or truthfully, that Rippi had found and chosen him. The man desperate to edge out over O'Neil, to take O'Neil's place as Marcus Daly's trusted confidant. And MacDonald... hell, he'd do just about anything to win out over his rival, and Rippi had provided him just the means to do it.

Cat let out a breath as the full scope of Norma's story took shape, solidified, and became truth. Somehow, even with her head swimming and the pain numbing her whole left side of her body, Cat kept her mind focused.

Abigail needed her.

MacDonald yanked Abigail closer to him. Abigail whimpered, her eyes closed so tight as if she didn't dare look at Cat.

"You really think you're so smart, Miss Cowboy Cat," he said.

"I think I guessed about right," Cat said. "You heard 'bout O'Neil letting loose some of Daly's plans to Norma, plans about keeping Clark out of the Senate. The kind of thing that your boss would be mighty upset to hear gettin' out. So you went and made sure Daly knew it, too. And Daly, he called on his good friend *Nadeau* to clean up the miss, to get Norma kicked out of the Gardens. He didn't ask for your help."

MacDonald sneered at her. "What did it matter? The deed was done. She was gone and out of our lives until, until that foolish woman decided to try again. As if blackmail didn't work the first time, why not try a second?"

Cat stepped forward and Rippi immediately brought his wooden slab up and pressed it right there, right on her shoulder.

She sucked in a breath but didn't back away.

Not an inch.

"Except that time, it wasn't you who learned of Norma's intent. It was Mr. Rippi. *He* who approached *you*."

MacDonald shrugged. "What can I say? I saw an opportunity and took advantage of it. It seems I wasn't the only one deceived and hurt by dear Norma."

Cat continued to breathe, then let it all back out again. Saw the story unfold, saw and felt the truth as it fit into its puzzle, all neat and tidy like there was only one way it could have fit to begin with.

"You learned Norma was dead," she said. "That had never been in the plan, not exactly, because deaths are a lot trickier to handle now. The law frowns on people just up and dying mysteriously. It was lucky Nadeau heard it first, and with his promise still hanging over him to Daly, he sent his doctor and his favorite police officer. But Nadeau being no fool, he remembered 'bout Norma's ties to O'Neil—and to you."

Yes, there was the puzzle.

She watched it turn in her mind's eye, seeing all those pieces, practically seeing the image Norma leaning against that grand piano, soaking up all them musical notes as if she were born to it.

Cat smiled at MacDonald then, and her smile was not kind either. "And that's where you made your mistake. Nadeau realized your part in all this, or suspected, and as we know, suspecting is enough to get one in trouble. So he tells Daly and now both you and O'Neil are on the outs. We don't exactly need proof in a town like Butte. Rumors... well, they're enough to cause some serious damage to a reputation."

"My reputation, Miss Cat, I assure you, is just fine."

"And see, that's where *I* went and stepped into this mess. There were a couple people looking into what had happened to Norma, people who cared about her, but that was manageable thanks to Mr. Rippi. Isn't that right, sir?"

Rippi didn't nod.

His gaze was so focused on her she was sure he could see right through her. Could see through her plan, weak as it was. As if staring long enough would reveal the whole truth she was trying to hide... about the girl, pressed now against the bottom of the window. Hidden just out of sight, with that little derringer clasped in her thin, shaking hands.

Rippi knew something wasn't right because Cat wasn't cowering, wasn't crying. She was standing there, hands pressed firm on her hips... well, much as she could with the whole shoulder that was throbbing so bad she was actually starting to see some stars.

But MacDonald, he had no idea the threat she was. No idea cause he really had no imagination, no sense or place in the world that someone like Cat *could* be worth while.

"You see," Cat went on, "everyone has their weak spots. Thanks to Mr. Rippi, you knew them all. Except for mine. And that's when your hands suddenly weren't so clean no more."

"I haven't the faintest idea what you're talk—"

"Officer White. He knew the truth. He knew the connections to you and Norma. And then I showed up and started asking questions. You had to keep me in the dark as long as possible, so you threatened Dusty with the one person he had left—Mrs. Allen—and then you poisoned White the same way Rippi had done to Norma. You were a friend of Nadeau's and that was enough for White let you in. And you, you offered him a drink. I'm guessing in thanks for his work handling Norma's case."

Cat could see it all clearly, the scene Blake had described to her. Two glasses. One empty, one full.

It was no great guess to figure out which one was whose.

"And that," Cat said, "that's where you slipped the poison in. And why not? If the truth ever got out... well, it'd be an easy thing to blame the miner who killed Norma in the first place, using the same method, in fact. The blame would never be placed on you."

Rippi glanced from Cat to MacDonald.

"Oh," Cat said, "you know it's true. He'd toss you aside faster than

Norma ever could and with a whole lot less regret."

Rippi grinned, as if welcoming such an opportunity. "Is not an experience he'd survive. It's one he may not yet survive."

MacDonald huffed. "Oh, don't listen to her. There's no way any of this is getting back to either of us. And frankly, my dear, you have no way of proving this, either. There is no official evidence and according to both reports, White and Norma died of natural causes, *not* murder."

"Thanks to Nadeau. Though I wonder how generous he'll be feeling towards your Marcus Daly when *he* realizes the depth of his own involvement. Covering up a murder is the kind of muck that sticks to any man, especially a businessman."

There was another shift on the floorboards behind her.

And... more too.

Not just from the girl with the stringy hair and nearly lifeless eyes, but the others. As if her words were causing them to pause, to think, to... to consider. As if, as if seeing Abigail, torn and broken, all her elegancy and finery stripped away to show them all the real truth.

The girls upstairs weren't to be envied, but at the heart of it, they were all still the same.

Cat included.

She kept her arms out, showing both MacDonald and Rippi she was unarmed, but then it wasn't a physical weapon she was aiming to use.

Madam Grace had told right.

Unite the girls. Show them they mattered. Show them they weren't alone.

And she did just that.

Using the only justice they had to them down here in the dark, down where the light didn't exist except what they kept nurtured and hidden and safe inside them.

Using the truth.

Because Norma's story, her truth, it belonged to them. These girls right here.

It was their story as much as Norma's.

There was another creak and this time it filled the narrow hallway, but... somehow... neither man noticed. They were too focused on each other, as if they hadn't really gone and thought through the whole story of Norma's as Cat now had, as if... not realizing the true part they'd each played and the depth of the consequences.

If... word ever got out.

A big if, right there.

Except for that slight creak as the boards covering the tunnel entrance were slowly, carefully, slid to the side. And then the slight shape, thin and silent, that crept right on out. They certainly missed seeing those blazing green eyes that pierced right through that blackness and met Cat's.

Eyes determined and filled with a righteous anger Cat knew all too well.

More emotions swirled inside Cat just then. Relief and joy, worry and some straight out, fiery hot anger because she'd expressly forbid him to come after her—

But later.

She'd sort through all those much later. When it was safe, when her head wasn't spinning so much, when she was at home resting with those who mattered most to her.

Cat stepped forward again. Purposeful. The pink dress, smudged and dirt stained and torn right along the hem, flaring about her like she really was some great princess or something, when really she was just a fallen woman who'd found the strength to get back up again.

"You're right," she said. "But I never said I was here to prove anything. Just that I came here lookin' for justice, lookin' to help those who couldn't get any."

"The courts won't listen to a word you have to say," MacDonald said.

"Oh, I know it, but then I don't really need them to. Justice down here, I believe, is it's own thing entirely."

MacDonald looked at her, confused. But not Rippi. Those sharp eyes of his, they widened. Coming alive with more than just darkness but awareness. Awareness of just what she was saying, as if finally sensing what he should have sensed a long time earlier.

Rippi came at her then. He raised his wood slab with those dark ribbons so high over his head, swung it down so hard like he was gonna crush Cat in one blow.

Too fast this time to dodge or block. And her shoulder, too injured to do much good, either.

But then she wasn't exactly trying to.

Instead, Cat shoved away from the window just as the girl with the stringy black hair stood. The tiny derringer, the little black thing that it was, fitting perfectly in her tiny hands, as if made for it.

The girl fired.

Once.

Only one shot in the gun, but one was all you needed. Especially standing so close.

The shot exploded in the narrow hallway. The window shattered. Shards of glass flew outward and more than a few dug hard into Cat's bare arms even as she flung herself away, protecting and covering her face.

The whole underbelly shook as if it was gonna collapse right down on top of them.

Screams erupted.

From the girls, for sure, frightened definitely, but also yells of anger. The viciousness and claws and souls that had been so tattered and used, they were simply *done* being tossed aside.

The girls came flying out of their cribs.

One grabbed Abigail. Just gone and yanked her away from MacDonald right as Dusty flew right at the other man. He grabbed MacDonald around the knees, taking him straight out and down in a tackle.

Meanwhile, there was Mr. Rippi. Standing for a moment in his dark, grease and grime covered overalls. And for a moment, there was nothing. Not blood that she could see... except... no, it was right there.

A small trickle flowing out his abdomen, a trickle that was so dark it blended right in with all the rest of him.

Rippi's eyes didn't leave Cat's and even as the light started to go on out, the darkness there remained.

"She... she was a mighty... fine lady."

Then he toppled first to his knees, and finally straight down in the dirt and grime he so deserved. Dying right there, in the under-belly of the Gardens, and no place more befitting than there.

Norma's home.

It was enough.

Norma, who'd never go on back home to her family, if she even had any family left. But she had Dusty and she'd never get to wrap her arms around him again, never get to hold him close, tell him how much he meant to her. And yet...

She had a feeling Dusty already knew.

Cat saw it, there in the ghost as Norma faded from view, and the final look she gave Dusty. One filled with longing and love and wishing too, that they'd had more time. And Dusty, his head snapped up and those green eyes of his looked right at where Norma was, where she was fading, and Cat swore she saw the glint of a tear in his eyes.

Then Norma was gone and the rest of the world, of time, caught up to them.

Or really, it was Cat catching Abigail, who about flung herself into Cat's arms. Which made Cat cry out and the tears and the pain renewed all over again.

"You came, you came—"

That's all Abigail seemed to say, not that Cat herself was makin' much sense, not the way her head was suddenly spinning.

Still, she saw enough.

Saw MacDonald down on the ground, a bit of blood seeping out from the side of his head and the shattered remains of a stained wash basin right beside him. Apparently some industrious young lady found another weapon more suited to her tastes.

Still, it sure did the job 'cause MacDonald wasn't moving, though he was breathing.

Justice, as far as Cat was concerned.

Then Blake was there.

She had no idea where he came from, just that he was suddenly there holding her upright, his strong hands on either side of her head, and she was staring into his blue eyes.

Not hard or determined but worried. Scared even.

And for sure, Cat thought that was just her head gettin' really fuzzy cause a man like Blake, a man who'd made his opinions about her and girls like her pretty well known.

And yet...

"You're alive," he whispered.

"Think so."

He touched his forehead to hers. Just a moment. Long enough to know that it wasn't just the world that was spinning, and this moment, this one right here, wasn't an illusion.

It was real.

Not that she'd believe it tomorrow.

"Good enough," he finally said. "Good enough."

Then Dusty, was tugging on her hand, and when she didn't respond in timely fashion—or at all, apparently—he got to tugging on Blake.

"She's got to go, Blake. Both of us. We've got to leave now."

Cat blinked.

Finally she heard the noises upstairs as her poor, tired mind tried to make sense of all of it. Lots of yelling... screaming... doors suddenly being flung open as if banging with the full force of an army behind it, and the unmistakable whistles of police.

Blake dropped his hands and glanced up. "He's right. You need to leave."

Cat's head might still be spinning, she might be seeing more black than just about anything else, but she was not letting go of him. Not yet. Nor was she in a place to question why either.

"Come with us," she said.

"Can't. It's my job."

"But you're not on the job."

Blake touched her again, right there on either side of her face, gentle, caring. And she knew that this wasn't all an illusion, not something her mind had made up like Rippi had done.

It was real.

"I'm always on the job," he said. "Just like you. Go. I'll tell them you left out the back when you went looking for Abigail. Everyone here will agree with that."

"But MacDonald—"

"Don't worry about him. Look. You've got to leave. You know damn well they'll try and blame this on you. Doesn't matter if you were defending yourself, you got Nadeau wound up in a right fury at the moment and he'll make sure you're buried for this."

"But—"

Blake dropped a hand to her shoulder, the uninjured side, and squeezed. Gently.

"If he can't get to you, he'll get to them."

Blake nodded at the girls, who were all crowded around together watching them, their gazes darting up at the noise and the clear, unmistakable pounding of feet...

Heading this way.

And each of those girls, they were still filthy, like they hadn't bathed in a month or more, still wore nothing but ragged clothes over their too-thin bodies. And yet to a one their eyes were now lit with more spark and fire than Cat had ever seen.

Still, she didn't want to leave them either, and she shook her head, which really didn't help with the black spots or the spinning.

But... Blake was right.

Dusty tugged at her again. "Cat, we've got to *go*."

She breathed in. Felt the last hold she had over her gift, the one her pa had taught her, and imagined herself lowering the rifle.

"All right. Let's go home."

Then she and Dusty were making their way down into the tunnels. Dusty doing both the leading and the dragging, cause she really wasn't in any shape to run, let alone stand. He also took possession of the derringer. It might not have any more bullets, but it was safer with him than her. And considering it was now a murder weapon... well, let's just say there were a lot of good hiding places along the way, the kinds of places no one, not even Dusty, could ever find again.

It felt like forever, felt like the pounding steps of the police would be right behind them any moment, though Dusty swore the police would never find them, not with all the twists and turns and sideways tracks they were taking. Some places so narrow it took nearly everything Cat had just to squeeze through, leaving scraps and bits of her dress behind every time.

But breadcrumbs of her dress notwithstanding, the police officers never found them, never caught up with them.

Still, when Dusty finally led her to the surface, shoving aside the metal grating over the exit, Cat took in a big, deep breath of that foul, ash-filled air and felt... relief.

Especially when two pairs of arms reached in and hauled her out. Chin and Fat Jack.

Together they helped Cat up and into Jack's waiting hack.

"Took you long enough, Miss Justice." Jack closed the hack's door behind her. "Thought I'd have to go in after you."

"Not today, Jack. Not today."

At least, that's what she thought she said.

Her whole body hurt, her arms stinging and burning from the glass that was still in there, and she hoped they had a doc waiting back at the boarding house. But for now, she was suddenly so very tired, and fighting the darkness of sleep just didn't seem worth it no more.

Besides, finally she was among friends and family.

Finally, she was heading home.

CHAPTER FIFTY-FIVE

Home was even better than Cat had remembered. Even better than the illusions and the dreams her mind had conjured up, imagining and daydreaming, wondering what life would have been like if her parents had lived, if Alice had never needed the marriage to Stan to keep her and her younger sister alive.

If... if... if...

Well, all those ifs were nothing compared to the real thing.

Even if her shoulder still hurt like a damn.

Cat half-lay, half-sat on Mrs. Allen's couch. Her legs sprawled out in freshly cleaned jeans, her feet cozied up in the warmest stockings imaginable, and a quilt draped around her just so while the folded up newspaper, the *Butte Bystander*, rested on her lap.

The scarf her sister had made, with its dyed pink now fading, tucked close to her neck and heart.

Chin had gotten the fire going again and had worked his magic on the whole room, in fact. There wasn't a single sign of what had taken place here, not a single dent or singe mark on that polished floor. But then the world outside didn't look much different, either. All the smoke and ash from those smoldering, burning heaps still going, still stinging her eyes even though she hadn't stepped outside since that night—forced to rest and recover, as ordered by the doctor. Those dark clouds which hung there just so, as if trying to drown out all bits and manner of light.

But the sun had managed to peak through a little bit today, and Cat, sitting there as she was, got to see it.

And smiled at the sight.

Maybe Nadeau was right. Maybe she really did have a thing about suns.

Or maybe the light just brought her hope.

Mrs. Allen's window had been repaired and in record time, too. It'd also been a gift from a mysterious benefactor, though in Cat's mind it wasn't quite so mysterious. Only a handful of options, really. Either Nadeau or Daly, seeing as how she had tied up two murders and neither man had gotten the finger pointed back at them. At least, not officially. Which was a bonus when you were a businessman of some importance.

But then again, could be the window came straight from William Clark seeing as how word *had* gotten out about Daly's little bit of trouble, and his business partner MacDonald who *was* being investigated for murder. Well, that had gone and renewed the town's support in favor of Clark for senator. So yes, she could see the would-be senator being a might bit generous with all of Cat's nosey digging.

Didn't really matter though, 'cause Cat got a chance to glimpse the sun today and really, it was those little things that mattered.

Mrs. Allen was home now and sitting across from Cat, drinking her tea. She looked about the same as when Cat had first met her, hair and face dusted with traces of flour. While she looked all calm and content, Cat could see the tightening of wrinkles round her lips, pure frustration at being forced to sit out of the battle that seemingly took place right in her sitting room.

Which in some ways, it had.

But frustrations or not, there was a freshly baked apple pie sitting there on the table to cool, the smells of which filled the whole house.

Just that perfect mix of baked apples and cinnamon was nearly enough for Cat to reconsider the state of her stomach.

She'd insisted earlier that she was full, seeing as how Mrs. Allen had done nothing but feed her these past few days. While Mrs. Allen, on the other hand, insisted that Cat keep on eating. She kept on quoting the doctor, who'd told Cat to rest and eat up.

In reality, feeding Cat had apparently become an acceptable way for Mrs. Allen to deal with her frustration at being safely tucked away in her nephew's home while the action had taken place. *And* that's she'd apparently missed Cat in her big moment, dressed and dolled up for the evening as she'd been.

She'd been particularly sour about missing seeing *Blake* dressed accordingly.

The dress, of course, had been a complete disaster and had been given a proper goodbye in tribute for the part it'd played in all this.

Cat had burned the corset.

However, she'd a feeling the opportunity would come again and Mrs. Allen would get her wish. And who knows, maybe Cat would get lucky enough to skip the corset.

No doubt Mrs. Allen had another on hand, and in Cat's size.

Dusty, on the other hand, didn't mind the change of place—or his new residence. He's moved right on in without anyone having asked him, as if he'd already known it was what they'd wanted. And apparently, it was what he wanted, too. He also didn't seem to mind Cat being stuck at home, staring out the window while he got to go running off and bringing back all those exciting rumors and details (and plenty 'bout her were sure flying around).

It seemed he liked doing his part, taking care of her.

He also didn't mind the enormous amount of pies Mrs. Allen was rolling out, as he was demonstrating right now, practically sitting on his hands to keep from grabbing the whole piping-hot thing and sliding it right onto his dainty little plate there.

Those green eyes of his just fixated on all that apple goodness.

It was another sight that made Cat smile.

She glanced down at the newspaper, thinking how such a simple thing had brought this all together. Her getting off that train and seeing Dusty... really seeing him for who he was, the kid with the shadow soul who now didn't look quite so shadowed.

Instead, it looked like he had a bit of his own light back and *that* made her smile.

"You gonna read it again?" Dusty teased as he nodded towards the paper with a full-on grin on his face.

Same grin he'd had on when he handed it to her this morning.

There'd only been one small piece, just a mention, really, of what had happened that night in Grace's Gardens, two days earlier, and yet she couldn't seem to put it down. Other papers had covered the event in greater detail, as great as they could seeing as how no one knew the whole truth except those who were there (and no one but MacDonald was talking—apparently one witness versus ten, regardless of his yearly earnings, wasn't enough to sway the justice system).

Still, it was this paper here, the *Bystander*, that was important to her.

It'd been the only one who'd mentioned Norma's death and now, it seemed, was the only one who'd mentioned her again.

Cat opened the paper once again, as if unable to help herself, unable to believe what was written there. The ink wasn't quite dry and had already stained her fingers... and she didn't really care.

... A police raid on the well-known Grace's Gardens found a banker of some importance in a compromising situation two days prior. When one of the working girls became threatened, the others rose up in defense of their situation. While the girl was unharmed, one man was shot and killed, and the gentleman in question detained by police for questioning.

An investigation by police officers, headed by Captain Jere Murphy, is ongoing and is looking into the connection with gentleman, who insists on his innocence, and the death of another officer.

The madam of the establishment had this to say about the incident:

"Justice was served for the death of one of ours. I have no doubt justice will be served again."

Of course there'd been no mention of the corruption and payoffs among the police, like Officer White in particular. Not in this newspaper, anyway. Just as this one was quite careful on keeping MacDonald's identity a secret. It'd probably been one last favor of Nadeau to Daly, pulling one last string, but in the end it really didn't matter.

The Miner had no such qualms about keeping MacDonald's identity a secret.

None whatsoever.

The Miner, which was owned by William Clark, went and told the whole story, in quite some detail, about Jimmy MacDonald of Daly's Bank and Trust, and the trouble he'd found himself in.

Daly would probably be throwing a few big parties in the near future, anything to garner favor among the town again, though Cat doubted she'd be on the guest list.

Butte... she sure was quite the town.

And there was no place quite like her.

Cat shook her head, her unbound hair sliding over her shoulder, the one annoying strand sticking right to her cheek. She moved it aside, not feeling the burn and sting from her shoulder as much, though she'd taken the doctor's orders to heart and kept it still.

Mrs. Allen set down her teacup, which clinked quietly against the little plate. "It was kind of Madam Grace to send you her doctor this morning to check up on you, see how you were doing."

Cat gave the woman a grin. "You just want to know what he said."

"Well, of *course* I do. I was out of the action this whole time, and in my own sitting room no less."

Cat shook her head. "You didn't miss much."

Dusty's eyebrows shot up. "Really? Like you almost getting a flaming rock smashed into your head. Or getting shot."

"I didn't get shot."

The girl with the stringy black hair had been a good enough shot for that, anyway.

"You *almost* got shot," he corrected. "You just got your shoulder smashed with half a tree."

Cat sighed. "You both just want to hear about the doctor."

"Of course we do," Mrs. Allen said. "And I'm tired of playing nice and waiting for you to get on to it. So, why *did* she send you the doctor? You've been patched up and takin' care of, we've seen to that just fine."

Cat shook her head, not bothering to hide her grin and the joy she felt singing through her. Joy that felt awful close to home.

"You already know why," she said. "Doctor Henry Griffin. He's the doctor they use at the Gardens and he knew Norma."

Cat looked right at Dusty, meeting those piercing green eyes of his, liking the bit of softness and joy she saw there. Not a whole lot, sure, but it was there and she knew she had her own answering light when before, before she'd come to Butte, she'd had none.

"Dr. Griffin was the one who found Norma," Cat said. "He's the one who tried to save her, and yeah, he told me he suspected it was poison. Told Officer White that, but... well, you know what happened there. Well, Madam Grace knew all about it and that's why she sent him. She wanted me to know the rest of her story."

Dusty closed his eyes for a moment and Cat saw a tremble on his lips, a slight shake of his shoulder. Then he opened them again and she saw more softness reflected there, more light.

Letting his sister go, finally.

Cat wanted to reach over and hug the kid but didn't. He wouldn't have wanted it nor welcomed it. Not yet, anyway.

Maybe... maybe one day.

But for now, this felt like enough. Even though not everyone was there.

Blake's spot at the table was empty, though Chin had purposefully laid out a plate for him, and mumbling something under his breath as he did so, while sending Cat a pointed look. It had made Dusty grin and Mrs. Allen laugh.

Perhaps it was a good thing she still couldn't understand the man.

And yet... yet she missed Blake's presence. He should have been here, should have been sitting right there and glaring at her as he liked to do from time to time, as if to remind them both what he thought about her and the life she'd come from.

... and if he still thought of her that way.

Maybe there'd be a day for that, too.

Besides, Blake was busy cleaning up all the messes Norma had gotten herself tangled up in. Norma with her legendary smile. All those ribbons, knotted and bound as they'd been, and somehow she'd found herself trapped in the center. There weren't a lot of officers Jere Murphy could trust and Blake clearly was one of the few.

He'd be busy for awhile, and maybe that was for the best, too.

Though she couldn't help but wonder, along with this little nagging feeling, almost like a tingle, that she should ask Mrs. Allen about where one could go to dance.

Dance and live and simply find joy.

Later, though.

For now, she'd rest and see what else life decided to throw her way.

Cat reached across and dumped the newspaper on the table.

"You know," Mrs. Allen said, nodding at the paper. "It has a nice ring to it. 'Miss Justice.'"

"I like Cowboy Cat better," Cat said. "A hell of a lot easier to live up to."

"I don't think it's going to matter what you call yourself now. They know who you are."

Which in and of itself was a weight, both heavy and light and... comforting, all at the same time.

"Maybe," Cat said. "Or maybe I'm still figuring it for myself."

Mrs. Allen reached behind her and handed Cat a stack of letters bound by a single red ribbon.

Cat fingered the ribbon and glanced up. "What's this for?"

"I think it's a good place to start, don't you? All those girls waiting to hear from their loved ones back home. And me? I'm too busy entertaining all these new guests and visitors who want to stay under the same roof as the famous 'Cowboy Cat.' I haven't got time to go around delivering letters."

The name 'Abigail' was addressed on top, the very one she'd meant to deliver that night when everything just about went to hell.

"What do you think?" Mrs. Allen asked. "You gonna stay for a spell? See what other kind of trouble you can get yourself into?"

Cat pressed the letters to her chest. She reached up and touched the scarf Alice had made. It rested there, keeping her warm and comforted, and for once there was no icy touch of Alice's ghost haunting her.

Nothing but love and... maybe... a vision for the future.

"Yeah," Cat said, "I think will. Stay for a bit, see what turns up next, see if anyone needs... needs someone like me."

"There will always be a need for someone like you," Mrs. Allen said.

Though her words were solemn, Mrs. Allen's smile was big and wide while Dusty's grin looked like it was about to fall off his face.

She laughed at them. "All right, all right. I'll stay! *But—*" Cat held out her empty plate. "Only if you hand over my slice before this kid eats the whole damn thing. I'm starving."

And the sound that met her words—the joy and laughter—was exactly what her soul needed to hear.

A place to rest and heal, and maybe the start of a new future.

Maybe even a new home.

AUTHOR NEWSLETTER

To keep up with Chrissy Wissler's new releases as well as information about her other works, please go to ChrissyWissler.com and sign up for her newsletter.

ABOUT THE AUTHOR

Chrissy Wissler's writing has garnered praise both from readers and professional writers. Readers love her characters and the emotional grip she engenders.

About her novel *Home Run, New York Times* bestselling author Kristine Kathryn Rusch said: "Wonderful book, chockfull of unexpected surprises. If you like sports novels, you'll like this—even if you don't like romance. If you like romance, you'll like this—even if you don't like sports novels."

Chrissy's short fiction has appeared in the anthologies: *Fiction River: Risk-Takers, Fiction River Presents: Legacies, Fiction River Presents: Readers' Choice, Deep Magic,* and *When Dreams Come True.* She writes fantasy and science fiction, as well as a softball, contemporary series for both romance and young adult.

Before turning to fiction, Chrissy also wrote nonfiction for publications such as *Montana Outdoors, Women in the Outdoors,* and *Jakes Magazine.* In 2009, *Inside Kung Fu* magazine awarded her with their 'Writer of the Year' award.

For more information about Chrissy Wissler's other works, please go to ChrissyWissler.com and sign up for her newsletter.

www.chrissywissler.com
chrissy@chrissywissler.com

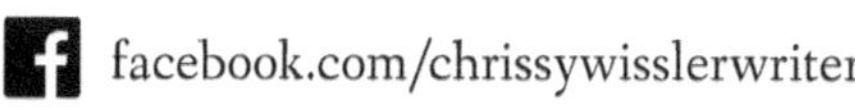

facebook.com/chrissywisslerwriter

ALSO BY CHRISSY WISSLER

Cowboy Cat Mystery Series

Women's Justice

Mother's Justice

For more information about Chrissy Wissler's other works, go to
ChrissyWissler.com